Praise for K. A. Bedford's Previous Books

"As with all literature, it's the questions that matter and in SF they are often the big ones. These are perhaps the biggest questions of all. What is life? What is intelligence? Is there a God? Is there such a thing as soul, or a personality? Are they different? Of what do they consist? Can you manufacture emotions?"
— Dave Luckett, author and reviewer for *The West Australian newspaper*

"Eclipse is an intelligent novel that will leave readers with much to think about."
— Victoria Strauss, *Sf Site*

"Bedford also raises some serious issues, using the interplay between disposables, synthetic minds, augmented animals, and a woman artificially enabled to live beyond her death to intelligently explore questions of free will, humanity, and the existence or nonexistence of the soul."
— Victoria Strauss, *SFsite.com*

"*Eclipse* works in all the ways that matter. It kept me turning pages way past bedtime. It has an edge of barely contained terror throughout; it has love, (sort of); it has mysterious, very alien aliens. It has a big picture that gets bigger as the story ends. It left me eager for more."
—Terry Baker, *Eternal Night*

"*Eclipse*... is a good read — very intense in parts, violent in others — and had me staying way too late in the evening when I had to get up early for work the next morning... I couldn't just put it down to finish tomorrow."
— Lisa Ramaglia, *scribesworld.com*

"This book has a delightfully strange feel to it, even though the setting and plot seem normal enough, as if any science-fictional world can be considered truly 'normal,' in line with a reader's actual experience."
— Lucy Schmeidler, *sfrevu.com*

"Bedford does an admirable job of world building and moving the at-times gory story along."
— Timothy Capehart, *VOYA*

"Finally, probably the best of the three is Australian author Bedford's *Eclipse*, a dark, brutal sci-fi tale that alternately recalls *Platoon*, *Lord of the Flies* and the aforementioned *Dick*. The novel follows the exploits of James Dunne, newly graduated from the brutal Royal Interstellar Service Academy, whose first flight into space turns out to be a violent nightmare. Dunne's battles with corruption read like a space-age memoir, offering enough vulgarity and blood-spray to satisfy more than just sci-fi fans."
— Bryn Evans, *Fast Forward News*

Books by K. A. Bedford

Orbital Burn
Eclipse
Hydrogen Steel
Time Machines Repaired While-U-Wait

PARADOX
RESOLUTION

by
K. A. Bedford

EDGE SCIENCE FICTION AND FANTASY PUBLISHING
AN IMPRINT OF HADES PUBLICATIONS, INC.

CALGARY

Paradox Resolution
Copyright © 2012 by K. A. Bedford

EDGE

Edge Science Fiction and Fantasy Publishing
An Imprint of Hades Publications Inc.
P.O. Box 1714, Calgary, Alberta, T2P 2L7, Canada

Editing by Brian Hades
Interior design by Janice Blaine
Cover Illustration by Martin Pasco
ISBN: 978-1-894063-88-3

EDGE Science Fiction and Fantasy Publishing and Hades Publications, Inc. ac-
knowledges the ongoing support of the Alberta Foundation for the Arts and the
Australian Council for the Arts for our publishing programme.

Library and Archives Canada Cataloguing in Publication

Bedford, K. A. (K. Adrian), 1963-
    Paradox resolution / K.A. Bedford. -- 1st ed.

ISBN: 978-1-894063-88-3
(e-book ISBN: 978-1-894063-89-0)

    I. Title.

PR9619.3.B46P37 2012   823'.92   C2012-902390-6

FIRST EDITION
(B20120507)
Printed in Canada
www.edgewebsite.com

Dedication

This book is for
my mum and dad,
Marie and Ken Bedford,
and for my wife, Michelle Bedford.
No writer ever had a better
support team.

CHAPTER 1

Aloysius "Spider" Webb did not look like a man who'd been to the End of Time and back. He didn't look like a man who'd been offered ultimate power, and turned it down. He looked ordinary, a middle-aged Australian bloke, a bit overweight, losing his greying hair, and with a bitter hardness about his eyes, a face that had been disappointed, and done the disappointing.

A long time ago, in another lifetime, Spider had been a promising young police officer. But then fate intervened and now he was stuck fixing broken time machines for (not much of) a living.

Though he hated time machines with the white-hot fury of a thousand suns, as they say, he did have an aptitude for the work. This surprised him very much. It helped that most time machine problems were stupidly simple, or indeed simply stupid. More often than not, Spider wanted to hit the owners around the head and shoulders with a copy of *Time Machines for Dummies*.

Spider's problem was that he was a good man living in a rotten world getting more rotten by the day.

Right now, he just wanted to get home to the Lucky Happy Moon Motel in Midland, but was stuck in traffic in Guildford. It was bucketing down warm rain when his phone-patch rang.

"Webb, go." Spider maneuvered his recumbent bike to the side of the road. It was late, and the Guildford traffic, improbably, was a seething mass of cars, bikes, and vans, all inching along, horns blatting and howling. It was almost a relief to get a phone call. *But who could be calling at this time of night*, he wondered. He needed to get home, get some sleep and get up early, fresh and chipper, ready to fix the city's endless supply of malfunctioning time machines. Spider barely heard the voice coming through his phonepatch.

"Al, it's me," said Molly, his very nearly ex-wife.

"Molly?" This was a surprise. "Um, hi," he said. Molly had always been the only person he permitted to call him anything resembling his actual first name, Aloysius. It was a name he had always hated, and which had got him into trouble when he was a kid in school. A friend at university nicknamed him 'Spider', and the name stuck. Molly, who he had also met at university, had never liked it, and insisted on calling him Al.

"Molly, just a tick, it's noisy," he said, imagining she was calling to make sure he had signed the bloody divorce papers, but no.

"Are you okay?" she said. "You sound tense."

Spider had always loved Molly's voice. It was one of the things about her that made him first notice her, perhaps even fall in love with her, once upon a time, a long time ago. He used to provoke her into arguments just to get her to talk to him. He knew he could have engaged her in ordinary conversation, but even as a callow Arts undergraduate, he noticed that Molly's thing was arguing. Prickly to a fault, she would *discuss* any damn thing; take any position, any opinion, just to be provocative, just to get a rise out of him, or out of anyone else within her blast radius. Somehow her passion was profoundly attractive. It was not until many years later that she had started to seem manipulative, annoying, and even cruel. The divorce had been Molly's idea.

"I'm in traffic, Moll," he said. "I'm on my way home."

Spider had talked Molly into a trial separation, instead of a divorce, during which, oddly, in the course of doing countless odd jobs for her, he wound up seeing more of her than when they had been properly married.

"Yeah, it's just, look, something's come up," Molly said.

"Uh-huh." Spider tried to concentrate on Molly's voice while ignoring the traffic around him.

"Can you come and do a bit of house-sitting for me, for the next, ah, two weeks, maybe?"

"Two weeks? What?"

"I have to go to America. Kind of sudden, I know."

For a moment Spider wasn't sure which part of Molly's statement required comment first. North America, these days, was terribly dangerous; and yes, this was a little bit sudden. Spider had seen Molly three days earlier, and there had been no talk of anything like this then. "Um?" he said in the end, always ready with the right thing to say.

"Yeah, I know. A gallery owner, from Mosman Park, has some contacts in New York, and he's—"

"What? Have you seen the news? New York? It's—"

"Look, if you can't do it, just say so—"

"It's not that, it's—"

"God, Al, this could be my big break and typical bloody you, all you can think of is your selfish self."

He took a deep breath, waited for his heart to slow, and tried to focus. "Molly, let's start again. You want me to house-sit? Is that right?"

"That's right. Stéphane wants me to fly out with him tomorrow. Business class, Al! Business class!"

"Stéphane?" he said, nearly choking on the pretentious name, and hating him. Hating that he had money, hating that he was on good terms with Molly, hating that he was taking her to New York, and hating that he had 'connections'. But most of all hating that he was probably sleeping with her. That burned, right there, that thought. Molly sleeping with anyone else. In Spider's mind, despite the divorce papers still waiting for his signature, he thought he could, maybe, one day, win her back. *Stéphane! Good grief*, he thought. He was losing her. And after everything he'd been through, that *they'd* been through, and everything he did for her, up to and including bringing her back from the End of Time, saving her from Dickhead's torture (never mind, he told himself, that it had been more or less his own fault that she had been caught up in that nightmare). But she wouldn't know anything about that; wouldn't remember it — in her mind that future had never happened.

In this timeline, their timeline, life was proceeding as normal — everything unfolding as it ought to.

"Al? Al, you there? Hello?"

"I'm here, Moll."

"So, are you excited for me?"

"Excited for you?"

"It's gonna be huge, Al. Just huge. There's talk they could get me into MoMA, for God's sake. Imagine that! Can you believe it?"

Holy crap, Spider thought, knowing what an exhibition in the prestigious Museum of Modern Art would mean for Molly's career as an artist. Knowing it could make her a success. Could set her up for life. A life in which he had no part to play, not even for doing odd jobs like rewiring her toilet system. He found himself, suddenly, on the edge of tears, his throat closing up, and his eyes stinging. Wiping at them with the back of his cold hand, he said, "Molly, that'd be brilliant! This guy can really do that for you?"

"Al, this Stéphane, he's bloody amazing! Just *amazing*!"

And in that one word, he thought, he could feel so much more about Stéphane's capabilities than simply his business skills. This Stéphane could give Molly everything she ever wanted, the things she most wanted, her heart's desires, in fact. All the sorts of things he had never been able to provide. Even when he had had a proper job, before things went bad, he'd made pretty decent money, never enough, of course; it was never enough for her, to set her up the way she wanted to live. His work in the Western Australian Police Service was so intense, so horrifying a lot of the time, and the police took so much crap from the public, all the criticism all the time about every single thing they did, and of course the government was always finding ways to claw back most of what they earned — which was a rant for another time.

What Spider did earn, particularly once he made detective senior sergeant, was okay. They'd been able to buy a house, a bit of a fixer-upper, with a big mortgage. Nothing flashy, certainly no luxury, but there was a separate room for Molly's studio, not all that big, but it was enough, and she toiled away in there, sometimes all night long, working on her bizarre stuff, stuff he never did quite understand, and some of which, let's face it, gave him the absolute creeps. The point was, it was home, it was theirs, it should have been enough for her, but it never was. Molly would complain about being stuck in the arse end of the world, which was Perth — the wrong city, in the wrong state, on the wrong side of the country. The arts world was in the east, in Melbourne and Sydney. That's where the coverage was, where the money was, the rich bastards who actually bought expensive avant-garde artworks were all over there. It was a long time since the collapse of Australia's huge mining boom back at the turn of the century, when China and India consumed every bit of rock that came out of Western Australia, and ordinary people in WA could get fabulously wealthy. Those days were gone, and with them, interest in the fine arts. Here, in the boonies, Molly had always been restless, frustrated — the word she liked to use, now he thought about it, was "alienated", a theme that showed up all the time in her work.

Spider thought, *Things are looking up for Molly. And the mature, grown-up thing to do, if he genuinely did love her, was to let her go, wish her well, and do whatever he could to help her out. Be a friend, first and foremost.* So Spider said, "Yeah, sure. I'd be happy to look after the old place." Once upon a time his old place, too. "Take three weeks, if it'd help. Those bastards in New York, they won't know what's hit 'em!" he said, perhaps overly cheery.

He could hear Molly smiling. "Thanks, Al. You're the best."

"One endeavors to provide satisfaction," he said, quoting the immortal Jeeves.

"What?"

"It's okay. Look, um, so what do you need from me?" He checked his watch, saw it was well after ten p.m., a cold and wet Thursday night in late April, rain pounding hard and loud on the bike canopy over his head. *What was she doing calling at such a late hour?* he wondered — and then remembered the time difference between Perth and New York; it was about twelve or thirteen hours, depending on daylight saving at the New York end. Molly had probably just got off the phone with Mr. Stéphane. Or maybe she and he had just had a fantastic evening in bed together in Mosman Park, and Molly had come up for air just long enough to call him, asking for a favor. It was a corrosive thought, eating through his mind, and he tried to unthink it, to get the image out of his head, but it wouldn't leave.

"Oh, one more thing, Al," Molly said.

"Moll?"

"It's Popeye."

"Popeye?" Spider said, surprised, thinking about cartoon sailors with improbable forearms.

"You know, Popeye. My fish! Mr. Popeye! I got him, oh, must be, two years ago, you remember! You were with me that day."

Oh, he thought. "Sorry, Moll. Not me. I'm sure I'd remember going fish-shopping with you." *Shopping with Molly, for anything at all was always such a lovely, stress-free experience,* he thought.

"Okay," she said, surprised, but not troubled. "Well, I've got this fish—"

"Mr. Popeye," Spider said.

"Yes, that's right. And, thing is, Mr. Popeye, he's—"

Spider understood all at once. He closed his eyes, waiting for the blow. "Let me guess, he's sick and you want me to look after him while you're away, right?"

"Well, yes, of course! It's just fin rot. So you have to make sure he gets his medication."

Spider was gobsmacked that there was medication for fin rot, medication which almost certainly cost more than the fish itself had cost. He sighed, pinched the bridge of his nose, trying to keep his breathing under control. "Okay," he said. "No worries! Just leave me instructions, it'll be fine. The little guy will be bright-eyed and bushy-tailed by the time you get back from your conquest of the Big Apple."

Then Molly did something Spider thought she would never, ever do, something that shocked him more than he'd been shocked by anything lately. Molly *squealed* as she said, "Can you *believe* it, Al! I'm going to *New York City*! MoMA, Al! It's just—"

"Unbelievable, yes, Moll," he said, and added, "Go forth and kick arse."

"Stéphane says its spring over there."

"Oh," he said. "Is that so?"

Then there was a pause on the line. "Al, you're not jealous, are you?" Molly said.

"Jealous? Why, no, I—"

"You *are* jealous, you are!"

Spider could imagine her smiling. "Silly Aloysius! There's nothing to be jealous about. Stéphane's *gay*."

Of course he is, Spider thought. "Sure. Okay. Um, cool."

"It's sweet of you to be concerned for my virtue, though."

Molly's virtue was the last thing he was concerned about, but he let her witter on in that vein for a while, as she told him all about the "lovely" Stéphane, how she met him, and how he'd introduced her to a bunch of his lovely friends in the art biz, some of whom, it turned out, went through Curtin University's Fine Arts program at about the same time she did, but she didn't remember any of them. It had been a long time ago.

And now she was about to be swept away into the glamorous world of New York art galleries, and from there, Paris? London? Frankfurt? *He would never see her again*, he thought, *except in news feeds that featured profiles of Australians who'd done well for themselves overseas and finally came back home after ten or twenty years — a huge success.*

Could he deal with Molly leaving his life like that? Could he deal with her success? He didn't honestly know.

Then, Molly said, "Oh God, look at the time!" Spider glanced at his watch; realized Molly had been talking for over half an hour. She went on. "Look, I'll be in touch with final arrangements about the house-sit, okay?"

"Fine," he said. "No worries. I'll be around."

"Good night!"

"'Night, Moll. Love you."

"You, too!" she said, and was gone, leaving him in cold silence, feeling like he'd woken up from a strange dream, to find himself tucked inside his bicycle, the rain beating down on the canopy.

He sat for a long moment, one leg keeping the bike upright, reminding himself that he had told Molly a number of times that he was always ready and available for whatever little odd jobs she might have around the old matrimonial pile. He had always told himself it was a good way, perhaps the only way, to stay in touch with her and her life. Maybe, he convinced himself, in the course of carrying out these odd jobs, she might notice once again that he was a good man worthy of her love. He thought of it as the "drip method", and told himself that a steady stream of water drops falling on a piece of concrete will, over time, break that concrete. Not that Molly was in any way like a piece of concrete, all grey and hard and lacking in tensile strength, really... No. Molly was merely her own person. She had allowed herself to forget that she and he had once been a fine pair of souls. He had hoped to remind her of this and it simply never occurred to him that his plan might backfire. The prospect of two weeks in the old home, tending to the needs of a sickly fish did not fill him with unalloyed delight. But he would do it. He would do it with something approximating a smile on his face. He had to be the grown-up. He was, after all, nearly fifty years old. It was more than time to behave like a grown-up.

The fact was, when he'd told Molly he loved her, he meant it, and she knew he meant it, but it meant nothing to her. He was her past, an issue to work out in her artwork. No matter what he said to her, no matter what he promised, or tried, he would never get her back. She would always, no matter what, just look at him, maybe smile a little, a sad look on her face, and tell him he was doing himself no favors with all this sad and pathetic nonsense. Molly had decided against him a long time ago, and it was just a matter of Spider grasping that, internalizing it, and moving on.

Back when he'd been a copper, he'd done his best to be the best, even, ultimately, at enormous cost to his own career. If he'd been prepared to go to the dark side, he could have saved his job, had money, better clothes, a nice car, all of it. All of the things Molly had always wanted. But that had not been who he was, and they both knew it. Spider wished, had always wished, that what he was would be enough for Molly — but that had never been the case. She always looked at him as if she were wondering how on Earth she had ever fallen for him in the first place — as if she didn't know what she'd been thinking.

CHAPTER 2

The following day, Friday, Spider was woken, yelling, by the cracking of thunder right near his — he hesitated at calling the Lucky Happy Moon Motel his "home" — domicile. Not really a motel; it was more what used to be called a capsule hotel, in which residents slept in plastic tubes mounted on several levels of racks. It was cold, never clean enough, always smelled funny, and Spider hated having to live there. It was the cheapest place in Perth. The only thing cheaper than this place was self-storage units, or maybe setting up a tent and a sleeping bag out in the baking bush somewhere. Bit far to commute to work, though. The storm kept up, booming and cracking over the city of Midland, pouring down hail and stinky rain and misery without relief, as Spider went about what he laughingly called his "morning routine," using the group shower, coaxing coffee out of a sad, broken down old coffee droid that made coughs of apology when Spider swore at it. At length, upright and mostly ambulant, Spider climbed into his recumbent bike — his only luxury, but also the cheapest way to get around — and set off, shivering, through choking traffic for Malaga, and the shop.

He arrived in Malaga, a landscape of bleak concrete tilt-up light-industrial estates, and found his way to Inverness Road, to his own place of work, Time Machines Repaired While-U-Wait. The shop's sign also included the words UNDER NEW MANAGEMENT and sported a snazzy new logo that, to Spider's mind, looked like a speeding clock mating with a spanner.

Spider shook his head, dismayed. It was bad enough that the name of the business made no actual sense, considering that, thanks to the magic of time travel, a repaired time machine was returned to its concerned owner mere moments after said machine was checked into the workshop. Now Spider's new boss, Mr. J. K. Patel, wanted him to figure out how to bring in more business by offering a paradox resolution service as well. Which, when Mr. Patel told him about this, he said, "Yes, sir, I'll get right on that," but in his head, Spider felt sinking, suffocating doom. Time travel was nothing if not a good, affordable way to create all manner of idiotic time paradoxes. The detailed and user-friendly manuals that came with every new time machine tried to explain, in simplified language, how the "Many Worlds Interpretation of Quantum Mechanics" worked. Complete with funny box-out cartoons of Niels Bohr saying, "Anyone who is not shocked by quantum theory has not understood it," and Richard Feynman exclaiming, "Hey, I said that!" But, unfortunately, almost no one believed that an infinite number of new universes would be spawned by every single decision ever made by every single person, all of the time. Fixing time machines was becoming frustrating and, as Spider pedalled up to the shop's main gate, he found himself feeling melancholy and nostalgic for "the good old days" of time machine repair.

This morning Spider noticed that two new signs had been posted on the shop's fence: NO CASUAL WORK and LOITERERS WILL BE PROSECUTED. *Signs of the times* he thought.

Spider was first to arrive, as usual, so he had the place to himself. He liked his own company: it meant there was nobody about pissing him off, bugging him with phone calls. He was, at least until Mr. Patel arrived, his own master. It wasn't much, as kingdoms went, but it was (mostly) his. He went around the workshop, checked the machines as they came online, and examined the tool systems, the automation, and the analytics. Everything worked the way it should. He had to give credit to the new owner for this. Mr. Patel, on taking over the firm, had replaced all of the archaic, dodgy hardware Dickhead McMahon, Spider's former boss, had insisted he use. Spider remembered when entire days of work would be lost because the quantum analytics scanner was stuffed, or when the database servers in the back of the building would suffer kernel panics and stack crashes because of a power spike. It was the stuff of nightmares, but he had stuck with it. Now, though, under the new regime, everything was different. The entire building had been given a fresh paint job. There were even new carpets in the office areas. And the best part: a new, multifunction, automated coffee droid. A coffee droid that would actually trundle on its tracks out of the break room, and come and find him, asking, very politely, if he was interested in a nice, fresh coffee. The first time Spider saw the coffee droid doing this, he just about wept big salty tears of happiness.

As he surveyed the workshop, Spider noted that only one of the three service bays was occupied — a Boron III needed some routine maintenance. Since Dickhead's disappearance last year, business had seriously gone off the boil. It was probably due to the world financial situation and the spectacular crash of the US economy. Businesses everywhere were going to the wall. But Mr. Patel reassured Spider that he and his coworker, Charlie, and their front office receptionist, Malaria, were safe from the sack. Would they still have jobs by Christmas? They didn't know. What they did know was that idiots armed with time machines were buzzing about in the timelines of the recent past, trying to engineer ways to keep this financial catastrophe from occurring. He imagined they were only making it worse.

Spider headed for the break room — time for his first coffee of the day. He was in the process of training the droid to recognize him, and to anticipate his coffee needs. The machine was smart, but smart like a border collie, rather than, say, a small child. And, like a border collie, it was very, very keen to please.

"G'day, Spider-san!" it said as Spider entered the break room. Its voice was almost natural, but not quite, and Spider was relieved. The last thing he wanted in a robot was a human-like voice. The machine needed to appear, at least to some extent, like a machine, he thought.

"Good morning, Coffee Droid. How are we this morning?"

"Very well, thank you!" Spider could hear the exclamation points. Something would have to be done about that. The thing did everything but bow at him; it was annoying. "How can I serve you today?"

"Just the usual, a double macchiato."

"I have the very thing, Spider-san!"

Spider stood there and sighed, staring out a small window, with its view of the car-park. It had always been a large car-park, much too big for the small number of staff here. Years ago, before Dickhead bought the premises to use for his time machine repair business it had been an auto mechanic shop. You could still sometimes smell the grease and the rubber, a ghost of jobs past. "Okay, Coffee Droid. Just don't burn the coffee this time, okay? Have you got that?"

"No burning! Yes, Spider-san!" The machine set about grinding fresh beans delivered from a large hopper that Malaria had to keep filled up.

Spider had often caught her eyeing the machine as it went about its polite and enthusiastic business. Malaria, a classically trained barista, who'd placed highly in national barista competitions, had deeply mixed feelings about the coffee droid: she liked that it made good coffee on a reliable basis, and that it would walk around, asking them if they would care for a refreshing beverage, but it also creeped her out and made her feel superfluous. Not that she would ever, except in the most exceptional circumstances, make coffee for anybody herself, but just the thought of this huge machine clumping about the building, taking care of everyone's caffeine needs, bothered her more than she could say, or even begin to articulate.

"Spider-san!" the machine said, fresh-ground coffee aroma filling the break room. "It appears I am out of milk. Please re-supply my milk reservoir!"

"Oh," Spider said, still floating about on the coffee fumes. "Righto." He went to the fridge, opened the door. Inside: several bottles of cheap Italian mineral water; disposable plastic boxes of home-brand instant noodles; several well-used Tupperware containers, all marked, "Property of Malaria Brown! Hands off!"; puddles of blood on the floor of the fridge; one plastic milk bottle, about half-full, but which might be past its use-by date — and, by far the biggest thing in the fridge, something huge and round, and if it had not been dripping blood Spider might have mistaken it for a particularly gross-looking melon of some kind. He paused a moment, deeply disturbed but not sure what had disturbed him so, and looked back — and looked back again. In fact, no matter how many times he stopped, looked away, and looked back at it afresh, it appeared, at least to Spider's coffee-starved eyes, to be a severed human head, facing forward, its eyes squeezed shut, its whole face locked up in an agonized grimace, cold and pale, a hideous grey non-color.

Spider stood there, his right hand on the door of the fridge, staring, tense, starting to feel faint and cold, but also thinking, *what the fuck is this*? He knew what it looked like, but there was no way in the teeming multiverse that it could in fact be what it looked like. Nobody would have broken into the building during the night and parked a severed human head in the break room fridge. That just would not happen. It was a non-starter, as ideas went. For one thing, the building had all-new security systems, with constantly scanning cameras in every conceivable location, watching the entire premises, inside and out. Certainly, Spider thought, nagging doubts starting to bubble up in his mind, the sort of doubts that told him that no matter how convincing the thing might be, it must surely be some kind of prosthetic movie prop, a confection of latex and paint and, and ... there was, if he leaned in close, the *smell*. And it was that smell that finally convinced him. This was a real head. It smelled like — oh God — like meat, reasonably fresh meat.

"Fuck a bloody duck," he said, barely breathing, staring at it, his legs starting to wobble, a cold sweat beading all over his own head.

He heard Charlie's jeep arriving.

The coffee droid said, "Spider-san!"

Spider screamed, and just about leapt out of his skin. Turning to the machine, he said, "Look. I need a moment. Just ... just wait up."

Then, as he turned back to see the head in the fridge, some-thing bad happened deep inside Spider's mind: it suddenly occurred to him, as he stared at the thing, that he *recognized* that head. Thought, in fact, it looked real familiar, and, thinking that, his stomach locked up tight, and he felt sick.

"No way," he said, "This is *not* happening! There's no *way* that's—"

Then things got much worse: the head's eyes began to open, with difficulty, as if they were all gummed up. They focused, and looked at him, filled with an unbearable sense of pain, bewilderment, and despair.

Spider gasped, startled, and stumbled back against the counter, staring.

The head spoke. It said, "*Spider...*"

Spider, hardly breathing, stared and stared at the severed head of Dickhead McMahon. It said, its voice barely a whisper, and with a great struggling, gurgling effort — Spider could glimpse the blackened tongue behind the teeth, something that nearly made him spew right there in the break room — "*Help me. Please ... help me.*"

CHAPTER 3

"It spoke to you." This was Inspector Iris Street, once of the Major Crime Squad, but now consigned to the misery of the Time Crime Unit. She wasn't happy about it.

"Yes, it bloody spoke to me!" This was Spider. He'd suggested they talk about the incident in the quiet of his office.

Iris was an attractive woman in her forties, short blonde hair, dark grey eyes, no makeup, dressed in an expensive black skirt suit, a crisp white shirt and sensible black shoes. Iris hated working Time Crime. She believed, correctly, her sideways promotion from the Major Crime Squad had been a "reward" for being, even in a strictly "just friends" basis, involved with Spider, and had told him so. Spider had felt bad about this ever since. There was no end to the mischief people tried to get up to with their time machines, though fortunately most of it was (a) juvenile, and (b) stupid, and (c) easy to foil. Of course there were "curly ones" — offences where specialist handling was called for — and Iris's team was needed. This business today did not immediately, in Iris's opinion, cry out in favor of a time crime interpretation. The uniforms who first responded to Malaria's emergency call thought it might be some sort of prank, even if a nasty one. Yes, it was a real human head, and that made the uniforms think there might be a freakish type of killer at work. The two cops had wanted to know if Spider had any enemies, and then were all confused because Spider wouldn't stop laughing in their faces, only it wasn't happy laughter; it was the sort of laughter that makes you worried that the person in question is about to break down. Clearly, they had not heard that he, Spider Webb, had once grossly offended the sensibility of the WA Police Service by testifying against Superintendent Alan Sharp, time-traveling pedophile. When these fresh-faced coppers doubted Spider's suggestions that some serious temporal malarkey was in the works, he suggested, very gently, that they should get Iris Street and her team involved. He was, he told them; pretty sure this was a serious crime involving time travel.

"Spider, the thing is half-frozen," Iris said.

Feeling all cold and clammy, wrapped in a fire blanket and sipping horribly sweet warm tea, Spider was attempting to give her his statement. They had been over the basic facts several times.

Her team and some blue-suited forensic guys were going over the scene in methodical detail. They even asked Spider to make the coffee droid go to the workshop and wait for further instructions. It shuffled off, "Yes, Spider-san."

It had been nearly two hours since Spider had found the head. He still had the shakes and was still imagining it there, in the fridge, its faint, hoarse voice whispering to him; its desperation and horror — the sense that the head was revolted at itself. *Bloody Dickhead*, he thought. *Always leave them wanting more, that's the spirit!*

"Iris, I'm telling you, I'm trying very hard to tell you, that, yes, it was Dickhead McMahon, of all people, and yes, he spoke to me. He asked for my help. He addressed me by name, Iris!" He knew Iris' forensic people had already gone over the camera feeds from the break room, starting from close of business yesterday, and found only the usual overnight contract cleaning crew, all of whom were vetted and cleared, and none of whom, in any case, had been seen transporting a freshly severed head into the break room and popping it into the fridge. There was no blood trail through the workshop or the offices.

Iris was staring at him, head tilted to one side, mouth pressed shut, quite unimpressed with the situation. "What is it about the shit that follows you around, Spider? My God!"

"I don't know! I've wondered the same thing myself."

"This is the kind of thing that the people in the Service — the ones who hate you — can't get enough of! 'That Spider bloody Webb, did you hear the latest?'"

Stay calm, Spider. Breathe. Take a moment. He said, at length, "I know. I do. But I also know what I saw."

"You realize we've been reviewing the security feeds. We see you coming into the break room, we see you faffing about with the coffee droid, then turning to the fridge, opening the fridge, and then you just kind of stand there, staring into the fridge for a while, and then you jump, screaming—"

"I did not scream."

"Oh, please, you screamed like a little girl."

"I was a little startled, that's all."

"Spider, come on. You jump, screaming, in the air, glare at the coffee droid, and then you go back to staring at the head in the fridge, and then you just kind of, well, collapse in a bit of a heap, and not long after that Charlie Stuart comes along—"

"I do know what's on the feed, Iris."

"Yes, but do you see how it looks, at least to me?"

He knew very well. "It looks like a stunt, like I'm having a lend of you."

"That head, I'll give you the point that it's a real human head, okay? And I'll spot you the point about it being a freshly severed head. No question. The blood's real, it's all legit. But so far my team thinks this is a stunt you've somehow put together using a time machine, and the thing I'm wondering—"

"Iris, please, that's—"

"No," she said. "Just no! I don't know why you'd want to piss me off like this. I think I've been a pretty good friend to you recently, for all the good it's done me, so I'm left wondering, you know, why you—"

"It's not like that! For God's sake, Iris! It's not."

The vehemence of this retort got Iris' attention. She stopped. "No?"

"I did not do this," he said, trying to keep from yelling. "I can't tell you enough times. This is *not* my doing. I did not set it up. I did not go out and cut off Dickhead McMahon's enormous head and somehow stash it inside the fridge, Iris! I don't even know where Dickhead is! The last I heard of him? The last I heard, he was off somewhere in his little empire at the End of Time, supervising the universe, tweaking everything to his bloody liking, so far uptime it was a miracle I managed to get myself back here — to the present. Iris, I need your help. I need your help like I've never needed it before, because yes, I do understand how this looks, and how it will play once word gets out. I'm in the shit, huge shit, and I need you to back me up, and speak for me. You believed I wasn't involved in that business with the woman in the time machine. I can't tell you what that meant to me. I just,

I just… Oh, for God's sake, now look at me," he said, struggling against the unstoppable and humiliating biological urge to start crying, right here, in front of Iris. He hated crying. It made him feel like he wasn't in control, like he was weak and useless, and — he started dabbing his eyes with the scratchy blanket. He felt his face on fire with shame, and he wanted to turn away from her.

Iris, on the receiving end of this speech, and seeing the state it had left him in, looked at the floor, abashed. She took a step towards him, tried to give him some kind of hug, but she wasn't a hugging kind of person, and he wasn't the type of guy who would respond well to a hug while he was doing his best to spontaneously combust to hide his embarrassment and anger. They banged their heads together, and there were arms everywhere, and in the end Iris backed away, and Spider slumped, covering his face with the blanket, his overheated mind awhirl, the sight of Dickhead's head still before him, and all the rest of his relationship with Dickhead, and what Dickhead had done to Molly in the other timeline, all of it, going around and around in a cyclone of misery.

After a long, awkward silence in which Iris pretended not to hear Spider's sobs, Iris said, "Spider, I'm sorry."

He nodded, exhausted. "Why would I—?"

Her hands up in front of her, Iris said, "Really, it's okay. It's fine. It's fine, Spider. It's just—"

"I know."

"This new gig they've got me on, all this 'Time Crime' bullshit—" (she was careful to indicate enormous air-quotes around 'Time Crime') "—it's…" She trailed off, lost for words, exasperated, staring out the window at the garden out the front of the building.

"I understand," he said.

"So, if it *wasn't* you—"

"Exactly," Spider said. "How did it get there?"

"There's no sign of tampering with the camera itself, nor its connection to the server at head office."

"Even if the culprit did use a time machine, I don't see how it could be done," Spider said, staring at the floor, still feeling fragile, longing for a double-shot macchiato, and wondering if Iris might oblige him.

"Yeah," she said. "Even if he used one of those base-station units, with the handheld remote to blip into the break room—"

"We'd have seen the guy arrive and do the deed."

"What about some kind of loop?"

"Chrono-forensics would have found telltales in the feed — splices or patches of digital noise."

Iris nodded.

"Well the bloody head didn't just turn up in there by itself!" Spider said, thinking the bleeding obvious — and the frankly impossible. Severed heads, even the severed heads of time travelers, did not do that sort of thing. Severed heads generally died fast. Spider remembered from a university course long ago that during "The Terror" of the French Revolution countless unfortunates were put to the guillotine, and the scientists of the day had conducted tests to determine just how long consciousness might linger — and found it to be about a minute. The severed heads communicated by blinking once for yes and twice for no. The heads had to be kept alert for as long as possible — sometimes with slaps to the face, often by shouting obscenities to distract the head from its physical pain. He shuddered, thinking about it.

All the same, it gave him a thought. "You'll be getting him, it, autopsied, right?"

The question startled Iris. "Yes, yes, of course. Mysterious death. Might give us a lead on finding the rest of the body."

Outside, a pair of black crows, perched on a street light, cawed, the sound like mocking laughter.

In life, Dickhead had been the kind of man who, while not actually obese, somehow managed to take up a great deal of room. He had only to enter a room, dressed in his customary style of cheap off-the-rack suits, for it to feel suddenly full, all means of escape cut off. Spider, who had once been a gamer and missed it badly, always thought of the wargaming concept of "zone-of-control", in which a unit occupying a given hex on the map exercised control of the six surrounding hexes, preventing enemy units from passing. Dickhead used this power all the time when he wanted to talk to you, even if you were alone, out in the open, with empty space all around, you were pinned and there was no escape until he went away. It was the most baffling, appalling thing.

And yet, despite everything that Dickhead McMahon had been up to — from his constant harassment of Spider over the firm's drooping key-point indicators to his final and terrifyingly unlikely desire to create an empire at the End of Time itself, including the manipulation of Spider into handing over Molly — Spider found that he actually *missed* the great git.

It had been months since Dickhead's disappearance, and not a day went by when Spider did not reach into his desk drawer and read again that letter Dickhead had sent him. The letter telling Spider that he now owed Dickhead a favor, and that he would be calling on Spider to collect it. That moment, he was thinking, looked like it had arrived: Dickhead's faint, whispery voice, clearly in agony, desperately asking Spider for help.

As if he'd known that Spider would be there at that very moment and had deliberately arranged for his severed head to be in the fridge, and still just barely conscious and able, after a fashion, to speak. The timing of it from the severing of the head to its arrival in the fridge and discovery by Spider suggested the most careful planning, and careful planning suggested a more than typically baroque Dickhead scheme, but why?

And what was Spider supposed to do about it? Keep Dickhead from having his head cut off? The idea made Spider laugh, which quickly turned to coughing. And then Iris was there, pounding his back until he held up a hand for her to stop. "I'm okay. I'm fine," he said, still getting his breath, all woozy, the room tilting and turning around him. He sipped some more of his sugary tea, now cold and vile. "Listen," he said. "Could you get a decent bloody coffee?"

Iris looked at him, head tilted to one side, hands on her hips, unimpressed. "Do I *look* like I make coffee, Spider?"

"Just get the droid to do it. It'll be fine."

"What? That robot thingy?"

"It makes really good coffee, Iris."

Iris berated him about how she wasn't his receptionist, and that his actual receptionist, Malaria, who knew her way around a coffee machine, was sitting just outside the office door, but Spider stared at her, his eyes huge and moist and sad.

"Oh no, not the puppy dog eyes, not that!" Disgusted, she stomped out of Spider's office.

"So, Iris," Spider said, between sips of his near-perfect double-shot macchiato, already feeling revived by its heady steam, "the autopsy report on the head...?"

"You want me to give you a copy as soon as I get it?" she said.

"I'm kind of involved, don't you think?"

"Spider, at this point, you're a witness, and that's it."

"A witness? For God's sake, Iris—"

"Count yourself bloody lucky you're not a suspect!"

He sat there, trying to control his temper.

Iris looked at him, her face unreadable. "In your statement you mentioned a letter the deceased sent to you a few months ago."

"That's right." He got up, put his coffee down, and went to his desk to retrieve it. The letter was a few sheets of expensive, heavy paper, printed from one edge all the way over to the other edge, with no paragraphs. It was, Spider thought, the essence of Dickhead. "Here, read it yourself."

Iris took the letter and skimmed it while he went back to his coffee. He watched her face, a little amused, watching her eyebrows dancing up and down, the minute shakes of her head, her wince of disgust. That was the Dickhead experience, that was. She scanned the letter into her handheld, tagged it, and very carefully popped it into a plastic evidence bag. "This is the first time I've seen it," she said, annoyed at him. "It offers material evidence of his state of mind. You know we've been looking for him." Apart from his criminal activities at the End of Time, he was also wanted in the present, for countless offences against the Companies Act. Apparently there were a baffling number of secret bank accounts, connections to dodgy Swiss financiers, mysterious shell company structures (which more closely resembled coral outcroppings than straightforward business interests) and it appeared that he had siphoned off close to ten-billion dollars from his numerous legal and illegal interests.

"What was I supposed to tell you, Iris? That I got a lovely note from good old Dickhead, Emperor of the Universe, from the End of Time itself! 'Things going well here at End of Time Towers.' Yeah, I could see you loving me sharing that with you!"

"Spider, like I said, it's his state of mind. Meanwhile, our forensics people could very likely have lifted evidence from the letter that might have helped us locate him, and at the very least would have helped us give his wife — his widow, I suppose — a bit of peace of mind. Did you think of that, Spider?"

Spider knew Dickhead's wife, Sarah, only slightly. Sarah McMahon lived in an expensive apartment in a tower development in South Perth, with a dramatic view of the Swan River. Lovely place, he recalled. Sarah McMahon had recently been in touch with Spider, asking if he'd seen Dickhead. The last message she'd received from her husband said he would be home for a flying visit in March, but he never did show. She believed Dickhead "traveled a lot for business", which was why she was always stuck at home on her own, and hardly ever saw him. She had no idea about his vast Zeropoint empire. If she'd heard the name, she probably thought it was some kind of software startup Dickhead had invested in. Spider tried to avoid her. He wanted to tell her the truth about her wayward husband, but he knew she would never accept it. Even though Sarah had her own time machine, a high-end Japanese unit, very expensive, parked in the secure underground car-park beneath the apartment tower, it would never in a zillion years occur to her that her erstwhile husband had an entire separate identity, a secret life to top all secret lives, a long, long way from the exclusive avant-garde world of Perth high society. And yet, when she called, that pitch in her voice, the loneliness, the pain, and, worse, that knowing tone: she knew Spider knew what was going on, and very likely where Dickhead might be. Why wouldn't he tell her? Why? *Because, Sarah, it would blow your tiny mind to Kingdom Come, that's why!* The number of times he'd nearly told her, had even started to tell her. The time he went over there one night after work, fully intending to lay it all out for her — but hesitated as he stood at her front door, and finally turned and left. He couldn't do it. She didn't deserve it.

"That was a pretty shitty thing you did there, Spider," Iris said, reading her scan of the letter again. "She deserves to know who she's involved with."

"I know, but you're wrong."

Iris looked at him. He hid behind his coffee.

There was a very welcome knock at the door. "Boss?"

Iris blinked, surprised, and turned to face the door. "Ah. Kevin. Yes. What news?"

This was Iris' new off-sider, Detective Senior Sergeant Mullens, a solid, middle-aged fellow about Spider's age, poured into a bad suit, a man with a "great face for radio", as Spider had once put it. A man who, on close inspection, resembled a building in a suit. Spider thought Dickhead himself would have admired such a suit. Spider knew Mullens of old. They were not pals. And now, as Mullens spoke to Iris, he did not so much as glance at Spider. Which was fine with Spider, of course. Though he did say, "Oh, g'day, Mullens! I see you still haven't done much about that face of yours, have you?"

"Spider!" Iris said, giving him one of her trademark Looks of Death.

Mullens' face went pale, and seemed for a moment to pucker with tightly controlled anger. Still, he refused to acknowledge

Spider's presence. He paused, gathered himself, and told Iris, "We're about done here. Any last requests?"

Iris said, "Righto. Check everything once more for good measure, and I'll see you back at the office."

Mullens nodded acknowledgement. "Boss," he said, and left, closing the door behind him.

Iris sighed and turned back to Spider. "You don't do yourself any favors, do you?"

"Mullens and his irksome ilk never did me any favors, let me assure you."

She shook her head, clearly dismayed at all the juvenile bullshit.

Spider said, "So, no can do on the autopsy report, then?"

"I'll see what's what," she said, as if making a concession to him that cost her years of her life. Spider had no official standing in the WAPOL, and certainly not in the Time Crime Unit. Yes, he had been consulting with Iris here and there on a few cases these past few months, but not in any formally approved capacity. He was given a VISITOR badge when he showed up at Headquarters, something that had happened exactly twice, and both times it had nearly done him in, just being there.

Then Iris said, "For argument's sake, let's say Dickhead McMahon's head somehow managed to come back in time, or whatever, to ask for your help, presumably with keeping him from getting his head cut off—"

"Yeah, okay," Spider said, glad to be back to the matter at hand.

"And let's say he meant business with what he said in that letter, that he did tweak the universe from the End of Time in order to make you beholden to him—"

"Uh-huh."

"The thing I don't get, if all that is true, is just what you are supposed to be able to do for him."

"I know. I'm only good at fixing time machines."

"Exactly. Other than the resources you have at your disposal here at the shop, you've got nothing. You don't even have a proper place to live!"

"Dickhead doesn't care about that. Read his letter again. He believes I'm his Champion or some damn thing, and I should be with him, at his right hand."

"Bloody delusional!" Iris said, shaking her head.

"Yes, apparently only I can make everything better for him. He's got all these people: experts, brilliant minds, commandos and his letter says he wants me. Well I don't want him. I'm still having nightmares about his acolytes at the End of Time, all dead because Dickhead told them it was time to partake in the Final Secret, to pave the way for the End of Everything. I can't save him and I won't die trying."

CHAPTER 4

Four days later, Iris called Spider. Her voice was low and urgent.

"I need to see you. Now. Today."

"Cool," he said. "I'll order some lunch."

A whirl of questions went through his mind, and he knew he could ask none of them, not over an open, unencrypted line.

"Good." She hung up.

Iris arrived at half-past twelve. Spider told Malaria to show the detective straight through to his office. "Good to see you," he said. "Coffee?"

"Mmm, please," Iris said, pale and frowning, and took off her gabardine raincoat, slung it over the back of the guest chair, and sat down, legs crossed.

Spider thought she looked like someone about to sit an exam for which she hadn't studied: unsettled, fidgety, her face tense. *Hmmm,* he thought, concerned, and popped his watchtop, opened the coffee droid's interface, and summoned the machine.

"I really shouldn't be here," Iris said, still frowning.

"You sounded kind of freaked out on the phone," Spider said.

Iris rubbed her face; she looked tired and drawn. "I don't know. Just a feeling."

There was a knock on the door. Spider jumped, startled; Iris's eyes went wide. "God," she said.

"It's open!" Spider called. To Iris, he said, "It's the coffee droid."

Iris swore under her breath. The door swung open, and the droid shuffled in. "Spider-san! And guest!" it said. "I bring coffee-production system to you! What is…" It hesitated for programmed dramatic effect. "…your poison?"

"Oh, kill me now," Iris said.

Spider ordered his standard double-macchiato. Iris said she'd just like a good old, straightforward flat white, thanks. When the droid asked about biscuits, Spider waved it off. "Very good, Spider-san!" it said, as plumes of steam vented from it, and it started grinding fresh beans, surprisingly quiet, considering it was right there in the room with them. After a moment, as the fresh-ground coffee aroma began to fill the room, cups appeared, coffee began streaming into them, then appropriate doses of steamed milk (very little for Spider's macchiato; more for Iris' flat white, followed by a creamy dollop of steamed milk froth). "Your coffee," the droid said with a certain dramatic flair, "awaits!" Spider got up, grabbed the coffees, shook his head with amazement, telling the machine that it was a "good droid, very good," and that that would be all for now. The droid said, "Very good, Spider-san! I am but a moment away!" and it shuffled out the door.

Spider handed one of the cups to Iris, who stared into the finely-textured foam admiring the way the droid had managed an artful design in the *crema*. "Nice work, eh?" he said. "Amazing, considering how little we're paying for the lease—"

"Spider," Iris said. There was an all-business tone in her voice.

"Iris?"

"You asked about the autopsy report."

"Yeah."

"The preliminary report's in."

"Oh."

"We're waiting on the DNA. Machine's down. Needs a part from Taiwan." She shook her head, sighed, took an experimental sip of her coffee, paused, looking down at it, then at Spider.

Spider knew about lab machines from the old days. "Uh-huh," he said. Back then he was always having to wait for crucial test results because the machine involved was stuffed; or the service guy responsible for it was on holidays; or some damn thing. The lab people always did the best they could under trying circumstances.

"Anyway," Iris said, "the thing is this: as far as we can tell, it is the one and only Dickhead's head, or at least a very good cloned copy."

"Okay," Spider said, sure there was more to come, and that it was something bad. The way Iris seemed to be working her way up to it did surprise him. She was usually more direct, even unto the point of blunt rudeness.

"But get this," Iris went on. "The wound to his neck, the pathologist reckoned it was consistent with the head having been sliced cleanly off, not hacked or sawed or chopped, say. And there was likely more than one killer. One probably holding Dickhead's head back — like this," she said, using her free hand to pull her own head back, exposing her pale throat. "While someone else, well..." She left Spider to imagine the rest while she went back to her coffee. "This is surprisingly good, by the way," she said, an afterthought. "We should get one of those things for the office."

Spider blinked. One moment, she was illustrating and describing a gruesome murder, and the very next moment, commenting on the coffee. Had he, Spider, ever been like that, switching effortlessly between the full grand-guignol horror that often went with work on the Major Crime Squad, and the banal details of ordinary life? Very probably, he thought. Hell, maybe, in that deeply-buried part of his mind, that vault where he stored his secret superhero identity, 'Spider Webb, Homicide Squad', with all its "Just the facts, ma'am," patter, he was still like that. You had to be, he always told himself. It was necessary. You couldn't let the nature of the work you were always dealing with smash your head in. You still had to function. You had to be able to leave it behind at the office when you finally, *finally* went home to your ordinary suburban life — or so the staff counselors always said. All of which sounded great, but it didn't bear close scrutiny. The truth was that "leaving your work at the office" was perhaps the hardest single thing a cop had to do, and the truth was he had never been able to do it. What's more, he didn't know many other senior coppers who could, either. Every night, they always said, your sleep, it's just shit. You shut your eyes, and go for a ride through your very own private museum of the vicious shit people did to one another, usually for the most stupid reasons in the world, or, worse, for no reason whatever. Every night. Most coppers Spider knew told their wives, and other civilians, that yes, it was fine. You just leave the job at the station and go home, everything's fine, and you just pick it up the next day, no worries. Of course, there were some coppers who said that, and meant it. They could attend a nine-car horror-smash, and be fine afterwards. How did they do it? Spider never knew. Wasn't sure he wanted to know.

"Yo, Spider!" Iris said, snapping her fingers.

Spider blinked, startled. "Sorry, million miles away. Right. Yes. You said," he stopped, tried to remember. "Yes, Dickhead's head."

"His wife identified him."

He winced, imagining Sarah's horror at the sight of her incomplete husband. "Right. I'm guessing she had no idea where you might find the rest of him."

Iris nodded. "Not a clue."

It had been four days since he'd found the head in the break room fridge. Four nights without sleep, dreaming about Dickhead's enormous noggin filling that fridge, dripping blood, staring out at him, with that sharp look of recognition in his eyes, his blackened, blood-swollen tongue moving around behind yellow teeth. A Lovecraftian shoggoth lurking behind Dickhead's lips; millions of tiny biting hungry mouths rasping out, "*Help me. Help me.*"

Chilled, he blinked, and reminded himself where he was, what he was doing. He got up, stretching, yawning, and tried to shake that image.

"Spider? You sure you're—"

"Yeah, fine. Go on. What else you got?"

Iris watched him, concerned, but went on laying out details about the decapitation process, that the wound itself was precise, smooth, and that there would have been profound blood-loss approaching exsanguination. Moreover, the head showed signs that Dickhead had not been well for some time — that he hadn't been looking after himself; the texture of the skin was poor, and he looked much older than existing photo records suggested he should look.

Other than a guillotine, Spider thought, *how the hell would you go about cutting off a head in one quick, clean cut?* Quite apart from some thick, ropy muscle tissue in the neck, necessary to support that enormous head, there was the problem of the spine, with all those gnarly vertebrae just waiting to catch a knife not wielded with extreme surgical care. And the spine was tough to cut through. He'd seen documentaries about Mary Queen of Scots, whose brutal decapitation had taken a long time because of this very problem. It was the kind of thing that made Spider's blood run cold, the sheer unbridled horror of the Middle Ages — which, meanwhile, were among the most popular time travel tourist destinations of all.

Iris wasn't finished. "You didn't hear the 'best' bit, about his autopsy." She indicated large air-quotes around 'best'.

"Do I want to hear this?" He took some deep breaths.

Iris hesitated, glanced about the room, at the ceiling, and took a couple of deep breaths herself. She said, her eyes shut, "There were *things* in his head, Spider."

"What? Like tumors? Some kind of infection? Prions?"

She sighed, annoyed. "No."

"Well, what then? Come on. You come in here looking like trouble, you dance around the bloody topic for ages, preoccupied like I've hardly ever seen you, and I figure something's up, something real bad, and then you come out and that's all it is? Something in—"

"Spider. There were *structures* in his brain. Man-made artifacts. Implants. Complex webs of some kind of thread. Things. Technological things."

He stared at her, feeling strange. "In his brain?"

"Some kind of, I don't know, the pathology people are baffled. All they could do was describe the structures—"

"Structures?" Spider said again, gripped, a gathering tension in his gut. "So, like prosthetics, implants, you know, like…" He was thinking about the neural interfaces he'd read about, where people who were paralyzed, or who were in comas but still awake inside, or who had degenerative brain disorders, blind people, all sorts of people benefiting from remarkable technological developments that, years ago, were the stuff of , in Spider's opinion, tedious cyberpunk tales.

So, given all this, and the fact that Iris still looked dreadful, like she was what, apprehensive? Scared, even? What on Earth could possibly scare Iris Street? What could a big oaf like Dickhead McMahon possibly have going on in his head that could make Iris look like this? Spider was starting to feel like he really did not want to know. It was going to be nothing good. Structures built into your brain? *Nothing good could come from that*, he thought. That look on Iris' face made him feel like the bottom was falling out from under his world, tumbling away into a void where any damn thing could happen, a void just past the End of Bloody Time, and he felt chills all over again. But there was one question he had to ask, and it embarrassed him that if he hadn't read all that cheesy science fiction when he was younger he wouldn't even think to ask about it now. He said, terrified of the answer, "Did he still … was it still … was it still his own brain?"

Iris said, "Something had been done to it. Something had been built in it and around it, woven all the way through it, fibers and threads and tiny gritty structures in key areas of the frontal cortex."

"So, maybe something from the future?" There were stories of people here in the present who had dreadful illnesses who used their time machines to blip off to the various points in the future in search of medical miracles, the way sick people had once trekked off to Thailand and the Philippines and Mexico in search of miracle surgery and drug treatments. Such people often did not return.

"No, Spider. Not at all. The pathologists said they had never seen anything like what Dickhead had going on in his brain. They consulted with other pathology specialists around the world, too—"

"Uh-oh," he said, realizing what she was going to say next.

"Before the government told them to stop."

He nodded. Yes, exactly. Just what he feared. "The government?"

"'Fraid so."

"Right." This was why Iris looked the way she had when she arrived. This was the reason for all the dancing about. Very likely Section Ten of the Federal Department of Time and Space had stepped in to have a quiet word behind the scenes. Section Ten was the secret branch of the Department, and existed to — well, Spider was not sure exactly. As far as he and everyone else these days had been able to establish, Section Ten existed to do whatever the hell it pleased, and the government let them.

"My apologies, Spider, for not coming more directly to the point. I just," she said, glancing about again, "have concerns about people watching in ghost mode, you might say." Ghost mode was the means by which time travelers could conceal their presence, usually in the past, in order to witness historical events, without interfering. In ghost mode you were effectively "not there" in any way, except you were.

"I understand," Spider said, now also paranoid about ghost moded public servants, himself. The temptation to wave at the empty corners of the room was nigh irresistible. "Where does that leave us?"

"It leaves us with this," Iris said, taking off her watchtop and handing it over to him. He took it; it was warm from contact with her skin. He looked at the scratched-up screen, which showed a document reader, loaded with what looked like a government-issued report. The data indicator reported that it contained video, text and images. The crest of the Australian Government, as well as the logo for the Department of Time and Space, DOTAS, were prominent at the top. The document came with various suggestions for appropriate action the government might or might not take. The file was open to the executive summary, the kind of thing prepared for the Minister responsible for DOTAS, a civilian politician who, Spider suspected, had no clue what went on in his own department. The executive summary had markings all down the left margin, indicating which paragraphs were subject to which levels of secrecy. Many of them were designations Spider had never seen before. Then he noticed the appended distribution list. "This one," he said, pointing at one of the baffling acronyms, "is that the Department of the Prime Minister and Cabinet?"

"Yes," Iris said dryly.

"And this one?" He showed her.

"Office of National Assessments." An intelligence agency, part of ASIO.

"Right. And this?"

"I believe that's the head of ASIO." Australia's domestic intelligence service.

"ASIO?" Spider said, gulping. "I didn't know they were interested in time-travel-related stuff."

"Anything that might threaten the security — or even the very existence — of the nation is their bailiwick."

"I thought that was Section Ten."

"It's thought that ASIO's Temporal Affairs Office acts in a supernumerary capacity over Section Ten. Nobody knows for sure, of course." She tapped the side of her nose in a very significant manner.

"So," Spider said, once he'd wrapped his brain around this latest development, "the contents of Dickhead's enormous head were so alarming that the nation's spy agencies were notified, and the Prime Minister himself was directly informed."

"That's correct, yes."

"And now here you are, with a copy of the report."

Iris flashed a cheery smile for a moment. "I have to keep up with things, Spider."

Spider imagined squads of black-clad SAS soldiers on the end of rappelling lines crashing through the windows and into the room, bearing flashbangs and automatic weapons.

"And that's just the *preliminary* report," Iris said, all the color gone from her face.

"Shit," he said.

"But guess what?"

"Iris, what are you doing with this? You could be in—"

"I don't officially have it. And I'm not giving you a copy. I pirate-bayed it from a site called The Memory Hole."

"Of course!" he said, now scrotum-pricklingly scared. Perhaps Dickhead was a Johnny Mnemonic, a courier for valuable data from the future. Was Dickhead doing that? But if not that, then what?

"All right", Spider said, trying to get a grip. "Where does this all leave us? What's next?"

Iris was checking messages on her watchtop. She glanced up. "It leaves us nowhere, Spider."

"Why am I not surprised by that?"

"I told you the government stepped in to shut down the pathology work?"

"Let me guess," he said. "They confiscated the head."

"The head, the fridge, the feeds, everything."

"Damn," he said. "Have to get a new fridge. Not sure if the budget will stretch to that."

"Spider!"

"Well, what do you want me to say? We're screwed!"

Iris looked at him for a moment; then she leaned forward. "Not just yet. Listen."

CHAPTER 5

Spider's phone went off. It was Mr. Patel's office, in the city. His boss's expensive robot receptionist informed Spider that Mr. Patel wanted to see Spider tomorrow afternoon, at two p.m.

"Why's that? What's up?" Spider asked.

The receptionist explained to Spider, in a soft, sing-song sort of voice, very realistic, that Mr. Patel wanted to discuss Spider's terms of employment. "Nothing to worry about, of course," the receptionist was keen to reassure him, using a tone that might otherwise be used to inform him that he was about to receive a slice of cake.

Oh, shit, Spider thought, staring around at the vast empty spaces in the workshop. The base-station time machines combined with the economic fallout from the world's financial system's long-forestalled ultimate collapse had come to make Spider's day, far sooner than he had hoped. "Okay," he said his mouth dry as outback dust. "I'll, um, right," he said, and touched his phone-patch to kill the link.

Next day, at two p.m., dressed in his best civilian outfit, cotton trousers and a short-sleeved blue poly-cotton long-sleeved shirt, but the same scuffed Doc Marten boots he wore all the time, Spider found himself on the sixty-eighth floor of a gleaming office tower on St. George's Terrace, a little woozy from the too-fast lift. Outside, it was a lovely day, an early taste of spring: bright, sunny, mild breeze; three small, puffy clouds. The views from the enormous windows were sublime: the swollen

Swan River, like blue glass, pressing against the concrete barrier walls erected along the city foreshore; picturesque yachts cruising about, sails luffing in the light breeze; the huge white apartment towers along the South Perth foreshore startling against the harsh blue sky. The door to the Perth office of the Bharat Time Machine Company of Mumbai stood before him, with its colorful logo that tried to combine the Hindu god Ganesh and a stylized time machine. He hesitated, not sure what to do, but full of a sense of impending doom.

Spider's coworker, Charlie, himself full of false cheer and bravado, no doubt waiting for his own call to come and have a chat with Mr. Patel, had taken Spider into the city in the shop's battered old Nissan fuel-cell van, and gave Spider a chummy punch in the shoulder telling him to "kick arse", and to "make sure the boss follows all the terms of the employment contract!"

Spider said that he would indeed kick arse and have a word with Mr. Patel. *If*, he thought, *he could*. The fact was that trade union membership in Australia was down to under ten percent of the workforce, and time machine repair technicians did not have any kind of formal union representation. Spider, Charlie and Malaria had had some legal protections and rights under the terms of their contracts with Dickhead, but when the Bharat Group, and in particular its business unit concerned with time machines, came to town, and took over the Time Machines Repaired While-U-Wait operation, and all its franchisees, the first thing they did was to instigate new individual employee contracts. Spider, who remembered the way that the trade union movement had taken care of his dad and grandfather, back in the day, felt vulnerable and scared.

He approached the glass entrance to the office suite; it swept aside, beckoning him within. Faint, haunting but very pleasant Indian music played at him, and there was a beguiling mélange of scents, spicy and exotic but not distracting, that carried him into the reception area. The sheer expanse of the space was magnificent. The Bharat offices occupied three floors of this build-ing, all of them arranged around a central glass atrium. From somewhere he could hear a waterfall, a real waterfall. There were beautiful rainforest plants everywhere. And the view! You could walk out onto a vast observation deck that projected out from the side of the building, all cantilevered engineered glass. Spider did not dare step out onto that platform. The height, the fear of the glass failing, it was too much and as it was he already felt a little woozy, a little buzzy, like he was not quite in his right mind.

The receptionist, a female-type android, skinned to look like a gorgeous Indian princess, all luminous saris, gold jewellery, caramel skin and dark, liquid eyes, with the red dot in the forehead he had never understood, floated across to him, a picture of serenity. "Mr. Webb?" she said, her voice very realistic, her accent Mumbai-meets-Oxbridge. Her face and form strongly suggested a beautiful young woman, without looking too much exactly like one. It was more that her appearance suggested those things, like a Picasso sketch of a beautiful young woman, rendered in plastic, vinyl, rubber and glass. The effect was disarming, but also a little disturbing, Spider thought.

"Hello, um, hi, um—" Spider tried to say, but found he could hardly talk. His mouth was dry, and now that he was here, moments away from his appointment, he was starting to feel numb, clammy, and not sure his legs would hold him up much longer. "Do you mind — a glass of water, and if you don't mind, I'll just sit over..." he gestured at a couch with a spectacular view of the river below. There was just one cloud visible from this position, small and discreet, perfectly art directed.

Seated, he felt a little better. When the receptionist presented him, with elegant economy, the glass of fresh water he had requested, he found he had to hold the glass with both hands, and even then, they shook so much he thought he was going to splash water everywhere. All at once, he felt ill, the way he used to feel just before exams at university, and in the police service when he was trying to get a promotion. This whole place, this perfection of space and design, was, he thought, oppressively beautiful. It was too much. It was no wonder they had a robot receptionist: a human receptionist would have found it too hard to take and likely would have quit after two hours. He compared it with the decidedly humble reception area back at the shop, with its naked brickwork, cheap laminate counter-tops, the posters and calendars up on the walls showcasing gorgeous high-end time machines, classic units from the previous decade, when designers put a bit of work into their drawings. Time machines that looked like they were going fast, as if they sped through time.

So, he thought, aware that time was slipping away from him, the way everything lately was slipping away from him, even his entire line of work, there's nothing left to do but take it like a man and watch the whole world, the world he had known all his life, go away, like colorful Christmas paper after all the presents are opened and revealed. It was a hard thing to contemplate, even harder to accept, the inevitable tide of technological progress, which even as it created careers for some, also destroyed careers for others. It felt, weirdly, like a punishment, Spider was thinking. He'd done his best, he'd always done his best, whether for his parents, the police, for Molly, for Dickhead. He'd struggled always to be his best self, to do what he had to do, and to always work in his own timeline, to keep from needlessly complicating the nature of reality. Even as he'd veered off into other realities for work purposes, he'd always come back here, to this world, to this time, because this was home. It was hard, now, to escape the possibility, as what he laughingly called his career hung in the balance, that he had been a mug from the beginning.

And now things were happening and changing so fast it was hard to keep up. These days even the small details of everyday life changed from moment to moment but nobody much commented on them. But with the Chinese doing their damnedest to sell off US treasury bonds as fast as they could possibly do it, not caring that they were sinking much of the rest of the world in the process, it was as if everything he recognized and understood about the world, and how the world worked, was simply going away. Even Molly was off in New York, squired about town with lovely Stéphane, chatting about "negative space articulation," and "alienated *weltanschauung*". It was all Spider could do to hang on against the receding tide, worried it might be the sort of receding tide that occurred just before an enormous crushing tsunami rolled ashore, spreading everywhere, sweeping everything aside in black chaos. He remembered the video he'd seen, years back, of the tsunami that hit Fukushima, the darkness of the water, spreading across the land like a cancer, claiming everything.

"Mr. Webb," the receptionist said, startling Spider so much he jumped and spilled the water all over himself.

"Shit," he said, getting to his feet, dizzy, hardly able to balance, feeling like a man about to be led to the gallows. "Yes, yes, sorry, look, sorry, I just — Mum always said I had two left feet," he mumbled, trying to make a joke of his embarrassment.

"Mr. Patel will see you now."

CHAPTER 6

Spider steadied himself, pulled his pants up a little, and switched his phone-patch to route any incoming calls and messages to his watchtop. Satisfied, he took a moment and polished the scuffed toe of each of his Doc Martens on the back of the opposite leg. "Right," he said. *Everything is going to be fine,* he told himself. *It might not even be bad news. It might be a promotion. It might be all kinds of things. Why assume the worst?* Spider made his way across the floor to Mr. Patel's door — was that real, living grass he was walking on here? — knocked once, heard Mr. Patel say, "Come in, Mr. Webb!" The door seemed to melt away to one side. Impressed, but trying not to blurt out stupid remarks, Spider said, quietly, "Whoa."

Then he stepped inside. He felt his scrotum tighten. The office, he thought, glancing about, was like a big white hangar, an immense space, with great dazzling blocks of harsh white light angling across opposing walls from the floor to ceiling windows. *The rent,* he thought, *must be crippling.* It was less a room, less an office, and much more a — what was the word? Yes, it was a *chamber*. For a moment he could imagine a symphony orchestra in here, playing something by Wagner, maybe.

And there was his employer, Mr. J. K. Patel, a small dark-skinned man in a big white room. In place of Patel's eyes, Spider saw he now sported the new and hideous black "eye-plugs" that served as a combination visual sensor array and high-speed data antennae. Despite this, Spider did have an impression that Mr. Patel looked like a man in his last hour of waiting on Death Row.

There was a strange heaviness to the otherwise immaculately dressed man, a weariness, that did not go with his youthful appearance. As far as Spider had been able to find out, Mr. Patel was only about twenty-nine years old. His short dark hair was already greying.

"Mr. Webb!" Patel said, calling from over by his desk, forcing cheery enthusiasm into his voice. "Welcome to the Bharat Group, to the Nerve Centre, if you will!" He managed a light laugh. "Thank you for coming. I trust you are well, that things at the Malaga workshop are proceeding smoothly. How are those key-point indicators shaping up, good I hope? Yes?"

Spider stood there, not knowing quite what to say. Mr. Patel was still coming across the great gulf of space between him and his desk, its smooth surface like a frozen pond of something sinister. Patel's vivid white teeth gleamed, betraying his other-wise well-presented Indian heritage.

There was, Spider thought, something odd about meeting Mr. Patel, in the flesh. In video conferences, mail messages, and his constant online exhortations to Spider that, even though Spider was doing a great job, he could still do better; Spider had an impression of his boss as a young man in a big hurry, keen to achieve great things for the company, as soon as humanly possible. He always seemed to have a billion items on his to-do list, and they all had to be actioned by close of business, or there would be consequences from his superiors in Sydney, and maybe even from the board, back in Mumbai. Spider always felt like he was taking up Mr. Patel's precious time, and Patel never did anything to correct that impression. His meetings with his boss had always been over and done with in less than two minutes. Messages he received from him filled no more than two lines of heavily compressed prose that sometimes resembled Orwellian Newspeak by way of phone texts.

And now here he was, coming toward Spider like something inevitable, like death itself, only smiling, and wearing a five-hundred-dollar business shirt, with the sleeves rolled up.

"I trust you had no trouble getting here today, Mr. Webb?" Patel said, almost there, beginning to stick his hand out for Spider to shake.

"Charlie drove me in, in the shop van. I hope that's okay, sir." Spider hoped that the thought of using work-related resources wouldn't be an issue.

Then, all at once, as if by magic, Mr. Patel was there, in Spider's face, smiling up at him with too many teeth, shaking his hand so hard Spider thought he was going to lose all feeling. It was those teeth, more than anything, so white, so luminous, and so many: for a moment Spider thought of sharks, with their rows and rows of spare teeth, all lined up like troops, ready to step into the front rank if one of the front teeth fell in battle. Another thing that was strange, and that Spider had failed to notice before: Patel's shoes made no sound on the glossy marble floor as he came over to greet Spider. You would have thought, if you were paying attention, and not simply freaked out over the whole situation, that in such a cavernous space, with such a hard floor, his footsteps would have boomed and rung and echoed about, multiplying — but there had been none of that. As if Mr. Patel had glided over, on a cushion of air. The impression added to the sense of eeriness, of stepping from a place of mere luxury into something unearthly.

As Mr. Patel made welcoming small-talk, his hand wrapped around Spider's right arm as if holding on to a life-preserver for dear life, he walked Spider across to a low, white leather sofa big enough to seat ten large people. As he sat down, and down, and down into the thing, knowing he was never getting out of this seat ever again, he happened to glance upward into the great vault of empty space above: *that ceiling*, he thought, *must be, what? Ten metres? Fifteen? Oh, what's that?* There was something up there, dangling by wires from the ceiling, some kind of large mechanical sculpture thing? *An ode to Victorian engineering?* He'd lived with a mad sculptress for long enough that he knew (believed, really) that much of what passed for art these days was bullshit, all naked emperors and nobody commenting on it. In any case, as soon as he registered, "ah, sculpture", he lost interest and looked away. But there was something about it that reminded him of something familiar.

Then, Mr. Patel was blathering — nervously, Spider thought, surprised — about offering Spider a beverage. "Tea? Coffee? Chai, perhaps? What would you like? Nothing is too much trouble for our VIP guests, Mr. Webb."

Spider felt as if he were floating in space, cut off from reality. VIP guests? "Nothing, thank you, sir, I'm fine," he said, hoping to get on with the business at hand. Patel bustled about the coastline of his desk, fussing with things, rubbing his face, brushing at imaginary dust on the great empty surface of that desk. He was clearly trying to convey a sense to Spider that things here at head office were going just swimmingly, and that he was an honored guest, but Spider felt there was something very wrong with this picture, and that he was about to find himself right in the white-hot center of that trouble, just as soon as Patel settled down. It was all he could do to keep from telling his boss to take a seat and get on with it.

At length, Patel took a small gold stylus from his shirt pocket and touched several points on the desk surface, which extruded various intricate structures. Patel watched these developments, frowned a moment, then tapped the structures twice more, which caused other, smaller structures to rise up, which he tapped with his fingers. That done, Spider watched the structures subside as the smooth surface of the desk returned. Satisfied, Patel set the stylus down on the desk, and leaned back, hands clasped across his stomach, making a performance of being relaxed and comfortable; a leader in charge of great things.

"So, Mr. Webb," he said. "It is good of you to see me today, so soon after I requested an interview."

This was something Spider had not expected. "I'm sorry, what was that?"

"I know you're terribly busy attending to business at the workshop there in Malaga, fighting the good fight, doing your best for the Group. You certainly don't need Management getting in your way, demanding your presence, now do you?"

"Actually," Spider said, not sure why he said it, "business is…" He was going to say, "business is pretty quiet, we've only got one unit…" but he hesitated before saying it in case Mr. Patel took that as evidence that Spider and Charlie were somehow slacking off, and that perhaps it might be an idea to review the staffing levels at the Malaga operation. Spider did remember that he had been summoned here today to discuss "the terms of your employment." If that didn't mean a reduction in hours, or a shift to part-time, or, worse, casual hours, Spider didn't know what did. It would explain Patel's erratic behavior. Spider knew that some managers were very uncomfortable with delivering bad news to employees, and would resort to all manner of weird measures to avoid it, or even to couch a "radical change of status" as somehow a positive thing for the employee in question. "An opportunity for growth!" such a manager might say. Maybe Patel was one such manager, knowing today was the day he had to fire Spider, but feeling terrible about doing so, particularly in the current awful business conditions. Who wouldn't? With all this in mind, Spider thought, *what have I got to lose, other than absolutely everything*? He was not a man who would beg to keep his job. If the axe was indeed swinging, he would take it and move on, somehow.

Patel said, "That is good to hear, very good to hear, Mr. Webb."
His boss got up again and stalked about, before settling at last, in
front of his desk, leaning against it, steepling his thin fingers. "Of
course. Which is why we must all redouble our efforts. We must
strive to achieve our greatest effort — do you see, Mr. Webb—?"
He broke off at this point, shaking his head, and then grinning,
a little sheepishly. "I cannot keep calling you Mr. Webb. Please,
may I call you Aloysius?"

Spider winced. "Um, look, sir. If you want to call me anything,
call me Spider. Everybody calls me Spider. This 'Mr. Webb' bloke
is my old man, right?"

Mr. Patel smiled. "Yes, of course. I know just what you mean.
It always bothers me when people call me 'Mr. Patel', for the
same reason." All the same, Spider noticed, Mr. Patel did not
invite Spider to call him by some friendlier name.

So far, so weird, Spider thought as he glanced around the office,
finally looking upward, at the sculpture thing up there — but
this time, he recognized it, and, pointing, said, "Wait a minute.
Is that…?"

Patel beamed. "Yes, it is, Spider. The original prop from the
movie."

"The original prop?"

"Ah, yes. It took a long time to find it, and then have it
restored," Mr. Patel said, also looking up, his face now radiant
with genuine happiness.

"There is no way that's the original from the movie! That was…
God, that was" He counted decades in his head. "Nineteen—"

"Nineteen Sixty," Patel said. "It took a great deal of finding, I
can assure you."

It was The Time Machine, from the George Pal 1960 movie
of the same name, complete with its great spinning disc, the
beautiful gleaming brass-work, the control panel from which
Australian actor Rod Taylor, playing the mysterious Victorian-
era Time Traveler, propelled the fabulous device through time at
breathtaking speeds, the world blurring past, mountains rising
and falling, cities forming and dissolving into dust, all the way
to the unthinkable year 802,701 AD. And now it was hanging
up there, tilted over at a rakish angle, to show it off. How could
he possibly have written that glorious thing off as just another
pointless bit of post-post-modern art? It was, well, it was a piece
of magic, right there.

Mr. Patel went on, "And guess what, Spider?"

"What?" Spider said, still staring up at it, captivated despite himself, all other concerns shunted momentarily aside.

"It works."

"It works? How can it — oh, wait! Did you—?"

"It is, of course, a film prop. Mostly made of wood, some cheap metal, then dressed up to look good on screen. When we had it restored, we used real brass, for example. We rebuilt it the way it should have been, if such a device had existed in the real world. And, yes, we gave it a fuel-cell, hidden under the pilot's seat, and a custom engine, combining scanning and translation into one unit, concealed in the control panel, and we rigged an interface for the controls, so that the original controls would work as they do in the film."

"And the big ... spinny thing?" Spider said, losing control of his speech capability for the moment.

"Spins very nicely," Mr. Patel said. "Purely decorative, of course."

Well, bugger me! Spider thought, but did not say out loud, still looking at it, this unexpected thing. He kept staring at it until he noticed his neck was getting sore, and he managed to look away, and saw that Mr. Patel had gone back to sit behind his desk.

Patel said, smiling, "I take it you are a fellow collector of time machines, Spider?"

"What? No, oh, God no, no not at all, sir. I just fix them. If you ask me, they're nothing but trouble. But that..." Spider paused, "is a fine piece of movie magic." From a time when movies *were* magic, the last days of the old Hollywood studio system. These days if a film called for a prop like that, it would most likely be rendered digitally; if it had to exist in the real world at all, it could be whomped up in a 3D printer, sintered from various powders, fused together with lasers — and utterly disposable, like most of the films that came along these days. Nobody would preserve such a thing; nobody would see the point in keeping and restoring such props. It was a sad thing, at least for people Spider's age, who remembered better times.

It was hard to go back to business, particularly when he saw the way Mr. Patel stared up at it, his black faceted eye-plugs drinking in the sight, enjoying the way the afternoon light reflected off the brass control handles. And in that moment, Spider noticed a strange thing. He found to his surprise that he did not dislike Mr. Patel. Which, obviously, was a long way from actually liking the man, but who knew? Maybe that would come in time. Yes, the man was annoyingly gung-ho about business matters, always sweating quarterly profit margins and business cycles and retail paradigms — to say nothing of those bloody key-point indicators — but, and this was the crucial thing, he was not simply a manager who had no grasp of what his company actually did or produced. Mr. Patel was, he saw, an enthusiast — a time machine enthusiast. Someone who, even if he had not wound up in the business, would still have been mad keen on the damn things, despite their trickiness, and their lure of false hope.

The thing Spider hated about time machines was that people got them, thinking they could fix everything that had gone wrong in their lives. Thinking they could go back and make amends for things they wished they'd not done. Thinking they could save loved ones from terrible fates, or magically improve their love lives. Too many people thought of time machines as magical "Get out of Personal Responsibility Free" devices. In times past, if you did something rotten, or hurt someone you loved, or didn't do so well with the ladies, you tried to learn from it, and maybe become a better person in the future. Now people who'd done those sorts of things — and worse — simply figured, Oh well, I'll jump in my time machine, and fix it. Which was fine, but in ninety-eight percent of such cases, time machine operators succeeded only in making their situations worse. Only two percent of time machine operators ever managed to achieve success, because they had taken the time to read up, both on the tubes and in countless how-to downloads, on time theory, which said, in part: If you tweaked the timeline at exactly the right *nodal point*, you could achieve just about anything. It was tricky, required expensive software and charts, but the ordinary home time machine operator could do it. Spider used to explain this to frustrated time machine owners who came to see him, wondering why everything they did with their time machines only made things worse. He told them what to read, which videos to watch on the tubes, where to get the appropriate software. He had, at one time, been very helpful to these people, because it was important to keep people enthused about time travel, because that helped sell units, and that meant more business. Except the great majority of them came back a week later, complaining that it was all Spider's fault. Yes, he thought, it was his fault. It was his fault for trying to help idiots.

Mr. Patel was roaming about the room again, talking, and Spider had not been listening. "I'm sorry, could you repeat that, please?" he said, worried that he'd missed his own sacking.

"It's all right, Spider," Patel said, a little sharpness in his tone. "I was just talking about my very first jump in time, years ago, with my father, shortly before he died."

"Oh," Spider said, embarrassed. "Right. Sorry."

Mr. Patel returned to his seat, sat there staring over Spider and out at the view across the swollen river, lost in his own thoughts, troubled, something weighing on him.

Spider let this go on for half a minute and then said, "Okay, um, look, you asked to see me today?"

All the joy had drained from Patel's face. "Yes, yes, I'm afraid I did — or rather, I do."

"The message I got from your receptionist said it was about the 'terms of my employment'."

"Oh," Mr. Patel said, annoyed, drumming the fingers of his right hand on the desk. "She said that? My goodness that must have terrified you out of your wits."

"It did give me pause for thought," Spider said, understating by orders of magnitude.

"Of course, of course. No, that is not quite the message I wanted her to pass on to you. My sincere apology. No, you see, I saw in your personnel record that you, at one time, worked for the state police service."

"That's right, yes," Spider said, astonished. Why on Earth would he want to talk about that? Was all of that going to catch up with him here, now, after all these years? He took a breath. *You don't know what Patel wants. Just hear him out. It's probably nothing.*

"I believe you did very well? High rank while still a young man? Very impressive achievement."

Frowning, worried, Spider said thanks.

"It says here," Patel continued reading something glowing in his desk surface, "that you became a whistleblower? Uncovered extensive corruption? Is that right?"

"It is, yes, sir." *Keep it together, Spider. Keep it together.* He could feel the old anger starting to boil.

"That could not have been easy for you, going against your own kind like that. The traditional lot of the whistleblower…"

"You're not wrong," Spider said, unable to keep from saying so.

"Good, very good," Patel said, nodding, glancing at Spider, and nodding some more.

"Okay," Spider said.

Mr. Patel said nothing for a long moment, his hands folded over his stomach, a terrible blank look on his face, or so it looked at least, to Spider. Those eye-plugs made Mr. Patel's emotions tricky to read. "Do you have any children?"

"No, sir. Not been blessed."

"Children can be a very great blessing," Patel said, staring out the enormous window behind Spider.

"I'm sure they can," Spider said, starting to understand what might be coming next. Something about Mr. Patel's kids. That his own police background might somehow be relevant. *There were only so many ways a set-up like that could play out, none of them good,* he thought.

"Of course, they can also be..." he trailed off, and glanced back at Spider. Eye-plugs or not, Mr. Patel was ashen. He fiddled distractedly with the gold band of his watch, trying to make it sit properly. He went on. "I — or, rather, my wife and I — we have only one child. A boy." The way he said it, using the tone of voice you might use to tell someone that you had three months to live, filled Spider with dread. All at once, he saw that whatever was going on here would soon be his problem.

"Uh-huh," Spider said, adopting a defensive voice.

"His name is Vijay. He's nine years old."

The man was clearly in pain and Spider was starting to feel a great sympathy for his boss. Only minutes ago, he'd been bursting with time machine geekery, lost in the magical glow of the movie prop hanging over their heads. *No trace of the time machine enthusiast now,* Spider thought. Patel had sunken into himself, retreating from the well-honed image of "business predator". *Broken, with all his stuffing ripped out,* Spider thought, as his own well-honed copper instincts for ferreting out the truth in any situation kicked in. Patel's body language practically shouted that his boy was dead, but Patel had said "his name *is* Vijay". So, if the boy was not dead, there were only a few other possibilities that would leave a parent looking like that.

"Whatever it is, Mr. Patel, I'm sure it's—"

Mr. Patel slammed a fist onto the glass table surface. Spider jumped, startled. Mr. Patel, now staring at him, moisture brimming along the underside of those eye-plugs, ashamed, said, his voice a hoarse whisper, "Spider, my boy is gone."

Oh, shit, Spider thought. He'd been right. "How long has it been?" He wondered if Patel and his wife were separated, and whether she might have taken the boy on a 'visit to meet the family', and simply not returned. It was a dismayingly common tactic employed by separated parents, typically in mixed marriages. Trying to get the child back from his abductor-parent could be, Spider knew, insanely difficult, negotiating the treacherous reefs of two countries' legal systems.

Relieved that this meeting was no longer focused on "the job", Spider said, "Pardon me for asking this, but was it your wife?"

Patel was shocked. "What? My wife? No, no, not at all. No, it's not that. He's not been abducted, nothing like that."

"No? Oh, well, in that case — oh," he said. "Then is he...?" This was unbearably awkward; he felt like he was intruding in the most delicate of matters.

Mr. Patel peered at Spider, confused for a moment, then understood, and managed a weak smile that never reached his eye-plugs. "Oh, you think — no, Spider. No, Vijay is, as far as I'm aware, still very much alive. I'm sure I would know if he had passed from this life."

Now Spider was confused. "So Vijay isn't dead, and not kidnapped — but he is gone? Um, sir?"

"He's taken off in my time machine, Spider."

"You have another time machine? Not this one?" He gestured up at the Machine overhead.

"Oh, yes, Spider. As it happens, I do have another machine, at home. I believe the term these days for such a time machine is, 'hotrod'? Yes? She is, so to speak, 'totally tricked out'." Mr. Patel smiled a little self-consciously, aware that he sounded like a fool.

"Oh," Spider said, dismayed.

"You're beginning to see the problem."

"He's nine years old, you said."

"Yes, Spider, and he's gone. And so is my machine."

Spider had heard stories, since starting to work in the time machine biz, of kids getting up to all kinds of mischief with their parents' time machines. Even quite young kids, though he had never heard of someone as young as nine making off with one. "How does a nine-year-old even know how to operate a time machine?" he said.

"He's my son. He shares my enthusiasm for all things time-travel-related. It's one of the few things we have in..." He trailed off, and dabbed at his eye-plugs. Spider looked away. Mr. Patel apologized profusely, and took a moment to compose himself.

"All right," Spider said, a little too cop-friendly. "Young Vijay appears to have absconded with your time machine. Fine. Can you please give me some details of the time machine in question?" Spider could hardly believe how easily he had slipped back into the old habits and professional demeanor of Detective Senior Sergeant Spider Webb. "Let's start with the technical side of things, so I have a baseline idea of just how far away in time Vijay might be." Spider knew some hotrod time machines could jump a few thousand years; others might travel even farther down- or up-time.

"She's a custom job. Very fast. Very powerful," said Patel.

Hotrods, once the domain of funky old cars given new life with sexy overpowered chromed-up engines and slick custom paint jobs, now included bog-standard old time machines, typically Tempos or Dolphins, which hobbyist tinkerers "fixed up": all-new, barely legal, radically overclocked, liquid-nitrogen-cooled engine units, often mounted in parallel, put together with long-range refrigerated hydrogen-slush fuel-cells, with just a two-seater cabin, all pimped out with custom fittings, and then the entire thing given a slick paint and polish job. If the hotrod's owner was truly on his game, he would likely have gone to the trouble of making the cabin air-tight, and organized some reconditioned Chinese EVA suits — just in case. Such hotrod time machine pilots sometimes liked to see just how far back in time they could go — the current record, for a single jump, was 74,200 years; but most hotrodders eventually attempted to jump into the Future. The farthest future jump — with the telemetry data to prove it — was a gobsmacking 142,000 years. It was far less than Rod Taylor had gone in the eponymous Time Machine. The pilot of that record-setting machine, a kid of nineteen, returned in a persistent vegetative state. Attempts to make sense of the contents of his extremely agitated but still conscious mind proved fruitless.

"So," Spider said, "you built yourself your very own hotrod."

"It's my hobby! Something to play about with in my down-time. It helps me think about things, provides a distraction."

"I see. And young Vijay helped you out, passed you tools while you tinkered with the components, listening to you, lapping it all up.

"Parminder," he said, shaking his head, "she's been after me to sell it for years."

"That would be your wife?"

"Parminder. Yes. Light of my existence." He affected a dull monotone, saying this, which Spider could not help but find amusing, thinking about his own history with Molly.

"She was concerned about Vijay getting into trouble with it."

"I'm assuming you had the unit pretty seriously secured, yes?" Spider said

"The starter unit was in a safe in my home office!"

Spider could feel a headache coming on. He shook his head. "When did you last see the boy?"

"Two days ago."

"Have you reported him to the police as a missing person?"

"No, Spider. I have not."

"Um, what?"

"I said, 'No—'"

"I heard what you said. It's just that I can't believe you said what you said. Sir."

"I am doing my best to keep the police from getting involved."

Spider thought a moment. "So you've heard from kidnappers?" Which made no sense, because Patel said the boy had not been kidnapped. So, if not kidnapped, and the kid had simply taken off with the machine to God knows when, why not tell the cops? "You are aware," Spider said, "that there is now a dedicated Time Crime Unit attached to the Major Crime Squad. I could put you in touch with—"

"Spider, yes, of course I know. Of course! I am not a stupid man."

Spider was up out of his seat, and leaning, on his fists, on the edge of Patel's desk, glaring down at his boss. "Then what are you not telling me?"

"Spider, please, sit. I will explain everything."

"You'll explain everything. Fine. Great!" Spider said, but inside, in his mind, he was thinking, *Bag and cat have now parted company.*

"It's a complicated affair."

"Of course it is." Spider sat back in his seat and rubbed his face, sure he was not going to like this next bit. "Complicated," he said. "Nothing's ever simple, is it? It's never, 'Oh well, I'll just download some fresh bloody drivers, and she'll be right'. Oh, no. It's always, 'Oh, Spider, look, it's complicated...'" He shook his head, eyes closed, feeling his beleaguered heart racing, aware of the adrenaline gushing through his body. He wanted to hit something, someone. *If only Stéphane were here,* he thought.

CHAPTER 7

Patel went over to stand by the billowing window, the glass darkening to ease the blaze of the afternoon sun, and told Spider everything. It was quite a story.

Patel had indeed built himself a superior hotrod time machine. It was, he said, "fully unlocked." Spider bit his lip. That meant the machine was unregistered. DOTAS had no idea it existed. That meant it could go anywhere, and the operator could do just about anything, unfettered by the usual restrictions imposed by governments everywhere on time machine use. "And your kid's got it?" Spider said, more to himself then to Patel.

"My work is extremely demanding, Spider. Business conditions are nearly impossible, and yet here I am trying to establish a Bharat Group presence in this country, intending to take advantage of that very situation. It is… It is hard. Very hard. Obtaining working credit in order to build, to hire staff, to buy plant and equipment — there is almost nowhere today you can get it at anything less than loan-shark rates, and even those sources are starting to balk. To be perfectly frank with you, Mr. Webb, I am not at all sure we can make a success of this venture."

If Mr. Patel were a soldier, he would be on the point of rout, ready to flee the field of battle. He was exhausted, Spider saw, beyond the point of utter fatigue, but Patel knew he had to fight on, regardless. How close was this man to a full-on breakdown? There was only so much pressure one could take before he snapped. Spider knew that only too well from his own experience. Push a man too far and you might damage him for life.

"Right, I didn't know things were in such bad shape," said Spider.

"That's business," Patel said, sounding like one of the many motivational videos Spider had been required to watch. "You take your opportunities where you find them. Work hard. Be diligent. Own the chronotechnology market."

Spider was all too aware of the impossible business conditions under which the Bharat Group was battling. Things started to spiral down when, to no-one's great surprise but awe-inspiring dismay, the United States president resigned from office, citing the "ungovernability of the union". The United States was "united in name only," the president had said. Vital legislation in the nation's interest could no longer be passed. The two legislative assemblies could no longer function. Bipartisanship was dead. So the president decided to fall on his sword, and he hoped his successor, his very surprised-looking vice president, might do better. International financial markets and institutions had not reacted well. The US dollar, already a mere shadow of its former robust self, crashed, blue-chip companies — businesses that had lasted a century or more, that had withstood the deadly rollercoaster financial crises of the past twenty years — laid off eighty percent of their workforce, or closed altogether, turned the lights off, locked the doors on their way out. It all happened so fast, the media — in any form — could hardly keep up. Suicide rates soared. People marched in the streets by the millions, waving signs, demanding the US be bailed out, and castigating the ex-president as a "quitter".

In the midst of the catastrophe, one product remained a strong seller, the one thing everybody wanted: time machines. Desperate people needed to think they could use the damned things to escape their predicaments. Millions attempted to use the machines for a one-way emigration back to the past, where they could set up new businesses, buy cheap land, and start over. It didn't matter that they might run into their past selves. They could exist in the same timeline without consequence. Spider knew this and supposed most of the time travelers just didn't care. Others opted to vault over the current crisis, hoping to land on the other side of it all, when things had settled, the US was saved, and it was back to business as usual. And, of course, no surprises, there were still others who simply wanted to meddle and speculate, either trying to keep everything from going bad in the first place; or hoping to find the critical nodal point that had set the catastrophe in motion. The United States had never been short on people keen to make money from ordinary people's fears of the future. These folks, the meddlers and the for-profit prophets were the ones who kept running afoul of the US government's Timeline Security cops, many of whom had gone private, and still, as in Australia, very keen to keep people from using chronotechnology to take any kind of financial advantage of their knowledge of how things have turned out. How could such time cops possibly know what 'simple, honest folks' were up to? It was a common question: just how *do* they know what I'm doing? The answer: they just know. That's all you need to know. And when you bought a new time machine, you had to sign a clause in the sales document specifying that you were aware of the government's regulations governing this kind of thing, and that you would indeed comply with it. Yes, they would argue, but if the government's collapsed, and the constitution's just a piece of paper, how can you prosecute me with any kind of validity? It didn't matter. Some rules were bigger than mere national constitutions.

CHAPTER 8

Spider stood, staring out the window. He saw that it was a beautiful sunny day, saw the way the river sparkled in the afternoon sun, how the traffic flowed along the swooping freeways, and marveled at the thrusting office towers all around. From Patel's office everything looked fine, a persuasive illusion. But in the office, right now, with Patel sitting at his desk, looking like a prisoner, things were quietly going from bad to worse to sheer, mindboggling catastrophe.

"When did you notice your boy was gone?"

"It was late, after a bad day. I got home, and I knew I had hours more work, three live videoconferences with my own bosses, and my wife, Parminder — well, she is the light of my existence, Spider," he deadpanned, "was waiting at the door, suitcase in hand, leaving to catch the midnight flight to India.

Spider raised one eye-brow.

Patel went on. "The trip had been planned weeks ago, Spider."

"Okay."

"So I kiss her goodbye and told her I'd say goodnight to Vijay, but Parminder told me not to bother: 'Your son is gone', she said, like it's nothing, like we've run out of milk."

"Uh-oh."

"I said, 'what do you mean?' And she said he is just gone. That he took *Kali*. That he was gone by the time she got home from shopping. I asked when that was, and she said about four in the afternoon. I pointed out, not unreasonably, that it was now almost ten p.m. Why had she not called me? I asked her if she called the rest of the family — we have a few cousins and such here in Perth that we visit socially — to ask if he might be with them? 'No', she said. She figured I would do it, it being my problem."

"I have to say, sir, and I'm sorry to say it, but Parminder does not strike me as overly concerned about her missing child."

"That is because Vijay, um, is not her son. As such. Biologically."

"Oh," Spider said, blinking, thinking about it. "I see."

"It is a long story."

Spider pressed on. "She said that Vijay took *Kali*? That would be the time machine?"

"*Kali*, yes. My pride and joy."

"You said you kept the starter unit in your home office."

"In a safe, yes."

Spider nodded. "So how—"

"He knew the code."

"He knew the code?"

"Once, some time ago, I told him to go and put the starter unit away for me. I gave him the code. It was a trust thing. And he was eight years old at the time. I had spent many hours of my life telling Vijay, over and over, drumming it into his head, that he must never, never, ever, touch *Kali* when I was not around. That he was not even to trespass in the garage itself without my permission, without my actually being there to open the time-locks for him. I went over this many times. No one needed to tell me that *Kali* was dangerous, Spider. Parminder — she had never understood. She told me Vijay would get past all my security one day, she had seen how clever he is, and that he was getting more and more clever as he got older. She told me, 'If the boy does take off in your time machine, it will be entirely your problem. It is not my problem. He is not my flesh. This will be your mess, and you will be responsible for it.'"

"Parminder plays for sheep stations," Spider said, mostly to himself, shocked at how Mrs. Patel could be so cold.

"She is difficult."

"Difficult. Right. Go on."

"I had to do something. The boy could be anytime, as you say, and he had a six-hour lead on me. So I got back in the car, and headed out to the dealership." The Bharat Time Machine Company of Mumbai sold highly desirable new time machines and related gear from a huge showroom in the Wangara commercial estate, alongside showrooms for cars and boats. "I finally got out there after eleven that night. Bad traffic. I spend two days a week at the dealership, supervising things, I'm sure you can imagine, so I have a key. I get in, have a quiet word with the night security staff, and head to the workshop, where we have plenty of time machines in for warranty maintenance checks. I 'borrowed' one, setting the coordinates for the driveway in front of my garage."

"So you could blip back to catch Vijay before he—"

"Exactly so, Spider. This is also probably why Parminder was less than concerned about the boy."

"Uh-huh."

"So, there I am, in the cabin of the machine, running pre-flight checks. Everything checks out. Funny cat smell I could do without, but otherwise, all green lights. I punch in a destination time that should catch Vijay in plenty of time, and I go — and arrive. No problem. Only it turns out to be a big problem. A very big problem indeed. Let me try to describe the situation, as I found it: my time machine, *Kali*, is there in the garage. Vijay — and a young girl, a friend from school, are there, too—"

"There's a girl as well?"

"In good time, Spider. They are both there. As of when I come through the side-door, the children are standing there, their backs to the wall of the garage, arms up, like this." He gestured. Spider had already sussed it. "Their hands are up because there is a team of men, wearing black, their faces hidden behind, what is the word? Balaclavas?" Spider nodded. "Yes. And they have guns. Assault rifles, pistols. Vijay is standing there with the keys to *Kali*. The general idea is for Vijay to hand these gentlemen the keys, so that they might take the machine."

"Oh. Shit," Spider said, starting to see what was going on.

"So I beat a hasty retreat, raced for the borrowed time machine, setting up a quick jump on my watchtop, so I could whack the go button and arrive one hour earlier — before Vijay arrived home from school and while Parminder was still out shopping. I check the garage: *Kali* was secure. So, I set up new security protocols for the garage, and for *Kali* herself — and I went to my firearms locker—"

"Shit," Spider said, shaking his head. Guns are not good. Not good at all.

"I had to take precautions, Spider. Anyway, I got the shotgun, and all the spare ammunition I could carry; pockets bulging, cartridges down my shirt and in a courier bag over my shoulder..."

"What sort of shotty you got?" This was professional interest, Spider's police-head talking, but also wondering just how much damage this guy could have dished out.

"Remington 870, twelve gauge. Double-ought buckshot. Fourteen-inch barrel," Patel said.

Spider whistled, hearing that. "Yikes." He thought Patel was acting altogether too much like an excited kid, talking about the best Christmas present he ever got.

"When I was a kid, I was in the Boy Scouts, you know," he added.

"I believe you." Spider had been in the Scouts, too, but didn't remember it as a fun experience.

Patel went on. "At last, I'm ready."

"You don't look like the shotgun type, if you'll pardon my saying so, sir."

"I got it during *Kali's* construction. I realized very early on that she would be a highly desirable machine, and that one day, no matter how careful I was, word could get out, and that word would spread like a wildfire. Yes, shotgun."

"Sorry to interrupt, but I need to know. Why do it in the first place? Why—" It was a question that fascinated Spider, and always had done, going back to his time in WAPOL. What makes a man go to the dark side? How does corruption start? Is there such a thing as only very slight corruption, or is it more like pregnancy: you either are or you're not.

"Go illegal?"

"Yeah. I'm curious."

"Ah. Well." He fiddled with his watch-band as he spoke. "I did not set out to do so. It happened, as one might imagine, gradually, over a long time. I wanted the best components. The best. I was prepared to source parts from anywhere in the world. I found myself facing situations where I would set out, having consulted catalogues and online reviews, to purchase top-spec component X, for argument's sake. Very high-end, bleeding edge technology, and just barely legal, DOTAS-compliant. But sometimes the vendors would say to me, 'Good sir, you are prepared to pay a great deal of money for this part. How would you feel about paying, perhaps, two percent more for the military version of that part?' The amounts of extra cost were tiny, Spider. Tiny! In some cases we were only talking about a few dollars here, and a few dollars there. For a long time I refused, insisted on paying for legal parts, a good boy in all respects. But these dealers, over time, they kept calling me, telling me that for a few lousy dollars I was denying myself 'the good stuff'. Denying myself 'the best'. 'Do you want to be the cool guy, or just a wannabe?' I told them I was not interested, not at any price, and that I would take my business elsewhere if they persisted. They would go away, I would go on my way, building my machine with legal parts — and then one fine day I was in the garage — this was a Saturday afternoon; I was listening to cricket: India was pasting the Australians — I found myself installing a Fenniak 3000GTi carbon separation buffer—"

Spider blinked. He'd never seen anything more impressive than the Fenniak 2000, long thought to be the gold-standard.

"There, you see! Yes, very nice. But that last guy had shown me a *F4000XXXp.*"

"Holy crap!"

"Only five percent more."

"He must have been offering a stolen military unit," Spider said, astonished to hear first-hand about something he'd previously only heard rumors about.

"Oh, yes. But it was enough. Parminder had been giving me grief about how I was neglecting the garden, the grass was dying, her precious bloody roses were parched, and if I lifted my nose out of the stupid time machine I would see that the house was falling apart. Truly, we were looking at either moving or renovating, a prospect I did not relish, believe me, because Parminder would not hear of hiring qualified tradesmen. 'It is nothing you cannot manage yourself, surely,' she would say, having watched too many renovation shows, with their easy, smiling reassurances that 'you and a mate and a weekend, you'll knock it up in no time at all.' You have seen these programs?"

"Yes, indeedy," Spider said. "My ex-wife loved the idea of me ripping out the old kitchen and installing a lovely new one for her, but I always turned out to be busy that weekend, pulling lots of overtime at the shop, don't you know."

Patel nodded, and pushed his glasses back up his nose. "Yes, well, then. You see how it works. I cannot tell you, Spider, how much I hate gardening. I am not at all an outdoorsy sort of man."

"Me, neither, really."

"Working on the time machine, it was like I was in another — well, you get the idea."

"You spent the extra money, and you got one illegal part, and then another, and then another still…"

"I swore, I told myself, that I would just get one more piece, something no DOTAS inspector would ever find."

"It's like eating potato chips, eh?"

Patel hesitated, then smiled. "Yes, yes, precisely. Next thing I knew..."

"Did it concern you, at all, that those shipments of illegal time machine parts were likely monitored by customs services around the world? By Interpol, even? That DOTAS very likely was getting reports from Australian Customs about what you were doing, and were just waiting until they could bust not just you but all your dodgy suppliers as well?"

"It crossed my mind, yes..."

"But you ... just kept on doing it."

"Spider, I was building the *best time machine ever!*"

"Yeah. And look where it's left you. No time machine. No son. Even worse: no son's friend!"

"I know. I know. I do. That's ... that's why we're here. You and I. We are going to fix this. I've figured it all out, Spider. I've isolated the correct nodal-point. I have a transient fix on *Kali's* TPIRB. I—"

Spider was so busy shaking his head, trying to keep his anger under control, lost in his astonishment at just how stupid Patel had been that he almost failed to hear this crucial detail. "You, sorry, you what? Did you say you had a TPIRB bearing?" The TPIRB was a government-mandated emergency rescue beacon. The original EPIRBs were waterproof, floating GPS receiver/transmitters used by survivors of boat-sinkings to help direct rescuers to the survivors. When the technology was adapted for use by time travelers, it required a means to communicate across time, rather than space, but the principle was the same, transmitting the stricken unit's Temporal Positioning System coordinates back to the present.

"*Kali* has a TPIRB, yes, of course. I'm not completely stupid, Spider." He sounded a little snippy, saying that.

"Okay, good. And?"

"They are out of range."

Spider closed his eyes and sighed, his moment of hope shattered. A fully-charged TPIRB beacon had an effective transmission range of ten thousand years, which, for typical time travelers, was usually more than enough capacity. "You said you had a bearing, though."

"The last known bearing, before the signal faded, was future-ward."

Spider knew it, he bloody knew it. The future. God, but he hated the future. Not that there was anything particularly cosy and reassuring about the actual past (far more confusing and dangerous than any history documentary would have you believe), but the future, by its very unknowability, its vulnerability to constant change from the ever-changing past, was terrifying. It was the darkest of dark woods, full of peril, particularly the sort of peril that would feed on children.

"Right. So we know they're more than ten thousand years out that-a-way," he said, gesturing forwards, ahead of where he stood. Now for the hard part."

"Finding them?"

"No, before that."

"Before that?"

"How did they end up inside your incredibly well-secured time machine?"

"I was trying to tell you..."

"You said you had your fancy shotty."

"Yes. So I pulled up a picnic chair, and sat there, me and my Remington, watching the time pass. But then I thought: wait a minute. If the machine wasn't here, it couldn't be stolen!"

"Good thinking."

"So, I jumped into the cockpit. But I still needed the starter unit, which was in the house. In the safe. But the starter unit wasn't in the safe. So, back to the borrowed time machine where I traveled back to early that morning. Snuck through the house — no one was up yet — opened the safe in my office, retrieved the starter unit—"

"You were crazy letting Vijay know the code, you know that."

"—And dashed back to the time machine outside. Blipped back to where I was before, and noticed a white van out on the street that had not been there previously."

"A van, huh? What sort? Logo on the side?"

"Appeared to be a van belonging to some home maintenance service, you know the sort. It was parked out front of the house next door, nobody in it that I could see. It looked perfectly harmless, but I couldn't remember it being there before I went back to that morning. Was I imagining things? I decide not to chance it, and head for the garage—"

"*Kali* still there?"

"*Kali* still there. I climb up into the cockpit, plugged in the starter unit, got green lights, and set up a quick jump. While I tried to decide which way to jump, the windows on either side shattered — rifle butts — and next thing I'm at gunpoint, no time to go for my own shotgun."

"They anticipated your move."

"Clearly."

"Damn."

"They pulled me out of the machine, shotgun cartridges spilling everywhere, pushed me to the ground and stood over me, guns pointed at my head. The man with the balaclava over his face asked if *Kali* was ready to go. I said 'no, no, it's not. You'll need the starter unit'. But one of the other men said 'it's already in the machine, showing green'. At that point I was sunk. Game over. The balaclava man said, 'Thanks, mate, sorry about this—' but just as he was about to hit me, another time machine appeared in the driveway."

"Another machine," Spider said, astonished. "And let me guess. Vijay and Phoebe?"

"Indeed so, Spider."

"Good grief."

"Vijay leapt out of this new machine, and yelled out to the thieves, waving the starter unit."

"Vijay's got the starter unit now?" Spider was trying to think his way around this whole thing. He figured that Phoebe's parents must have had a time machine, and the kids used it, in ghost mode, to blip back to the garage and snatched the starter unit while the thieves were concentrating on Mr. Patel. *If that's what had happened*, he thought, *it was an incredibly ballsy and stupidly dangerous thing to try*.

Mr. Patel went on. "So Vijay's standing in the pilot's door of this new time machine—"

"So there are now three time machines," Spider said, trying to keep up.

"That's right. And Vijay's waving the starter unit, calling out to the thieves to leave me alone. I'm on my knees, but look up when I hear Vijay. The thieves are startled and two of them head for Vijay and Phoebe, but—"

"They vanish."

"Quite so, Spider. Only they pop up inside *Kali's* cockpit, plug in the starter, and they're gone before the thieves know what the hell is going on."

"I know the feeling."

"The leader of the gang, the one who was about to hit me, wants me to tell him where the kids have gone, but I don't know. I really don't know. There's the emergency exit button on *Kali's* dashboard that blips the machine off on a random futureward jump, no setup required. I told them Vijay might have done that, but otherwise I didn't know, and couldn't say. I was just damned proud of my boy. And ashamed, Spider. My boy and his friend were exposed to all this, because of me. Proud and so ashamed, I cannot even tell you."

Spider nodded. "I'm guessing that's when they hit you."

"Oh yes. The leader bashed me quite thoroughly in the side of the head with the butt of his rifle."

"Good grief," Spider said.

"When I came 'round *Kali* was gone, and so was the time machine the children had borrowed."

Spider nodded. "What time of day was this again?"

"About four-ish. I waited and waited. Parminder returned from shopping. She was horrified when she saw me, and made a fuss, thinking I'd just been mugged, and at first I did not disabuse her of this notion. But then, of course she noticed the time machine *I'd* borrowed, which I'd tried to hide, and the empty garage. *'What have you done?'* she said to me. *'What have you done?'* It was, oh it was brutal, Spider."

"I can imagine."

"She put two and two together, and figured out that the me standing before her, as small as an ant, was a time traveler. 'What have you done?' she said again, and marched into the house. But then she wanted to know where 'your boy' might be. Was he staying over at a friend's house? I did not think so, but I didn't know. Then we got a call from the parents of a girl. Her name was Phoebe, a girl Parminder said she had met a couple of times when Vijay brought her round after school to play. Parminder thought she was a lovely girl, but not suitable for Vijay. It seemed this Phoebe had called her parents on the way home from school and told them she was having dinner at our house, and would be home later. But Phoebe had not come home, nor had she phoned to say she would be late. They wanted to talk to her."

"What did you do?"

"Parminder turned to me. She told me that this was my mess. She transferred the call to me, and went to the bedroom, and began packing."

"Packing?"

"She wanted to clear out before Phoebe's parents started an investigation. Me too. I told them I'd call back. Then I hopped into my borrowed time machine and blipped back to the dealership, returned it, and drove home. On the way I started thinking that you, of all people, could help me out. I'd read your file and knew you had been a policeman and your employment record showed you are a time machine genius."

"Christ," Spider said, not happy. "Thanks."

"I know, I know. But I've got no one else to turn to."

"Right. Okay. How many guys did you see, before they knocked you out?"

"There were at least four."

"The one who spoke to you, was he Australian? The way you described what he said to you, it sounded Oz."

"He was, I think, either Australian or a Kiwi. Maybe British."

"Good grief," Spider said. "So how tall, do you think? Tall as me? Shorter than me? Tall as you, maybe? Like a jockey? Or some kind of lumbering great bloke?"

"Tall, yes, taller than you. And lean, quite fit, I think. Like perhaps a player of Australian football."

"You're sure about that? He wasn't my sorta height, but really thick-set, made of cement, no neck, like a rugby player?"

Patel laughed. "No, he could have played AFL."

"What about the other guys?"

"I didn't get much of a look at them, sorry."

"Yeah, fair enough. Okay, here's a touchy question. What, um, race were they, these guys?"

"What race?" Patel stared at him.

Spider was embarrassed. Here he was, well into the twenty-first century, and race was still the hardest thing in the world to talk about, particularly when talking to a person not of one's own race. "I'm really sorry, all right? But I have to know. Was he a whitefella like me — or what?" Having said this, Spider stopped a moment and wondered what on Earth possessed him to use the term "whitefella", something you generally only heard in discussions involving or about Aboriginal people. Spider wished he could climb under a rock and pretend he hadn't said anything, but he couldn't. The word was out there, hanging between them, like a lingering fart.

"Oh," Patel said, getting it, but not happy. "He was white. From what I could tell."

This was getting murky, with layers and layers of cause and effect, whole realities being created and eliminated right there in Patel's garage. It looked as though Patel's garage was either a naturally occurring nodal-point, or it had become one as a consequence of all the high-powered time-travel-related activity that had happened there. Either way, all kinds of possibilities branched off. It made Spider tired just thinking about it. It also occurred to him, once he saw that Patel wasn't going to hold Spider's clumsiness with language against him, that it was possible, in Spider's present timeline, that Vijay and his girlfriend might simply have taken *Kali* for a joy ride, and any thieves in the here and now would simply have found an empty garage. It was like a card game with all the players slapping down cards that completely changed the nature of reality every turn, and the turns happening blindingly fast, leaving the final winner almost impossible to figure out. "Phoebe's folks must be climbing the walls."

"They have contacted the police. Phoebe is now officially missing, and I am the chief suspect. I have had my house searched, my property examined, and I have been interviewed at length. Of course they don't know about *Kali*"

Spider could imagine. The police would look at the facts, and come up with all manner of possible theories to explain what had happened, and in the end they would go where the evidence led them. All the same, among those theories they would have to explore was the one in which Mr. Patel, possibly with the complicity of his mysteriously absent wife, had done a vile thing indeed, not only with their own son, but with another child, too. Even if Mr. Patel eventually confessed to building a hotrod time machine, the coppers could think that Patel was simply creating a distraction, and that Vijay and friend might well be somewhere here in the present, and very possibly have come to a bad, bad end. Spider had to keep that firmly in his mind. It was a lesson he had learned on the job: things are not always as they seem. Sometimes, even most times, they are far stranger than you'd imagine, and most likely more perverse than you'd care to consider.

Spider believed there had once been this fabulous hotrod time machine, called *Kali*. He believed, with difficulty, that Mrs. Patel had shot through to India to let her husband take all the flak. He believed that Patel was a genuine time machine enthusiast. You only had to look up at that glorious machine hanging above his desk to see that. That right there was solid platinum geek-ware, he thought. But geeks could still be killers and worse. When children were involved, you had to take every possible care, follow every procedure, make damned sure you were interpreting the law correctly to the nth degree. Because you would be tested on it. You could very well wind up in court, defending the integrity of your findings while the defendant's lawyers did their best to destroy your credibility. How awful would it be if you presented an account of kids having absconded in Dad's illegal time machine, only to have the truth turn out to be simply that Dad killed them in his bathtub, or in that great big two-car garage, and buried the bodies in a shallow grave out in the bush somewhere? The thing was, correlation did not necessarily imply causation. Yes, Patel's time machine, and these two children, were gone. But it did not necessarily follow that the missing kids were with the missing machine. Spider had to be on his guard here, the way he had to be on his guard years ago, when he was tracking Superintendent Sharp and his pedophile buddies to early twentieth-century Perth, when they were interfering with local kids and getting away with it because they weren't locals. He shuddered, remembering that, and seeing that right here, he could be up against similar trouble.

So, what to make of Patel? Spider thought. There was something madly admirable about his desperate determination to push through and succeed, no matter what; but there was also something sinister about that desperation that left Spider feeling uneasy in Patel's presence. How far could such a man go in order to make a losing proposition pay off? What would such a man be prepared to do? Was there anything he would *not* do? What kinds of deals would he make, if it meant great glory? Or even, maybe, simply getting away with murder? He scribbled some notes on his watchtop, and decided to change the subject. "What's the name of the officer leading the investigation?"

"O'Connor. William. Bill."

"'Wild Bill' O'Connor? Right. Okay." Spider knew the guy. Very professional, and most likely clean, not having been part of Superintendent Sharp's group of special chums. This meant Spider might, possibly, be able to talk to O'Connor about the situation, without too much of his own history getting in the way. Or so he hoped. Spider had been away from WAPOL for a long time now; he didn't know how his legend might have spread or waned in the interim. If Iris' accounts were to be believed, the general mood of the local service was still very much anti-Spider, at least on the surface. Was it possible that O'Connor might talk to him, professional to professional? Or was he, Spider, just as likely to get drawn into the whole thing and treated as, at the very least, a Person of Interest?

"I'm going to need your help," Spider said.

"There are limits to what help I can provide, Spider. My position here is not what it was."

"Yeah, I get that. But you're still here, you can still requisition stuff, right?"

"What did you have in mind?"

"I'll need a unit. A time machine. And I can't do anything without money. The pittance you pay me for my work at the shop is not going to cut it."

"My authority to requisition such things is—"

"Curtailed, yeah, okay." That didn't leave Spider many choices.

"As for money, I can pay you out of my own savings. What else?"

"I need a leave of absence from the shop, so I can work on this full-time."

"I'm afraid not, I'm sorry to say."

Spider could not believe his ears. "No?" He stared at Patel. "No? You expect me to slave over bloody time machines *and* argue with idiot owners *and* rescue your nuts from the fire in my spare time?" *When not tending to poor Mr. Popeye for Molly, of course*, he thought with more than a trace of bitterness.

Mr Patel said, "I assumed you would make use of a time machine to get all the sleep you need without it affecting your duties at the workshop. Full shift at workshop, hop in time machine, go off and get eight, ten hours sleep, something to eat, a bit of rest and downtime, perhaps, and then pop back to the present and carry on working on the case for the rest of the evening."

"Just like that," Spider said, disgusted at the way Patel had it all figured out.

"It did not seem like a problem in any way, I thought," he said.

Spider went to object, but he knew, as always, resistance was useless. He shook his head. The shitty deal just got shittier. Perfect. "What about you?"

"What about me?" Patel said, the color of doom itself.

"Probably only a matter of time before you're arrested and charged."

"That seems very likely at this stage. I have already retained a legal team."

"I see."

"All is not yet lost, of course," Patel said, glancing at Spider, allowing himself the tiniest of wry smiles.

Spider remembered a detail. "You said you had a nodal point all sorted, didn't you?"

"With a bit of luck, I can make all this so it never happened, even if I have to wait twenty, thirty years to do it. It just depends on you, Spider. You must find Vijay and Phoebe."

"What about the machine?"

"I do not care about the machine. Bring it back, destroy it, whatever."

This made Spider lift his eyebrows. "I'll come over to your place tonight, late, to have a look at the premises."

"I should be there any time after nine."

Turning, getting ready to leave, Spider glanced up at the Time Machine hanging above. He needed a working time machine to find the damned kids. "Ahh … as for the coppers…"

"I shall keep you posted."

Spider looked back at Patel, a little guy in big trouble. Trouble that he was only too happy to spread around. This could go very badly for Spider, he knew that. It would be too easy to find himself caught in the same vortex that was taking Mr. Patel down the plug-hole. He could wind up an accessory, or even an accomplice, in the eyes of the law. Certain officers of WAPOL might well think, justice has caught up with that traitorous scumbag Spider Webb at long last. He had no doubt that there would be people out there only too happy to doctor evidence, to change statements, anything at all that might help seal his fate. "We never picked you for a bloke interested in little kiddies, there, Spider. Very nasty. How the mighty have fallen." He could see it all now.

As he left Patel's office, and emerged once more onto the hectic bustle of St. George's Terrace, dodging panhandlers, Hare Krishna groups, doomsayers bearing apocalyptic signs raving on, mobs of grave-faced office workers in rumpled shirts bearing boxes of personal effects, Spider thought, *Gonna need some help.* And no sooner had he thought that than he noticed a white "Jim's Custom Pets" van parked across the street. The hairs on the back of his neck stood straight up, and he felt cold. Then he noticed people who seemed perhaps too obviously just standing around casually, chatting on phones, fiddling with their watchtops, eating takeaway. In all this hustle and bustle, with so many people moving around him, people standing still stood out. And yet, he told himself, doing his best to keep calm, that even though the government almost certainly knew about Mr. Patel's hotrod time machine, there was the possibility that Patel had been so clever that he'd pulled off the seemingly impossible, and nobody knew. As impossible as it must have been to keep such a project secret, it seemed equally impossible that government agents worth their weight in dark sunglasses would look quite so obviously up to something like these people he saw. Real government types, Spider thought, proper professionals, would indeed blend in. Which was a line of thought that did not help. And that wasn't even taking into account those watchers out there monitoring him in ghost mode. Spider told himself he wasn't being paranoid, but the fact was he was now involved in two separate situations in which the government had probably taken an interest: Dickhead's mysterious "upgraded" severed head; and the hottest hotrod time machine ever built. He hated this kind of thing. It reminded him of the long secret campaign against Superintendent Sharp, when he could only speak to his control officer about the case, worried all the time that the control officer was somehow also talking to Sharp, and it was all going to crash down on his head. The tension made him sick all the time. And now he could feel that tension settling in the pit of his stomach all over again. But here he was, thinking, "you're not paranoid if there really are people out to get you".

Spider popped his watchtop and called Iris; told her he needed to talk to her, tonight, at Trinh's Vietnamese cafe, about eight. This was code they both understood. A "meeting at Trinh's" was in fact a meeting at the Kid's Adventure Playground in the depths of Kings Park. Iris went on to ask what was going on, but he cut her off, and headed off to catch a taxi back to the shop. It was nearly five p.m.; the sun was diving for the western horizon, beyond the hulking mass of Kings Park, going underground.

CHAPTER 9

As soon as he walked in the door, Malaria popped up, looming over him. "Spider! Thank God!"

He glanced about, on edge. "Something wrong?"

"The coffee droid's died."

He felt himself sag with relief. All the way home, after calling Iris, he'd been tense, coiled up, to the point he had to ask the taxi driver to pull over because he thought he was going to be sick. After some dry heaves, a coughing fit, and a foul taste in his mouth, he got back in the car and they carried on. It was a telling sign. He was in trouble, and knew it. There was an excellent chance Iris Street might arrest him tonight, and bring him in for questioning, with the aim of turning in Mr. Patel. He hoped he had enough connection with Iris that she would instead at least listen to him, and decide what to do about it later.

But now? The coffee droid was dead? The office clock said it was five-thirty. Spider felt knackered. Long, long day. Too much going on. What he wanted was a nap, but doubted very much he'd be able to sleep even if he tried. It was such a tempting thought. Failing a nap, a lovely double macchiato would have hit the spot instead. "All right", he said. "How dead? Show me."

Malaria showed him. The machine was still operational enough to greet him, "Spider-san!" But there was also something of humiliation in the way it stood there in the workshop, tucked away in a corner. Malaria left him to it.

Charlie came over. "How'd it go with the old man? a bit of a joke with them since Patel was young en Spider's son.

"Same old," Spider said, evading the topic, making a show of inspecting the droid. "Know anything about this?"

"Yeah, I went to get a flat white while you were out. Coffee came out cold, tasted of shit and chemicals, and this nasty stinky smoke — it smelled like burning plastic, tell the truth — started pouring out the vents."

"Really?" He looked at the machine. "Coffee Droid—"

"Spider-san?"

"Feeling a bit sick, yes?"

"Coffee production functionality currently not online. I am … ashamed."

"Machine intelligence," Charlie said, shaking his head, disgusted.

"It's all right, Coffee Droid—" he said, and turned to Charlie. "We seriously need a better name for this thing."

"Right now," Charlie said, "I'm voting for 'Useless Box o' Gears'."

Spider felt a pang of embarrassment on behalf of the coffee droid, which itself stood there, venting noxious steam, some-how conveying to Spider a sense of profound shame that clearly Charlie did not or could not detect. To the droid, he said, "Coffee Droid, I—"

"Spider-san! How may I serve you?"

"Good fucking grief," Charlie said. "I'll leave you to it. Meanwhile, is there any of that jar of instant left in the — oh, shit." A few months ago Malaria had bought a small jar of instant coffee to get through a crisis with their last coffee droid. Only problem with that was that that jar, as far as Charlie and Spider knew, was still in the break room, and the break room was still cordoned off with blue and white WA POLICE CRIME SCENE DO NOT CROSS tape. "I'll go talk to Malaria."

"Top plan," Spider said, and turned his attention to the droid. Diagnostics shed no light on the problem. Auto reset didn't help either. The only thing left to do was to open it up, and have a poke about. Which, this close to closing time, was a prospect that did not appeal much, but it seemed better than stewing in his own tension, brooding about Patel and his meeting Iris at 8:00. All in all, the coffee droid's problems seemed much more attrac-tive, and even more so when Charlie appeared bearing a big steaming mug of searingly hot instant coffee for him. "Malaria had the sense to put the jar of instant in her desk drawer!"

Spider blew on the surface of his brew, and dared a sip. It was hot enough, but also eye-poppingly strong. "Oh, Charlie! My hero!"

"Weren't nothin', ma'am," he said, miming doffing his hat. "Anyway, thank Malaria!"

"I will, I will," Spider said, inhaling instant coffee fumes, which certainly smelled better than the steam coming out of the coffee droid. They stood there a moment, taking minute sips of their coffee. "Looks like I'll have to open him up."

"Betcha anything you find a dead cat in there."

Spider laughed, but in the process inhaled coffee, and now had what felt like white-hot coffee scalding his sinus membranes. "Oh, God! Oh, God!" Tears streamed from his eyes. "Oh, God!"

Charlie laughed and laughed, and ran off in search of something that might help.

After closing up the shop, Spider biked to Molly's place — how long had he been thinking of it that way, as Molly's place, he wondered. It used to be his place, too, long ago, when dinosaurs roamed the Earth, wasn't it? He parked his bike in the garage, stretched, and felt the beginnings of a migraine starting to bang away behind his forehead. His old man, whenever Spider visited his folks, would offer to go out to the shed and get his power drill. "Soon sort out that bugger, you watch!" his dad would say with a smile, an old routine, more intended to get a smile out of his son than to provide actual assistance.

Then, he was there, on the front porch, facing the locked front door, and flashing back to the past, long ago, when he found the door ajar, and one of his Future Selves warning him not to go in. *Those guys are a pain in the arse*, Spider thought, *time travelers from the future, always meddling; wanting me to do things I don't want to do, always for the very best of reasons, at least to them, no matter what it winds up costing me.*

He worked his way through the layers of security he had installed for Molly, disabled the security cams, the motion tracker, the heat sensor, and in the end, made his way into the entrance hall. "Hi honey, I'm home!" he muttered under his breath. The whole house smelled like clay, wet Swan River clay. When he lived there, Molly confined her hideous, breathing, stretching artworks to her studio, a converted bedroom in the back of the house, with its view of the tiny backyard and the back fence. Now, they were everywhere. She had taken over the huge open plan family room, and turned it into a full-on workshop. All around the room, Molly's sculptures, her *HyperFlesh* creations, the very things she was right this minute hoping to exhibit in New York, loomed around him, watching him with their agonized eyes, things that looked like what he and his mates at school would once have called "transporter accidents", and now looked altogether too much like unimaginable creatures in terrible pain. It seemed as if they knew he was there, in the room. The ones with eyes followed his movements, and recoiled in something like fear if he came too close.

He turned to the aquarium, under the main window, where poor, sick Mr. Popeye swam back and forth, back and forth, his bulbous eyes staring up at Spider. Spider thought of tapping the glass, but didn't. "Two careful drops of the prescribed medicine," Spider said to the fish, "and yummy fish flakes, too. Gotta keep your strength up. Yes you do. Yes you do." The fish did not react, and continued swimming and staring, looking to Spider like he was bored and depressed out of his tiny fishy mind. "Yeah, mate. Know what you mean," Spider said, nodding sadly. He made a note in the treatment log Molly had left for him to fill in, to provide a record of what he was doing for Mr. Popeye. "Good grief," he said.

That done, Spider turned around and tripped over the coffee table, knocking a large manila envelope to the floor. It contained the divorce papers Molly wanted him to sign. He carried it into the kitchen. Spider hadn't signed them when she first presented them to him and he wouldn't sign them now, not while she was away. Of course he knew that signing them was the right thing to do. His initial plan, to make himself available, to do all manner of odd-jobs for her, had not worked out. He had wanted her to know that he was over all the pain and wretchedness that had followed his departure from the Police Service. That he'd moved on, found a new career — he laughed a little, thinking about that — and was, in all respects, a New Man. Well, hadn't that worked out well! In the process Molly had acquired a handyman who was available whenever she needed him, who never charged her anything, who even refused the money she tried to offer for his services (which were, at times, nothing short of heroic, and above and beyond the call of duty, but he was trying not to dwell on that). He did allow himself to be offered coffee and a biscuit, as a compromise, and still he hoped that it was only a matter of time before she came to realize the folly of her ways, and that he was really a New Spider, and that maybe they could, slowly of course, a bit at a time, negotiate their way back to some kind of relationship. Obviously, he told himself at night when he couldn't sleep, it would never be the same. He was realistic enough about that, he thought. He'd seen too many families with warring parents, some of whom did manage to find a new common ground, a new energy level, where they could once again build something together — but it was never the same something. It made him think of a time machine that had been in a wreck. If it wasn't fixed just right, it never really worked properly again. Yes, it would run, and you could use it, but it wasn't truly fixed. Of course, beyond a certain point of trouble with a broken time machine, you just had to ditch the thing and get a new one.

Spider knew all this, knew it in his bones, but when he was with Molly, doing some stupid odd-job for her in the middle of a wintry night, he didn't care. He watched her, trying not to be obvious about it, of course, for signs that she might be thawing towards him, at least a little. Sometimes it did look that way. Sometimes she was warm and caring. She smiled, even laughed if he managed to crack a particularly witty joke. He loved her laugh. He remembered how, when they were together, he often thought there was no finer purpose in life than making Molly laugh, because it was so rewarding, the way she would dissolve in fits of laughter. It was the best feeling in the world.

Spider just stood there, in the kitchen, over the sink, eating cold baked beans out of a tin, hardly even noticing what he was doing. "A good man, eh?" he said to himself. All he could see was a man in direst danger of surrendering his honor, his principles, even his sense of who he was as a person, in order to help his employer climb out of the deepest pit in the world. Because if he didn't, if he refused, what would happen? Would Mr. Patel shrug, shake Spider's hand, and tell him, "Oh well, Spider. No worries. Just wanted to sound you out." Would he do that? Or would he instead give Spider the sack? And, into the bargain, spread the word on Spider in the time machine industry that here was a man who was not to be trusted? Or, hey, why bother with such puny smears when he could simply go to the police and accuse Spider of having made off with *Kali*. With Mr. Patel's connections and expertise, he could certainly engineer Spider's timeline where it turned out everybody believed that he had gone bad and stolen the precious machine, and, who knows, maybe interfered with those children somehow as well? Spider could see how his entire existence might be upturned in an instant.

That's why he had to meet with Iris tonight. To talk to her before he agreed to do anything for Mr. Patel; to show her his file, and prove to her that Mr. Patel should be the person of interest here, and that he, Spider Webb, wasn't an accomplice. She would possibly ask him to wear a wire when he next spoke to Mr. Patel. Now there was a quaint term, now wasn't it? There were no wires these days. Undercover operatives had a tiny device injected under the skin of their faces and later retrieved under local anesthetic. It monitored everything the user saw, said, heard, everything, weeks and weeks of audio, video, you name it.

"Well, Iris," he said out loud, there in the kitchen, between mouthfuls of beans, "my boss has done this hugely illegal thing, and now it's all backfired on him something chronic, and he wants me to get him out of it, and will probably find ways to implicate me in the whole affair if I don't go along with it." Said aloud like that, it did sound crazy. "Oh, and Iris, there are two missing children in the mix as well." He shook his head, found he'd lost his appetite for baked beans, and dumped the rest into the garbage. "Shit," he said, and shuffled over to the family room.

He sat down on Molly's couch, surrounded again by all those "things" watching him, feeling uncomfortable, as if each one knew he was being a damned fool and was trying, each in its own repulsive way, to tell him so. "Yes, I know, I know! Leave me alone!" He wondered if he could turn them around to face the wall without somehow damaging them. "Hi, Molly, glad you're home, hope you had a lovely time in New York, one small thing, um, I inadvertently broke a bunch of your sculptures because they were being all accusing and mocking at me," he said, and rubbed his stubbled face. Sad, more than anything else, he opened his watchtop, and piped the display output into the ceiling projector.

Patel's file was an impressive document. There were countless photos of young Vijay, a shy wisp of a kid, always busy with handheld game machines; crouching to look at tiny marine creatures in rockpools; and leaping, arms flung wide, off jetties at Crawley to splash in eruptions of white froth in the river. There were photos of the whole family together, in happier times: at Hindu festivals here in Perth and back home in India, covered in brightly colored powders. Patel's wife was a tall, serious woman, who never once, not in any of the provided images, looked happy. Never cracked a smile. Not even a smirk. There was one where she appeared serene, a formal portrait, standing there with her husband, and a very young Vijay on a chair before them, looking at something behind the photographer with rapt attention. Again and again, Spider's attention went back to Mrs. Patel, regal, posing in luminous sari and golden jewelry, a vision — but not a vision of joy. What was her problem? Spider thought, and then felt a little ashamed. One thing he had learned as a police officer: you can't judge people just from a few images. That was true, he knew that, but all the same, he thought, poring through these images, there was something about the family dynamic that, even allowing for cross-cultural differences he barely understood, still struck him as odd, nagging at the part of his mind that noticed little details: the way the knuckles on Mrs. Patel's hand, resting on Vijay's shoulder, looked tense, like she was holding the kid in place by main force ("or else!" added a little voice in the back of his head).

What else was there? Details of Vijay's school, an expensive private school in Nedlands, but one that let the students go home each day, rather than board. There was an image of Vijay's current class, Year Four (G). Spider didn't know what that was, so he phoned Patel, who told him, "It means he is in the Accelerated Learning Program, for Gifted Children. Very advanced. Robotics, calculus, symbolic logic!"

Spider swore, thanked Mr. Patel, reminded him that he'd be around later, and said that he was taking a moment to review the file. Patel said that was good, but don't take all night about it. "Yes, sir," Spider said, hating himself. In the class photo, the kids were all standing in well-ordered rows, in the school library, but deliberately pulling funny faces, sticking their tongues out, sticking "V" signs with their fingers behind the heads of the kids in front of them. Enormously gifted children, but still children. Spider felt himself wanting to smile — but there was Vijay, in the back row, one of the taller kids, frowning, worried about something.

As well as a hefty dossier of Vijay's school reports and class assessments ("easily distracted", "could try harder", "great facility with electronics"), Spider found a comprehensive dossier on Mr. Patel's illegal, custom hotrod time machine project. *Oh, my*, Spider thought, flipping through, having a quick look. The man had documented everything, down to the last fastener, the last memristor wafer. The minute details were the things that struck Spider the most, the man's astonishing attention to such things. Maybe, he thought, Mr. Patel was more like him than he wanted to believe. He happened to glance up, and saw again those monstrous eyes, and things without eyes but which seemed somehow to look straight into his soul, and moved back to the kitchen, where he could make himself a coffee while he watched the screen.

As to the machine in question: Spider was impressed despite himself. Boutique brands, and frequently the most exotic, high-end components available. No expense spared. It was breathtaking. Where had Patel found the money for this project? It must have cost a fortune — not to mention the additional payments for bribes and "facilitation expenses" to import illegal parts. According to the appended work log, documenting the construction of the unit, Patel had built it — with the help of his boy — over nearly three years. He'd started it while they were still living in an outer suburb of Mumbai, where it appeared he'd rented space in a local workshop. Then, when they moved to Perth a little over a year ago, they'd had to find a home with a double-garage, just to have space for the growing monster: there was an image of Patel's car, an old Toyota, stuck on its own out on the paved driveway, while the beast took shape in the garage. Spider thought about it, the scope of the project, what it must have meant in terms of planning, organizing, talking his wife into it. Three years of snatched bits of time on weekends, late nights and early mornings, tinkering about in the garage.

Patel had started with an old Hyundai Boron One, the original, big and boxy, not pretty at all, a unit whose primary virtue was that it was one of the very first consumer-level time machines available in Australia, or anywhere else. Prior to the Boron One, time machines and time travel had been the exclusive province of labs, governments, and corporations. There had also been a fledgling commercial time tourism industry, originally founded by Richard Branson, offering crazy bastards with too much money the opportunity to travel as much as *ten years* in either direction, and come home again after staying one hour. *The early days of time travel*, Spider thought. *Crazy times indeed.* Crazy because, and this was the weird thing, it turned out that the most happening, most up-to-date, post-modern thing a person with way too much money could do was to lob himself back ten years in time, to swan about in the recent past, all, "Hey, babe, I'm totally from ... *The Future!*" Nothing was more futuristic than the recent past.

The Boron One retailed, on its first day on sale, for fifty thousand dollars, give or take. If you wanted "all the fruit", you'd be looking at up to $150,000, and for that kind of money you could, and this was the cool part, you could travel as much as *one hundred years* into the future or the past, and stay, oh, four hours! The Boron One was the unit that introduced the wonder of ghost mode. The only drawback, which in those days nobody thought much about, was that the fuel-cell was only good for two, maybe three such hundred-year hops before it needed re-charging, and that, in the early days of the hydrogen economy, was expensive. That was the Boron One, the killer app in time travel. And here, Spider saw, in the work log, was the cracked and battered hull of the Boron One Patel managed to find in a salvage yard in Mumbai, an empty carbon-fibre hulk whose hardware had already been harvested by machine-recycling bots, stripping out all the stuff worth anything, leaving this sad, broken thing. Spider was struck afresh at the sheer size of the engine bay, which back in the day had housed not only the hydrogen fuel-cell, the considerable bulk of the scanning engine (the first version of the Boron One could only take one time traveler because the scanning engine did not have sufficient processor or storage power to handle passengers), but also the legendary Chronotek 5000 translation engine, the machine that powered a revolution, that was to consumer time travel what the previous century's Xerox Alto had been to personal computers. At the time, the CT5K had been a world-beating quantum poly-processing computing device, just barely capable of reading and modifying the quantum state vector data of every single particle in the vehicle and its occupant. Spider remembered that it was a colossal technical achievement, a genuine breakthrough, bring-ing time travel to the masses. Nowadays, almost fifteen years later, you only ever saw CT5Ks in engineering museums, turned into fetish artwork, or repurposed as avant-garde furniture.

As much as Spider hated time machines and the whole rationale of time travel generally, he had learned enough about hardware and machinery these past several years that he could begin to appreciate what the Boron One meant, what a break-through it had been.

Clearly, Mr. Patel felt the same way. While he had found the hull of the Boron One at a salvage yard, he had not been so struck with nostalgia as to dig up an old CT5K engine; he had looked at his budget and opted for a very big Chinese-built ex-military combination scanning/translation unit, and, of course, had it chromed. The images of the finished unit, Spider had to admit, with that fully exposed engine bay, the long-range super-cooled hydrogen-slush fuel-cells (you could clearly see them, wreathed in white frost, with icy fog flowing all around); the feral bulk of that mil-spec scanning/translation engine, all gleaming in chrome, and the whole thing sprouting all those long yellow-and-black heat sink fins — Spider thought the finished unit looked like a machine-porn lion fish you might have designed while off your face on cheap designer hallucinogens. It did not look like any time machine Spider had ever worked on. It actually looked, and he was surprised at himself here, kind of cool. In the course of pimping-up the hull — extreme glossy moral-panic red with blazing yellow lightning slashes — Mr. Patel had had the name *KALI* stenciled on the vacuum-tight doors. Checking Wikipedia, Spider found that Kali was the Hindu goddess of destruction, but also of creation, and even all eternity itself. *Kali* was as much about the universe, and the temporal continuum, as she was about sheer, mindless, physical destruction. Shit, he thought, impressed afresh. That was a lot of metaphorical freight for one machine to carry, even one as, frankly, *shiny*, as this one. Spider checked the projected range of the thing: *unknown*. He felt a chill crawl up his spine. "One hundred thousand years, possibly two," Patel had written in tiny, intense handwriting. "We have not tested the unit yet, but all simulations suggest robust jump-range."

Incredible. There was one, final, image of the thing, with Mr. Patel and young Vijay standing in front of it, Patel in filthy overalls, eye-plugs, with his data-glasses pushed up on his forehead; Vijay lost in tracksuit pants and a brand-name-printed sweatshirt, and his own pair of data-glasses, too big for his face, also pushed up on his forehead. Both Patels stood there, arms folded, doing their geeky best to look tough and masculine. It made Spider smile despite himself. As for the machine? It looked, with its tripodal articulated and jointed legs, like an exotic, tropical insect, packing more than a mere sting.

Spider stood there a long time, staring at that final image, man and boy and the beast they had built together. He could well believe that Vijay could pilot the thing, and that he would be sufficiently excited about working on it that he would inevitably tell someone at school, maybe even show them an image, who knows? No kid on Earth could keep a secret like that, Spider believed. Patel had been a naïve fool, at best, and, at worst, might end up being responsible for the destruction of the universe.

But wait, he thought. Mr. Patel had told him that *Kali* had gone beyond the range of its onboard TPIRB, beyond ten thousand years. Patel had also told him he had managed to get a brief, transient TPIRB signal from *Kali* as it blipped out, and that it was heading futurewards. It was hard to think about the idea of two children stuck more than ten thousand years away in an utterly alien, terrifying future. *How cool a customer might Vijay be as a time machine pilot?* Spider wondered. All things considered, particularly since the boy had a girl with him, Spider reckoned there was a very good chance Vijay had simply launched *Kali* on some crazy trajectory across the great gulfs of the future, headed who knows how far away. *Yikes*, he thought, trying to wrap his mind around it. Although it was true that he had been to the actual End of Time itself — so far uptime that numbers no longer bore any relevance and matter itself was long gone, other than weird things brought there by time travelers — the only time machines Spider had ever used himself either belonged to customers, were borrowed, or were the short-jump Jiffy booths at the airport. Spider's travels to the End of Time itself were not his choice, and he, even now, had terrible dreams about that void, where he fell and fell, unable to tell in which direction he was heading. It was so far in "the future" that it was hardly futuristic at all. But ten thousand years? Now that was a number you could maybe begin to deal with. You could start to get your brain around it. Ten thousand years? You could be looking at a new Ice Age, maybe. Or maybe global warming gone gonzo, drying up the oceans, baking the land, humanity barely hanging on, living on not much more than dirt. And even with that, Spider knew, the truth was that the children could be way, way beyond that point.

Would they try to come back? There was a fresh thought he could have done without. Suppose the idea was just to take the machine out of the garage for, say, a day or two; blip off to the unimaginable future and come straight back — arriving a few days after leaving. Or perhaps do a stupid little two-week jump, point to point, boom, and right back.

Except there was that TPIRB signal. They'd gone far, far away. What if the plan was to come straight back, but they got stuck wherever they wound up? Or, oh God, he didn't need this thought, captured, somehow, by whatever locals or others who might be there. For some reason whenever Spider thought of "people of the far future", he always thought of them as "Morlocks". He never imagined such people as the peace-loving, soporific "Eloi", living their attenuated, blissy lives. No, it was always Morlocks, tough mofos, built to persist and struggle, no matter what. When reading Wells' *The Time Machine* as a child,

Spider had always liked the Morlocks way more than the point-less bloody Eloi.

Not that such thoughts filled him with any hope for the missing children. Any kind of self-respecting Morlock-type residents of the far-future would eat children like Vijay and Phoebe for lunch.

Furious at finding himself dropped in this latest mess, Spider called Patel again. "You bloody moron!" he said without preamble.

"And a very good evening to you, too, Spider."

"Do you have any idea what might be happening to Vijay and Phoebe right now? I mean, do you? Did you stop to think, even once, when you were building your deathtrap, that maybe it was too dangerous, that it really shouldn't be allowed to exist—"

"Spider, I was able to finish the machine. Nothing stopped me. The universe and the gods let me do it."

Spider rolled his eyes and tried to control his temper. "So because nobody stopped you, including no time travelers from the future coming back to stop you doing it, you figured it must be okay to continue and finish the bloody thing."

"Correct, yes, of course."

"Even so, the thought that your own child might be in danger from it never crossed your mind?"

"Yes, of course it did, Spider," Patel told him, clearly nettled. "I told you, I gave Vijay the strictest instruction in safety and security!"

"Yet you let him know the access code for your safe."

"A son must feel like his father trusts him, Spider. This is a fundamental thing, do you not agree?"

"A son, surely, must also be protected from his own impulsive urges to fiddle with things he has no business fiddling with."

"I took every precaution. Every care. I had the best security."

"Yeah, and look where that's got you."

Patel had nothing to say to that. Spider was right. Then he said, "I have of course attempted to go back, to warn myself, my earlier self, you understand, about the children and everything that happened that day."

This was something new. "Yeah, and what did your earlier self tell you?"

"He—"

"Let me guess. He told you to bugger off. He knew what he was doing. He had the very best security money could buy. Everything was going to be fine. I bet he told you that until you got fed up and left. I bet you went back again and again, taking all this documentary evidence with you, to show yourself what happened, and what past you would have to guard against, and still you ignored you, appreciated the warning, and would beef up security in the garage, but otherwise told you to go the hell away and let yourself finish. Right?"

Patel hesitated, and Spider could hear him breathing. He said, "You are broadly correct, yes." His voice was very small.

"Christ, I hate time travel," Spider said.

"I am swiftly coming to share that view."

"You could still go back, you could get some of your dodgy mates to fit you up with some simple explosives, nothing special, just something easy to use. Blip back to the recent past, and blow *Kali* to bits. Destroy the file. You could do the universe a favor. Might even save your marriage."

"Oh, nothing can save that, Spider," Patel said in a low voice.

"Anyway, what do you reckon? You tee up some explosives, and I'll come with you. It'll be great. You, me, a bomb, and we can sort out this whole mess, once and for all, before it even happens. It'll be brilliant."

There was a long, tense silence. "I cannot do it. I'm sorry, but it simply … no, Spider. I can't."

"Okay, fine. She's your pride and joy, and clearly much more important to you than your son, which is fair enough. I mean, yeah, children are expendable, and there's probably too many around the place as it is, taking up resources, getting in the way, growing up into teenagers, being all sullen and bored, and who needs that sort of grief, right?"

"Are you quite finished, Mr. Webb?"

"I don't know. Am I? You're the one who thinks your bloody time machine is more precious than your own flesh and blood, not me."

"It is an outrageous lie. How dare you suggest I do not love Vijay!"

"You said it yourself, in your own words, just then."

"Vijay is my son. I went through a very great deal of, of, *shit*, yes, shit, to make sure he was brought up properly, to give him the opportunities he deserved. The things I—"

"Still, given a choice of giving up either your machine or your son, you picked the machine ahead of your son."

"For gods' sake, Spider!"

Spider found, to his great surprise, that he was quite enjoying this. "You love Vijay?"

"Yes, of course! What a—"

"Then destroy the machine. Or let me do it."

"You don't understand. It is more—"

"More complex? Yes? I don't understand? How can I possibly understand, I'm a simple Australian bloke?"

"It is, yes, more complicated than you imagine."

"Destroy *Kali*. Give the order. You told me yourself, just today at your office, to destroy it, you even used the word, 'whatever'."

"That was the heat of the moment. I have had time to reflect, you might say."

"You complete bastard," Spider said, stunned.

Spider could hear Patel trying not to cry. It was a dreadful thing to hear. He understood only too well what the guy was going through. The thing that shocked him was that, for whatever murky reasons he didn't want to go into, he still wouldn't destroy his stupid time machine if it meant saving his son. Spider remembered the time Dickhead McMahon wanted him to do something he did not want to do, until he found the one thing Spider cared about more than life itself, and used that against him. Spider caved instantly, and had been hating himself ever since. That was the thing, though. Spider would do anything for Molly. He would lay down his life, if it would help her. Yes, she didn't want him. Yes, he probably would sign those bloody papers, fine. But even though he had lost her, she was still his Molly, the love of his life, he would always love her, and he would die for her. Spider saw this as only natural. It was honorable. It was damned crazy, and Molly would not thank him, but it was, he thought, the right thing. This attitude of Patel's? Now that was crazy. He didn't understand it. How could you sit there and allow what had happened to actually happen, considering what was at stake — his own son? What kind of man would think that way? He didn't think it was some weird Indian ethnic thing, either. He believed that Indian people, like people everywhere, loved their children like nothing else. No, Mr. Patel was something different. Something was wrong. It was at once fascinating to see it in action, but also utterly revolting, loathsome. He could not get away from it fast enough.

"So," Spider said at last. "You're prepared to sacrifice your son in order to save your machine. Yes?"

"No, it is a false choice! You are misrepresenting—"

"No, no, you stop right there. I'm out. I'm done with you. I quit. I resign. I refuse to help you. I'm not getting involved with all this, and if you attempt to smear me, harm me, or use recordings of our conversations against me in a court of law, be aware that I have my own evidence, my own resources. I want nothing further to do with you, with time machines, with your company or any of its designated subsidiary properties. I am done. I'm gone. I'm getting the hell out of here. I would also draw your attention to the fact that I have your file, the whole thing, the entire history of your precious *Kali* project. I will waste no time in giving that to DOTAS, to the Federal Police, to the State Police. I—"

"Are you quite finished?"

"No, just getting up a good head of steam."

"Fine. Now listen to me. That file?"

"Uh-huh."

"Is deleting itself as we speak."

"It's ... *what*?"

It was true. The image up on Molly's wall showed FILE NOT FOUND. TRY AGAIN. Spider worked the interface from his watchtop. The file was gone. File recovery. Nothing. Nothing at all. "Shit," he said, cold all through, staring at the wall. He was counting on showing the file to Iris.

"I accept your resignation, Mr. Webb. Effective immediately. I will make sure you receive your outstanding entitlements forthwith, minus whatever liabilities are appropriate."

Vast forces swept and whooshed around Spider. This, he knew, was bad. He'd been sort-of bluffing. Patel was meant to cave in and see things Spider's way, do the right thing, and give Spider his blessing to go back and destroy *Kali*. He hadn't been expecting this. He hadn't prepared for this.

"Fine," he said, feeling unsteady on his feet. "Good."

"Thank you for your service. Good-bye."

Mr. Patel killed the link. Spider stood there, his knees weak, feeling cold and ill, clutching the edge of the sink with white-knuckle hands.

Then his phone went off. Spider figured it was Patel again, calling to warn him off trying some kind of private operation of his own. It wasn't. When he tapped his patch he heard, "Spider! Listen. Change of plan for tonight." It was Iris.

"Okay," he said, hardly listening.

"Something's come up. I need to see you right away, so I'm sending a car to pick you up. You're at Molly's, right?"

"Yeah," he said, absently.

"You all right, Spider?"

He could hear traffic noises, people yelling, police radio squeals, in the background. "I'll be waiting outside."

CHAPTER 10

An unmarked cop car, a late-model Holden, big fuel-cell engine, rims, bland paint job, swept into Molly's driveway. Spider saw a young Chinese-Australian woman in the driver seat, in uniform, no cap. She smiled and waved at him as he approached and slid into the front passenger seat. He smiled back, said hi, felt numb, and then felt a firehose torrent of memories blasting through his mind as he glanced around the car's interior, but it was that smell, that unique and distinctive cop car smell that just about did him in. How he remembered that! That mélange of body odor, hints of leather, industrial vacuuming, the out-gassing of synthetic carpet — it was like being in a taxi, only there was a vague subliminal vibe of *authority* about it.

"Mr. Webb?"

He started, blinking. "Sorry, what? Yes?"

"You don't look well, sir. Can I get you anything? Some water, maybe?" She was young enough to be his daughter, pretty but with a serious face, narrow data glasses, and her black hair, glossy under the overhead light, pulled back in a bun. She smelled faintly of something a little exotic that he couldn't place. Just looking at her; the uniform, all those patches and pins, the symbols and markings, her badge number, the crisply pressed folds in the blue fabric, the utility belt and sidearm. How that took him back, took him back to such an extent that he nearly forgot all about that row with Mr. Patel, and how Patel had left him washed up, shipwrecked, on a rocky coast.

"Oh. Right. Okay, sorry. No, I'm fine. Just … fine."

"You're sure?"

"Let's just go."

So they went. The young officer driving, whose name was Wu, expertly handled the car, and dealt with radio chatter with a level of banter and directness that Spider remembered well. Then, during a quiet lull as they sped down Tonkin Highway, she said, "It's quite an honor to meet you, Mr. Webb, if you'll pardon my saying so."

"Uh-huh," he said, getting over the worst of the contact high from finding himself in a cop car after all these years and starting to feel more like his usual self, which was to say, a decent guy up shit creek. "Thanks." He wondered what game the girl might be playing with him, but didn't care much. He didn't care much about anything at the moment.

Wu went on. "We studied your case, at the Academy, actually."

This got his attention. "What?"

"The Sharp case, and the aftermath. The way you were frozen out."

"You," he said, starting to say something, then stopped, confused. "You studied me?"

"Yes, sir. Strategies and Tactics for Fighting Internal Corruption."

There was a course, at the Academy, about internal corruption? In his day, everyone was assumed to be clean and virginal going in, and the in-service training courses only touched on corruption in the workplace. And, if Spider remembered correctly, many of those that he attended were run by several of Superintendent Sharp's oily minions, which rendered the entire business laughable at best. Ah, the good old days. "Okay," Spider said, not knowing what else to say. "So what do you do when you're the only officer not actually in on the 'joke'?"

"Sir?"

"Suppose you find that every copper you know, or even know of, everybody's in on it, they're all getting their payoffs, and everybody's happy about it — all except you. You find an envelope full of cash in your locker, just like everyone else, only you decide to burn it, to make a point. Suppose further this renders your position, to use a polite term, 'untenable'? Then what?" Spider could feel himself getting angry. It felt to him like it was never over, never finished. Like a dead body thrown in a lake, weighted down with cinderblocks, yet bubbling back to the surface, stinking up the whole world.

Wu hesitated a moment. "You keep detailed records: photos, fingerprints, everything. You go public."

"They're teaching this at the Academy?"

"Yes, sir."

"Good grief," Spider said, not sure how to feel. "I'm a case-study in a textbook."

"I think you did the right thing, Mr. Webb."

He stared at her, astonished. "Thanks." What else could he say? "Yeah, and look what it got me?" or maybe, "What would really help is if the fucking government would come to the party with whistleblower protection laws. Now that would help!" But no. All there was was the bitter knowledge that bright-eyed young recruits were being taught to Just Say No. Maybe, Spider had often thought, the real problem was that people were naturally corruptible. Maybe corruption was normal, and staying clean was deviant and wrong. Maybe he'd been wrong on the issue. He thought about Mr. Patel, lured over to the dark side by the promise of the best hotrod time machine ever. Just a few percent more, just a few percent. He sat and stewed, and said nothing.

"You're welcome. I hope I have that much courage one day."

"Courage is the bloody least of it."

The body had been torn to pieces.

It was, or had been, a white male, in his thirties, with longish dark hair, and a goatee beard. Where Spider could see the man's skin, there were the beginnings of what would ordinarily become heavy bruising. Every piece of the body had been punctured with holes, more like big bite marks than entry or exit wounds. The remnants of a black tracksuit, a cheap red skivvy and old running shoes long gone grey, lay strewn about. Something had ripped it apart like it was a piece of blood-soaked paper.

At length, Iris took Spider aside, out of the glare of the portable lights. "What do you know about this guy?"

Spider was so stunned he did not know what to say. "This guy? *This* this guy?"

"He knew you."

"I — what?"

Iris showed him a cheap black vinyl wallet containing seventy-five Australian dollars, the bills well used, and genuine; and a total of fourteen Canadian dollars, consisting of a ten-dollar bill — very colorful — and two two-dollar coins which looked like a copper coin set inside a larger silver coin. The wallet also contained some Canadian ID: a driver's license issued by the Province of Alberta to one John Stapleton, of Calgary, Alberta. The photo broadly matched the face of the victim. According to the stated date of birth, Mr. Stapleton should be in his middle-forties, but did not look older than mid-thirties, as far as anyone could tell based on what was left of his face. The reconstruction guys had a job ahead of them. Next to the photo was a torn piece of plain notepaper, the pulp and texture clearly visible, suggesting some kind of boutique paper mill, perhaps even a hobbyist supplier making paper sheets the old-fashioned way? Except on the paper, written in blue ball-point, was Spider's full name: ALOYSIUS WILLIAM WEBB, AKA 'SPIDER'. There was also Spider's usual address, the Lucky Happy Moon Motel, which, Spider did not need to be told, was less than fifty meters to his right. Everything suggested that Mr. Stapleton was attempting to find Spider, and had been told to look for him at the Motel. Spider stared and stared, peering at the note. Why would a Canadian guy be looking for him? Most troubling: what on Earth could have come along and done this to him?

"So you don't know him?"

"Never seen him before."

"You're sure."

"Yes, I'm sure." He felt cold all through, and a little shaky. *Why would he be looking for me?* Spider thought to himself.

"We also found this in his pocket." Iris reached into her raincoat and produced a plastic evidence bag containing a translucent red plastic six-sided die, the numbers marked out in white dimples. "Does this mean anything to you? Have you seen it before?"

"It's a D6," Spider said. "What do you want me to say?" Back in his gaming days, Spider had quite the collection of plastic dice: everything from four-sided D4s to six-sided D6s and on up to the ten-sided D10s, and the icosahedral D20s. All kinds of games required different sorts of dice, but none so much as old-school *Advanced Dungeons and Dragons*, *AD&D*, before the D20 upgrade. Back in the day, *D&D* was all about dice, lots of them, as many different types as you could find or borrow. The D6 Iris had in the evidence bag looked more like the kind of die you would find in a casino, at a craps table. Iris handed it to him, bag and all, and he took it in his hand, weighing it, examining the vertices and edges for signs of wear, and found plenty. This D6 had been around, seen some action, one way or another.

"Yeah, I know it's a D6, Spider. Been there, played that. But hold it up to the light, have a look inside."

Spider did so, squinting against one of the lamps, and noticed, faintly, that there was something in the heart of the D6, regular, blocky, but small. "Oh, hello, what's this?"

"We think it's portable memory. I had my watchtop open earlier, and it noticed an unknown storage device, unknown size and format, that hadn't been there before. Definitely this thing."

Spider was still playing with the D6, checking to make sure it followed the D6 rule, which was that opposite sides had to add up to seven. The three was opposite the four; the six opposite the one. It wasn't much, but it made him smile a little, thinking about happier times.

"So," Iris said, "Guy turns up, bearing both Canadian and local money, Canadian ID, one D6, your address, and gets torn to bits."

"Bad day."

"Bad day gets worse."

"Worse?"

"Does not get a mention in the International Traveler's database. Doesn't get a mention anywhere."

"Canadian records?"

"What we've found so far is this: name and prints and photo are a match to a physics teacher from Calgary who worked at one of the universities there—"

"Uh-huh," Spider said, not liking the way this was heading.

"Disappeared more than ten years ago. Paff, gone. Wife, too. Just vanished. Officially listed as a missing person, and declared legally dead by the Canadian RCMP. Memorial service three years ago."

"And it's definitely the same guy."

"DNA will confirm, of course, but..." Iris looked tired and annoyed.

"The DNA machines—"

"Got it in one."

Spider looked around, the forensic and chrono techs dressed in white anti-contamination jump-suits were busy with their examinations, running their tests, and taking their samples; all of them shocked into whispered silence. This whole area was a park, recently converted and beautified by the local council. Once, years ago, a tilt-up office block stood here, but when the first waves of wild financial times hit, the businesses in it went toes-up, nobody bought or leased the building, so eventually the owners had it demolished and tried to sell the land, but nobody wanted even that, so at last the Midland City Council took it off the owner's hands, and turned the site into a lovely park, with a beautiful lawn, rose beds, meandering paved paths, wrought-iron benches, and now perhaps the grisliest murder scene to have come along in recent WA history.

Spider could smell the blood. A perverse gremlin deep inside his mind chirped at him, telling him that blood would be good for the roses and the lawn. Beyond the blood he smelled acid. As bad as the physical destruction of the body was, whatever had attacked Stapleton had also used acid. Inadvertently, Spider flashed back to the classic *Alien* movies of the 1980s and '90s, creatures with acid for blood, eating their way through the decks of spaceships. At the time, and in many fan discussions long since, he had maintained the position that acid blood was a dumb idea, that it was far too dangerous. But here, with this poor bastard? He looked around. Apart from this park, between two office blocks, the rest of the area looked much as it always did, grim and lifeless. Which was to say, normal. There was a major road, heavy traffic at all hours, like it or not. Planes overhead coming and going from nearby Perth Airport, making windows rattle. Across the road, shops, cafes, a service station, a vet clinic. And, of course, a gathering crowd of sightseers, ghouls, people with cameras.

Uniformed officers had put up barricades and taped off the area, but still, so many people wanted to see what had happened, and what would happen. There were catcalls and rude remarks, jokes in poor taste — and traffic backed up a long way, horns blaring, as the exclusion zone spread onto the road. Any minute now the media would arrive — but then, looking around at all those people with their watchtops open, each one with a video camera built in, there was a good chance the media was already on the scene. Iris left Spider at one point to confer with the team's Intelligence Officer, who was busy taking note of the bystanders and gawkers, watching for ratbags, performance artists, serial pests, and all the rest of the public circus this sort of high-profile incident brought out.

Then Iris was back. "Some new developments," she said.

"Let me guess," Spider said. "There's no official record of this guy entering the country, under any pseudonym: no fingerprints, no arrival card, nothing. He's technically an illegal immigrant."

She arched an eyebrow at him. "Exactly."

"He's a time traveler. Right?"

"Well, obviously. We just have to check every little detail."

"So you're all wondering: where's his machine?"

"We're looking. We've notified DOTAS, and they're looking, too."

Spider nodded. "Great. A time traveler who knows me, but who I don't know, at least not yet. Oh joy. And what about—"

"We've got uniforms going door-to-door, checking for witnesses."

"Witnesses to the event itself?"

"Somebody must have seen this happen."

Spider reckoned they'd be lucky to find any witnesses. He could only think of two things that could have done what had happened to Stapleton. One was some kind of heavy industrial machinery. The other? Well, the word "monster" is so overused, but Spider figured some kind of monster was the likely culprit. Which, of course, was utterly preposterous. Absurd, even. One did not, ordinarily, encounter actual for-real monsters outside the realms of movies, games and cheesy books. One did not encounter actual monsters in a lovely park in the middle of Midland in the course of an ordinary evening. Say you're a typical member of the public, going about your ordinary member-of-the-public business, and lo, out of nowhere as you make your way down the street with your shopping you see some big nasty thing tearing apart some hapless man. You likely run like mad away from the scene, and pretend you saw nothing, and say nothing, because you're worried that whatever that thing was that you totally didn't see, might decide to come after you and yours.

Sometime around midnight, after the pieces of the victim had been taken away, and after the scene had been processed and sampled and examined and photographed to within a nanometer of its life, and after the last of the hopeless gawkers and murder fans had been sent on their way, Iris and Spider stood there, in the ruins of this park in Midland, drinking bad coffee from a roadside van, talking. They were both, for different reasons, shaken up, tense, trying to recover, to relax — *and nothing says rest and relaxation like drinking strong, bad coffee after midnight*, Spider thought, sipping his and wincing.

"So," Iris said, at one point, "you wanted a word with me today? Earlier?"

"I did, yeah."

"Yeah, sorry about that. It's just, this all came up, and we're flat out, we're—"

"No, honestly, it's fine. I understand. I just wanted to talk to you."

Iris was watching him over her plastic coffee cup. "What's wrong? Something's wrong, it's obvious."

He felt embarrassed that he was so easy to read. "Not, well, not wrong, exactly."

"Talk to me, Spider. It's not getting any earlier, and I have to be at the office by seven, so spit it out, mate."

"I got sacked today."

"Oh?"

"Yeah."

"Sorry to hear it. I thought—"

"I quit, in fact."

"Oh. You quit. Now I am surprised."

Spider started to tell her what happened, about Mr. Patel wanting to see him, about his special project for Spider, about *Kali*, the children, the whole thing, including the smoking-gun file documenting the entire thing, which he no longer had. It took quite some time to fill her in. He wanted only to give Iris a bare outline of the situation, but the more he talked, the more he had to talk, and, after they moved to a nearby bench, he told her everything, in detail. When he finished, he sagged back against the seat, his legs out in front of him, starting to feel cold in the wind coming off the nearby river.

Iris sat next to him, compact, serious, thinking hard. "You know how to pick 'em," she said.

"How was I supposed to know the bastard was gonna drop me in all this?"

"By now, Spider, you should just be immediately suspicious of pretty much anyone you meet, I reckon. It's like everyone who meets you turns out to be trouble in some way. Have you noticed?"

"Yeah," he said, and managed a rueful smile, which Iris shared.

"So you are in fact out of a job."

"Out on my fat arse, yes."

"What are you gonna do?"

"How should I know?"

"Just a question. Trying to get you focused on what's important."

"I don't even know where to begin"

Iris nodded. "I'll alert DOTAS about this *Kali*. It went future-ward, right?"

"Yes. At least ten thousand years."

"Okay. No worries. We'll set up an amber alert and start looking for the children, you know, just in case."

"He'll deny everything."

"They all do. But he can't deny reality. All DOTAS has to do is blip back a few days in ghost mode, and behold, there it is, the machine itself, in the garage, and Mr. Patel looking all guilty and remorseful, etc. etc. in front of the damn thing."

Spider was dismayed at the image Iris had painted. He imagined the photo of Patel and Vijay standing in front of *Kali*, having finished the build, looking all rugged and tough, all "Look at what we made, here!" And Spider, surprising himself, felt a strange urge to defend Patel. Yes, the guy was a criminal, and yes, he'd built a machine way too powerful for its own good, one that could be used as a weapon, and yes, he'd been criminally irresponsible regarding his own and someone else's child. Sure, there was all of that. But Spider did kind of like Patel. Despite everything. Not that he would warn Patel that the Feds were coming to bust his chops. It was more that he understood the guy, at least a bit. Recognized things in Patel that he saw in himself.

"Never good when children are involved."

"Tell me about it," Spider said.

Iris slapped his leg. "Yeah, sorry about that."

"Me, too." His leg burned where she'd touched him with her warm hand.

They said nothing for a while. Spider yawned. He was knackered. After a few minutes watching the traffic inching back and forth along the jammed-up road in front of them, Iris said, "So what are you gonna do?"

"Dunno."

"You could go crawling back."

"Screw that."

"You need a job, Spider."

"I'm not going crawling to any bastard."

"It may have escaped your notice, but the entire world is burning right now. Pretty soon just about nobody's going to have any kind of job at all."

"Yeah. Challenging job market. I know."

"Last I heard," Iris said, "the time machine biz is one of the best prospects for employment; at least in the near term."

"I said—"

"I know what you said. But still."

"I know."

"Maybe you could try the competition."

Spider was about to shoot down that suggestion, too, and tell Iris that Dickhead will have seen to that, poisoning the entire rest of the industry against him — until he remembered: Dickhead was gone. He was reduced to a severed head, now under lock and key at Section Ten. Dickhead wasn't so mighty or so all powerful anymore. Maybe Spider could get a gig at one of the other time machine firms. If Patel hadn't already spread the word against him, of course. Still, it was worth a try. "Yeah," he wound up saying, scratching his face, staring off.

"Meanwhile, I'll have a chat with some of my mates. Who knows?"

"Iris?"

"I'm saying nothing. Okay? I'm saying nothing at all."

He stared at her, puzzled, wondering what on Earth she was on about.

They went quiet again. Spider's mouth tasted foul. "That poor bastard tonight, Stapleton. How soon do you reckon he'll be autopsied?"

"We put a rush on it, maybe tomorrow, late, maybe."

He nodded. "I'd love to hear about it."

"You'll be the first person I tell."

"Thanks."

"Why'd you reckon he was looking for you, of all people?"

"Buggered if I know. I haven't met him yet."

"Only you, Spider!" Iris said, slapping his leg again. She got up, stretched, yawned, and shook her head. Spider could see her breath pluming in the cool night air. He stood up too, and walked her back to her car. "You know," she said after a while, as they walked through dewy grass, "we could probably find you more work, maybe even as a paid consultant. You thought of that?"

"Yeah, and how's that gonna go over with everyone?"

"We'll see," she said, tilting her head from side to side.

Spider remembered Constable Wu, who told him she'd studied "his case" at the Academy. Who told him she admired him for what he'd done. Maybe, he thought, things might be changing.

He opened Iris' car door, making a show of it. "Oh, thank you, good sir," she said, smiling wearily, and getting in. He closed the door, and she lowered the window. "You gonna be okay tonight?"

"Yeah. Back to Molly's. Gotta look after the fish."

"There's a fish?"

"Yeah. Long story."

She flashed him a wry smile. "Fair enough. Now go. Before you catch your death."

He watched as she backed out and drove off, and kept watching until her tail lights disappeared into the teeming traffic.

Later, much later, that night, Spider was back at Molly's place, on her couch, trying to sleep, but pretty sure he wasn't going to get any. Between the row he'd had with Patel, losing his job, and the dismembered time traveler, Spider was feeling done in. Buggered, in more ways than one. Exactly what *was* he going to do in the morning? His resignation, Mr. Patel had told him, was effective immediately. There was an excellent chance that, should he show up at the shop, there'd be security goons at the gate. There'd likely be a new head technician there, too. And, what about all of his stuff, his "personal effects"? He supposed they would be chucked into a box and left for him to collect — or maybe not.

Now, at two in the morning, and not feeling remotely sleepy despite his aching fatigue, he felt a dull, throbbing ache in his head, like something huge banging on a castle door, trying to break in and kill everyone — only this was something trying to break out. Something that might tear a person limb from bloody limb.

He snapped awake, wide-eyed, realized he'd just been sort-of dreaming, that it was now almost half-past three and his phone was ringing.

He tapped the phone-patch, still stuck to his face. "Hello..." The voice of weariness itself, fed up with the entire universe.

"Al! Hi! It's me! How are things?"

It was Molly.

"Is that... Is that you, Molly? It's—" He checked his watchtop.

"Yeah, hi! Just thought I'd check in, see how you're going, what's happening, see how poor Mr. Popeye's faring — you know if he dies and you replace him, I'll absolutely know, you can't fool me!"

Was it his imagination, or did she have a bit of an American accent now? There was something weird about it. And loud! He fumbled in the dark with his watchtop interface, trying to find the control for lowering the volume. "Molly, it's, oh God, it's really late here. What time is it there? It must be…"

"So how is my little fishywishy? I hope you've been giving him his medication, Al. He's my special little guy, and I'd hate to come home and find he's died."

"He's fine. Sends his regards. Wants a bigger tank."

Molly actually laughed. Spider lay there, blinking, thinking about that, trying to remember the last time he'd heard her laugh. She said, "Aren't you the funny one!"

"One tries," Spider said, still all half-dead, but not sure which half.

"So have you signed those papers yet?"

"Papers? What — Oh, those papers. No. I have not as yet—"

"Oh, come on, Al. You gotta let me go! I have to move on, be free!"

He wanted to ask her, who are you and what have you done with my real sort-of ex-wife? This did not sound like Molly. It sounded like, he thought, he wasn't sure what. "How's New York, then? Busy?"

"Oh, Al, it's fabulous! You have to come out and see it for yourself, you'd love it! I've met all these lovely people!"

Last news Spider saw showed how much of New York City was in a process of economic and even physical collapse. There were riots, huge protests. It was, Spider thought, like 1980's Beirut. There was nothing "fabulous" about it, and he failed to see any of these "lovely" people Molly mentioned. He said, "Okay, that's nice, love."

"Oh, gotta go, Al! Someone's calling for me. Talk to you soon!"

"Um, see ya," Spider said, and heard the click as the line went dead. He lay there, staring at the ceiling, at the cobwebs in one corner, his head ringing with Molly's voice, full of that strange enthusiasm. Had she been high? That might have been it. She might well have been completely off her face on something one of her dubious new pals had given her, some party drug. It was certainly the strangest conversation he'd ever had with her, in all the time he'd known her. For another thing she had also been far happier in that call than at any time in their entire relationship. Even on their wedding night, she hadn't been that happy. Something, he knew, was wrong.

The alarm on his watchtop went off at six-thirty. He'd been lightly dozing, having terrible dreams. "Oh, God," he said, feeling his heart starting to settle down. "Errgh." Shafts of molten brass light came slicing through the windows, casting stark shadows on the ceiling.

"Coffee. Must have coffee." He lurched to his feet, went to the loo, splashed cold water on his stubbly face, considered shaving, thought better of it. "Hmm. Food. Food good." In the kitchen, the light was far too bright for decent people. Even the light in the fridge was too damned bright. And he was very pleased to see, as he rummaged for milk for his coffee, that there was no giant severed head in there, asking for his help.

Later, showered and dressed in yesterday's overalls, he got his bike out of the garage, popped the polycarbonate canopy, and climbed into the framework, easing his aching self into position. It was as he snapped the canopy back into place that he stopped, staring at nothing in particular, and looked at his watchtop.

That call from Molly, he thought, squinting to remember. *There was something—*

Time-gaps. There had been no time-gaps when he was talking to Molly during the night. Spider, in the course of his former job, had to talk to people overseas all the time — parts suppliers, manufacturers, sales reps, international regulatory bodies. And when you spoke to such people overseas, there was always a slight gap between what you said, and what they heard, and vice versa. It simply took a small amount of time for the voice signal to make its way around the bulk of the planet. No matter how you tried to compensate for the gap, it was still there, tripping up the people on each end of the call.

But Molly had been speaking to him with no such gaps, as if she had been calling from next door. He realized that, aside from the fact that Molly had sounded not at all like her usual bristling self, the absence of those tell-tale time-gaps meant Molly, strange, weird, off her face Molly was almost certainly here in Perth.

CHAPTER 11

Spider pedaled off to the shop. It was all he could think of to do, and he arrived with no memory of the journey. The whole way there, his mind was filled to bursting with the thought that Molly was, for some reason, back in Perth, off her face on some damn thing, but keen to make him think she was still in New York. What was that about? Why would she do that? What had happened to her over there? She'd only been there a week. Surely the first couple of days she'd have been too jetlagged to do anything but just lurch about, wearing dark sunglasses, experiencing the city as if dreaming, the sort of dream where very little makes sense.

As he rounded the corner onto Inverness Road in Malaga, he very nearly ran into a white semi-trailer coming the other way, blatting its horn at him. He snapped back into default reality in time, swerved the bike, avoided the impact, heard the hissing air-brakes on the truck blasting away over his head, and next thing he was tilting over, the canopy popping — there was a mighty thump as he and the bike hit the ground — and he tumbled out, landing in a heap on the dried out grassy verge in front of the abandoned tire place that used to be next door to Time Machines Repaired While-U-Wait. He lay there a long moment, dazed, his shoulder and hip hurting, his nose full of the smell of dead brown grass, and glancing back, saw the semi-trailer turn and head for Malaga Road. He saw, not quite understanding it, the Bharat Group logo, huge along the side of the shipping container mounted on the back of the semi. Spider stared as the truck disappeared. In the time he'd worked at the shop since Bharat had taken over, he'd never known the company to send out a bloody great truck like that. Certainly, the company had sent out some new equipment, but that stuff fit on the back of a one-tonne truck, no problem, and still left room for the driver's kelpie dog.

Spider struggled to his feet, wincing; rubbing at his shoulder, wanting to make sure his hip would still take his weight. *So far, so good.* Inspecting the bike itself showed it was none the worse for the spill. The front gate was only a few meters away. If he still had his job, he would have been on-time, more or less. It was not until he saw the front gate that he began to understand the reality of this new day.

The gate was chained and padlocked. There was a sign, from a commercial real estate firm, saying the property was up for lease. OWNER WILL REDEVELOP TO SUIT TENANT, it said. The shop's front door was closed, with anti-intrusion tape across it. NO TRESPASSING. As he stood there with his bike, staring and staring, he heard the *basso profundo* booms of big dogs barking, going nuts, in the distance, and thought, *Oh, no.*

Three big black dogs, each the size of a truck, came boiling out from behind the building, thundering towards him, slobber flying, eyes crazy. They flung themselves at the gate. Spider stumbled back, numb with shock. The dogs hurled themselves at him, again and again, desperate to get at him, and tear at him — he flashed on the remains of John Stapleton and for a moment wondered if he could have been done in by something as ordinary as a pack of wild monster dogs. Spider, backing away, could not believe how high they could jump.

Feeling sick, shaky, and cold inside, Spider turned his bike around and slowly pedaled to the nearby lunch shop, a place he'd visited just about every day since he started working at Time Machines Repaired While-U-Wait. The girl behind the counter, Sheri, said, "G'day, Spidey, how's it—" She stopped, once she got a good look at him. "Spider, God, what happened, mate?"

He went to speak, but couldn't. He gestured, trying to indicate the workshop, not looking at her, not looking at anything. He felt his eyes stinging, and his throat tighten up, and he realized he was going to cry, and that wasn't on, so he tried to smile, and went to leave, waving to Sheri to let her know that everything was fine. Except that Sheri wasn't stupid, and she came after him, "Spider! What the hell's going on?" She grabbed his arm; he tried to pull away from her, but she hung on. "Spider! Talk to me!"

So, taking his time, and thanking her for the tissues and the coffee she gave him, he told her that just yesterday, he'd inadvertently quit his job, but he figured Mr. Patel would just replace him and things would go on. He never ever expected that the company would shut the place down. What about Charlie and Malaria? What about them? They hadn't done anything wrong.

Other customers came and went, wanting the usual morning pick-me-ups, and they all, to a man, ignored the stubbled figure in the corner, turned away so nobody would see him. He was thinking of heading to the city to talk to Patel. Not, by any means, to beg for his job back. That was not going to happen, not if Spider lived to the End of Bloody Time. No, he wanted to see Patel and, maybe, just maybe, give the swine a good kicking. Yes, Mr. Patel might be angry with Spider, fine, no problem. He could respect that. But closing the shop? Taking Charlie and Malaria's jobs, in the current economic climate? Was that entirely necessary? Anger, Spider could understand, but cruelty, too? It wasn't fair. And Spider needed to tell him that. Now. In person.

Leaving the lunch shop, his coffee unfinished, Spider steered his bike onto the Mitchell Freeway, slotted into the bike lane, got a nice low gear going, and cruised towards the rising towers of Perth, forging a new, hard anger in his heart. Thinking, with every stroke of the pedals in front of him, just what he was going to say to Mr. Patel, rehearsing the entire thing in his head.

But when he got there, got into the Bharat Group office tower, the Ground Floor receptionist would not let him pass. "I'm sorry, Mr. Webb. I cannot allow you onto the premises. I have specific orders."

"You have orders. Oh, good, you have orders. Fine. Good for you." He pushed past the reception station, across the gleaming floor to the elevators. "I'll give you bloody orders," he muttered to himself — and then found he was facing a pair of heavy-duty security officers, stun-guns leveled at his chest.

"Mr. Webb. Please leave at once," said one. The other joined in, "Let's not make a scene, what do you reckon?"

Spider took some breaths, doing his best to control the frantic, booming, beating of his heart. The adrenaline fizzing through his system, he could do nothing about, and he knew that his entire body was, right now, up for a fight, you just watch, he could totally take these two clowns. He remembered all the unarmed combat training he'd gotten as a copper. Two guys? No worries. Two guys with stun-guns? Okay, that would present difficulties, but if he was quick, and zigged when they were expecting him to zag, well, who knows? He smiled at them. His best, most disarming smile, lots of teeth. Look at me, I'm harmless, no threat at all. He had his arms and hands out, to show he was just a regular bloke, nothing to worry about. "Now, look, fellas, I just want to go and talk to my boss, okay? That's all I want."

"Your former employer, sir," the goon on the left said, taking a step towards Spider, the stun-gun still leveled at him, "does not wish to see you. If you do not leave immediately, we will take action, and we will hand you over to the police, and have you charged with trespass, and whatever the hell else we can think of to have you charged with. Now you don't want that, do you, sir."

"But I just need—"

The darts hit Spider. He went down, shaking, in agony.

When he woke, he was sitting in a plastic chair, feeling dizzy, and everything hurt. A voice to his right said, "What am I going to do with you, Spider?"

Squinting, he saw Mr. Patel, sitting at right-angles to him, on another plastic chair.

They were in a small, windowless room; it looked something like a first-aid station, with a high narrow examination bed, some simple medical equipment, a medication cabinet on the wall with a big red cross on it, a full-size plastic human skeleton, grinning at him. He could hear the air-conditioning; it was loud, and was making the already stuffy air in the room smell bad. Seeing Mr. Patel was a shock. The man was dressed in a business shirt, sleeves rolled up, no tie, and no data-glasses. He looked, Spider noticed, as bad as Spider felt. "You," Spider said, and wished he hadn't. Fresh waves of pain crashed in his head as he spoke. He clutched at his forehead, his eyes closed. Once again, an image of something huge and monstrous trying to escape the bone prison of his skull filled his mind, and when he opened his eyes again, he saw Patel, still there. "You shut us down."

Patel shrugged, trying to appear calm and rational, but in fact looking like he'd had no sleep. Spider imagined the guy spending the night trying to figure out what he was going to do. The cops breathing down his neck, the man he'd chosen to sort out his troubles gone, Phoebe's parents screaming at him. Yesterday, Spider had been sympathetic. Today, no. Today, Spider wanted to strangle him. "How could you do that?" The words boomed in his head, and he winced.

"Spider, it was an underperforming node in the network. The KPIs were flatlining. Revenue was down sixty percent on last quarter, and forecasts suggested it would continue to decline and ultimately crash. It was a mercy killing."

"There was no need," Spider said, clutching his head, his eyes squeezed shut, "to sack Charlie and Malaria."

Patel was surprised by this, and peered at Spider. "They are not fired, Spider. Far from it. They are valuable Bharat Group assets. We moved them to new positions at our Morley dealership. Malaria Brown has been inducted into our executive training program. Charlie Stuart has his own department in the workshop."

"I beg your pardon?" Spider had heard what the man told him, but he did not believe it. "Why should I believe you?"

"Believe what you like."

Spider said nothing, sat there, aching all over, soaking in the pain.

Patel said, "I suppose you've come to get your job back."

"No chance of that."

"Quite so."

"Wouldn't be caught dead."

"I have had a box containing your personal effects couriered out to your last-known domicile."

My last known domicile? Spider thought. *Molly's place, or Mrs. Ng's?* He'd have to check. "Thanks," he said, grudgingly.

"You are most welcome."

Again, the silence settled between them. Spider heard the air-conditioning wheeze. There was a faint odor of something like damp socks.

"Any word of Vijay?"

"What do you think?"

Spider nodded, gently. "Three days now."

"No need to tell me."

"You'd think he'd come back, if he could."

"You think I've not had that same thought?"

"Sorry." Spider was finding it hard to stay angry with the man.

"I am sorry, too."

"I told the cops. Last night."

"I know. I have already heard from Inspector Street?"

"Time Crime Unit."

"So she said."

"How'd you play it?"

"Full cooperation. What else?"

"She'll look after you."

Patel nodded, staring at the floor. Spider wasn't sure, but it looked like the guy had more grey hair than he'd had when he spoke to him yesterday. His face was drawn, with bags under his eye-plugs. "This morning I got a note from Parminder."

"Bad news?"

"Yes and no. She has decided she wants a divorce."

"I see what you mean."

"How are you feeling now?"

"Like a bag of shit."

"When I heard what they did…" Patel said, referring to the stun-gun attack.

"Not my first time."

"Even so."

"Whatcha gonna do if you don't hear from the children?"

"The matter is out of my hands now."

"Yeah, but what are *you* gonna do? You can't just sit on your thumbs."

"Inspector Street has cautioned me not to leave the State, or the present. They are, she said, 'checking things'."

"Did you give her your file?"

"I did."

"Right thing to do."

"Oh, shut up," he said, tired, worn down, not meaning it. It was the kind of thing, Spider thought, a friend would say to another friend, which, all things considered, was odd.

Spider nodded, and rubbed at his face. "I could murder a coffee."

Patel went out and returned a few minutes later, with a coffee for Spider, and a chai for himself, in paper cups with plastic lids. "These things make me feel like a baby," Patel said, detaching the lid. "I think I've outgrown sippy cups, what do you think?"

Spider's coffee, a simple flat white, smelled good but was burnt. He sucked it down regardless. "Thanks," he said.

"Do you realize, Spider," Patel said, "they've even confiscated the Time Machine from my office."

"The cops?"

"The company. I led the effort to track it down and get it restored, but it was always company money, and it was always company property."

Things moved fast in the Bharat Group, Spider thought, sipping coffee. It was too bad, really. For a while there, Spider had had his eyes on the Machine as a possible solution to his need for some kind of unit with which to go after the children. "Don't suppose you've heard from any future versions of yourself?"

"Whatever I'm doing in the future, I'm not sufficiently disturbed to consider warning myself here. Or, possibly, I'm unable to warn my present self. I just feel so, so cut off, like I'm missing a limb." Patel sat, hunched forward in his chair, fiddling with his gold wedding ring. Spider could feel the heat pouring off the man, his brain churning constantly, trying to figure out how he was going to get out of the very deep hole he was in. Spider also had the sense that Patel wanted to ask him to get back on the team, at least in his capacity as a private investigator, looking for the children, but could not bring himself to say so, and Spider did not feel particularly much like making it easy for him. The fact was, he thought, the man, when presented with the choice of saving his boy (and the girl), or losing his precious *Kali*, was prepared to sacrifice the children. That right there was not on. That was the kind of thing that made Spider want to go out and find the damned contraption specifically so that he could blow it up, to stick it to Patel, to tell him, "It's just a machine! It's not your flesh and blood. It's not you. It's not your immortality. It's just hardware."

"Guess you're feeling pretty helpless," Spider said, deliberately trying to nettle his former boss. *That'll teach you for getting me burnt coffee*, he thought, full of mischief.

"Yeah, helpless and without much to go on. I do have the coordinates for a nodal point located four years in the past, when I was still living in Mumbai. It was the day I first had the idea for building *Kali*. I remember that day very well, I wrote of it in my personal log. If I was going to go and visit my past self, that is the day I would visit."

"What if that version of your past self tells you you're full of shit and to bugger off?"

Patel looked at Spider. "At this point, the way I feel right now? I would pull out a gun and shoot the smug bastard."

Spider was so surprised he damn near choked on the dregs of his coffee.

Later, back on the freeway, heading to Midland so he could visit Mrs. Ng's Lucky Happy Moon Motel to see if his personal effects had been returned there, Spider was pedaling in cruise mode, his legs still aching from residual stun-gun effects, when he got a call from Iris. The autopsy findings on the body from last night were in. Spider told her where he was heading. Iris said she'd meet him there.

"God, what happened to you?" she said as he limped towards her on the path outside Mrs. Ng's.

"Bad day, Iris. Getting stun-gunned was kind of the least of it."

"Somebody zapped you?"

"You said you had autopsy findings?"

"Yeah, and something else."

"Do tell."

She produced the evidence bag containing the D6. "Hold this a minute." Iris reached into a pocket in her raincoat and pulled out two pairs of vinyl gloves; she put her pair on with practiced ease, took back the D6 in its bag, and handed Spider a pair of gloves for himself. He had noticeably more difficulty pulling them on. It was as if all his coordination had left him. He'd never felt clumsier. At length, and with a little help from an exasperated Iris, he got them on. Iris filled him in on the autopsy results. "Guess what we found in Stapleton's brain?"

At first, frustrated over the business with the gloves, and not in a mood for stupid games, Spider suggested, "green cheese?", "kittens?", and, "psycho death-kittens?"

She made a face at him. "Remember I showed you the report from McMahon's head?"

It took Spider a moment to realize she was talking about Dickhead. He remembered that conversation very well. He remembered the paranoia he felt, knowing he was reading a document he had no right to read. "Yeah, it was full of some kind of artificial structural stuff."

"Same stuff in Stapleton's head."

"You're kidding me?"

"People in high places, Spider, are exceedingly concerned, you might say."

He finished with the damned gloves at last, and flexed his plastic-covered fingers, which rustled quietly. "Some poor bastard's had to get the PM out of bed again, yes?"

"No, he was already up this time. But yes, not happy."

"Two people with some kind of weird hardware in their heads?"

"Did McMahon have any Canadian business interests?"

"Not that I know of, but who knows? I mean, this is Dickhead McMahon we're talking about. Looking at him, you think he's

just some mid-level corporate drone in a cheap suit and a bad but
expensive haircut. Then you turn around and he's the Emperor
of Bloody Time Itself, fiddling about with the threads of history
to make things go his way. The way he supposedly saved my
wretched life last year."

"That was a hell of a scar you got."

"Still itches sometimes, at night."

"So you don't know about his offshore business interests, is
what you're saying."

"I can tell you all about his End of Time business interests, no
worries, but Canada? No idea."

"Okay, hmm," Iris said, and made a note on her handheld.

"What am I doing with this?" Spider said, holding up the bag
with the D6. "Isn't it kind of really not on for you to be wandering about with bits of evidence like this?"

"Open the bag. Take it out."

He stared at her, surprised.

"That's why you've got the gloves."

It took some fumbling, but at length, Spider got the bag open,
and dropped the D6 into his gloved hand. Up close, out of its
bag, and in daylight, it looked even more like a D6 that had seen
some heavy-duty gaming in the course of its short life. Some of
the white-spotted dimples had lost their paint; the edges and
vertices were worn and scratched. If Spider were still a gamer,
he would never have allowed the use of a D6 in this condition: it
wouldn't produce reliably random results. "Okay, then," Spider
said. "I have the D6. I have the wicked power of pseudo-random
number generation right here in my hot little hand."

"Roll it."

"What?"

"Roll the damn die."

"You came all this way to talk to me, and this is what you've
got?"

"Don't forget the machine shit in Stapleton's head."

"Yeah, yeah," he said, frowning at the D6 in his hand. "Where
do you propose I roll this thing? I'm pretty sure you don't want
me rolling it on the pavement, getting evidence all contaminated
and everything."

Iris reached into her shoulder bag, and produced a Tupperware
lunch box, which she opened, and removed from it a bundle of
plastic cling wrap, and a banana peel, already going brown and
blotchy. She shook the box out, emptying it of sandwich crumbs,
and handed it to Spider. "There you go. Knock yourself out."

The thought of Iris eating lunch was enough to make Spider's own stomach grumble. So far today he'd only had some Vegemite toast, a few coffees, a shot from a stun-gun, and not much else. "What sort of sandwich was it?"

"Just roll the bloody D6!"

It rattled around the plastic box, and came up showing the number three: three dimples arranged in a diagonal pattern across the upper surface of the D6. "Oooh, a *three!*"

"Roll it some more. Maybe, say, five times. Make a note of what you get."

So Spider got busy. He got a one, a five, another one, a two — and a *"B"*. It was a capital B. Much of the white paint had been chipped away from the dimpled surface, as with the numbers. He stopped, staring at it. "That's…"

"It's…" Iris peered into the box. "Yes, that's a B."

"Yes, I can see it's a B, Iris."

"Good. Full marks for observation."

"But it's a B!"

"Yes, and?"

"D6s, in my experience, such as it is, generally produce numbers between one and six, on a more or less equally distributed basis. If you have two D6s, and you add their results, you can get a very nice normal distribution curve, where—"

"Spider, you're babbling."

"What the hell is a B doing in there? Is this a trick? Have you fiddled with—"

"Yes, it's a trick. No, I had nothing to do with it."

"No, I don't believe it! It's rigged."

"Okay. Roll it some more. See what you get."

Spider did some more die-rolling. It was just like the old days, rolling up damage from a fireball in *D&D*, say, when he was an unpopular fat kid in high school, playing the game with other social misfits in the school library at lunchtimes and he didn't have much money so he only had the one D6, a white one with nice black dimples. Rolling 10D6 damage with only one D6 could take a long, tedious time, he remembered. Now, rolling the thing in Iris' plastic lunch box in front of the Lucky Happy Moon Motel, Spider felt a little self-conscious, but mostly he was baffled out of his mind. Then Spider rolled an *"F"*.

"Oh, hold the phone," he said, staring into the lunchbox.

"What'd you get?"

"An F. I got an F."

"What about the other rolls?"

"Just numbers." He stared and stared at that F.

"So that's a B and now an F."

"Uh-huh."

"What does that tell you?"

Spider tore his gaze away from the F and looked at Iris. "Do you propose letting me in on this game at any point, or what?"

"Last night, when I finished all the paperwork on everything, back at the station, cataloguing all the physical evidence, not that there was much, this D6 in its little plastic bag was the only thing left on my desk not filed away. And it was showing the letter 'D'."

"D, you say?"

"Kind of appropriate, in a way. Remember when Perth detectives were called 'the d's'?"

"Yeah, dimly. But…"

"Listen. It was showing a D, like I said. The letter D. And it was all chipped and worn, like everything else on this D6—"

"Suggesting it was a result that had come up many times before, as part of the die's normal operations. Like these other letters."

"Exactly. Yes. So I picked it up, real carefully, keeping the D in sight at all times, and I had this thought. The Rule of Seven."

"Opposite sides add up to seven."

"Yes."

"So you…" He picked up the D6, showing the F, and with great care turned it around so that he could see the opposite surface. And was so shocked, he dropped it back in the box, and very nearly dropped the box itself.

"What did it show?" Iris asked.

"Minus five." It looked just like the usual five-dimple X pattern, as worn as all the other results, but with a small minus sign near the center dimple.

Iris nodded. "F is twelve, and minus five plus twelve gives you seven."

"You seem very calm about all this, Iris." He was holding the D6 again, looking at every surface, and only seeing six distinct sides, numbered from one to six. There was no trace of letters, and certainly no trace of negative numbers. How the flying hell was this innocuous little thing doing that? Was it that strange little device you could barely see deep inside the D6, in its murky heart? He remembered that Iris had told him that the thing itself appeared to be some kind of portable drive, but that it showed up on her watchtop interface as using an unknown format and could not be read. What did the weird business with the numbers and letters have to do with whatever it had locked inside? Was there a password? Something you had to enter based on a sequence of these numbers and letters? It didn't make a lot of sense — at least, he thought with a tiny shudder, in this universe. What if this was the sort of artifact someone like Dickhead might use to influence the strings of time? He didn't like to think that something as ordinary-seeming as this could secretly be one of the keys to the universe. And, thinking that, he put the D6 back in Iris' Tupperware box, and gave it to her, not wanting anything to do with it. Whatever the hell it was, it was bad juju. That much, if Stapleton's fate was any guide, was only too clear.

Iris said, "Other than his wallet, this D6 was the only thing Stapleton was carrying."

"Well, good for him," Spider said, watching Iris put the thing back in its evidence bag, certain that now that he'd handled the thing, even with plastic gloves on, it would soon be just one more thing in his life giving him grief.

"Yeah, that's what I thought — until I started thinking about it."

"Oh, shit, that's never good."

"Two guys, both dead, both with all this hardware in their heads. Two guys who just turned up, out of nowhere, in bad shape."

"And then some."

"You know, Spider, and this is just between you and me—"

At that, Spider put his hands over his ears. "Oh, no you don't. I'm not hearing it. Whatever it is, I'm not listening! La la la la la la la! You can't make me hear it, I don't want to know!"

Nonplussed, Iris waited for him to finish. "Spider, shut your gob and listen, all right? This is important. You're my consultant. There could be money in this for you."

That got his attention, with the greatest reluctance. "Uh-huh."

"Last night, after everyone went home, it was just me in the section, like always, right?"

"Please don't tell me you got a visit from a future version of me with dire warnings."

"No, nothing like that."

"Good," he said. Because, he remembered only too well, the last time a version of himself from the future came back to visit Iris, his Future Self ended up sleeping with her, much to Present Spider's aching chagrin.

"So I was sitting there, playing with the D6, just like now. And with gloves on, of course. Rolling numbers, writing them down, seeing what I got."

"Uh-huh."

"I got all the numbers, from one to six, you'd expect to get. But I also got the letters A to F, and a bunch of other numbers, from minus one to minus five — and zero."

"Zero? As in—"

"As in a side with no number on it. No dimples. Blank and smooth, like, well, like a very smooth and blank thing indeed."

Spider felt things moving around in his head, trying to take all this in. He was tense, on edge, absolutely sure this harmless little red cube was nothing but trouble. To take his mind off this conviction, he worked through the numbers. Between the regular numbers, the minus numbers, the letters, and the zero, he came up with 24 sides for that harmless little D6. "So it's a hypercube," he said, not happy.

"Yes, and there's more."

"Oh, lovely."

Iris leaned in close to him. She said, very quietly, so only he could hear, "I had a hunch, Spider."

"Uh-oh."

"I took my glove off, and, very carefully, went to pick up the thing."

"You could be charged with tampering with evidence, Iris."

"Spider, listen to me."

"How do you know the killer didn't plant that on Stapleton's body?"

"Will you shut up?"

"Iris, you can't do shit like that!"

"Spider!" she said, grabbing him to make him pay attention to her. "Listen to me! The thing *burned* me when I tried to touch it."

"It did what?"

"It burned me."

"How bad? Are you okay?"

Iris showed him a distinct red mark on her right index finger and her thumb. "I ran it under some cold water, it was fine."

"Good. You had me worried—"

"Yeah, the thing is—"

"I can't believe the little bastard burned you!" He stared at it in Iris' evidence bag, looking all innocent. He was starting to think of it not as an 'it' but as a creature, dangerous and far from tame.

"The thing is, it was only when I tried to touch it with unprotected fingers. When I tried the glove again, it was fine."

Spider took this in. "So it was like it knew you were the wrong person to handle it."

"Yes," she said, nodding, "it was exactly like that."

"But that's crazy!"

"Crazy, sure, but you saw it yourself."

He was still watching it, hanging there in the bag, full of extra-dimensional menace. "Did you try to pick it up again, without the glove?"

"I did, with my other hand, and got burned again." She showed him her other index finger and thumb.

"Shit!"

"But you know what's weird, really weird?"

"Because all of this isn't quite weird enough?"

"It was — and hear me out here, okay? — it was like the thing reached into my head, during that moment of contact. I could feel something in my mind, like that feeling when you know someone's behind you, watching you, and you turn around. Only on steroids. Something reached into my head, figured out I wasn't the right.person, so it burned me."

Spider stared and stared. "Iris, are you—"

"For God's sake, Spider."

Iris was the coolest, most composed person he knew. Nothing rattled her. But this little plastic cube was freaking her out, and that freaked him out. "Ditch it."

"I can't ditch it, Spider. Evidence."

"Yeah, yeah, I know."

Then Iris said, "Spider."

"What?"

"I need you to do me a favor."

"You want *me* to do *you* a favor?"

"Stapleton was looking for you."

"You think."

"He had your name and address on that bit of paper."

"So you're thinking...?" He was pretty sure he knew what Iris wanted from him, and didn't like it.

"I think the D6 wants to meet you."

"Out of all the possible people out there."

"I know, but would you try?"

"You want me to contaminate evidence?"

"We know Stapleton was a time traveler. And we know he didn't have a time machine, or at least not one we could find. Even the chrono-forensics guys couldn't spot one." Spider knew those guys used tools that would reveal a ghost-moded time machine, if they stumbled across one. "They searched out to a five-k radius. Nothing."

"He had Australian money. He might've got a taxi." Spider was staring at the D6 in its bag. There was no way on God's green Earth he was going to touch that thing. Not with his naked skin, anyway.

"The thing that reached into my head, I've been thinking about it, trying to remember the sensation, what it was like."

"I'm not doing it, Iris."

She looked at him, and could see for herself that he'd made up his mind. She put the evidence bag back in her raincoat pocket. "Could be important, Spider."

"Could be a one-way trip to winding up dead like Stapleton, too!" It had occurred to him that the thing that killed Stapleton might have been looking for that D6, for whatever unimaginable reason. "Any further information about what killed the poor bastard?"

"We're setting a regress for tonight. You want in?"

A "regress" was the coppers using time machines of their own to rewind time to see just what happened at the crime scene, at the time of death. "Ghost mode?"

"Wouldn't have it any other way."

"What if whatever killed Stapleton—"

"It won't."

"The way Stapleton finished up, nothing ordinary, conventional, did that, you realize that, right?"

"Forensics reckons that kind of damage might have been done by a harvester, like on a farm?"

Spider nodded. "Should be easy enough to spot a whacking great John Deere agricultural harvester rampaging along the street here."

Iris made a face at him. "I'm pretty sure it wasn't any kind of machine."

"Yeah, me, too."

"Weird thing to think about. Actual, you know," Iris said, uncomfortable at the very idea. "Monsters. Not just things under the bed, or in the wardrobe."

Spider was more concerned about, as he saw it, the bleeding obvious: Stapleton was trying to reach him before this thing caught up with him. It strongly suggested that pretty soon Spider, too, would be trying to get away from it. "Yeah."

"We'll be armed to the teeth, of course," Iris added.

"Good. That's real good."

"You don't think we can take it?"

"You saw the guy, Iris."

"Yeah, I saw him all right. I'll be seeing him all the rest of my days, I reckon."

"Great job. Career opportunities."

"Complimentary post-traumatic stress disorder. So, you're definitely in, then?" she said.

Maybe they could grab Stapleton before he got hit, and take him off somewhere safe and talk to him. Find out what the hell's going on. Find out what's up with that damned D6 of his. If, in fact, it was his. Time machines, for all that Spider utterly hated them, and hated what they did to people's heads, were brilliant for dealing with ordinary crime, including murders. It was the easiest thing in the world: go to crime scene. Activate time machine. Wind back through time until you catch the murderer red-handed. Spider knew there was a vexed philosophical question over the issue of what should be done about victims of crime: do you try to prevent the crime, or do you let it happen, and then prosecute the offender? You can't charge a person with a crime he has yet to commit — unless you have incredible evidence suggesting that said person is deep in the planning stages of a premeditated crime. That was a separate case, and presented its own problems. The WA Police Service's Office of Philosophical Analysis, once the province of ethics graduates and constantly mocked by the real-world coppers they worked with, was these days a vital center of study into the question of just what was police work about. The current view was that police work was primarily about solving crimes, and only secondarily about preventing crimes, if possible. It turned out to be very good PR for the Service to be seen by the public arresting murderers red-handed. That played to the media extremely well, and the politicians loved it — whereas catching a guy who was about to kill someone rather lacked the same impact. Yes, you saved a life, but those people saved had a strange way of going on to die anyway in terrible accidents. It was an example of the cussedness of time travel. At what point was the prevention of crime actually about preventing bad things happening at all? Should people be protected from everything that could happen to them? On this issue the Office of Philosophical Analysis was, at least at the moment, quite clear: police can only follow the current law, and arrest people who offended against the law. Anything else started to become babysitting, and nobody wanted that. "Yeah, I'm in. Like I could say no. I mean, an actual, for-real monster. Gosh."

"I imagine the technical term would be more like some kind of extra-terrestrial lifeform, or some damned thing."

"Not necessarily," Spider said. "It could be indigenous fauna, just from the way far future or something evolved from crabs, maybe."

"That's one big crab."

"Yeah."

"About the D6," Iris said.

"I said I wasn't going anywhere near the bloody thing."

"I was just thinking it might help."

"It might help," he muttered, shaking his head, not happy. Iris stood there, not looking at him, with her hands buried in the deep pockets of her raincoat, staring at the teeming traffic; Spider stood there, too, feeling guilty for not helping Iris. She really had done a lot for him, he knew that. But this thing, this bloody D6! It could be dangerous! It could be... He sighed, staring at passing traffic. What was the worst that could happen? He could get a bit of a burn? Well, no. The worst that could happen was that he could wind up dead, in small bite-sized pieces. He rubbed his eyes, and knew what he'd say. "Iris."

"Yeah?"

"Gimme the damn thing."

She handed him the bag, a wry look on her face. "If it was dangerous, surely one or other of us would have come back from the future to warn us about it, right?"

He was fumbling with the ziploc seal of the bag; Iris had to help him. His coordination was still crap. At last, the bag open, Spider closed his eyes and tipped the D6 into his gloveless hand.

"It's not burning me," he said, blinking, surprised. The thing just sat there in his hand, currently showing a four. "It's not doing anything!" He even flashed a rare smile, and laughed a little.

Iris joined in. "Thank God!" she said.

"Oh," Spider said, after a moment, the smile vanishing. "Oh, what's that?"

"What's what? Spider?"

"I've got this, sort of, ooooh, there's something going through, oh this is very weird, it's like someone's rummaging about in my head..." He stopped, touching his forehead, and looked at Iris. Then, he looked at his hand again. "There's this warm, tingling sort of feeling, in my hand, no, now it's in my arm."

"There is? Oh, God, I'm so sorry, Spider!"

"It's, it's not unlike if you have to have radioactive dye injected into your arm before a CT scan or an MRI. The way you can feel a hot sensation moving up your arm. It's like that. Weird."

"It's doing that? Should I get help?"

Spider smiled. "No, no. It's not unpleasant. And that feeling in my head, now there's this kind of warm, beneficent sort of feeling, like whatever the hell it is is happy. The weirdest thing!"

"Spider, are you sure? I can get help—"

"No, it's fine. Oh, it's up in my shoulder now, and..." He touched the side of his neck. "It's heading for my head. Uh-oh." *This*, he was starting to think, *might be trouble after all. In fact*, he thought—

Spider passed out and collapsed, just as the warmest, dreamiest, most wonderful feeling in the world bloomed in his head.

"Spider!"

CHAPTER 12

Spider dreamed — it had to be a dream — of red-checked paper tablecloths, and shiny steel cutlery wrapped, mummified, snug inside paper napkins. A small bottle of Heinz Ketchup. A small, boxy metal gadget from which one could control a jukebox, with flippable pages listing songs he didn't know.

There was a rich smell of coffee, and he saw that there was a large white china mug of black coffee before him on the table, on a plastic placemat. There was a small saucer containing sealed plastic cups of "half-and-half". There were sugar cubes, arranged in a neat little pile, as if awaiting an engineer to build them into something impressive. He was sitting on a vinyl cushion, on a wooden seat with a high back — he realized he was sitting in a booth, in a diner, like diners he'd seen on American TV shows.

"What the hell?" he said, and slid out from his seat, stood up — his balance and coordination were okay, he noticed, and his head felt fine — and looked around. If this was a diner, it was empty. There were no staff he could see, and no smell of food cooking, nor sound of people bustling about. There was a blackboard up behind the counter, listing the various offerings, many of them dishes Spider had never heard of. What the hell was *"poutine"*? Turning, walking around, he went to the front door. It was a big glass door, with a sign on it, the kind of thing you can flip between OPEN and CLOSED. Right now it was CLOSED. "No kidding," Spider said. The big glass windows either side of the door both featured switched-off neon signs. *"The Daily Grind"*, he thought one said, in cursive script. And under that, the lettering arranged in an upside-down smile-shaped curve, *"RESTAURANT"*. *No shit, Sherlock,* he thought, and pulled on the door handle. A small silver bell over the door tinkled. He looked outside.

The diner was on the corner of a city street. The city appeared empty. Tidy, but empty. There was a breath of wind; it smelled faintly of pine trees and earth and sunlight. It was, he noticed, despite the end-of-the-world creepiness of the people-free city, a beautiful day, though the light was strange: Spider was used to the hard-as-bloody-nails sunlight, what some called "Mediterranean" light, in Perth. The light here was different. The colors not so startling. He counted four white fluffy clouds. There were no birds that he could hear. There was a traffic light thing hanging down over the center of the intersection he saw, and that was so unfamiliar he just stopped and stared at it for a long time. The traffic lights should be mounted on yellow poles by the side of the road at intersections. Why were they hanging down over the intersection like that? Surely that was danger-ous. He saw, too, colored steel boxes with windows in front containing folded papers. It looked as though you had to insert a coin, or something, into a slot, so that you could retrieve a copy. There were several such boxes, in different colors, with different names. *Calgary Herald,* said one.

Newspapers! he thought. "Bloody newspapers!" Spider had not seen an actual newspaper, in print, on actual paper, the ink coming off on your fingers, in years and years. These days if you wanted to know the news, you hit the tubes, like everyone else, with the device of your choice. Nobody published a print edition.

He checked his watchtop, looked up Calgary. Biggest city, but not the capital, of Alberta Province, Canada. "If this is Canada, where is everybody?" He walked up and down a while, looking in windows, examining cars — and saw that drivers would sit on the left side of these cars. "Now that's just wrong," he said, shaking his head. Some of the cars looked sort of familiar; some didn't. Hmm, License plates, dated various years, clustered around the period 1999-2003. Then he stopped, thought about where he'd just been, and what he'd just been doing. Something in the hypercube D6 had done this to him. The D6 they got from that dead Canadian guy. Hmm. At that point Spider started to understand that this was not a dream; it was more like some kind of hugely elaborate and detailed simulation. So detailed, in fact, his watchtop appeared to work.

"So," he thought, "this is a representation of the past." With no dust on cars. No bodies in the street. And no birds in the sky.

Spider retreated to the café — no, the *diner*. Yes, the diner. Right. He opened the door and stepped inside, squinting to see in the relative dimness inside.

"Spider! Hey, over here, man," said an unfamiliar voice, which startled him. He'd just spent half an hour wandering about the abandoned streets of Calgary, getting used to the idea that he was the only person here, at least that he could find. So he stood by the door, peering into the diner, waiting for his eyes to adjust, and waiting for his beleaguered heart to settle down.

"Back here. Hey!"

Spider saw someone waving an arm. That voice had sounded a little familiar, too, but the fact that the only other person he'd found, so far, was sitting here, apparently waiting for him, was not, he thought, a good sign. What to do, what to do? He thought, Okay, outside, in the real world, I'm with Iris. She gave me the D6. Then all this happened. Lucky me. More weirdness coming right up, step this way, sir.

"Look, I won't bite, okay? Promise."

Which, Spider thought, was a funny sort of thing for the guy to say, but there was something in the voice that undercut any possibility of humor, something bleak, even grave. Spider's suspicions started to shade, a little, into sympathy, just hearing that tone. So, certain he was going to regret it, certain it would all end in tears, and likely with his own horrible, screaming death, he stepped further into the diner, moving down the aisle on the left, his footsteps loud on the checkered linoleum floor.

The new arrival was sitting on the opposite side of the booth Spider had occupied earlier. He was a tall guy, slumping a little, portrait of a tired man. Yup, Spider thought. This is Stapleton. But he was in one piece. This was a guy with a story to tell. *Poor bugger*. And he was smiling at him — as if Spider was a long lost friend who had finally turned up to rescue him, or some damn thing like that. "Hey," Stapleton said, as Spider slid awkwardly into the seat opposite Stapleton. "How are you doing, eh, Spider? It's damn good to see you, buddy."

Spider nodded thanks, but felt at a loss — and now, in this booth, pinned down in a way he had not felt when he was here earlier. "Hi," he said, uncomfortable. This guy had gone to a lot of trouble to find and talk to Spider, and that, right there, made him curious.

Then this Stapleton guy sat up straight, all at once. "Oh, sorry, Spider. I forgot. You don't know me yet. We haven't met. Geez. Rookie mistake." He stuck his hand out. "John Stapleton. Pleased to *meet* you, Spider."

"Mr. Stapleton, yes. I know who you are. Nice to see you in one piece," Spider said, and winced, thinking that was a stupid thing to have led off with. He tried to cover the gaffe with a nervous smile, but it was no good. Stapleton stared at him. Spider then added, "Hello, nice to meet you at last." Stapleton reached a hand across the table, but Spider did not shake it, and he was not sure why, exactly. It was just a gesture of greeting, so why the reluctance? Was it that Spider had already seen this guy in blood-soaked pieces in a park in Midland? That there was something of death itself hanging over him? Actually, Spider thought, yes, that might be it. It was like meeting a ghost. Stapleton retracted his hand, and looked embarrassed for a moment. Now that Spider was close to him, he could see that Stapleton had been living rough. His skin was drawn and tight, more greyish than anything else, and pale, as if he were sick. There were three or four days of greying stubble around his jaw, and his hair, worn long in a ponytail, and starting to thin, hadn't been washed in some time. He wore cheap, op-shop clothes, an old skivvy and trackpants. But for the bizarre circumstances of their meeting, Spider would have sworn the guy was long-term unemployed, living hand-to-mouth, eking out a living.

"Well?" Spider said. "This is your meeting."

"Yeah. Okay. Look. I'm sorry about all this. Things are, well, not exactly ideal, just now, where I'm putting this thing together. I'm a little distracted."

"All right. Fine. Just, I don't know, here's a crazy idea, why don't you start at the beginning, wherever that is, right? And just go from there. I can't see a way for me to get out of here, so I'm pretty much a captive audience, right?"

"Oh, yeah, okay, sorry about that, I shoulda said. If you just write, using your finger, or whatever you can find, just write 'ESC', on any surface, wherever you are, the system will dump you back into your real world."

"Just like that?"

"Yeah. You're not a prisoner, Spider. Didn't mean to freak you out, but, well, I could see how you, well, feel free to punch out anytime."

"Okay, good," Spider said, frowning, suspicious. Something here was off, he thought. Something smelled bad, and it wasn't coming from the kitchen. Watching Stapleton, sitting there, hunched forward, hiding most of his face behind clasped hands, Spider noticed that he looked twitchy, shaky, like he was cold, or under some kind of heavy-duty medication, maybe, and, now he thought that, Spider thought he could feel Stapleton's leg, under the table, bouncing up and down, something Spider remembered his dad used to do when he was under the influence of certain medications. *You poor bastard*, Spider thought, trying to keep his face blank.

Stapleton said, "You saw me in pieces?"

Shit, Spider thought, embarrassed. He shouldn't have said that. "It was, yeah, it was pretty bad. Sorry. You were ripped apart by some monster."

"Shit," Stapleton said, nodding, closing his eyes a long moment, thinking about something Spider didn't want to know about. "That hasn't happened yet, in my subjective time. Hmm," he said, scratching his chin, shaking his head a little. "How'd I look? Other than that?"

"About the same, more or less. Same clothes, I think. You had a goatee beard, going a bit grey. You had a bit of notepaper, with my name and address on it, and you had a hypercube dressed up to look like a regular six-sided die, only it really wasn't. And there was something inside it—"

Stapleton managed a weary smile. He reached down under the table, into one of his pockets. "You mean this?" He produced the D6, and rolled it on the table surface; it made a familiar clattering noise; there was a blur of numbers and patterns of dots flashing past, before it came to rest, showing the letter "*A*". "It's part of a game we play. It's also a mainframe, as you've no doubt discovered. A hundred terabytes."

Spider, staring at the innocuous cube, took in what Stapleton said about it. A hundred terabytes wasn't a lot, by current standards, but it was more than enough to pull off an illusion like this. "It was obviously trying to find me, and it burned my friend Iris—"

Stapleton interrupted. "Iris? Your friend Iris?" he said, his face neutral, but something was wrong.

Spider noticed this. "Yeah, she's a cop I know. A good egg."

"Right, yeah, okay, sorry. Go on."

That was odd, Spider thought, but decided to leave it be. No doubt he would soon enough find out all about whatever the hell was going on. "Anyway, when Iris tried to pick it up, it burned her, but when I picked it up, it didn't burn me. I got this warm feeling, going up my arm, and this sense of soothing rightness, like the thing was somehow *happy* to have found me."

"Okay," Stapleton said, listening. "Fair enough. Good to know."

"Why the hell are you looking for me, of all people?" Spider asked. "How do you know me?"

"You? I've known you for a while, mate, if you'll pardon my use of the term." It was entirely wrong hearing a Canadian trying on the Australian "mate" like that. The wrong emphasis, the wrong tone. It sounded, from him, like "meet".

Spider made a face and then regretted doing so. Stapleton looked, for a passing moment, embarrassed. "I've already figured out I meet you up in the future someplace."

"Yeah, that's right."

"So how do I wind up there?"

Stapleton said, "Yeah. That's a long story. Kind of involved and I'm pretty sure you won't like where it goes."

"I already don't like it," Spider said, annoyed.

"Spider, you're right. You're absolutely right. Of course you have no reason to trust me, you don't know me, you've never met me before, I get it, I really do. Of course. I'm sorry. I'm just … I can't tell you, I just can't tell you how hard it's been, just getting here, to put this little show together for you. I just assumed, in my fried little brain here," he said, indicating his head, "I just assumed you'd be the same guy I knew in Colditz, where—"

"I beg your pardon," Spider said. "Did you say "Colditz"?"

"I did, yeah—"

"The Nazi prison? World War Two? Crazy bastard prisoners in one of the towers building a glider out of cardboard and rubber bands? That—"

"Not that Colditz, no, sorry."

"So I'm not going to World War Two?"

"No."

"Good. Relieved. That was a worry."

"No. I'm talking about a—" He hesitated, thinking hard, fidgeting, then said, "It's kind of a prison, a detention facility. Colditz isn't the actual name, it's just wound up with that name."

"Um…"

Stapleton hesitated a moment, watching Spider's eyes then added, "Eight-point-four million years from now, your time."

There was a long, long pause. Spider sat there, the index finger on his right hand itching to scribble ESC on the red and white checked paper tablecloth. "Eight-point-four million years," he said, sure Stapleton was having a lend of him.

"Give or take."

"Oh, okay," Spider said, nodding, playing along, sure this was all bullshit, but the sort of bullshit that was going to wind up causing him nothing but pain and misery. "I'm sure you're just dying to tell me all about it." *Eight million years*, he was thinking. *Nothing good could come from something like that.*

"Yeah. One of the other detainees called it Colditz, and it kind of stuck."

"Okay," Spider said, maintaining a façade of good cheer, going along with it. "Damn."

"We were, you and me, and some others, lost time travelers mainly, were being held there."

"I was there? In a prison?"

"That's right. A detention facility for time travelers."

"Shit," Spider said.

"Yes," Stapleton agreed. "That's it, exactly."

"I don't think I want to end up there, if that's okay with you, John."

"The thing is, though, Spider, you do. And soon."

"Like I said, no, I don't think so."

"Neither of us had a choice."

"What, we're just minding our own business, wandering along one day, and boom, zapped off to Time Travel Prison for no good reason? Eight million years from now? You seriously expect me to buy that?"

"The next time you use time travel, boom, just like you said. 'Eight million years, do not pass Go,' is what you said when I met you. You were pretty pissed off, understandably so."

"I was, was I?" Spider was looking at the tablecloth, thinking he'd had just about as much of this as he could stand. "What about you? What did you do to wind up there?"

At this, Stapleton sat there, looking across at Spider. Spider had the impression that Stapleton knew he was losing, that Spider was about to bail out of this lovely virtual world he'd built, and not come back. But then Stapleton came up with this: "What did I do to wind up in Colditz?"

"That appears to be the question currently in play, Mr. Stapleton."

"Spider, I met Dickhead McMahon."

And with that, Spider was hooked.

CHAPTER 13

"You told me, Spider, about how, years ago, in your own subjective experience, you were going through some hard times. You were more or less homeless, you were separated from your wife, you were out of a job, and the circumstances of how you lost that job, in the police, no less, and that you had enormous trouble trying to find another job. Things were pretty bad. Then, one night, you were in a pub, back in Perth, nursing a beer, and you met this weird guy, who insisted you call him Dickhead, and who, in the end, offered you a new job, in fact a whole career, fixing time machines. He even covered your expenses to go back to school and get qualified to fix time machines. It was extraordinary. This big, strange guy in a cheap suit — I remember you told me about how he had this 'zone-of-control' effect. 'Dickhead', you said, 'was like that. If he got you in conversation, you were stuck there. There was no escape.'"

Spider was gobsmacked. "Your research is good; I'll give you that, Mr. Stapleton."

"But wait, there's more! Because of how things were at the time, you took Dickhead up on his offer. You went back to school. You started fixing time machines. It was mostly okay as work went, and you soon wound up as head tech at..." He seemed lost for a words for a moment.

"Malaga. North of Perth. Light industrial area. Tilt-up hell."

"Yeah, Malaga. That's it. So, there you were, working for Dickhead. Well, guess what? Me, too."

"You fix time machines, too?"

"No, God no — oh, wait, I don't mean to suggest there's anything wrong with that kind of work—"

"No, of course not," Spider said.

Stapleton looked genuinely pained. "Look, sorry, Spider. No, what I mean is Dickhead offered me a job, too."

"Uh-huh," Spider said, interested despite himself.

"A bit about me. Okay, um. Okay. First, I'm in physics. PhD. Condensed matter physics. I was teaching at a Calgary University, and doing a bit of research on the side, but mostly teaching undergrads. Boring as hell, but essential — students need a good foundation to build on. Hook them at the start, and they'll follow you anywhere, right?"

"You tell me, Doc," Spider said, who'd been thinking that if Stapleton was from Calgary, it explained this virtual world he'd built. A little taste of home. It also explained Stapleton's accent. At first, Spider had mistakenly thought, despite knowing the guy was Canadian, from his ID, that he was American. His voice sounded a lot like the accents he heard in American movies, but it wasn't quite right. The vowels were a little off — when he said anything with an "out" sound in it, it came out more like, "oat", and the sound of the letter "a" came out sounding more like an "e" than anything else. Spider had never met any Canadians before, and knew very little about Canada as a country.

"So," Stapleton went on. "One night, in April, it was late, I was tired, and I hit this bar I like in Calgary, Moose's, for a refreshing beverage before taking a taxi home. Beautiful evening. Crisp. Spring, with a hint of summer coming. Minding my own business, cold beer, cozy bar, things were looking good. Then, boom, out of nowhere, there's this big guy, bad hair, cheap suit, with the most enormous smile, and he's got a couple of fresh brewskies, expensive imported stuff. Did I mind if he shared my table? The place was packed. Monday night. Hockey's on the tube, Flames playing the Leafs. Sure, no problem, I say, pull up a chair. There was something odd about the guy, though. Weird accent I couldn't place at first? British, maybe? It turned out he was from Australia. 'Long way from home,' I said, making polite conversation. 'Further than you think,' he said, and introduced himself. 'Name's Dickhead. Dickhead McMahon.' Well, I nearly choked on my beer, let me tell you. 'Your name's Dickhead?' 'Sure,' he says. 'Everybody calls me Dickhead. It's me name!' And he laughs, this big laugh, and for a moment it's all I can hear — even over the commentary guys on the hockey, louder even than the people in the bar cheering. That's loud. It made me look at him, feeling a bit uneasy, like there's something not quite right about him. I remember when I first told you about this, when we were at Colditz, you said it was like even his smile was too big for his face, like it was glued on."

Spider blinked. "Right, yeah, that's Dickhead, for sure."

Stapleton nodded. "Hmm, this is thirsty work. How 'bout a coffee?"

Spider pointed out, gently, that there was no wait staff — but by the time he finished pointing this out, a new white ceramic mug, full of steaming black drip-filter coffee, had appeared before him, and in front of Stapleton, who reached over to grab two of the small sealed cups of half-and-half, peeling them open, and pouring the contents into his mug, along with two sugar cubes. Spider watched, fascinated. "What is that stuff, that half-and-half?"

"Half cream, half milk," Stapleton said, nudging the bowl of the little cups over towards Spider, who made use of them. The same magic that caused the coffee to appear also caused spoons, gleaming stainless steel, to appear just when needed.

Stapleton resumed his story, describing his first encounter with Dickhead in the bar, how they got to talking, and how Stapleton felt like he couldn't leave Dickhead's presence, that he was somehow trapped. "After a while, though, you know how it is, you need to use the washroom. So I get up, go and do my business, and the whole time I'm gone, I'm thinking, this is all too weird. And it's late, I've got to be at the university early in the morning, I really shouldn't be out this late, Ellen's gonna kill me — oh, Ellen's my wife. So I start thinking, well, it'd be pretty rude, but why don't I just head out of here the back way, call a taxi, and go home. No harm done. At worst I've offended an Australian, but it's not like it's gonna be an international incident, our prime ministers on the red phone, yelling at each other."

"Right, I wouldn't think so, no."

"So that's my plan, but then I realize, my briefcase is still out there at the table"

"So you went back."

"Back to the zone, yeah."

"He's good, that Dickhead," Spider said, trying the coffee. It wasn't great, a bit weak, kind of watery. He wondered if Stapleton here could wish him up a macchiato.

"So, back with Dickhead. While I've been gone, Dickhead's been buddying up to some of the other locals, too, 'shouting them a round of the bar,' he said, and again, the expensive, imported stuff."

"Bloody Dickhead," Spider said, shaking his head.

"So there we are. Dickhead's having this fantastic time, everybody loves him, toasting him, sending him beers, and he's starting to get into the hockey, rooting for our team, really fitting in well. And all I wanna do is just get the hell out of there, go home, and try and get some sleep. But you know what?"

"You don't."

"That's right. Next thing I've got a fresh beer and Dickhead's there with me, his big arm around me, laughing it up, and I'm laughing it up, and we're having the worst good time ever, you know?"

"Oh, yeah," Spider said.

"Then, after a while, and I'm starting to feel particularly well lubricated, and no longer worrying too much about Ellen, even though my cell's going off in my pocket, vibrating away, she's trying to call me, Dickhead says to me, 'So, John, mate, look here. Do you want to spend the rest of your life trying to get idiots to understand the beauty of the universe — or do you want to *participate* in the beauty of the universe? Do you want to know the Final Secret of the Cosmos?'"

"Shit," Spider said.

"I said, 'The what and the what now?' And he told me again. He explained the whole thing. The universe, he said, was going to be torn down, burned to the ground, rebooted, so to speak. 'Creation 2.0', was how he put it. But, and this was the best part, once the universe was all destroyed, nothing but particles and vacuum, these special messengers, these Angels of God, called 'Vores' were going to impart one, final, ultimate, mind-blowing piece of wisdom to the Chosen, the Selected, the Ones Who Got It, who stood back during the burning, and let it happen. Dickhead said to me, and he was leaning right over the table, right in my face, like this, Spider, he was right there, I could see right into his eyes, and there was this light there, this mad light, and right then, I knew, I knew in my heart of hearts, I knew two things: one, that this guy was absolutely the most crazy bastard who ever lived, and two, that I wanted in. I wanted that Final Secret, man. What a prize! What an idea! The key to everything. The final knowledge. The universe explained at last."

Spider sat there, feeling bad for the guy. "So you signed up."

"Well, not exactly. First, Dickhead bought another round. He asked if I was up for a little wager between mates. He'd wager a hundred Canadian dollars, he said, that I couldn't down the whole beer in one go. When I hesitated, he said, 'All right, two

hundred dollars!' This went on a bit. Pretty soon he was up to
one thousand dollars, and the whole place was watching me,
yelling out, either joining in on the action or yelling out dares. I
felt ridiculous. How'd all this get so out of hand? But Ellen and
I, we could really use that thousand bucks, I was thinking. You
don't make much teaching stupid undergrads. So I chugged the
whole damn thing. The place erupted, cheering, applause, people
yelling out, and Dickhead pounding my back, always with that
creepy smile And then there was this burning, feverish feeling,
in my stomach, then sort of everywhere, all at once — and then
in my head."

"Oh, shit," Spider said. "He spiked your drink."

"He did, yeah," Stapleton said, mouth twisted, embarrassed.
"Next thing, it's like, stuff is happening in my head, I'm sitting
there, sweating, the sweat just pouring off me, and I've got the
worst headache ever, like something was squeezing aside my
brain to make room."

"So what happened?"

Stapleton took a sip of his coffee. "I thought I was having a
stroke! I told Dickhead to call emergency, but he's suddenly all,
'it's okay, John. Just relax, let it happen. You'll be fine. It's just
the immune response to the installation. Once the new system
stabilizes, everything will be much clearer, okay?' I tell you,
Spider, it was one of *those* moments. You just stare and stare at
this guy, this guy who as far as you can tell is killing you, and
he's talking about something 'installing'? God!"

Spider thought about how the D6 seemed to have installed all
of this in his own head. "Yeah, I know the feeling."

"Mmm, yeah, well. So, the thing is, I must have blacked out
for a moment, or something, because next thing there's a voice
in my head—"

"Oh, a voice! How nice."

Stapleton continued under the withering gaze of Spider's
scorn. "Yeah, this TV announcer-type voice, like that movie
trailer guy, Don LaFontaine—"

"Sorry, who?"

"You know, the guy who did all the movie trailers, with this
heavy, gravelly voice. 'In a world where madness has a name...'"

"Oh," Spider said, getting it. He remembered that voice from
when he was a kid, going to movies. "Him."

"Yeah, only that voice is in my head, and it's talking to me.
'Welcome, John Stapleton, to *Time Voyager*, your gateway to the

wonders of the past, and the mysteries of the *Future*!' And you could hear the italics in 'Future', too."

"Wait a minute, just wait one minute. Time Voyager? What the—?"

"Time travel without a time machine, Spider."

"Without a time machine?"

"No machine, no problem."

"No way," Spider said.

"I'm telling you the truth," he said. "Scout's honor!" Stapleton held up two fingers to illustrate. "And it works. You tell the thing where you want to go, and you go. Boom. Just like that. No machine. No hassles."

This started to explain a few things. Like Stapleton turning up in Midland without a machine. Like Dickhead's head turning up in the break room fridge.

Spider was trying to get to grips with the idea. "So, what? You've turned your brain into a time machine?"

"Kinda, but not really. It's more that your existing brain now has new functionality. You can see Time itself. You can step outside the flow, and you can see how what we perceive as time is mostly illusion, an artifact of the way parts of our brains are structured."

"Bull-hyphen-shit," Spider said, sitting back in the booth, stunned at what he was hearing, and not believing a word of it. "No way. Just … no way."

"Spider, there's a considerable body of neurophysiological research backing this up. Time, as we have always known it, is an illusion. It's not a fundamental part of the universe, the way we always thought."

"But," Spider said, feeling his own brain starting to ache as it tried to digest what he was hearing. "But what about Einstein? What about—"

"Yeah, I know. It's okay."

"It's bloody well not okay! It's not okay at all!" Spider said, getting heated. "No, I'm not accepting this in any way, shape or form! What you're talking about is bloody magic. You're talking about wishing yourself hither and yon in time, for God's sake!" He was up out of his seat, pacing, clutching his head, trying to remember there was some trick to getting out of this world, and back to his own world, but what was it? It was the simplest bloody thing, but now that he wanted to use it, he couldn't remember it to save his useless life. This, this "Time Voyager" nonsense was squeezing everything else out — or, maybe, it was more that all the sensible contents in his brain were retreating quick-smart from such an outlandish and frankly insane notion, boycotting the idea, perhaps even waving handmade protest signs and chanting. It just was not on, Spider thought. You could not simply wish yourself about in time. Even with the sorts of time machines he worked on every day, time travel was still massively difficult, the computations involved were of staggering, breathtaking complexity. Only the unbelievably powerful computer hardware of recent times was up to processing the white-water torrent of particle-state-vector data for every particle in not only the time traveler's body, but the particles of the time machine itself, and even the air inside the time machine. All of the data for all of those particles had to be rewritten in the translation engine, a computational task that once only God could possibly have performed, and probably only with a really good calculator.

Now, Spider thought, everyone will be able to go anywhere in time; anywhere in the Manifold. It was unthinkable, to have such power. He turned to Stapleton. "What about ghost mode? What about historical events?"

"Like what?"

"Let's say, the Crucifixion." It was the number one time tourism destination, even if you could only go in ghost mode so tourists couldn't interfere with Christ's suffering, much as some often desperately wanted to do. The consequences of messing with the Crucifixion were considered by world governments to be far too dangerous to let mere mortals interfere with it. "What about that? Can Time Voyager—"

"No problem. Go back. Hang with the locals. Eat the food, drink the water, get lucky with the ladies, talk to Jesus, heck, talk to the Disciples, you name it. Whatever you want to do, you can do it."

"So you could keep Christ from getting crucified."

"It's tricky and you'd be hard pressed to stop it, at least by yourself, but yeah, it could happen."

Spider could barely think. He had to hold his head. His heart boomed in his chest. Spider was thinking about the consequences of Time Voyager going public, going viral. He thought of guys like bloody Mr. Patel, who'd spent all that money and all that time building his Best Time Machine Ever, now needing only to drink what amounted to a bloody *potion*. It was too much, too much power, too much influence. The temptation to meddle would be unbearable. Governments around the world had no chance of stopping it, not once the instructions got pirate-bayed.

Reality was done for. Every clueless moron who ever bought himself a time machine for the express purpose of using time travel to scam reality out of big bucks could now rampage about in history, screwing things up, creating great turbulent change-storms rippling all over the Manifold.

Then Spider stopped. "So there you are, a mild-mannered Canadian physics guy, minding your own business. And you meet this amazing guy, who gives you an amazing superpower. A bloody superpower that allowed you to appear in the middle of Midland..."

"As easy as stepping in and out of your timeline."

"So where'd Dickhead get it?"

"Dunno, you'd have to ask him. He never said."

"Well, since the git in question has been separated forcefully from his enormous great head, I don't see much prospect of asking Dickhead much of anything."

"Um, what?" Stapleton said, startled.

"Dickhead. Someone's cut his head off. Wound up in my break room fridge."

"In your fridge?"

"Yeah."

"A fridge."

"Yes, a fridge. God, do I have to draw you a diagram, Physics Genius?"

"How the hell would it get in your fridge?"

"Me, I reckon it was time travel," Spider said.

"Why would someone time travel a severed head into your fridge?"

"I think Dickhead did it himself."

"You — what?"

"Dickhead's head. Gets cut off. Lots of blood. But this Time Voyager thing is in his head, like it's in your head. First chance he gets, post-slice, he blips away from wherever he is, getting parted from his body, and winds up..."

"In your fridge."

"Yup. Just like that. Which means...?"

Stapleton saw where Spider was going, and was clearly thinking hard about it. "Why would he wait until after his head was severed before blipping out? Why wouldn't he just blip out at the first sign of trouble?"

"Exactly."

"Hmm," Stapleton said, a little pale, amazed at the very idea. "A head could do that, on its own?"

"Severed heads are conscious, more or less, for anything up to a minute after they're cut off from fresh blood and oxygen, depending on how the cut's done," Spider said, and went on to explain about the experiments conducted on guillotined heads during the Terror. "As for Dickhead, well, his head comes off, and all the blood pours out, and that'd be bad — but there might have been just the merest speck of life left in that enormous noggin of his, just enough, that he could punch out, and find me, good old Spider, lucky Spider. Spider who owes Dickhead a big favor."

Stapleton was lost in thought for a long moment, frowning, fiddling with his bitten-back nails. "You told me in Colditz that Dickhead saved your life once."

"More than once, really, if you factor in giving me the job in the first place. Less dramatic, but it was a good deed, even if he did have an ulterior motive at the time. Just like he must have had with you, that night in Calgary."

"Well, yeah, since you mention it..."

"He put the hard word on you while you were all ga-ga over the Time Voyager thing, right?"

"He said he'd just upgraded my brain, so I'd be able to deal with this big project he had cooking, this really big special deal."

"Was it called Zeropoint?"

"Yeah, that was it."

"Got the same offer."

"So you got the—?"

"No. No I did not. And I wouldn't have accepted it, anyway. Would have done everything in my power to get it the hell out of my head right then."

Stapleton nodded, looking sad and tired. "I should have, too."

"Regrets?"

"I've got a few, yeah, you might say that. One or two."

"Shiny future not quite so shiny?"

"Not shiny at all."

"You could have just bugged out, though. Time machine in your head. Nothing to keep you there, at the Arsehole of Time with Dickhead, right?"

And here Stapleton looked at Spider, and for the first time Spider saw some vulnerability, some fear. "You know about his cult, right?"

"Oh, yeah," Spider said. "Been there. Saw the bodies. Got the t-shirt." He was being flippant about it, but in his head, where he still saw those frozen bodies every night when he tried to sleep, the silence of Dickhead's abandoned flagship still boomed in the big empty spaces of his mind, cold and hollow. "You were there?"

"Spider, we were on the Gold Alpha Protectorate Team."

"Cool. Did you get special glow-in-the-dark badges and secret handshakes?"

Stapleton ignored him. "It was our job to carry out the ascendancy operation."

This made Spider shut up and adjust his attitude. "Oh," he said in a small voice. "You had to..." He nodded towards Stapleton, indicating the obvious.

"That's right. We had to acquire the drug — the 'eucharist', if you like — work out dosages versus body weights for each member of the Ascendancy Team." His voice was quiet, almost inaudible; his eyes were staring at something far away Spider did not want to see. "But there was a problem. Some members of the team were allergic to one of the ingredients in that formulation of the drug. We had to recompile it, test it, to make sure it was safe—"

Spider sat blinking slowly, unable to believe what he was hearing. "Make sure it was safe," he said, trying out the sound of each word. "Safe," he added, now shaking his head. "You were going to kill people."

"It had to be painless. It had to be free of any kind of unpleasantness, sickness, pain. It had to be like going to sleep, or people would refuse to take it. Dickhead was extremely clear about this. Taking it and succumbing to it had to look — and here Dickhead was very specific in his choice of words. He said it had to look, 'inviting, even tempting'."

Spider thought he might be ill. "How could you...?"

"Spider, we didn't."

"What?"

"We didn't."

"I saw the fucking bodies."

Stapleton could see the look on Spider's face. He said, "Some of us, Ellen, me, Deb, Lee and Lyn, we hatched a plan."

"Ooooh, a plan! Was it a cunning plan?"

"Well, it worked. How's that, Spider? Huh? It worked. It got us out of there. We stole one of Dickhead's timeships and blipped out of there, we—"

"Why not just blip out with the Time Voyager thing?"

"Time Voyager doesn't come with a battleship's worth of cross-time weaponry."

"Ah. Good point."

"So there we were, hurtling across the Manifold. It was Ellen, in the beginning. She saw what we were doing, and she just plain refused. Me, I was still a loyal acolyte. Yes, Dickhead, sir, whatever you say, Dickhead, and all the rest, but Ellen took me aside, and she, well, she tore me a new one. Told me she did not marry a monster, and she would not become a monster herself, just to satisfy some madman from Australia with a Jim Jones fetish."

"Ellen sounds nice."

Stapleton smiled, but then the smile broke. "Yeah," he said, and wiped his face, looking at his empty coffee mug.

"You've lost touch?"

"Dickhead's people came after us. They used all kinds of custom hacks to break into our ship. They sent chronovirus attacks, causality bombs, scatterboys, chum-chums, you name it — and we were doing the same, trying to crash their Time Voyager installations to keep them the hell away from us, chasing illusions and false leads, hopping timelines, switching universes, sheaves of alternate realities, bouncing back and forth, back and forth, sometimes hundreds, thousands of times per second, desperate to keep ahead of them, to get some distance, to change our identities. The speed of it, Spider. Hot pursuit! Burning through billions of years in a moment. Wiping out entire nascent cultures with every other step, but then inadvertently causing life to sprout on some dead, ancient rock the next. It was a rush, to be honest, a blur of adrenaline, calculation, blinding speed, dazzling power — and in the end, yeah, we lost the pursuers..."

"But you also lost...?"

"Yeah. Yeah..."

"Is she—?"

"No, or, well, I don't know. We got separated." He stared to one side. "And that was that. No time to check. No time to loop back."

"Mate," Spider said, feeling for him. "I'm sorry."

Neither said anything for a long while. Spider wished he had another coffee. He got up, wandered around the diner, admiring the small details, the textures, the play of light and shadow. As virtual worlds went, this was a good one, though too heavy with silence at moments like this. After a while, as Spider played with the cash register, he said to Stapleton, "So what happened next?"

"That's just it. I don't remember." He got up, and came over to the counter, as if he wanted to order something. He was studying the menu on the wall behind Spider.

"How can you not remember?"

"Memory, Spider. It's a funny thing. Easy to get tangled."

"So how'd you wind up in Colditz?"

"Don't know. There's this gap in my timeline. A big gaping hole. Time traveler goes in, nothing comes out. One moment we're fleeing for our lives, blazing across the Manifold. Next moment, we're cooling our heels in Colditz, and we realize we've been there a while."

"Eight million years from now."

"Yeah."

"You think Dickhead built it, or had it built?"

"Dunno. Don't think so."

"But if you've got all that time travel stuff in your head..." Spider said, thinking aloud.

Stapleton finished the thought. "How do we wind up stuck anywhere, least of all there?"

"Crossed my mind."

"Colditz security system. Interfered with Time Voyager, rendered it inoperable. The only way out of there, well, getting out of the facility wasn't actually that hard. In some ways the guards even encouraged it, since it cut down the numbers of prisoners — sorry, detainees. The only thing was: The atmosphere was frozen and had collapsed. Outside of Colditz, if the vacuum didn't kill you, the temperature would."

"Someone stole the sun?"

"That's what we were told, yeah."

"But you can't just go around stealing whole stars! Who could do that?"

"Dunno. We were too busy trying to survive and get out of there."

"Fair point." Spider stared at him, horrified. "So, at minimum you'd need an EVA suit."

"And a ship, or at least a decent high-end time machine, good for really heroically long jumps."

Like a hotrod, Spider thought, thinking about Mr. Patel and *Kali*. "But," Spider said, "somehow, whether by luck or good fortune, or whatever, you managed to get out of Colditz."

"Yeah," Stapleton said, sipping a mug of steaming coffee he'd just magicked into existence, not looking at Spider.

"You got out of the inescapable prison."

"No prison is ever escape-proof, Spider," he said, meeting Spider's gaze over his coffee. "You and I were on the escape committee—"

"There was an escape committee?" Spider said, eyebrows raised, astonished. "And were there a couple of flinty guys up in one of the towers building a glider, and everything? Or maybe an elaborate tunnel system underground?"

"There was an escape committee, like I said. No gliders or tunnels, but there was the secret construction of a one-man, one-shot time machine."

Spider was amazed, but tried not to let it show. "Which, I'm guessing, you're going to tell me actually worked, and here you are to tell the tale?"

Stapleton couldn't resist a satisfied smirk at this. "Something like that," he said.

"Okay," Spider said, frowning, sensing something wasn't quite right about all this, that there were quite a number of details Stapleton was leaving out. "That's all fine and good. But the thing is, like I said, you were torn up pretty bad, John. And I'm talking limb-from-limb here. The cops reckon, to the extent that they can even think about what might have happened to you, someone turned up with some heavy-duty piece of industrial hardware, because the alternative — that there's some kind of rampaging monster stalking the streets and parks of Perth — is just too unthinkable. This is *Perth* we're talking about here." As if it would be far more plausible for such a creature to be rampaging about the streets of Sydney.

"Yeah, that. Hmm," Stapleton said, scratching his chin, staring into his coffee. "That's going to be problematic to explain."

Spider rolled his eyes. "How bad could it be, at this point?"

"Badder than either you or I would ever want, believe me."

Spider watched him, thinking hard, trying to evaluate what he was hearing. Some of it sounded all too plausible, even likely. But some other parts? Stolen suns? Earth drifting through space, its atmosphere snowed out and lying around on the ground? Sounded like madness and delusion talking. Spider wasn't sure quite what to do, but he had to hear the rest of it, if only to find out what he might be up against. "So why don't you tell me some more about it," he said at last. "Leave nothing out."

Stapleton nodded, finished his coffee, set the cup aside. It didn't vanish. "Things were bad, Spider," he said, hunched forward, trying to meet Spider's gaze. "Everything was breaking down. The guards had left. Why did they leave? I have no idea.

I never even knew who or what they were. That thing you say killed me? That was another prisoner, kind of."

"Just tell it, John."

"Most of the prisoners were doofus humans like me and you, time travelers who wanted to see the future. But there were some others, not so familiar."

"Aliens?"

"For want of a better term, yeah."

"Good grief."

"This particular prisoner, this alien thing, was very different from the rest of us. So different it had its own holding facility. You've heard of the Vores?"

Spider's jaw dropped, he was so surprised. He knew it was a bad move in a situation like this, to reveal any kind of reaction to what you're hearing, but it had been a long time since he'd first been told about the Vores, and the very idea of them still haunted him. "You're saying..."

"It was a *captured* Vore, Spider. Near as we could tell, the entire facility was built to capture and keep this thing. The rest of us, regular dumb human time travelers, we were never meant to wind up there. We were swept up in the same net, like jellyfish."

Spider did not know quite what to say. Dickhead had told him about the Vores. He'd described them as things, whether creature or machine, Dickhead didn't know, busy eating the space-time fabric of the universe itself, but spewing out waste matter and energy to the outside of the universe. It was as if Vores were ticks, embedded in the surface skin of the universe, with their gruesome mouthparts appearing in the universe, while their bulging abdomens protruded from the outside. And, Spider remembered, there were all manner of weird creatures, indeed a whole ecosystem of such creatures, living a precarious existence on the outside surface, relying on the Vores' excreta to live.

The thing was, Dickhead had never given Spider any idea of their size, or actual appearance, or explained just exactly how it was that they could consume space-time itself. That, on its own, did not appear to make much sense. The only similar things he could think of were singularities, deep inside black holes, that consumed everything within reach of their enormous gravity wells. Were Vores somehow like black holes? Living black holes? Spider felt his brain hurting as he tried to think about it, and tried further to think about what kind of trap you would need to catch such a thing, particularly since, in the case of a captive black hole, surely the thing would eat the trap, you, everybody you know, and ultimately the whole universe itself. So, a bit of an engineering challenge, then.

"So, um," Spider started, thinking hard, "this place has a Vore on ice. But, strangely, the Vore manages to free itself. Oops. Small design flaw. Suddenly, you've got all manner of trouble rampaging about."

"Hence the need to use the time machine built by the escape committee."

"Okay, yeah, got that. You manage to get away, and leave everyone else to be digested or otherwise killed by the Vore itself. Not such a good look for you there, John, eh?"

"The idea," he said, clearly stung, "was that I would go and get help, and come back in time to save everyone else."

"Ah," Spider said, seeing the full design at last. "And this is where I come in?"

"In a manner of speaking, yes."

Spider suddenly felt like a rain of shoes was about to come screaming down out of the sky, and pound him into the dirt. "What's the catch?"

"The catch, well, it's not a big catch," Stapleton said, now looking all discomfited.

Spider remembered, finally, the ESC command. "Tell me now or I'm out of here and never coming back." He had been full of sincere compassion for Stapleton earlier, the thought of losing your beloved in the course of escaping the worst trouble in the universe — that was tough. But now, Spider was starting to feel like he had been manipulated from the start.

Stapleton said, "The captured Vore?"

"Spill it or I'm gone."

"It was no longer just a Vore. It had changed. Something had happened to it."

Spider was ready to write ESC at a moment's notice. "Come on." He was trying to act all tough about this, but he could see from the look of horror on Stapleton's face, and the way his hands were starting to shake, that something about what he was going to tell Spider was seriously not right, not right at all. Spider was dead sure he was going to hate what came next.

And, sure enough, he did.

Visibly trembling, unable to look Spider in the eye, Stapleton managed to say, "Spider, the Vore…"

"Get on with it, damn you!"

"It's merged itself with Molly."

It took Spider a moment to twig to what Stapleton was telling him. To fully grasp the true scale of it. "M-Molly? My Molly? That Molly? Eight million years from now?"

Stapleton nodded. "I'm so sorry, I—"

Spider cut Stapleton short and slipped out of the booth, hot with bitterness, fury, and, most of all, confusion. He stood there, staring back at Stapleton, who sat there still, his hands up, as if to ward Spider off. "I'm sorry. I'm so sorry. I can't tell you, I—"

Spider did not trust himself to speak. The bastard had set him up, fabricated the whole stupid story. Spider could barely think. Molly? His almost ex-wife Molly? There was no way his Molly would let herself wind up in a situation like this. Like Colditz. It would simply "not do...", he could imagine her saying in frosty tones, "...not do at all."

The thing was, though, he was thinking, his overheated brain blazing with the speed of his thinking, it was one of those things that was so utterly crazy that it might be possible. If all she had to do was travel in time when the vore-net was deployed, and boom, next stop, Colditz. But why would Molly and this Vore connect? And how would they even begin to strike up a conversation? Without, that is, her being pulled into the Vore's lethal event horizon. Without her being destroyed? It made no sense. And it was that lack of sense that made Spider, in the back of his mind, start to believe everything was possible.

Then, Stapleton was up out of the booth. He was in Spider's face. "I didn't do this, Spider. It's not my doing. You gotta believe me, okay?"

Spider struck out and hit him good and hard. It hurt, but felt good.

Stapleton fell backwards, hit his head, and slumped to the floor. Spider stood over him.

Hitting people like this, he knew at least in the real world, was stupid and counter-productive. But this was not the real world; far from it.

He went up to the blackboard menu, found a bit of chalk, wrote, "ESC", and left, rubbing his knuckles.

CHAPTER 14

He woke gasping for breath, confused, his eyes hurting from the glare; he spied Iris, who looked worried sick, and saw that he was in an upmarket café, and there was a fabulous aroma of fresh-ground coffee in the air, and—

He remembered what Stapleton told him. *It's merged itself with Molly.* What the *fuck* did that mean?

"It's all right, Spider. It's all right!"

"It fucking well is not all right!"

"Okay, just breathe, nice and slow. Nice and slow now."

"I have to talk to Molly!"

"You said Molly's in New York—"

"No, she's—" He tried to get up, but was too dizzy, and collapsed back into his chair. "Oh, oh God. What now...?" He felt like someone had installed a gigantic refrigerator inside his skull, against all advice that there might be insufficient space. Something, right behind his eyes, felt huge, like it was taking up every cubic millimeter of space back there. Surely his actual brain, such as it was, would be oozing out his ears, and he was so stunned and disoriented that he actually checked his ears, and found nothing out of place. He wiped at his face, and glanced around. He was quite the object of embarrassed curiosity, which embarrassed him. *Must settle the hell down.* Right now he looked like the town drunk, he imagined, like those guys he used to see on the bus, when he was a kid. So, with Iris hovering next to him, ready to help, he said, "Could you get me a coffee, please?" Said it like it was the most important request a man ever made, like the fate of the universe hung on the outcome. Iris told him one was on the way. Already he could hear the Italian espresso machine gurgling and hissing, emitting wonderful steam, attended by black-clad baristas, men and women who knew their stuff, for whom coffee actually was the most important thing in the world. It was comforting, oddly.

His heart was starting to settle down, easing back into his chest, and resuming its residence, crisis sort of over, at least for now. "Iris," he said, and she was right there, sitting next to him, one of her arms around his slumping shoulders. She smelled the way the Major Crime Squad offices used to smell, back when: bad coffee, late nights, too much time in front of computers, lousy overworked air-conditioning.

"I'm right here, Spider," she said.

And she was indeed right there. "Iris, I have to talk to Molly."

A waitress brought over Spider's coffee, a double macchiato, two shots of espresso, a dab of milk, a pattern in the *crema* resembling a spiral galaxy. The aroma hit him, and he gasped. "Oh, my! Oh, my, yes!" He decided to try a sip; his hand shook so he used both hands, and managed to get some. It blazed in his mouth, but it was smooth, multilayered, rich and... He stared into the cup. "This could be the best cup of coffee I've ever had," he said, and looked up at the team manning the machine, the others serving the long line of customers, and realized where he was. "This is the Pure Bean café, isn't it?"

"Well, yeah, it was the closest place I could take you when you spazzed out like that. They helped me carry you in. The coffee's on them, by the way."

The Pure Bean café was near Mrs. Ng's, but Spider had never been inside. A simple flat white there would have set him back almost twelve dollars. He simply had never been able to afford it. Even now, thinking about what money he had on him, he doubted he could cover the cost, and that was important to him. He wanted to tell the staff that the double mac was superb, but didn't, worried that he'd embarrass them and himself. He really would be like those old drunk guys on the bus if he started doing that.

So he sat there, clutching the mug in both trembling hands, taking in the restoring steam, feeling more and more like his usual self with every passing moment. It helped. Iris had done the very best thing she could have done for him. There was nothing, at least in Spider's experience, like coffee for making things better. "How do I contact someone," he started, still staring into the coffee, "who likely doesn't want to be contacted, Iris?"

"Why would Molly not want to hear from you?"

"It's..." he started to say, "It's complicated," but knew that if he were to try that gambit, Iris would come back with, "So explain it to me," which would result in a counter-move from him along the lines of, "It just is, trust me," and so on, and so on, and nobody would get anywhere anytime soon, and right now, as far as Spider could see things, based on what he'd been told, time was crucial. Instead he asked, "Is that regress still on for tonight? It is tonight, right? I haven't lost a day, have I?"

"It is on tonight, yes, we're planning to hit the rewind button at eight on the dot. As for you, you were out cold for all of about three minutes, give or take. Lucky you didn't hit your head when you collapsed."

"You didn't think to call an ambulance?"

"If you didn't come round in a couple more minutes, then yeah, absolutely."

He nodded. "Right. God, my head, Iris. It's just..." He looked at her, trying to figure out how to convey to Iris the sheer scale of what he could now feel in his head. Not that it hurt in any way; it was simply the sensation of great mass and size, as if his actual head were now heavier, somehow. As if when he swung his head back and forth, it had more momentum, and required more effort to swing back the other way. He wondered, briefly, if he was going to get a sore neck and shoulders at some point.

"You're not exactly impressing me with your calm, composed and rational self here, Spider."

"I know, yeah, sorry." He had some more coffee. God, but it was good. "It's just, I was in there for ages, it felt like maybe an hour, two hours?"

"In where?"

"Virtual environment, constructed inside my head. The whole thing was incredibly detailed—"

"Virtual environments are not exactly cutting edge tech, Spider."

"Yes, but inside your head? The man wanted to explain things—"

"Man?"

"John Stapleton. He built and recorded this thing while he was on the run, before he wound up here." Spider filled her in on the basics, how he knew Dickhead, his part in Zeropoint and the final massacre, how he and a few others escaped, followed by Dickhead's goons, zooming across time, all to come here, to find him, Spider Webb.

"Why you? What are you supposed to do?"

He explained about the Colditz facility, full of trapped time travelers, and one, presumably very unhappy, Vore.

"Wait, you said last year, these Vores, they eat the very substance of the universe, the fabric of space and time itself. Is that right? That Dickhead thought they were these incredible angelic beings, intent on tearing down the universe so God could start over with, I guess, a new, no doubt improved, Big Bang, now with even *more* Bang?"

"Yeah, that's it. When Dickhead was a little kid, he had this, hmm, 'religious experience', I suppose you'd call it. For all we know his little wee brain might just have had a stroke or some damn thing. Upshot, though, was he thought an actual angel appeared before him, and told him all kinds of neat but apocalyptic stuff about the universe, about God's decision to start over, and that only the very few, the Chosen, could be part of it, and thus find out about the Final Secret of the Cosmos."

"But that's bullshit, surely."

"The Vores seem real enough," Spider said. "How what happened in Dickhead's childhood bedroom has anything to do with things that can devour space and time itself, I don't know. Dickhead thought he knew. And all these trusting people believed him." Again, in his head, the memory of bodies lying there, wreathed in hoarfrost, perfectly still in the silent vacuum of Dickhead's flagship. He had some more coffee, needing to warm himself up. The coffee was starting to make him feel more or less human again, his bloody great huge head notwithstanding. "This guy Stapleton said that Colditz had been built to hold one of these things."

"And just incidentally, oops, bit of a design flaw, caught all these clueless time travelers as well?"

"Yeah. And maybe Mr. Patel's *Kali* and the children, too."

Iris stared at him a moment, a sour look on her tired face. She got up from her chair, and went to order a double-macchiato for herself. When she got back she sat facing Spider, shaking her head a little. "If this was anybody but you, I would think that's the biggest bloody load of bollocks I'd ever heard in my life — and I've heard some serious, professional A-grade bollocks in my time, let me tell you. I've heard the very best, top-shelf bullshit, from some of the masters, blokes who could bullshit for Australia in the Olympics, they're so damn good."

"I know," Spider said, in a small voice. "There's more, though." And he told her what Stapleton had tried to tell him just before Spider punched out, that somehow this imprisoned Vore had "merged" with, of all people, Molly.

Iris pinched the bridge of her nose. "It's a bloody good thing they hadn't made my coffee just yet, or I would've just sprayed it all over you. God!"

"My thoughts exactly."

"Molly!? *Your* Molly?"

"I think this is why Stapleton wanted to reach me, as you say, of all people. He needed me because of Molly."

"But…" Iris could hardly contain her disgust at the very idea. "Molly? Passive-aggressive, mad sculptress Molly? Molly who's always got you on a short chain so she can get you to fish daddy long legs spiders out of the toilet bowl? Molly who can't see what sort of a decent man you are, who doesn't know when she's on a good—" Iris cut herself off at that point, her spluttering outrage brought to an abrupt halt, and she appeared, at least in this light, to Spider, as if she was blushing. Not that Iris ever did anything as undignified as blush, of course. She got up and fetched her coffee, without saying a further word. Spider watched her go, stunned all over again, staring now at her back. Had Iris just said what he thought she'd just said? Not that she would admit to having said anything like that. That would be unprofessional. She was just, he supposed, badly in need of that coffee. Yeah, that was it.

Iris returned with her coffee, sat and stirred three sugars into it, studying the process closely, like she was mixing nuclear isotopes in a lab, and could not look away from it, lest the whole place be destroyed. Spider watched, amazed at her, and trying not to smile, at least a little.

He said, "Yes. My Molly. She of the endless 'little jobs around the house'. Of the whingeing and the complaining. Molly who's supposed to be in New York right now, but who I'm pretty sure is right here in Perth." Spider explained about the call last night.

"She must have been off her face!"

"Yeah, I thought so, too," Spider said, and sloshed around the last bit of his own coffee, now gone almost cold.

"But now you're not so sure?"

He told her about the lack of gaps between speaking at his end and the message coming through from the New York end.

Iris objected. "I don't hear any gaps on international calls."

Spider frowned. "I always get gaps. Drives me nuts."

"Maybe it's your dodgy service provider?"

"Regardless, I just know Molly's here in Perth."

"You just know. Right," Iris scoffed.

"It was just like talking to you," he said.

"Oh, thanks muchly," Iris replied, arching an eyebrow.

"In the sense of talking to someone right here in town, is what I meant."

"Yeah, I know," she said, allowing the most minute curl of her lip as she drank her coffee. A smear of *crema* foam clung to her upper lip, Spider noticed.

"It was the weirdest thing. Not at all like her to be like that. She doesn't even drink. Doesn't want her creative process 'polluted' — her word — by any kind of outside influence."

"Nothing at all?" What Spider was suggesting was almost unheard-of: an Australian who didn't drink, not even a bit, not even on a special occasion?

"She takes her 'artistic practice' very seriously."

"I see," Iris said, thinking, her brow furrowed. "So why don't you call her? You've got her number, don't you?"

Spider had had the same thought. He winced, his teeth clenched. "I kind of don't wanna be right."

Iris put her coffee down, wiped her mouth with a napkin, put her hands on the table, and gave him The Look. "Mate, for God's sake."

"What if she's..." He stopped himself. He had been going to say, "...up to no good?"

"Spider, has it occurred to you that maybe you just don't know her anymore?"

His first impulse was to leap in and deny any such suggestion. Of course he knew her. He saw her all the time. They talked, had coffee together. Except, now that he thought about it, he had not known before that late-night call last week, when she said she was heading off to New York, and would he mind looking after poor Mr. Popeye, that she was even interested in getting a goldfish. Had not known she was even interested in keeping a fish as a pet, until she told him that night. Molly had always been deeply anti-pet — again because of the time and energy a pet would take from her work.

Was it possible that Mr. Popeye was a symptom of a much larger problem? That Molly had moved on from anything that included him, except as a sometime handyman who would work for peanuts? That she had a whole new life. He felt the full weight of the idea hit him hard. What was happening to him today? Everything was coming undone.

Then again, he thought, wait a minute. Surely, just as she had
moved on from being the person she had once been, at least in
his mind, it was possible that he had done the same thing, without Molly noticing his change. She only ever saw him the way he
had been when they lived together, when he'd been a disgraced
police officer, depressed, angry, a man who always looked like he
wanted to hit something, and sometimes did. Molly had never
seen in all these years since those bitter days, that he'd managed
to move on, at least a bit. He'd gotten himself cleaned up, found a
new line of work, started to establish a whole new career, paying
his bills, making rent each week. When they talked these days,
he knew, she only ever saw in him the Broken Spider of the past,
who had been such a good man that it cost him everything he
had, ultimately including his wife. She still looked at him with
pity in her eyes, he realized, because she could see what he'd been
doing all this time, making himself always available for those
stupid jobs of hers, so she would see what a good egg he was, so
she'd maybe forget about getting a divorce. Spider began, at last,
to realize that the Molly of today had no reason at all to regard
him with any sort of renewed respect. How had he not seen this
before? Yes, he got it now. He could see what she had been trying
to tell him all this time, he could see it like he could see the sun,
blinding and painful. She was on her way out of his life, just as he
was on his way, for good or ill, out of hers.

He felt inexpressibly sad. What a day. Sitting there at the Pure
Bean café with Iris, looking at his empty coffee mug, watching
Iris sorting out police business on her watchtop, deep in a meeting of some kind. Around him, café patrons were scribbling away
on their handhelds, ignoring their coffees. The world was ending,
but life went on. Probably most of these people were scrambling
to find new jobs, or keep the ones they did have. The future was
here, right now, not a singularity of incomprehensible technological progress, but instead one of economic catastrophe. From here
it was impossible to see what lay beyond the wall of the future.
Spider remembered, years ago, when there was first talk of the
impending arrival of something called "Depression 2.0", and how
it had never quite turned up. Now? It was on its way, an unstoppable crushing force that would level much of the world, as he
knew it. Though probably not for long. Someone would seize the
initiative and find a way to make everything go again, and he
knew there were time travelers trying that very thing right now.

Nobody knew exactly who or what, some years ago now,
had sent the now-famous Email From the Future to all those

technology firms, the one with the instructions for constructing the first working time machine. Attempts had been made to jump forward, to try to find the source, without success. Spider was not alone in thinking maybe it had been a terrorist operation from the start. Step One: provide world with wondrous technology from the future. Step Two: stand well back, and watch the whole world go completely nuts. Probably, in the timelines where the world had chosen not to build time machines, where all those companies had deleted those emails as obvious spam or trolling, the financial catastrophe had still turned up, but much later, and with less severity.

Which didn't help Spider right now. A quick survey of his life situation, as of this moment, was not good, and the prospects for his immediate future were even worse. All of which was assuming he didn't get killed this evening while helping Iris and her Time Crime Team with the regress operation to find out what had killed John Stapleton. As things stood, it occurred to him that might even be a good result, and would solve a lot of his problems. No job? No money? No wife? No problem.

So what did he have, exactly? Right now Spider had $132.00 in the bank, for as long as the bank lasted. The federal government had announced that they would guarantee customer deposits in the banks, as they had once before, years back, to keep people from panicking. Mrs. Ng's was about the cheapest place to stay in Perth, but even those rates were steep when you had nothing coming in. There was limited help from the government for unemployed people, but generally these days, with businesses going under and newly unemployed people flooding the streets, hoping for any kind of work at all, there was little to no prospect of any kind of government assistance. In fact, there was a growing likelihood that the government would soon find itself bankrupt, and unable to secure bridge-financing from the global markets, because they'd be broke, too. So, no help there, either.

This did not leave many good options. In fact, Spider could see that in the end he would have to throw himself on the mercy of his aging mum and dad. Both in their seventies, neither all that healthy, his parents would almost certainly take him in, but even then he'd be expected to contribute towards household expenses, which again would involve money, which he did not have.

So, what else did he have? His health? This wasn't even funny.

He slumped in the chair, and took in the full sweep of how very screwed he was. Mr. Patel had been going to pay him for tracking down Vijay and the girl, Phoebe, but of course that had fallen through, too. Well played, Spider, with your ethics and integrity and your self-righteous bullshit. He could easily have taken Mr. Patel's money for looking the other way about the illegal hotrod time machine, and all the rest of it, and sure it would have made him complicit, even a conspirator, but he'd have a job. He'd be able to buy these absurd twelve-dollar coffees.

He slumped in his chair, exhausted and beaten. He felt naked and cold. It was even hard, now that he'd thought about all this, to look Iris in the eye. She was, he knew, taking time out of her busy day to look after him, and help him with this latest crazy thing in Spider's long history of crazy things. What she was doing was charity, he thought, and that stung.

So what could he do? Seriously, now.

1. Find Molly and talk to her. Find out what the hell was going on. Not to try to woo her back — hell, he'd sign those bloody divorce papers for her right now with no reservations. It'd be good to get that over and done with, so they could both move on. No, he wanted to talk to her about what was going on with her. Why a man from the far future would tell him that Molly and a Vore had somehow "merged". That needed some explanation, or, preferably, some convincing refutation.

2. Go back into that diner in his head and talk some more to Stapleton about Molly and this alleged Vore thing. Surely the man was bullshitting, but why would he do that? He used to work for Dickhead, so maybe he was deliberately winding Spider up, as part of some labyrinthine scheme of Dickhead's.

3. And, thinking that, Spider thought: he needed to have his head examined, only literally. Maybe Iris could help with this. Something enormous had been installed in his head, and he was increasingly sure it wasn't just the run-time code for the virtual environment. Maybe his brain was now like Dickhead's and Stapleton's. Maybe he was now, like it or not, a "Time Voyager". The thought made him feel ill. Look at me, Mum! I can travel in time, just by thinking about it! I'm a bloody time machine! If it was true, he needed to get that shit out of his head, pronto.

They all sounded like good ideas. He asked Iris if she could help organize a brain scan for him. She said it should be no problem. "Let me make some calls," she said. "What'll you do if you find out you've got it, too?"

"Dunno, to be honest."

"Oh, Spider," Iris said. "It'll be okay. *We'll* get through this."

He was all set to offer a sour rejoinder, all, "Yeah, sure," but he didn't because he noticed that Iris had said, "we'll get through this." That they both would get through it. "Okay," he said, not sure what else to say. "Good, then."

"What else can I do?"

At first he hesitated, not wanting to burden Iris when she had so much else to do, but she again gave him The Look, and he blurted out, "If Molly is back in Perth, she must have come by air—"

"Check arrival details, all airports, someone named Molly Webb?"

"Her full name, her maiden name, was Mary Margaret Huddlestone." He gave her a description.

Iris made notes. "Right. Got it. I'll let you know this evening."

He checked his watch. Seven-thirty was only a few hours away.

"Gives me time for a restorative nap," he said. *Anything to get this endless day out of the way.* He'd had it. He could catch some z's, maybe snag some instant noodles, have a scrub, and then go over to the park, where Stapleton had died, in time for the regression.

They got up. Iris took their empty mugs back to the counter. Then, outside on the crowded pavement, as Spider was about to say "see ya!" Iris suddenly stepped closer, enveloped him in a tight, brief hug, said, "God, Spider, I thought I'd—" then broke off, not making eye contact, her mouth pressed shut, as if mortified at what she'd said. She stepped back, hands in her deep raincoat pockets, nodded, as if unsure what to say, and said, "Tonight, then," and turned to walk quickly away, disappearing into the crowd.

Spider stood there a long moment, a rock in the endless torrent of passersby, watching. Had he heard right? She thought she'd ... what, exactly? And what was she talking about? When he passed out? But he was only out for a couple of minutes, she said. She saw you do something that might have been crazy dangerous, and which made you collapse. She was thinking you could have died. Oh, he thought, standing there, speechless, stung with guilt. He remembered Iris's other uncharacteristic lapse while they were at the café. Confused, tired, and not sure what to think, he made his way through the teeming, smelly pedestrians and occasional bike messengers, and at last reached the entrance of the Lucky Happy Moon Motel — where he found a sign on the door:

> *"Due to unforeseen circumstances beyond our control, Management must inform all current clients of the Lucky Hapy [sic] Moon Motel that we will be closing our doors in seven (7) days' time. Please collect your things, and pay outstanding service fees and rent. During the next seven (7) days, clients can only pick up personal effects. You may not sleep here. We are sorry. —Mrs Ng, for Management."*

CHAPTER 15

Spider tried calling Molly. Through the phone-patch under his ear he heard her phone ring a few times, then cut to voicemail. Molly's gorgeous cut-crystal voice, with its ringing enunciation, reported that she was offline right now, but callers should leave a note and she'd get back to them as soon as she could manage it.

Spider killed the link. *Okay,* he thought. *If I can't reach Molly, maybe I can reach Stéphane himself.* If she'd left New York earlier than planned, he would know, and might possibly even tell him. Or, if they'd come back together, likewise. Spider popped his watchtop and hit the tubes, found Stéphane Grey's art gallery in Mosman Park, winced at the minimalist, too-exclusive-for-the-likes-of-you design of the site, and after some poking about found Stéphane's contact details. It took a lot of patience, having to talk to a clueless receptionist with a too-squeaky voice and patronizing manners, but eventually managed to persuade the girl, whose name was "Vinyl Rose," to let him speak to the boss directly, even though said boss was, she said, "still in New York."

Which itself was useful intelligence, Spider thought. She gave Spider Stéphane's phone details, and said she could connect him directly. He heard the North American ringing tone, some clicks, then a female sounding voice, all weariness and irritation, in a blunt New York accent, saying, "What?"

This surprised Spider. After a moment's hesitation, he said, "Hi. Uh, I'm looking for a Stéphane Grey? Australian art gallery guy, supposed to be at this number?"

"D'you know what time it is, 'mate'?" Her pronunciation of the iconic Australian word sounded more Cockney than anything.

"Well…" No, Spider did not know, but now that he thought about it, he realized it must be something like zero dark o'clock in the morning. "Look, I just need a moment of Mr. Grey's time."

"Shit," she said, and he heard the woman mutter something at someone nearby, who grunted and muttered in the background. She said, "Just a moment," and at length, a male voice, thick with thwarted sleep, emerged on the line. Spider guessed the woman had heard Stéphane's phone go off, took the patch from under his ear and stuck it on her own head so she could take the call and let the great man enjoy his slumber. But since Spider really did need to talk to said great man, she had to go and stick it back on his head somewhere, and, he guessed, she'd stick it on the guy's forehead, right between his eyes. She sounded just that pissed off. "Stéphane Grey. Who the hell is this? It's… God, it's nearly five in the morning!"

"Mr. Grey. Hi. Hello. This is Spider Webb. You don't know me, but—"

Stéphane interrupted him. "Wait a minute, wait just one minute. Spider Webb? Aren't you Molly's—"

"Yeah. Molly's ex. I'm just—"

Stéphane's tone phase-changed right away. Where a moment ago he'd been all annoyed at getting disturbed at this hour, now things were different. "Oh, shit. Mate, mate," Stéphane said. The man sounded wide awake, and full of some terrible species of grave sympathy. His rendition of "mate" carried weight and feeling. Hearing it, Spider felt cold, and wasn't sure what to say next. Stéphane said, "You still there, Mr. Webb? Hello?"

"Yeah, yeah, I'm here. I'm here."

"Molly talked about you all the time," Stéphane said.

Surprised, Spider blurted out, "She did?" But then thought, what was with the past tense?

"Yeah. Um. Okay. Look, Mr. Webb, can I call you—"

"Please."

"God, this is difficult." He could be heard whispering to the woman to put some coffee on. "Look, Spider. I have to tell you."

"Tell me? Tell me what?" Though, hearing that tone in the guy's voice, Spider already knew. There were only two possibilities that would inspire that tone, neither of them good and wholesome.

"Molly's disappeared."

Spider took that in for a moment. "Disappeared? As in—?"

"Well, yes. The cops are looking for her right now."

"The cops are looking for her?" Through the connection, he could hear no fewer than three different wailing sirens in the distance, and rattling, intermittent machine-gun fire. The thought of Molly in the middle of that gave him chills.

"It's, oh God, look. Let me send you an email with all the details. Okay? I can't do this over the phone."

The cops were looking for her, the guy said. Spider tried to take that in. He said, not sure as he said it, what exactly he hoped to achieve by saying it, but it was the first thing that came to mind, "Nobody told me she was missing."

"Spider, I wanted to call you. It seemed like the decent thing..."

"It's okay. I get it," he said, trying to maintain control, shaking his head. "Look, can you, I don't know, can you just give me some idea of what happened? Anything at all? Maybe I can use some contacts at this end, it might help?" *Maybe I should contact the Australian Embassy*, he was thinking.

"Molly told me you were a cop once."

"Yeah, once," he said.

"She really admires you, you know."

This cut through to where Spider lived. "Molly said what?"

Stéphane repeated the claim. "She told me, I hope you don't mind, she told me what happened to you. I'm sorry, man." He sounded genuine.

"Yeah, um, thanks," he said, confused and baffled. Molly admired him? What the hell was that about? She admired him? She *really* admired him? He went to press Stéphane for further details, but at that moment his phone-patch died, out of power. Nothing. Silence. And it was his last phone-patch, too. Typically, he'd throw away the dead ones, but this one had Molly's voicemail message on it. He peeled it off his jaw-stubble, looked at it, a thing the size of a ten-cent piece, and dropped it in his pocket. He touched that pocket. That phone-patch might now be the only piece of Molly he would ever have.

Forget that, he told himself. Focus. What was important was that Molly was gone, who knows where. And he was too busy basking in the glow of Molly's supposed high regard for him to press Stéphane Grey for whatever details there might be about Molly's disappearance. Had she just vanished, into thin air? Had she been bundled into a black van? Had she just gone for a walk one afternoon, not leaving contact details, and simply never returned? Had she gone underground, assumed a false identity, and slipped away on a night-flight to Switzerland or some damn thing? Iris was right. He really didn't know her anymore. Any of those possibilities could be true. It was a frightening thing to contemplate how little he really knew of his once and former wife. Even so, he thought, finding the focus of concentrating on Molly's disappearance helpful, what could he do from here? *I should probably*, he thought, *buy some phone-patches*. In the meantime, he still had tube access. He checked his watchtop to see if Stéphane's email had arrived, but there was just noise, porn, and scams.

First thing was to get in touch with Iris. He dictated a quick note, sketching in the few details he had about Molly's disappearance, and sent it off.

What was next? Food? Shower? Check on Mr. Popeye. Yeah, good idea. He got into his bike, closed the canopy, and headed off to Molly's house. Was it his imagination or was there even more traffic on the roads — vehicles and bikes — than he'd ever noticed before? Everyone seemed in a ball-tearing hurry to go places, even if just to the nearest bank to pull out all their savings. The smell of barely suppressed panic rode the air, a pong distinct from exhaust fumes and dust and smog.

At length, pedaling hard to keep up with the flow, Spider's mind spun with Molly's disappearance. It did occur to him that Stéphane might be having a lend of him, for whatever Byzantine reasons. Who knew, maybe Molly thought it might be a fun jape to mess with Spider's head in return for not signing those bloody divorce papers in a timely manner! Was Molly capable of such cruelty? He supposed, thinking about her recent HyperFlesh works, "Studies in Suffering", she called them, strange robotic half-creatures bent over or huddling in all the various kinds of pain Molly could imagine, and that were altogether too effective at conveying the central, red-hot idea, that yes she was indeed capable of such cruelty. He had to shake his head to clear bitter memories. The things people said to one another, full of bile and spite, things they could never take back, that left scars.

All in all, though, Spider had a feeling deep in his guts that Molly really had vanished. It was no clever jape. It was, most likely, serious crime. Which in turn led Spider to imagine mobster types abducting her and holding her to ransom, chopping off her fingers, one by one, to send to her agonized parents, all that kind of thing. It disturbed him how easily he was able to dream up these scenarios. But why would mobsters be interested in her? An Australian sculptress, of all people. She had next to no profile, and certainly no money. Her main asset was the family home, fortunately all paid off long since. Was it just that she was a middle-aged woman in pretty good shape who didn't know enough about life in post-crisis New York City to watch where she was going, and make sure she had at least five heavily-armed beefy bodyguards with her at all times? Could it be as simple as that? As naïveté? *Oh, Molly*, he thought, *surely not that*. The Molly he knew never had a naïve bone in her body, probably not even when she was a precocious kid going to all the best private girls' schools. Never afraid of anything, always able to talk her way clear of anything, and God, could she talk.

He knew that things in the US these days were bad and deteriorating fast, with each day bringing fresh news of shocking chaos and collapse. Yes, Molly went over there. It seemed preposterous, but it also seemed like Typical Molly. Crumbling social order? No problem. I'll just talk to people, make them see sense! He could imagine Molly saying that, dismissing all concerns as alarmist nonsense, and rejecting all concern for her well-being as barely disguised jealousy, because she might finally be successful. The thing was, Spider knew, as soon as Stéphane or one of his "lovely" mates had floated the idea to Molly that her work might find its way to MoMA, that would have been it. It was a name to conjure with. The Museum of Modern Art, the beating heart of twenty-first century art, an institution doing its best to hang on in a world gone mad, selling off parts of its famous collections to finance the institution's defense. Molly would not care about that. Even if the media these days was much more interested in documenting the end of the world than publicizing the work of a little-known Australian sculptress, all Molly could see was the idea that she would be in MoMA, even as MoMA itself, like so much else, was going under. "I was there, I was there!" she'd say.

He thought back to Thursday night, when she'd first told him about all this, and remembered the squealing joy in her voice — Molly, squealing with joy! — as she told him all about it. It occurred to him that if he had a time machine, he could go back to that night, and try to talk her out of it. Molly, you can't go. Something bad is going to happen to you! No, I don't know what. No, I'm not making this up, I'm really not. Honestly. I'm not just thinking of my lying, selfish self. I'm not. You just can't go, because, well, who the hell knows? Just, that's right, Something Will Happen to You. Something Not Good. No, not even in an "Adventure Travel" sort of way. Yeah, that was going to fly, wasn't it?

The worst part of all this? Molly actually *had* her own time machine, sitting there in the garage at her place. Whether it was operational or not, he didn't know, but it would be easy to check. Besides which, he knew very well, unless he went to the trouble of finding the nodal point in the timeline to go back to warn Molly, all that would happen was she'd end up disappearing somehow, probably. If trouble was coming, it was not easily put off by clever bastards with time machines.

His head hurt, and there was still that heavy sense of something big and serious going on inside his skull. Then again, what if he didn't need to borrow anybody's time machine? What if he really did have one right there, in his too-heavy noggin? It was an unbearable thought. It was the kind of thought that made a fellow want to grab a spoon — a very narrow spoon — and start digging in through his ear. Maybe a power drill would do the trick, and Spider knew his dad had quite a range of suitable power drills. Well, Dad, I need to borrow your drill because there's this thing in my head — yes, that's right, in my head, some kind of hardware that shouldn't be there. Well, long story, so can I borrow the drill? Promise I'll clean the bit after I'm done. Yeah, he could imagine that conversation. Iris said she was going to organize a brain scan for him to find out just what the hell was going on in there, but who knew how long that might take to set up? What if there were immune system problems with all this hardware clashing with his body? He could die of some horrible infection before he'd sorted out anything! As it was, he was starting to feel a bit clammy, and that couldn't be good.

Besides which, suppose he did have some kind of whizzy time machine thingy installed in his head right now. He still had no clue how to use the damned thing. Stapleton never bothered to tell him how. And that was assuming the thing really was in there, and his head wasn't just full of the runtime code for virtual Calgary. It occurred to Spider that he had punched out of his conversation with John Stapleton a little precipitously, and had no clue how to get back to ask a few pointed questions.

Shit!

What to do, what to do? He checked his email to see if Stéphane had sent him that note yet. Nothing. He checked again, immediately. Still nothing. He pedaled onwards, watching traffic, trying to concentrate, awash in chip-shop-smelling exhaust fumes, aware of the passage of time, thinking about Molly, thinking about Vijay and Phoebe, maybe caught in that trap in the year eight million AD, stuck in "Colditz" with all those other hapless time travelers. Hell, he was even thinking about Dickhead's severed head. *"Help me, Spider..."* "Help you with what, exactly, you great git?" Spider muttered to himself. "Keep you from getting decapitated? Keep you from being captured by someone intent on killing you? Keep you from killing all of your loyal Zeropoint followers, for no good reason? Fuck, Dickhead, where do I even start?"

At length, feeling dismal, his stomach grumbling, still a little clammy, but that could just be sweat from making his bike go, he got off the freeway, and made his way to Molly's place. Yes, he noted, it was still there. Good. The bike secured and locked, he hauled himself up the steps onto the porch—

The door was ajar.

Uh-oh, he thought. And, as he stepped closer, he noticed a strong, nasty odor wafting out from inside, an odor he recognized, not in a good way. Oh, shit. That was the odor hanging around the scattered remains of John Stapleton. Damn, damn, damn. So, first thing: call the cops. If he stepped foot in there without the police securing whatever the hell had happened in there, he'd be in deep shit. He popped his watchtop, and went to tap his phone-patch, and remembered that he was out of phone-patches. Ah, but wait: the phone-patch he did have, the one in his pocket with Molly's voice-mail message on it, despite being dead, could still be used to make emergency calls, but that was it. He held the patch against his prickly jaw to maximize the bone-conduction, and told his watchtop to make the call. He called, the cops said they were on their way, and he was instructed to touch nothing.

A WAPOL cruiser turned up bearing two uniforms, a sergeant (male) and a young constable (female). The sergeant, his blue uniform bristling with leather pouches for equipment, reminding Spider, as always, of Batman's utility belt, approached Spider, keeping it professional, all, "Good afternoon, sir. What seems to be the trouble?" Spider watched the guy's face, waiting for the sergeant to realize he was talking to the legendary scumbag and traitor Spider Webb, but either the sergeant didn't know (possible) or didn't care (also possible). The sergeant asked Spider some questions about the situation, nodded a lot, made notes on his handheld, and had the constable patrol around the front of the property looking for anything unusual or suspicious. She set off and, Spider saw, looked like she was doing a thorough, by-the-book job of inspecting the premises. The sergeant noticed the odor. "Nasty pong, eh?" he said to Spider. When Spider agreed, saying nothing about last night, the sergeant added, "I'm sure it's nothing to worry about, sir, but please wait out here until we give you the all-clear, okay?"

Spider wanted to get inside and find out what the hell was going on. Knowing that odor, knowing that the thing which produced that odor had torn a man apart, filled him with fear for these two fresh-faced young coppers. They didn't deserve to wind up in pieces, for no good reason. *Well, shouldn't you clue them in*, Spider thought to himself. *Shouldn't you tell them to at least check with Iris? If they go in there and wind up dying, it'll be on you.* In the end Spider could think of no good reason not to tell them, so he approached the sergeant, as he was talking to the constable, planning their entry into the house, and told them about last night, and that they needed to talk to Iris Street about it.

"Is that right?" the sergeant said, looking him up and down, nodding, and shooting a glance at the constable, who was staring at that open doorway, rubbing her upper arms. The sergeant got on the radio, worked his way through the system, and at length made his way to Iris. They talked for a few minutes. When he mentioned Spider Webb, and the domicile of Molly Webb, Spider heard her demand to speak to Spider, pronto.

Spider took the radio mike. "Hey, Iris. Guess what?"

The radio crackled. "Spider, I can't leave you alone for one bloody moment, can I?" She told him she was in a meeting, but that she'd be there as soon as she could. This turned out to be over an hour, involved a meeting she couldn't easily get out of, and then getting stuck in rush-hour traffic. When her car pulled into the drive, Spider saw Iris and her junior, Detective Senior Sergeant Mullens, he of the "great face for radio", and the barely controlled loathing of Spider. Spider watched him get out of Iris' unmarked Holden, met his carcinogenic gaze, and could imagine the conversation in the car between Iris and him as they had made their way here. Iris came over, got briefed by the uniforms, and had a quick look around. "That is indeed that smell again," she said, wrinkling her nose, looking at the house. "Oh, good." She told the uniforms to set up a perimeter, and to call out the rest of the team to start door-knocking the neighbors up and down the street to see if anybody saw or heard anything unusual.

Then she turned to Spider, who was leaning against the uniforms' cruiser, arms folded, watching everything. "Can't get rid of you today, can I?" she said, coming over, Mullens in tow.

"Must be a sign," Spider said. "Hey, Mullens. Cheer up, mate. Might never happen."

Mullens shot him a look, said nothing, and stood there, taking up space, slumping in his bad suit, clearly wishing he was anywhere but here. Spider, surprisingly, was amused to see the big lug behaving like this. He'd been extremely impressed with the professionalism of the uniformed coppers, appreciated that they did not give him grief on account of who he was, and did their jobs. By comparison Mullens looked sour and churlish, a very poor example of WAPOL service — and Spider was also quite sure that Iris noticed it.

Meanwhile, Iris took Spider aside. "Listen, hate to be the bearer of bad news, but—"

Spider felt himself tense up. "Let me have it. I'm big and strong." He coughed for comical effect.

"Tonight's regress op?"

Uh-oh, he thought. "Yeah?"

"It's off. Mission scrubbed."

"The hell!?"

"Out of my hands, Spider. DOTAS got wind of it, and that was it. They're handling it now. Something about 'clear and present danger', 'national security risk', 'too big for local pretend-coppers like you lot.'"

Spider heard the venom in her voice, telling him all that. "Fucking Feds!"

"Apparently, if any of us, and in particular you, Spider Webb — believe it or not that there was a specific mention of you in the memo, and how you were not to be allowed anywhere near the scene — even think of showing up, we'd be in danger of suspension."

Spider was gobsmacked. He stood there, unable to speak, for a long time. "They mentioned me by name?"

"I'm only telling you what I heard."

"How on Earth am I any kind of threat?"

"You're personally involved with one of 'the principals', apparently."

At first he was baffled, thinking this thing tonight meant a possible encounter with a rampaging Vore, but then remembered his chat with Stapleton, and remembered, too, Stéphane telling him that Molly had gone missing in New York. He had chills, thinking about it. "Meaning Molly?"

"You did say Molly and this Vore thing..." she said, still skeptical, still watching him, as if trying to spot some evidence that Spider had lost his marbles.

How on Earth did DOTAS know that Molly was even involved? he thought. He'd only told Iris, and he was sure she would not have told DOTAS anything they didn't need to know, and indeed, would not have done them any favors at all. "Bloody DOTAS," he muttered, dismayed. And dismayed, too, thinking that of course DOTAS, with their spies everywhere across time, would know everything, and know it before he did, most likely.

"The way they see it, and here I'm just relating what they had to say in the memo, okay? This is not my view, though on this point I think they may be onto something—"

"Get to the bloody point," he said.

"The thing is, they reckon there is a real chance that this, whatever the hell it is, this 'Vore', or whatever, this thing that happened to Stapleton last night, is way, and I mean, *way*, beyond anything we can realistically handle. Even with the whole Tactical Response Group on hand. Even, for God's sake, if we had the Army involved. We just don't know what we're up against with this thing, Spider. They reckon even nuking it wouldn't be enough to slow it down."

"DOTAS knows about Vores?"

"I suspect it's more Section Ten that knows about them, but yeah."

"Nukes, huh? Hope it doesn't come to that." Last Spider heard Australia did not possess nuclear weapons. Not officially.

"Yeah. Me, too."

"So," he said. "A quiet night in, then." He was shaking his head, disgusted. He had been sort of looking forward to the regress op, terrifying peril aside.

"DOTAS said they would pass along a full report, as a matter of courtesy."

"Decent of them," Spider said, fuming.

"You think it's at all possible Molly's involved?"

"I'm not sure what to think at the moment, to be honest."

"But surely there's just no way—"

"Yeah, I know. And yet, that's what Stapleton told me."

"And you believe him?"

"Yes, and no. I dunno."

Iris shook her head. "Jesus, Spider. The shit you attract, it's incredible."

"Must be my aftershave." Which was very glib and all, but inside, he was seething. DOTAS had specifically mentioned him, a washed-up cop/time machine repairman, of all people, in their memo! It was infuriating. He tried a bit of pacing back and forth, rubbing his face, trying to figure out what to think. What if Stapleton had lied to him about Molly and the Vore? What if he was just messing with Spider's head — yes, but why would he do that? He was trying to win me over, to get my help to save his life. It made no sense for him to lie to me about Molly. If he really had met me in Colditz, he'd know my feelings about Molly. And, thinking that, he had a moment of chilly clarity: *yes, and he'd know Molly was my weak point. Yes*, he went on, thinking hard, *but even so. He'd have to know how I'd react when he mentioned her; that I would do what in fact I did, and just punch out of the entire thing. He can't have wanted me to punch out. Could he?* Spider stood there, frowning, struggling with the crazy ideas that were his current reality. For only the *nth* time today, he wished he could get back into the Calgary simulation to talk to Stapleton in a "safe" environment. "Hey," he wanted to say to the guy, "what did you mean by that crack about Molly 'merging' with this captive Vore? You just pulling my leg, or what?"

"So," he said to Iris, "did the DOTAS memo say just what they'd do if we, well, I, show up tonight anyway?"

Iris rubbed the skin under her eyes. She looked exhausted. "I suspect they could do anything from taking you into custody as a possible terrorist, and letting you stew in a Section Ten dungeon for a week or two with no light and no contact with anyone, to simply shooting you dead."

"Because I'm such a terrible threat to them?"

"Because you're too personally involved."

"Because of Molly."

"They clearly know stuff I don't, is all I can think," she said, stretching and yawning. "God, I could go for a coffee right now. Last one's worn off."

So, he thought, that's that, then. The Feds stick their noses in, decide that helpless, pathetic little WAPOL couldn't run a chook raffle, let alone handle a major incident like this, and he, Spider, was stuck. It felt like a personal rebuke, the hand of the federal government reaching down from the clouds above and pushing him back into his proper place. Which only left one key question for him, one he did not share with Iris, who was staring at Molly's house again, shaking her own head with dismay, no doubt thinking she was going to have to go in there. Spider was thinking about the Feds: *you want me out of that regress op tonight? Try and bloody stop me.*

Yeah, and what if in the process of trying to find out what had happened to Stapleton he wound up drawing the Vore to him, all, "Oh, there you are!" Which presented a conundrum all of its own: *how to save the Canadian's life?* Could it be done? He doubted it, if he was honest with himself: *Lone time machine repairman up against something from beyond the universe.*

"So, what's the story here?" Iris said to him, pulling out her handheld. She already had a copy of the statement he'd given to the sergeant, but wanted to hear it from him. Spider, now that he had some kind of half-baked plan for tonight, settled the hell down, focused on the present situation, and did his best to explain what he could, that he'd come here and found the house in its present state. Door ajar. Nasty stink. Bad vibe. Probable trouble. Iris nodded, and said that was pretty much her impression, too. Spider thought it was remarkable that she could put aside her own feelings about having the regress op taken out of her hands, and focus on the job at hand. He doubted he'd be able to compartmentalize the two matters quite so effectively, given the same situation. He watched Iris and Mullens confer a moment about the best way to get into the house, then she sent Mullens around the back. Iris left him at the car, with strict instructions to stay put until she gave the all-clear. Spider sulked a little. But as Iris approached the door, the strength of the odor was too much. She recalled Mullens, and got him to grab the respirators from the boot of the car. "Right, take two!" Iris said, her voice muffled by the respirator, and approached the front door while Mullens once more went around the back. Sidearm drawn and ready, Iris eased the front door open, stepped inside, and was soon lost to view. Watching her go, Spider found himself feeling like he should be right there with her, or even instead of her, that if there was trouble in that house, he couldn't bear the thought of Iris on the receiving end of it. And that stopped Spider cold, thinking about it. He knew Iris was capable of looking after herself; it wasn't that. But that he "couldn't bear the thought"? What? His heart boomed in his chest, and he was biting his lip. *Spider, mate, what the hell's going on with you?* he was thinking, and the truth was he no longer knew for sure.

CHAPTER 16

Spider watched and waited. Fidgeted. Paced back and forth. Tried not to brood about the canceled regress. Tried not to think about the great knot in his chest. The way things were going today, the worst day Spider could remember in a long while, he could wind up losing Iris, too.

Iris had kept him going these past several months. She'd helped him with the terrible dreams he'd started having after he returned from the End of Time, and got him some free counseling and treatment. She was one of the very few good friends he had. And now she was in that house, where whatever the hell it had been that had killed Stapleton might be waiting (what if, he thought, it wasn't a Vore at all, but something else?). The thought was too much. He decided to hell with it, he was going in, regardless, but he hadn't taken two steps before the young female constable appeared before him, her gun-hand resting on the butt of her holstered Taser, ordering him to wait by the car until further notice. She was a tiny thing, all of 150 centimeters, and probably weighed about as much as a pencil, but that look on her face and the tone in her voice, stopped Spider where he stood. The last thing he wanted was another Tasering. He went back to the car, his hands up, *look, officer, nothing to see here, I'll be good*. He did say, "It's just, it's my ex-wife's house."

"Just wait here until Inspector Street gives the all-clear, Mr. Webb."

So he waited, and waited. Five minutes passed, then ten. Wasn't it taking a bit too long? Shouldn't Iris and Mullens have emerged by now? What if they'd come to some kind of harm? Then again, he'd heard no sign of any kind of trouble: no gunshots, no screams. Just that vile odor that stung his nose and made his eyes water. When fifteen minutes had passed, Spider could hardly bear the tension. He started edging his way down the brick-paved path to the porch, *just so I can can hear better*, he thought. Who knows, things might be such that Iris and Mullens couldn't call out, and maybe never had time to get off a warning shot, or maybe—

Just then, the front door eased open, and the two senior cops came out, holstering their sidearms. They pulled off their respirators once they were clear of the house, but even so, they still coughed, and when Iris came over, Spider could see her eyes were red and she was sniffing as if with a head cold.

"Good God," she said, shaking her head. Mullens, Spider saw, stood a couple of meters back, hands on his knees, coughing hard. Spider thought the bloke might throw up, and secretly hoped he would.

"So, what did you find?" The suspense was killing him. It was all he could do to keep his voice calm and reasonable.

Iris was taking in great, deep breaths of fresh air. "God, I can still smell it, I think it's on my clothes, God…" she said, wiping her nose, "It's bad. It's real bad."

"How bad? Are there—?"

She grabbed his shoulders to settle him down. "It looks like our mystery-thing has trashed the place. Like in a frenzy. All of those, artworks? The ones you told me about? They're utterly destroyed. It's like they were the focus for the attacks. Sorry, Spider."

"Her sculptures?"

"Yeah. Just, just…" She struggled for a word that was both suitably descriptive and yet not too disturbing for Spider. "Just awful."

"God."

"Mind you," she said, wiping at her nose again with a tissue. "There was one thing."

Mullens piped up at this point. "The goldfish is fine. No worries! Swimming about in his tank, fins look a bit rough around the edges, and, God, those eyes, geez."

It took Spider a moment to grasp what Mullens had said. "The *fish* is all right? Everything else is trashed like a bomb hit it, but the fish is all right?"

Iris said, "It's baffling."

Spider grasped the ungraspable, and he began, at last, to see. "It *is* Molly," he said, amazed to have confirmation, looking at the house, thinking about Molly's disappearance in New York, and that weird phone call that he had been sure was a local call. "This is Molly's doing."

Mullens looked at Iris, hoping she would clue him in, but Iris was focussed on Spider. She said, with the greatest compassion, "Spider, no, just no. Even if she is here in Perth, and so far my inquiries have not indicated anything suggesting she is — there's nothing in the system to suggest she re-entered the country recently — Spider, it's just not possible—"

"It *is* Molly. I'll bet you a million dollars. Why else spare the stupid bloody fish?" *I'll place a fair-sized bet on the divorce papers still being intact, too,* he thought.

"No. You don't understand. The scale of the destruction, it's—"

Mullens said, "It's like someone stuck a chunk of C4 on each of those sculpture things. There's just … there's just nothing that could do that, not a middle-aged female artist, anyway."

"And anyway," Iris pointed out, "if it was Molly — and I don't really believe it was, okay? — but if it was, why would she destroy her own work like that?"

That was a good point, and he had no ready answer. Molly had sweated blood over those ghastly things. They were her life. They were the work that got her noticed by Stéphane, and that led to MoMA. Why destroy them? Surely they meant more to her than Mr. Popeye, who was, as far as Spider could tell, a passing fancy at best.

Iris was beaming photos she'd taken inside the house over to Spider's watchtop, which chimed as they arrived. Spider flicked through them, noted the destruction. The house was no longer habitable, he could see that. It would have to be demolished, or rather, the demolition would have to be completed. The furniture had been reduced to splinters and bits of unrecognizable wood and metal. The sculptures did look as if they had indeed been blown up. Spider zoomed and panned around some of the wide shots, and found recognizable bits — fingers, arms, and legs — embedded in the living room wall. And yet, even with all of this shocking destruction before his eyes, Spider struggled to feel the full impact of it. There was so little in these images that he recognized it could have been any trashed house. The only thing missing was foul and unimaginative graffiti on the walls. Then he found the shots of Mr. Popeye, caught in a thoughtful moment, perhaps, contemplating his crazy owner as she rampaged about the house destroying everything that had ever meant anything to her, as if she was ruling a line under her old life, *all* of her old life, as if she was never coming back.

Yes, that. Exactly. As if she was never coming back. Spider had dreaded, when she'd told him she was going to New York, that she would never come back to boring old Perth.

Only Molly would have spared Mr. Popeye's life. An entity from beyond time and space wouldn't care, but Molly would. It reinforced the thought that the Molly part of the Mollyvore merger might be reachable, that she might actually have some control over what the Mollyvore thing did, which was a startling thought in itself. How had she not simply been destroyed in the process of merging with the Vore? How had she survived to have this much control over their activities? Would a Vore, left to its own devices, even bother with trashing a suburban home in Perth? *Molly,* he thought, *might be reachable.* That led him to wonder if, maybe, the merging might be reversible. Could he get her back? The thought left him standing there, agog, staring at the dying grass on the front lawn. Could Molly be rescued? What if what she/it had done here was Molly's way of crying out for help? Drawing attention to the most personal part of her life so that the likes of Spider... He let the thought peter out, unconvinced. *Really, how desperate are you, Spider,* he thought, *that even when presented with the clearest evidence in the world that Molly has more than moved on with what passes for her life, you still imagine yourself a knight in shining armor, ready to steal her back from the clutches of the fiendish bug-eyed monster? Just how sad is that?*

Chagrined, he began to question his decision to try and crash the regress op. He thought, *is it really, in the end, any of my business what's happened to Molly? Even if the merging happened against her will, did he really have any standing in the matter? Would she thank him for interceding? Probably not,* he thought, in a moment of understanding that left him feeling a little unsteady on his feet, beginning at last to adjust to the idea of a life without Molly.

"Spider," Iris said, looked at him hard. "Spider, what aren't you telling me?"

"Iris?"

"Spider, come on now. This is getting ridiculous. I'm spending all my time chasing after you in one crazy situation after another!"

He could see she had a good point. "Yeah, sorry, Iris. It's been a weird few days."

"Weird few days is right! Christ!"

"I said I'm sorry. It's just…"

She held up a hand. "Just get yourself sorted out, Spider. I can't keep coming to bail you out of this shit."

"I understand, I—"

"I used to be in Major Crime, Spider!" she said, trying not to shout. "You know what that means?"

He felt small. "I know what that means, yes." Homicide, kidnapping, armed robbery, the big stuff, the glamorous stuff. The cases that made the news, that made coppers look good. Even though the Time Crimes Unit dealt with similar matters, it was not the same. They were second-best, handed the leftovers of the media coverage. He knew the demotion would burn an ambitious cop like Iris.

"Now I'm stuck on bloody Time Crimes, and it's all this bloody bullshit, every single day, time machine this, time machine that. God! The stupidity! And that's just on a 'normal' day, Spider." She made very elaborate, sarcastic air-quotes around "normal". "And now all this! One crazy thing after another. Dickhead's severed head, Patel's missing kids! This business with your ex, for Christ's sake Spider, your *ex*! Take the hint: Molly's *gone*. She's moved on. She's not coming back. Open your stupid eyes Spider, see what's out there, you might get a surprise!"

It stung him to hear all this. He knew she was right, dead right. He was abusing their friendship. It was a humbling thing to face up to. He slumped against the car, and said nothing, feeling guilty.

Iris was next to him checking her messages on her watchtop, shaking her head, breathing hard, biting her lower lip.

"You're right," Spider said.

"Am I?"

"Yes."

"Oh, good-o!"

He pushed himself clear of the car, and went to get his bike, which he wheeled across Molly's lawn. "I'll be off, then. Sorry to bother you." Not that he had the first clue what he was going to do next, but it seemed like the right thing to do.

Iris looked up, confused a moment, then understanding. "Oh, now hold it right there, soldier. You are not dismissed."

That tone in her voice stopped him. He glanced across at her. "I'll take care of everything," he said. He'd imposed too much on Iris. It was time to stand up for himself. "I'm sorry I got you involved."

She came after him. "Oh, no."

"None of this should be your problem, Iris."

"Yes, you're right, but it is. Because I'm the Time Crime Go-To Girl, so it all winds up in my lap, regardless."

"Even so. I have to move on, like you said."

Iris grabbed the frame of his bike, took it out of his grip, and wheeled it back to the front of the garage. She came back, took Spider by the shoulder, and marched him to her car, where she pushed him against the driver's side door, hard enough that he nearly lost his balance. She said, "You are staying right where I can see you, full bloody time, starting now. You got that?"

"What?"

"You heard me," she said, coming closer, sticking a finger in his chest, her face like thunder.

"But—"

"Suppose I let you slope off on your own, you with the huge bullseye on the back of your head and a sign that says, 'Kick Me!' How long would you last out there, on your own? The way things are going, you'd wind up dead within about…" She checked her watch. "Maybe half an hour, tops. Most likely because of some stupid time machine bullshit, again. So, my problem. As usual. Therefore, you stay with me. And don't give me any of that Basset Hound face bullshit, either, with the sad eyes and the moping, yeah, that face right there!"

He had not been aware he had been pulling any face other than, "shocked". He went to speak, but Iris was not done yet.

"You think whatever the hell happened here at this house was done by your precious bloody Molly—"

"Not just Molly, she's—"

"Stop right there," she said, holding up her hand. "Just give it a rest. You're going to give me that bullshit about Molly and this, this, "Vore" thing, getting together, like that Stapleton guy told you, aren't you! Because a perfect stranger is so trustworthy, and all. The guy who told you — and you believed him! — that Molly's disappearance from New York landed her in the way far future, only not really, and now she's here and trashing everything she ever valued—"

"Except the fish."

At this Iris slumped against the car, and managed a bitter sort of laughter, coughing it out. "Yeah, except the stupid fish."

He went on. "It's true. Molly and this Vore thing. And it was them last night, with Stapleton."

"You are most likely right," Iris said, at last, after careful thought. "Certainly DOTAS thinks so, after all. I just can't see it myself. I'm sorry. My poor old brain won't go there. You're talking about monsters, Spider. Monsters! Now come on. Help me out."

Spider took a breath, knowing none of this talk was going to make a difference. Iris was rooted in the here and now. He no longer had that privilege. He'd left all this behind, and gone to the End of Time, and seen things he never should have seen. He'd never felt properly anchored to this reality since. It was as if a part of him was still there, left behind at the End of Time, caught up in all the Zeropoint intrigues. All the same, he took a shot at it, starting with the basics. "Stapleton was at the Colditz detention facility where they had the Vore on ice."

"Until it did the nasty with your ex, of course!" Iris said, one eyebrow arched.

Spider ignored that, or tried to. "And Stapleton escaped. He said the prisoners built a time machine—"

Iris clapped her hands, delighted. "Of *course* they did."

"So he got away, and came to find me."

"And the big beastie came after him, and caught him, before he got to you."

Spider had been wondering about this all day. Why *would* this Vore, having escaped from its detention, go after a mild-mannered Canadian physicist, of all people? Stapleton told Spider that he needed Spider's help, though he never quite got around to exactly what kind of help, did he? And now there's this Mollyvore, which, of all the things it could have done after escaping from its captivity, chose to chase Stapleton across time, to keep him from reaching me. *Like I'm some huge threat!* he thought, which itself was clearly absurd. What am I going to do? Kill the Vore part of Mollyvore with a spanner? Hit it with heavy-duty sarcasm? Hmm. And then, he thought, following the thread where it went, when this unimaginable thing did catch up with Stapleton, it didn't just kill him, did it? It *destroyed* him. Spider remembered the sensation of crazed viciousness hanging in the air. The Vore, or Mollyvore, had it in for Stapleton, Spider was thinking. And that was the puzzling thing. What could this guy have possibly done to so piss off an otherworldly being?

Spider thought about his frustrating little talk with John Stapleton, in the Calgary diner simulation, and despite Spider's best efforts, was damned if he could remember Stapleton explaining just how it was exactly that *he* had wound up in

Colditz. Spider remembered the business about Stapleton, his wife Ellen, and some confederates, people who'd been part of Dickhead's Zeropoint operation, bunking off, fleeing across time in one of Dickhead's enormous fleet of timeships — but there was that big gap in Stapleton's timeline just before he had been caught up in the space-time-twisting driftnet that was Colditz. That gap, Spider thought, was going to be trouble, and it likely concealed all manner of things Spider would rather not find out about. As it was, there was still the question: why build something like Colditz? Eight point four million years in a cold, dark future. What was that about? And what would it have taken to build such a place, in such conditions? What would be the point of capturing one of these Vore things? It would take limitless money; world-consuming resources; relentless drive and determination over a godawful long time. An effort along the lines of the construction of the Pyramids or the great Cathedrals: backbreaking effort over lifetimes. It seemed to Spider like a lot of trouble to go to in order to capture and hold this thing. The more he thought about it, the more gobsmacking it seemed, just trying to wrap his feeble 21st-century mind around the idea of far-future technology. Then again, he thought, maybe Colditz was nothing more than a very big, very elaborate bug trap, like the kind of thing you'd use to trap and kill pantry moths — only writ larger than large, with a strong dose of super-science. What did the freezing people of the bleak Earth of the Year Eight Million want with idiot time travelers from the distant past turning up, wanting to take photos of them and their quaint folkways? Maybe trapping those pesky time-travelers — and killing them? — was the idea. He remembered that Stapleton told him that he, Spider, or at least a future version of himself, had also been there. It was because Stapleton and this Future Spider were friends or at least allies in Colditz that made Stapleton come back to now to try and reach him. Yes, that was right, Spider thought, trying to keep it all straight in his overtaxed mind. *Something to look forward to, then*, he thought.

Bloody hell, he really needed to talk to Stapleton again, and, this time, get some actual answers. He'd tried everything he could think of, on his own, to reactivate the diner environment, without success. The idea that everything he needed to know was, right now, this very minute, actually stuck in his brain, in a locked compartment, was driving him nuts. He thought again about his dad's power drill. *Tempting, real tempting.*

Then, a brainwave: what if John Stapleton, the physics professor, had not been just this unlucky time-traveling guy caught in the Colditz trap, but had been the secret mastermind of the whole thing? No, that was bollocks, he thought. Where would Stapleton get the resources for something like that? Spider had met the man. He was just this regular bloke, very brainy, sure, who'd been swept up in Dickhead's insane cult, but who came to his senses and got out, just him and a few others, including, Spider remembered, Stapleton's wife.

Yes, all true, at least as far as it went. Spider had met his share of murderers and assorted scumbags during his time in WAPOL. He knew there were the ones who would blab everything as soon you looked at them; that there were the ones who wanted, badly, to unload this terrible burden they were carrying; that there were the ones who denied everything, and would continue to deny everything, no matter what the courts decided, until the heat death of the universe; and there were those who would just sit there, arms folded, eyes dead, staring and saying nothing; and then there were the tricksters, the ones who would bury you in details and factoids and narratives that sounded incredibly compelling and believable, about how they were the innocent party in all of this, and you need to be out there chasing after these other bastards, and they really, really sold it, and made you believe it. Spider had met them all.

But, thinking about it for a second, Stapleton had worked for Dickhead. Stapleton was the guy in charge of administering the poison — oh, wait, sorry. Poison, Spider thought, was a bit harsh. The facts were that Spider's Far Future Self, Soldier Spider, and his time marines, were all set to storm Dickhead's Zeropoint flagship, and Dickhead knew it. So he brought forward the "ascendancy operation", in which his acolytes were told that it was finally time to partake in the Final Secret of the Universe, and that this meant drinking a lovely, tasty beverage. Stapleton and his wife had been part of the team assigned to prepare and distribute the stuff to the adoring crowds on all of Dickhead's ships. Stapleton was part of Dickhead's Inner Circle, one of his most trusted people. *Hmm*, Spider thought, *maybe there was a lot more to Stapleton than he had hithero suspected*. Spider remembered his first sight of the interior of Dickhead's flagship when he and the time marines arrived — the frost-covered bodies of hundreds of people, all of them believers, all of them dead because of their faith in Dickhead's ravings about the bloody Angels. *Focus, Spider*, he told himself.

What if Stapleton had been much more Dickhead's man than he'd previously let on, or Spider had suspected and was one of these trickster bastards? What if he, for whatever demented purpose of his own, wanted to get his hands on this Final Secret without having to wait, or die? Spider could imagine it. "Hey, Dickhead," Stapleton would have said at some point, "what exactly is this Final Secret thingy, exactly?" and Dickhead would have given him all manner of magical bollocks about angels and God and the tainted world that needed rebuilding, and all of that, and Stapleton would have asked, because he was a scientist, a man of reason, "No, really. What's in the actual Secret itself? Have you had any, for want of a better word, spoilers?" Spider was pretty sure that Dickhead had no idea what the Secret might actually contain, but he could guess what Dickhead would tell Stapleton. He'd look at the guy, that weird, messianic light in his eyes, sweat pouring down his enormous great head, and grab Stapleton by the shoulders, and say, *"Power, my boy. Knowledge is power, you mark my words!"*

"Oh, dear God," Spider said, thinking it over, seeing how all the parts might fit together. And thinking, too, that Molly, *his* Molly, was right there, in the burning, crazy heart of the whole thing.

He had to go there. There was nothing else for it. *"Bugger!"* he muttered, kicking at the pavement. "Bugger bugger bloody buggery bugger!"

Iris did her best to conceal a look of amusement, watching Spider carrying on. "Something wrong, Spider?"

He looked at her, none too impressed to see that his troubles amused Iris. "Just the usual."

She nodded. "Sorry I yelled at you. It's…"

Spider held up a hand. "No. No, don't apologize. I was out of order." He was still staring down at Molly's driveway. Fitful weeds were struggling through gaps between the paving bricks here and there. He felt a strange urge to go and get a shovel and get rid of them before Molly came home. Then he remembered, glanced up at the house, thinking about the devastation inside, that the whole place was now a crime scene, and would be taped off. This presented Spider with a problem, he began to realize. Where the hell was he going to sleep tonight? Now that the Lucky Happy Moon Motel was closed, Spider was homeless. He hadn't fully taken it in, earlier, when he saw the sign on the Motel's door, that they were closing down. Now the enormity of it, the prospect of actual homelessness, began to close over him. *Oh, God,* he thought, wide-eyed, trying to think. "Um, Iris, listen." Oh, he hated that tone in his voice.

Iris was way ahead of him. "You could crash on my couch; it'll be like old times." Strangely, though, she didn't sound too enthusiastic about those "old times". He remembered how actually living in Iris' small flat was good, but awkward, and none too cozy. "You know," she added, "just until you get something permanent sorted."

"Sure. Of course," he said, nodding. "Absolutely." *Or until I get killed, whichever comes first,* he thought.

"S'pose it would kill you to move back in with your mum and dad."

"Like nothing else. It'd be like bloody kryptonite." Spider's parents had been bugging him in recent months about doing exactly this. They'd told him they could not abide the thought of their son living in Mrs. Ng's dreadful place one minute longer. "You're better than that, son," his mum told him. "Where's your sense of dignity?" and Spider had told them that dignity cost money he didn't have.

"Where's my bloody team got to?" Iris said, leaving Spider at the car while she went to stand in the middle of the yard, on the phone, yelling at people to "get their precious arses over here, pronto". Spider could imagine that the prospect of attending a crime scene at Spider Webb's old domicile was not filling Iris' team with enthusiasm.

"Look, Iris," he called over to her. "Why don't I just duck out to get something to eat. I'm bloody starving. What about you?"

She ordered him to stay put, and said she'd send a uniform to get him something, and that he, Spider Webb, was not leaving her sight, not now, not later, not bloody ever, and was that understood? He wanted to answer, "Yes, dear," but knew he'd be atomized if he tried it.

CHAPTER 17

Much later that evening, once the scene at Molly's house had been sampled, sniffed, skimmed, vacuumed, scanned, probed, and otherwise investigated as far as was considered safe for Iris and her team, Iris left Mullens in charge of the continuing examination of the front and back yards, and the interviews of all neighbors out to a radius of about half a kilometer. Mullens was in for a long, long night. Iris, meanwhile, grabbed Spider. "Hungry?"

"I was hungry hours ago," he said. He was reading a message he'd just received from Stéphane Grey about Molly and her disappearance.

They wound up at a late night fast-food place, a franchise operation run by spotty teenagers in ill-fitting uniforms, where what passes for "ambience" is drowned out by constant beeps, hums, howls, chirps, and klaxons going off as various automatic food-production machines finished their cycles. The smell of hot grease and burned meat made Spider's stomach rumble. Iris looked right at home, Spider was surprised to see.

Once they were settled in an out of the way corner of the restaurant, Spider tried to explain to Iris what Stéphane had to say about Molly's disappearance. "The key thing, right, is that Molly seems to have met this old woman."

"Name? Description?" Iris dabbed at her mouth and wiped her fingers.

"No name given. Description, well, elderly, but upright, strong, in good nick, I guess you'd say."

"An old woman, eh?" Iris said, with a small sigh.

"Yeah, that was my thought, too."

They both said, as one, "Future Molly."

"So did Old Lady leave a name and contact details with this art guy?"

"No. He only heard about her in the first place after asking around when Molly failed to show up to a lunch meeting he'd organized. He went back to the hotel where they'd been staying, looked around, and found a note."

"So long and thanks for all the fish?" Iris asked, tired but sense of humor still intact.

Spider was amused. "Something very much like that, actually. Just, 'thanks for the opportunity', was pretty much all she said." Spider didn't mention that the note, a copy of which Stéphane had attached, had been signed, "*Love always, M.*" He went on. "She'd taken one of her suitcases, her handbag, and that was about it. Stéphane started asking around, talking to everyone on the hotel staff he could find, which is how he found out about the old woman, very well put together, elegantly dressed, accompanying Molly through the lobby, into the lifts and, presumably, up to Stéphane's suite."

"So this woman was actually in his suite. If it was Future Molly, it'd be hard to tell, fingerprint- and DNA-wise."

Spider said, "What about microbeprints?" This was a new thing, only recently accepted as evidence that would stand up in court. The idea was that people carried patterns of microbes, bacteria, on their hands and fingertips, and that as people went about their business, touching things, they left samples of these microbes behind, which could then be matched to their owner. Microbeprints were not considered an absolute proof of identity, since a person could go through several microbe patterns in the course of his or her life, and in this particular case, involving a version of a person from some far off point in the future, it was entirely conceivable that Future Molly and Present Molly would have different but similar microbeprints.

Iris lifted her eyebrows. "You're well-informed."

"I try to keep up."

"Still, you're talking about a hotel room. In New York, right now. Have you seen the news? If those rooms are getting cleaned at all, I'm guessing management's doing it."

Iris was probably right about that, Spider thought. She went on. "So where did Molly meet this woman? Did he say?"

"He said, earlier that day, he had a bunch of meetings, so he left Molly with strict instructions, an armed minder, and some transport credit—"

"Wait, she had a minder?"

"The minder says Molly went to one of the few remaining Starbucks to get a coffee, while she, the minder, stood out by the entrance. She added, by way of covering her arse, that she insisted Molly wear antiballistic armor, which the hotel provided as a courtesy service. Nice, huh? Anyway, Molly goes into Starbucks. A while later, Molly and this woman emerge. The old woman, the minder commented, looked a bit like she could have been Molly's mother or grandmother, with the coloring, bone structure, that kind of thing, and wore sunglasses. She also, this old woman, did not have any apparent body armor or sidearm protection, but then didn't look like she needed any, either. Minder said, quote, 'she herself wouldn't try to take down that bitch,' unquote."

Iris said, "Shit."

Spider said, "Apparently, the old woman looked all confident, self-assured. Molly looked pale — okay, more pale — maybe a bit anxious. The minder asked Molly to introduce her to her new friend. By way of answer, Molly dismissed the minder."

"Dismissed her. I see."

"My thoughts exactly," Spider said.

Iris said, "So what did the minder do?"

"She's getting paid by the hour, no hazard pay, not much more than minimum wage, so she cleared off back to wherever she came from to get a new assignment. Probably got a cab and left."

"So Molly goes into Starbucks to get a coffee, gets accosted by tough-as-nails old lady, and they wind up leaving together, and ditching the minder. Next they're spotted back at the hotel, going up to Molly's room. I'm guessing nobody saw either of them come down again, right? Yeah, thought so. Then Stéphane himself comes back, expecting to find her, and finds Molly gone, that note, and some missing luggage."

"That would appear to be the whole thing," Spider said.

"Did this Stéphane go to the trouble of trying to find people who might have sat near Molly and the old woman in the Starbucks, who might have overheard them talking?"

Spider looked at her. "Get serious. In a city like that? In the current situation?"

"Yeah, I know." Iris finished her second coffee, and looked like she wanted another. "A lot of those old buildings in New York have those fire escapes, don't they? Could Molly and—?"

Again, Spider just gave her a look.

"Worth a thought," Iris said. "Someone's gotta look out for the sensible and rational."

"You're suggesting I'm neither?"

She smiled at him, the sort of smile an exasperated mother would give a kid who couldn't stop screwing up or was always hurting himself in stupid attempts to fly or climb trees. She got up to order another coffee. Spider asked her to get him one, too. While she was gone, Spider stretched and yawned. He felt full, but he would not confuse that feeling with any sort of satisfaction. The food filled his stomach the way a bad argument fills your head with persuasive but ultimately nonsensical claims that are hard to refute. He suspected that later tonight, trying to sleep, he'd be plagued with heartburn and indigestion. *Good-o!* Meanwhile, the idea of Molly meeting a future version of herself, just the way he had met various future versions of himself, managed to both tickle his fancy, and fill him with dread. In the time machine business Spider knew he could expect all manner of space-time nonsense. But Molly, in stark contrast, was an artist, grounded in the here and now, at home with wet river clay under her fingernails. People from the future, Spider knew, could be intimidating and persuasive. To most people, the thought of meeting a time traveler was exciting, maybe too exciting. It was something like the shock and awe of meeting a hugely famous celebrity in real life. People from the future had an inherent sexiness to them, a glamour. Knowing Molly, she'd need some serious convincing, but then, Spider thought, she'd be arguing with an older, crankier, more disagreeable version of herself. Future Molly would practically force Molly to believe, simply to get on with things.

Iris came back and presented him with a coffee which, already, just smelling it, he could tell was badly burned and bitter. *Damn.* Iris sat, made herself comfortable, and sipped her own coffee.

"The bloody future!" Spider muttered. "What's it ever done for us?"

This made Iris laugh, an actual, proper laugh. For a while they swapped favorite bits from Monty Python, laughed, corrected each other's misremembered quotations, had a huge flaming argument over the Spanish Inquisition sketch, which led the restaurant manager, who looked all of eighteen, to turn up and ask them to settle down or take it outside. Iris and Spider stared at this manager kid, and laughed, banging the table with the flats of their hands. They took their coffees, got up and left, still laughing. They ended up outside in the carpark. It was near midnight. Getting a little chilly. The night sky was clear. Stars blazed and glittered. Iris and Spider sat on the bonnet of Iris' car, sipping their coffee, watching the heavens.

After a pleasant, companionable moment, Iris said, "What's it like, out there?"

"Horrible," Spider said, not wanting to talk about it.

"You know, when I was a kid…"

When Iris trailed off, Spider looked at her, and found her looking back at him, her eyes huge, and gleaming with reflections from the carpark floodlights. She looked, he thought, different, but familiar. He knew that look. It reminded him of… He tried to think. Iris interrupted him, and said, looking away, staring at the ground, "Nah, you'll just laugh."

"No, what? When you were a kid … what?"

"If you laugh I'll hit you with my Taser."

"Why would I laugh?" he said, watching her. She was smiling, even as she blushed.

"You'll think it's stupid."

"Iris, for God's sake!"

She looked back at him, and he could see she was actually worried about his reaction, biting her lower lip, to a degree he found hard to believe. Iris had never been one to worry about what other people thought of her, at least in his experience. "I wanted to be an astronaut. Oh, God, I said it. Oh, God!" She clapped a hand over her forehead, shaking her head, looking away from him.

"You wanted to be an astronaut?" He didn't think this was remotely funny, or even embarrassing, and yet it was all he could do not to laugh. He struggled to master himself, and managed, at length, to say, "Cool. Why didn't you pursue it?"

"Oh, piss off. Don't patronize me, Spider."

"No, seriously. Why didn't you follow it up? That would've been great!"

Iris looked back at him, scowling. "If you're taking the mickey—"

"I've been Tasered once today, all right? I've no intention of doing that again. Look. I Promise. Cross my heart, hope to die." He even held up two fingers in a Boy Scout salute, which, he admitted to himself, was possibly pushing it a bit far.

Watching him now, lips pressed together, she seemed to decide he might be genuine after all. In any case, after a moment of staring at him, holding up those fingers like that, she burst out laughing, and kept laughing, great loud booming laughter that made Spider smile, and he felt warm inside, for the first time in a very long while.

He said, "I really do think it's cool that you wanted to be an astronaut."

Once she got herself back under more traditional Iris Control, she said, "I never had the marks. All that hardcore science, just couldn't hack it in the end."

"Sorry to hear it."

"Just made my brain hurt."

"Why'd you think I'd laugh at you?" This was the most in-depth conversation Spider had ever had with Iris. Even way back, when they were both young coppers, and had their brief-but-intense affair, they'd never talked like this. They'd always been too busy for mere talking, even once the affair began to end. They'd been a secret white-hot item for ten days, the first four or five of which had been incandescently fantastic for both of them. But then doubts, and guilt, started settling in. Spider had already been having trouble with Molly, early in their marriage, and what he needed at the time, really, was someone he could talk to, but he couldn't talk to Iris, not that version of Iris — Past Iris, he guessed he could think of her — all she would talk about was her plans for the future, her towering ambition, to make Inspector before she was forty. It was dismaying, finding himself as if magnetically attracted to this extraordinary, flinty woman, even as he realized she was not what he truly wanted. Once their affair was over, they drifted apart: Spider found himself on the career fast-track, while Iris languished as a uniform cop, which also became a problem that neither of them could talk about. In fact it was only last year that Spider and Iris met up again, as part of the police investigation into the business of the dead woman from the future who had been found hidden inside a faulty time machine. For the longest time Spider found it impossible to trust her. He imagined, wrongly, she had been one of the WA police who hated his guts. That she was not, and that she still cared about Spider, had been very hard for him to accept.

"I don't know, I just…"

He nudged her shoulder with his arm. She nudged him back with hers. They went back to staring up at the stars, the ones they could see despite the carpark floodlights.

Spider said, "You'd still be up for it, though, eh?"

"Oh, yeah, like a shot."

He sighed. "Be careful what you wish for."

"True," she said.

There was a commotion nearby that distracted Spider. Some git with a big trailer on the back of his four-wheel-drive had slung his vehicle off the main road and into the carpark, and was hurtling at surprising speed in their general direction, high-beams blazing, spotlights flashing, and, as the vehicle got closer, the driver was hitting the horn. Bystanders scrambled to get out of the way.

"The hell?" Spider said.

"There's always someone wanting to ruin a lovely evening."

Then Spider recognized the driver, and began to understand things. Before he could tell Iris, the four-wheel-drive rushed up to where they were sitting, and came to a sudden, brake-squealing stop surrounded by a cloud of its own chip-shop exhaust. The vehicle was a monster, a recent model, the serious sort of four-wheel-drive actually intended for off-road driving, the kind of thing you'd want for driving across a flooded river, or inching your way down a tricky, perilous mountainside. It was the trailer — and the tarp-draped object on the trailer — that had Spider dismayed. He got up, shaking his head, swearing loudly, throwing his unfinished coffee aside.

Iris got up, too. "You know this idiot?"

"You don't recognize him?" Spider said, watching as the driver got out of the vehicle, his hand already out to greet Spider, a big nervous smile on his face, and he said hello to Iris.

Iris realized, all at once. "Oh, it's…"

Spider said, "It's trouble, is who it is."

"Trouble?" said Iris.

"Spider!" Mr. Patel said, coming up to him, taking his hand, pumping it hard. "You're a hard man to find!"

"Evidently not hard enough."

"I couldn't get you on the phone, so I had to track the GPS in your watchtop," Patel said, still pumping Spider's aching hand.

"Phone's cactus," Spider said, taking his hand back, rubbed it a moment, and told Iris what was going on. "Inspector Iris Street? I believe you've met my former employer, Mr. Patel."

Iris said, "Mr. Patel," in a quiet, cautious tone.

But, Spider was thinking, something was wrong, beyond the obvious. This, he thought, was not the twenty-nine-year-old Bharat Group *wunderkind* who had built *Kali*, and who had just today wound up the Time Machines Repaired While-U-Wait shop in Malaga. This guy was middle-aged, his face all hollowed out, with deep lines carved in the coarsened skin, and bags under his eye-plugs. This guy sported a goatee beard gone salt-and-pepper, and his hair, which Spider remembered as receding, was now all gone, his scalp shaved back to aerodynamic smoothness, and there were two or three worrying-looking scars, pale against the brown skin. This version of Patel was much older, and hadn't eaten well; he was much thinner, and he had already been a wiry whippet of a guy when Spider knew him, just yesterday. It was moments like these, with their jarring temporal dislocations, that bugged Spider most of all about time travel, the way they messed with your internal models of how people look and behave. Still, wherever this Patel had been — and Spider was betting it was nowhere good — the man had not lost his energy or enthusiasm. Right now, meeting Spider and Iris, Spider found he still kind of liked the guy, even though he was obviously full of trouble, and had not gone to the bother of tracking Spider down via GPS just to hang out and shoot the breeze about old times. The thing on the trailer under the tarp was meant for him, Spider knew that only too well. And what's more, there was only one thing in the whole world that would look like that shape.

To Patel Iris said, "Any word of your son and his friend, sir?"

He said, "As it happens, yes, and that's why—"

This got Spider's attention. "You've heard from them?"

"It was the faintest signal, terribly red-shifted and attenuated almost all the way into the infra-red. If I hadn't been scanning the TPIRB channel, I'd never have found it. And even then, there was so much cross-time chaotic noise, it was hard to pick out the signal, but I'm sure it was them. Very brief, repeated over and over!"

"Coordinates?"

"Coordinates. Last known TPS position."

"Let me guess," Spider said. "Eight-point-four million years from now, give or take."

Iris was looking at Spider. "You said—"

"Yes, it fits with everything else. Shit!" He was looking at the object under the tarp again. "Is that what I think it is?"

Patel flashed him a broad smile, full of nervous pride. "It is, yes, very good. It took some doing, once I got out of prison, to get my hands on it, some intense time-trickery, which of course only seems appropriate, considering—" The man was talking so fast Spider was having a hard time keeping up.

Iris said, "You went to prison? Over the missing children?"

"That is correct, Inspector. I am currently on parole, so…" He shrugged, unconcerned, knowing he was going back to prison just as soon as the future police tracked him down. Spider had no doubt they were coming.

He said, "So you stole the Machine, and—"

"I *borrowed* it, Spider. The company had it stored with some other sculptures and artwork. They had no idea it was a working machine. The fact that it's company property is a legal anomaly. And in any case, I do fully intend to return it."

"For fuck's sake, Mr. Patel!"

Iris was trying to follow the conversation. "What's he talking—?"

Spider said to her, "Looks like I'm going on a little trip."

Patel was just about bouncing up and down on his toes, he was so keen to get moving. "Spider, I've got the TPS coordinates. You've got to get going, my past is depending on you."

"Damn," he said, not happy about this one bit.

"My time here is short, you must understand. The police are coming. The plan did not go quite as smoothly as we had hoped."

"Plans can really suck that way," Spider said. "But can this machine go that far? Eight million years, I mean—"

"I have taken the liberty of replacing the power supply, the translation engine, and uprated the primary operating system. She's as bootstrapped and bodacious as I know how to make her. So," he said, bouncing on his toes again, full of bubbly intensity, "I need to know. What's it to be? Are you a man of your word?"

Iris interrupted. "Now just wait a bloody minute here, sir. You would appear to be telling me that you are in possession of a stolen time machine?"

"Well, yes, but—"

"You are talking, let me remind you, sir, to the senior inspector in charge of the Time Crimes Unit of the WA Police Service."

"Yes, *but*—"

"Mr. Patel, I am at this point well within my purview to place you under arrest on numerous charges, to say nothing of your own freely admitted breaking of the terms of your parole. Do you understand me, sir?"

Patel was sweating under the floodlights, looking at Iris, looking at Spider.

Spider said, "Inspector Street has a point, Mr. Patel. She's got you dead to rights."

Then Iris said, in the same forbidding tone, "You claim that Mr. Webb can use this machine of yours to locate your lost son and the girl?"

"Yes, that's—"

"And that he can, in fact, bring the machine back, having retrieved said children?"

"Of course! That's what—"

Iris said, "Which would nullify the original charges against you, which in turn would shunt everything to a new timeline."

Spider was watching Iris think her way through this. She said, in a tone like death itself, forbidding and dire, "I do have a small degree of discretion in the way I carry out my duties and responsibilities as head of the Time Crime Unit, sir. It seems to me that if you sign an affidavit, explaining what you propose to accomplish—"

"Actually, Inspector, if we stay here, in this timeline, and Mr. Webb goes off in the Machine…"

Spider, full of mischief, was enjoying Patel and Iris's strange dance around the law. "He did say it's borrowed, Inspector…"

Iris ignored him. "And he brings back the kids…"

"And," Spider added, "if you, sir, can convince your younger self, here and now in this timeline, to give me my job back, we might have a deal."

Patel's face lit up. "Of course, Spider. Leave it with me. I will do my best."

Hmm, Spider thought, the statement filled him with no confidence at all. *Fair enough.*

Iris interjected, "But you're talking about going more than *eight million years* into the future?"

"Yeah," Spider said. "It's where all the fun people are hanging out."

Iris stood there, speechless.

"I'll be back in a few minutes." Spider said, moving down to the trailer, looking up at the hidden shape. He started unknotting the lines holding down the tarp. Patel went around to the other side, and did the same. Before long, they'd pulled the tarp free, and the Time Machine stood revealed, its brass framework gleaming under the carpark floodlights, just as it had once shone under studio lights in 1959. The thing that surprised Spider, seeing it before him, was how small it was. It had only one seat, a plush, deep red, well-upholstered chair, more of an armchair from which to view the shifting epochs humming by as it plunged off into the future. There was the great, concave disc, easily two meters wide, and marked with cryptic glyphs around the edge, with intricate filigree at each of its cardinal points. Then there was the modest white cylinder mounted behind the pilot's seat, itself decorated with that lace-like filigree, from where the Machine drew its power. He could see that it had been modified in the process of converting it into a working time machine, and modified still further as Mr. Patel had turned the Machine into a hotrod version of its former sedate self. Spider could well believe that this new form of the beast would indeed have the legs to make an eight million year jump. Of more concern was the sheer lack of space. If he was going to get the two children home in this Machine, things would be a little too cozy for his liking. "Here, kids, just sit on Uncle Spider's lap while I lay in the coordinates for home!" The thought of two nine year olds, climbing all over him, filled him with dread. Then again, it was quite possible that Patel's *Kali* machine might simply need repair. Something he could easily do and then Vijay could drive *Kali* home with Phoebe. *Sure, that could work*, he thought. But, he reminded himself, time machines are nothing but trouble. They play up. They can seem to have minds of their own. They can have dead cats inside them that you can never ever find. They are the incarnation of trouble itself. There was a more than excellent chance that this would be a one-way journey. The fact that the children had not returned already weighed on him. Why had they not come home? What was keeping them? Could they come home? Were they even alive? Were they caught in John Stapleton's space-and-time-distorting Vore trap? Stapleton had told him there was an escape committee. It sounded so collegial, so chummy. Not like an isolated, endangered human outpost on a dead world drifting through dead space towards who knew what kind of fate. And here you, Spider, are planning to go to this so-called bloody Colditz, with an ulterior motive of your own. Would you go if there was no prospect of Molly being there? If it was just about the children? Would you put yourself into that much jeopardy, just to rescue them? He wasn't sure, but he told himself he would, yes, definitely. It was one thing for grown adults to wind up stuck in a trap, but children didn't deserve a fate like that.

Even so, Spider knew, he was practically begging to come to a bad end with this thing. Where were the safety systems? Where was the TPIRB? Where were the pressure suits in case he really did wind up in a howling freezing vacuum? He thought about all those other time travelers who'd set off on voyages into the future, intending to find solutions to all their troubles, whatever they may be, and never returned. Some had likely wound up in this Colditz facility, he figured, but most, just about all, would have died, whether from sheer exposure, from hostile locals, from God knows what. And here he was proposing to head out into that great void in this thing? A souped-up movie prop?

Yes, all of that was true, he said to himself, now climbing up onto the wheel of the trailer so he could have a closer look at the Machine. Patel had taken the liberty, in the interests of saving time, of getting it powered up for him. The disc was starting to spin. The power was building. There was a crackling, ozone-scented hum in the air, with electricity snapping and causing static discharges along the Machine's framework. The great unlikely contraption was now starting to vibrate, Spider noted. This was unlike all other time machines he'd ever encountered. None of them had ever had this tremendous sense of nigh-unlimited thrumming power. The hair on his fore-arms was a-tingle, standing on end. It was the most uncanny, even uncomfortable, sensation. He felt weird in his guts, and it belatedly occurred to him this might not be good for him. But just *look* at it! Look at the workmanship, the intricate craftsman-ship, the artistry of it, the touches that were there purely for aesthetic appeal rather than functionality.

Yes, but it will get you killed, you stupid man!

This is where Spider remembered something his dad would say, whenever he was warned about eating too much cake. "What a way to go!" he would say, beaming, shoving a great huge chunk of cake into his mouth. "What a way to go!" And, frankly, Spider thought, his life, as of this evening, was going to shit. He thought of the way he and Iris had made fun of that restaurant, and the kids working there, and the teenage manager who'd ejected them. At least those kids had actual paying jobs, he thought, feeling a pang of shame. They had more than he did, he'd have to give them that. Maybe Patel could fix things up, and maybe right now, this minute, was the right nodal point to change the future. The fact was, Spider was screwed regard-less of what he did. He looked back at Iris, who was talking to Patel, who was waving his arms a lot, looking very animated, defensive, and then he saw Patel signing something on Iris' handheld, which she examined, nodded once, and shook the man's hand, apparently satisfied. Then, before Spider knew it, Iris was climbing up the other side of the trailer. "Are you really thinking about doing this? For real?" She was shouting over the rising howl of energy; her own short blonde hair swirled around her head. A crowd started to gather around them.

"Yes," he said, shouting, back at her.

Iris stood, staring at him, and he was astonished to see that she looked achingly sad; she was even, if it wasn't a trick of the light and the thundering energy, on the point of tears. "I can't let you go, not like this," she said, her eyes shining.

"I haven't got a choice!"

"Yes, you have got a choice! Stay..." She didn't complete the thought, and looked down at the ground, where stray bits of napkins, plastic drink containers, empty phone-patch rolls, tumbled and churned. Nearby, car alarms were sounding off. One of the floodlights blew. When she looked back at Spider, he could see tears in her grey eyes. "Please, stay!"

Spider faltered, seeing her that way. His heart turned over. His mouth went dry. He'd never seen Iris like this. When they'd had that brief but intense affair, once things reached the point where they were wracked with guilt and recriminations, she'd always looked at him like he repulsed her, like the thought that they had, only a few days earlier, desperately wanted each other, made her sick. She had not been able to get away from him fast enough, even as something treacherous inside her still, despite everything, still wanted him. Spider, looking at her now, did not know what to think or how to feel. *Of all the times for a moment like this!* he thought.

Mr. Patel was behind him, on the ground, checking something on his watchtop, shouting up at him. "Now! You've got to go now, Spider!"

"Promise me you'll make everything right," he shouted down at him. "Promise!"

"I will do my best, Spider. I give you my word as a time machine engineer."

Then, Spider looked at Iris, who was climbing up onto the framework of the Time Machine itself. She had pulled on her leather driving gloves. "Iris, what the fuck—"

"If you won't stay here with me, then I'm coming with you!"

He was speechless. He found he was shaking, nervous in a way he had never been before, or at least since he was fifteen, and managed, accidentally, to sleep with a girl. He remembered shaking so much he could barely control himself. This was like that. "But—"

She cut him off. "Come on!"

It was one thing to risk his own useless life on a crazy adventure, but Iris? Who was the sensible one of the two of them? Who had a career? Who had, God, a future? A home to go to? A cat? A whole life, in fact? "Iris!"

They were both clinging to the frame of the Time Machine now, standing on the polished wooden platform that formed the Machine's floor. The static zaps were driving Spider crazy, but he had to hang on. Someone had to get in the pilot's chair. "What?" she screamed at him, tilting her head, indicating, as the great disk spun so fast you could no longer make out the detailed markings, as the world beyond the Machine seemed to get a little blurry around the edges, as he felt himself getting a little blurry around the edges, his skin tingling all over.

"You'll have to sit on the front rail there."

"You can't give me a dink?" she said, smiling at him.

God, that was something he hadn't heard since he was a kid, where you could carry friends around on your bike by having them sit on the handlebars, trying not to get their legs caught in the spokes of the front wheel.

Spider climbed into the plush red control chair. It was firmer than he expected. He remembered Patel telling him that the fuel-cell was under the seat. Iris was having trouble getting properly settled, and wound up with her backside propped against the front of the control panel, just in front of the three domed status lights. He admired her sheer crazy gutsiness.

The controls were simple. The target date and coordinates from the TPIRB had already been entered; it surprised him that the registers went as high as dates in the millions. The original Time Traveler in Wells' story "only" went as far as 802,701 AD. Here, he was proposing to beat that by an order of magnitude. And there was the direction lever, forward for *Future*, and backward for *Past*, all beautifully engraved in the brasswork. A flare of light overhead made him glance up, and he saw the great blinding spotlight of a police helicopter searchlight swinging towards him.

Patel was up on the trailer, hanging onto the framework of the Machine. "Travel safe, Spider."

Spider said, "I can't make any promises about *Kali*, you understand that, right? It's just the two children I'm interested in."

"Yes, Spider, of course!" he said, watching the helicopter. "You have to go now!"

Spider couldn't see a thing with Iris right there in front of him. "You okay up there, Iris?"

She flashed him a thumbs-up.

Spider pushed the direction lever hard forward, and saw for himself the whole world beyond the framework of the Time Machine flicker and blur, then—

CHAPTER 18

Then Spider dreamed, or thought it was a dream. It was hard to say. First there was a jarring sense that something in the Time Machine had gone catastrophically wrong. How exactly he knew this, he could not have said, since he was something other than conscious, perhaps perpendicular to consciousness. Something, though, was wrong. He felt the Machine lurch to one side. He thought he heard Iris cry out, "Spider!"

Then, he had this dream about Dickhead McMahon. It was the strangest thing, and the first he knew about it was the smell of a cold winter's night in the French countryside, late at night: rich soil, bugs, a waft of lavender on the wind — and he was sitting, alone — where the hell was Iris? Wasn't Iris with him just a moment ago? — in a familiar chair at a familiar desk in the middle of an empty pasture. There was a chill wind, and he thought he heard sheep bleating, off in the distance. Up in the sky, the stars looked all wrong; there were very few visible, and those burned so far into the red, he knew they were close to death. Much of the night sky was awash with luminous reddish cobwebs. The end of the visible universe was at hand, he thought, but did not know how he knew that. "What the fuck?" He got up, took a few steps, his Doc Martens sinking into the rich soil.

"Hello!" he said, calling out into the night, trying to rise above the sound of the crickets and frogs. "Hey! What's going on? Iris?" Of more concern: where was the Time Machine? He peered into the darkness: no Machine. No Iris. He knew what this was: this was the Display Room on Dickhead's command vessel, the timeship *Destiny*, at the actual, for-real, End of Time. This was where Dickhead took his VIP guests to overwhelm them with his extraordinary power, to show off, as Spider's mum would have put it. And if Spider was here, then things, in a word, had gone to shit, and he, Spider, was standing at the very hypocentre of it, about to be blown to smithereens. Where the hell was Iris? If he was here, why wasn't she here with him? He had a faint echo of a memory of something happening to the Time Machine in the instant between pushing the lever forward, and the landing.

As if on cue, Spider heard heavy footsteps, labored breathing, faint under-breath muttering, somewhere behind him. He turned, and yes, there he was, the man, the mass-murderer, the legend in his own lunchbox, the one and hopefully only, Dickhead McMahon. Spider was used to seeing him in a cheap K-Mart suit, heavy on the synthetic fibers, but here Dickhead was in a grubby old t-shirt; tattered, dirty tracksuit pants; and what looked to Spider like surfer thongs on enormous feet. Dickhead was having a hard time making his way through the soft soil, but once he saw Spider, he yelled out, "Spider! You made it, mate! So good to see you!" He came up to Spider, his arms spread, hoping to go for the big friendly embrace. Spider stepped back to avoid him. Dickhead noticed. He stopped, looked at Spider, for a moment shame-faced. "Yeah, well," he said, and lowered his arms and managed a vague wave. "Hi, Spider."

"Dickhead."

"Look. Thanks for coming. Know you're in a bit of a rush. Things to do, places to go, yeah, I know how that goes, been there, done that, got the t-shirt, know just what you mean, oh yes I do, I haven't fallen quite that far yet, I have my pride, you mark my words I do—"

"Dickhead? What am I doing here? I was travelling with a friend. Where's she gone? And where's—"

"Look, I won't keep you. I've rigged up a thing. It'll get you back to where you were—"

"What the fuck are you talking about?"

It's on a timer, you see. Pretty clever, if I do say so, considering what I've—"

"Dickhead!"

"Look, I just wanted a quick word, all right?"

Spider, dismayed, even embarrassed for the guy, could see he wasn't going to get any satisfaction from this ragged, aged version of his former boss, so he went back to the desk and resumed his seat. "This *is* your meeting."

"Yeah, well," Dickhead said, non-plussed, unsure of himself, looking at the desk, taking in the scene around them. He sighed, and sank into the chair across from Spider. "Well," he said.

"Got a hot date with a time machine, Dickhead. Make it brief."

Dickhead nodded. "Yeah. Got that. Um, look. It's um…"

"By the way," Spider said, interrupting. "Sarah says hello, and are you ever coming home? She's been a bit worried, you might say."

"Ah. Yeah. Sarah. Hmm. Okay. Fair comment. I'm on it. It's on my to-do list, I've got it down right here, you mark my words. I know the poor thing must be out of her mind—"

"I've nearly told her about your adventures, you know—"

"You didn't."

"Not yet, no. She'd never believe me, anyway, would she?"

"Yeah, point. Yeah." Dickhead managed a weak smile. God, but he looked rough, Spider thought.

"You know the shop's gone, right? New owners wound it up. Things are pretty bad back home."

"So I hear. Damn shame. It really is, it really really is."

"You could have tweaked things a bit, couldn't you? Made all that come out differently? Save the day?"

"You have to kill John Stapleton," Dickhead blurted all at once. "I've tried, like you told me, but he's using the ship's systems against me, and now he's personally trying to take me down, Spider. It's a mutiny! Can you believe it? A mutiny, against me? I'm a good boss, aren't I? Tell me I'm a good boss. Who'd want to take me down, after all I've done for everyone! I'm on the run here, I've been on the run for years now. Been some tight scrapes, some near-misses. Stapleton's goons are good, Spider, damned good, my word they are. They nearly got me a few months back, and I barely got away in time. For now I've looped back here, to the old flagship, the last place and time they'd think to look for me. It's all I have left."

"Dickhead?"

"You can only crash on the couches of your friends while you've got friends, eh?"

"That's true."

"Still," he said, shifting in his seat, glancing about, "They're bound to find me. So, it's either this or abandon Zeropoint altogether, and I can't do that, Spider. Not when there's still work to do." He was babbling, watching for enemies real and imagined, mopping his brow. It looked like it had been at least a week since Dickhead had shaved last. Spider could smell the man from where he sat, and it wasn't pleasant. He'd always known Dickhead's personal discretionary fragrance to be bold, assertive, just this side of offensive, a cologne he liked called *Thrust*, but there was nothing at all cologne-like about the odor coming off his former boss now. Nothing too discretionary, either, for that matter.

"Like I told you? What?" Spider said, sitting back, arms crossed, studying Dickhead. "I don't—"

Dickhead planted his huge hands on the table surface and leaned forward, his eyes huge. "For God's sake, man, he's out to get me! You have to stop him. You understand? You have to stop him."

"You? Who'd want to kill you?" Spider deadpanned.

Not getting the gag, Dickhead proceeded in all seriousness. "John was one of my people, my crew, in Zeropoint. Back when. Years ago now. My right-hand man. He had the job you should have had, Spider! If only you'd said yes. If you'd said yes, and joined us here at the End of Time, everything would have been different, it really would, you mark my words, everything would have been brilliant!"

"But, um, surely you could've just tweaked things a bit, and got me here regardless — if it was that important. I mean, you saved my life — and thanks for that, by the way, very decent of you, much appreciated — so why couldn't you just flip me over to where you wanted me to be? I don't see the problem. Man with your godlike power, ruling over the whole of history, all of Time itself, well, and of course, staying so modest all the while never letting all that power go to your head. That's what I've always admired about you, Dickhead. You never believed your own publicity. Very impressive. A role-model, that's what you are, mate. A role-model!"

Dickhead hardly heard any of it. He tuned out after the first sentence, looking around into the darkness, listening, watching. "You hear that?" he said, looking off to one side. "You hear that?"

"Hear what? All I hear is you sweating." Which he was, even though the 'conditions' were those of a winter's evening in rural France — exactly what Dickhead's obsession with France was about, Spider had no idea, but suspected some version of what used to be called the "cultural cringe" — and Spider wished he had a jacket. Dickhead, meanwhile, was sweating. His thinning hair damp and stuck to his bulging forehead; the collar of his t-shirt wet. Dickhead was bursting out all over with the cold, dank funk of *'oh shit, I'm gonna die!'* "You sure you can't hear that? Yes, there! Right there!" Dickhead said, turning and pointing off behind him.

"I see nothing. I hear nothing. Just, you know, some crickets, a few lonely frogs, and you going on and on."

A tiny crack, as of a snapping twig, somewhere off in the cold, dark distance.

"Okay," Spider said. "That I heard."

"There! You see! There! Get up. We can't stay here."

"But it's comfy, sitting out here in the middle of a field in the middle of the night, chatting with an old pal," Spider said. "I thought you could order up some food, some wine, it'd be like—"

Dickhead was up. He pulled a pistol out of the waistband of his sweatpants. Spider watched him efficiently check the magazine, work the slide, and flip the safety. Spider felt a twinge of dread; something might actually be going on. He got up. "Plan?"

"Kill the fuckers before they kill us."

"Sound plan."

"Come on."

They set off, away from the dim light surrounding the desk and chairs, and into the darkness. Spider, with his boots, managed okay; Dickhead, in thongs, had a harder time of it. After a moment, Dickhead paused, and with a quick motion, stepped out of the thongs. He was now barefoot, and made better progress across the field.

Spider, trying to keep Dickhead in view in the moonless dark, slogged on. He was reasonably fit from all his cycling, so he expected to go a while before fatigue set in, but the soft ground was proving more challenging than he expected. Then, Dickhead stopped, turned to Spider, and said, "If the worst happens, okay? I need you to be ready. Promise me, Spider. Okay? Promise me."

"Promise you what?"

"Spider, you owe me, remember? You owe your life to me. This is when you pay up. If I go down, you have to, you know..."

"I have to what? Eat your bloody heart and bury you in a cairn of stones?"

"You have to avenge me."

"Avenge you? *Avenge* you?"

"Spider. Promise me."

"But—"

Then everything went silent, bugs, birds, frogs, the slow tick of the simulated universe overhead. Dickhead stood up straight, his eyes huge, frightened. He looked back at Spider, and mouthed something Spider couldn't quite make out. Spider felt foolish, clomping about in a field like this at night. If anything, he felt more at risk from Dickhead's gun than from any unseen enemies — but out of nowhere there was a high, fast swooping sound, Dickhead said, "Oh, fuck," and turned to Spider, gushing blood from his throat. Spider could not actually see any wound there; the blood, nonetheless, was coming out. "Help me, promise me." Dickhead mouthed, stricken, clutching at his throat, as if to hold it together. Before Spider could react, before he could even move, John Stapleton and two goons in black stepped into faint view. One of the goons relieved Dickhead of his unfired gun. Dickhead stood rooted to the spot, still gushing blood darker than the night, the metallic stench unbelievable and hot. "But—" Spider said, stupidly. Stapleton reached out, grabbed Dickhead's huge head. He said to one of his goons, "Make sure you get a good shot of the head, okay?" and the goon produced something Spider guessed, in stunned panic, was a camera. But as Stapleton first slid Dickhead's severed head sideways, then lifted it by the hair clear off his hemorrhaging body — Dickhead's body stayed rigid for a long, horrible moment, then collapsed at Spider's feet — the head disappeared out of Stapleton's hand. *Gone.* Just like that. Spider thought he saw, in that moment, before the head vanished, Dickhead flashing a wink at him. It occurred to Spider that right now, even as he stood there, quaking with fear, Dickhead's head would be popping back into existence in the break room fridge, ready for his Past Self to find it when he went to get some milk for his coffee.

Stapleton, standing there with his arm up, as if he were still holding Dickhead's enormous head, looked ridiculous. Gobsmacked, he stared at his hand, then he turned to his two goons. "Did you see that?"

Of the goons, one said he had seen the head vanish; the other said he was trying to get the camera settings right and missed it, but, "whoa, you — where the fuck did he go?"

"If I knew that..." Stapleton said, lowering his hand, and turning to Spider. The observant goon leveled Dickhead's pistol at Spider's head. Spider could smell the gun oil on it. He could just make out the huge hexagonal barrel, blacker than black. He felt his bladder wanting to let go, but he just stood there, knees on the edge of failing. His mouth dry. Tongue, thick and useless. He wanted his heart to settle the hell down, and he was breathing much too hard. Only too well he could see Dickhead's headless body lying there in the dirt, still gushing blood in nasty spurts. He decided, at length, that the better part of valor indicated the sticking up of his leaden arms, and even that proved harder than he'd ever have thought.

His arms felt like bags of cement, but he got them up.

Stapleton stepped over to Spider, furious. "Where'd he go?"

"Buggered if I know," Spider managed to say.

"Pardon me?" Stapleton said, surprised at Spider's language.

"I said, 'Buggered if I know.' As in, you know, haven't a bleeding clue. Don't know. Not in the loop."

"You were obviously working with him."

"I wouldn't say that."

"You must know where he went."

"Must I?"

"Where did he go?"

"I don't know."

"Where?"

"Fuck off! I don't bloody know!"

"You're lying."

"Why would I lie in a situation like this? I ask you."

"You were his friend. You must be in on his plan."

"I was *not* his friend!" Spider said, with considerable emphasis that surprised even himself.

"So where'd he go?"

"I told you, I don't know. Don't. Bloody. Know!"

Stapleton fidgeted with a gadget that appeared, in the dark, to consist of two small knobs which he kept pulling apart and letting snap back together. Spider heard a faint sound as the two knobs came together. Some kind of monomolecular wire, he guessed. "You don't know. Right. Okay. Sure." Stapleton nodded, glanced at his two goons, each of whom looked like the unfortunate result of breeding industrial refrigerators with sides of water buffalo meat. The goons nodded, going along with the boss. The one with the camera appeared to have sorted out his technical difficulties and was now filming the scene, moving around to find the best angle to shoot from. Stapleton said to Spider, "He was your boss, is that right?"

"Past tense. Yeah. Yours, too, I gather."

"I'm sorry, what did you say?"

"He was also your boss. Zeropoint. End of Time. Fun with Vores. Dodgy woo-woo with angels. You remember!"

"He told you—"

"No, mate. You told me."

"I told you?"

"Sure. We had a big meeting."

"I don't seem to recall such a meeting. I'm pretty sure, in fact, this is the first time I've ever—"

"My past. Your future," Spider said, interrupting.

Stapleton quit fiddling with the knobbed device. It zipped back together, and he dropped it into a jacket pocket, all the while watching Spider. "What'd we talk about at this meeting?"

"Oh, well, everything. It was great! You whomped up this whole virtual environment, and you planted it in my head, see—"

"I planted something in your head…?"

"No, you will. Stay with me here, John. Now—"

"Who the hell are you, anyway"

"Look, I'm just passing through. I'm not from here."

"Nobody's from here."

"Yeah. You, for instance. Calgary, Canada. Early twenty-first century. I know."

Stapleton was clearly irritated at Spider's knowledge. "What else did I tell you?"

"Everything, mate. Bloody everything. Went on for ages, pardon my saying so."

"Why would I come and find you? I don't even know you."

"Ah, but you will eventually know me, and to know me is to love me," Spider said, and smiled.

"Let me hit him," said the goon on the left, the one without the camera.

"This is the Zeropoint flagship. We have the best security. We—"

"Don't look at me. Dickhead dialed me in. Wasn't my idea."

"Fucking Dickhead," Stapleton said.

"Yeah, I know. I couldn't agree more."

"Okay, so tell me what you know, starting with your name."

Spider's arms were getting heavy and sore. "Look, could you get your minion here to lower the bloody gun? It's a bit off-putting. Not exactly conducive to a nice chat."

Stapleton gestured; the gun went away. Spider took the hint, and sketched out the key points. "First thing, my name's Spider. Spider Webb. Yeah, I have heard that. I fix time machines for

Dickhead, or I did. Long story in itself. Broken time machine comes in, fixed time machine goes out. Rinse, repeat. One day, just recently, you came looking for me, in my time. Stuff happened, and I wound up with this D6 of yours—"

"A D6? You mean, what? A six-sided…?"

"Yeah, like you'd use for gaming. A D6."

"What was I doing with a D6 in your timeline?"

"Anyway, not an ordinary, everyday gaming random-izer. This one was also a portable drive, and had twenty-four sides. Multidimensional. Kinda nifty. Liked it when it came up blank. Oh, and it had some nano-shit on it, targeted to my DNA. Thanks for that. A lovely surprise. Turns out that what's on the portable drive in the D6 is the installer for this whack-ing great huge virtual environment you hacked together, a diner in Calgary. Nice place. Magic coffee. So I'm wandering around, and eventually come across you. We get chatting. It's nice. You tell me how you met Dickhead. One Monday night in a bar in Calgary, early 2000s. You're a frustrated, bored physics professor. Overworked. Clueless undergrads. Then this loud Australian turns up, somehow charms everyone, including you. He drugs you with something, and later you develop crazy time travel powers, and Dickhead puts the hard word on you to join up with his insane crusade here, in the future, at the actual, for-real, End of Time. You and your wife Ellen sign up — because hey, why the hell not? — and off you go. Only, you find out that Dickhead is more Jim Jones than anybody ever suspected, and pretty soon things deteriorate to such a state that he orders you to organize the poisoning of all the Zeropointers. Everybody. Millions of people. Big job. Starting with the crew of this ship, the flagship. Apparently this is called the 'ascendancy' event. Woo. Sounds like a lot of bullshit to justify mass-murder, you ask me. Since you've just murdered Dickhead, I'm guessing there's a lot of dead acolytes just outside this room, and now you're trying to decide what to do next. My big tip is this: there's about to be a shitload of heavily armed time machines coming to say g'day. You probably don't want to be here. Might be an idea to take poor old Dickhead's body with you when you go. Mind you, at the time you were telling me your story, you weren't the murderer. You guys supposedly were the conscience-stricken pacifists who couldn't hurt a tiny wittle fwy, so you rounded up your like-minded buddies and left, with Dickhead's loyal troops in hot pursuit. Cool. Big chase and running battle ensues across time. Very exciting. Is any of this sounding familiar?" He hoped it was, because his bladder was killing him, and his mouth was still dry.

Stapleton looked at Spider with interest. "I told you all of that?"

"Yeah. Talkative bloke. Like you had stuff to confess, only what you confessed was a bunch of bullshit, pardon the, um, French." He flashed a phony smile.

"Excuse me?"

"You heard me."

"And what makes you think I was — will be — lying?"

"What, apart from my standing right here while you've murdered Dickhead?"

"Why would I tell *you* all of this, bullshit or not? Why would I do that?"

"Because, moron, you want to get me on side, seeing you as, oh look, another tragic victim of evil Dickhead's megalomaniacal ways, so I will do a job for you."

"What job?"

"Long story. Involves my ex-wife."

Stapleton burst out laughing. His laughter sounded weird out here in the cold night. "Your ex-wife. Now who's bullshitting?"

"Yeah. My ex-wife. Molly."

Stapleton appeared not to be sure whether Spider was telling the truth or having a lend of him. He conferred with his goons, both of whom thought the thing to do here was simply to kill Spider and move on, because time, they said, was short. Dickhead's own goons would be on the move at any moment, and they had to get away if they were going to get away at all.

Spider, meanwhile, had begun, very slowly, taking subtle care, to edge away from the guys. Exactly how he might get out of Dickhead's Display Room, he didn't know, but he figured there was an entrance somewhere. He just had to find the edges of the room and work his way around until he found something that might be a way out. This was likely going to be complicated by Stapleton's goons, and possibly Stapleton himself, having some kind of facility with infra-red or night-vision. It stood to reason they might have such a thing, considering the way they had approached Dickhead. So, Spider thought, not much of a plan, but better than just standing here waiting for Stapleton to kill him when he was of no further use. Then there would be the additional, extra-credit, problem: once he got out into the corridors of the ship, there'd be a cold, hard vacuum. Dickhead's people had arranged to open the whole ship to space before the time marines appeared, making sure any stragglers who didn't take their poison did in fact die. This Display Room was probably the only pressurized area on the whole ship.

Stapleton turned back to him. "You're coming with us. Eric?" he said to the goon who had the gun, and gestured that Eric should secure Spider.

Eric nodded, very efficient; a huge building of a guy, and as he took a step towards Spider, Spider headbutted him, not that successfully, but well enough to put him off-balance. Spider took off, running as fast as possible across the open field; getting up a decent turn of speed despite his heavy boots and the soft soil. It was hard to see where he was going; there was no moon, and the near-infrared starlight was so weak as to be worthless. At full-tilt in pitch darkness, breathing through his mouth, his heart in his throat, banging away much too fast, Spider started to cover some serious ground. *God, the wall had to be around here somewhere.* Meanwhile, he could hear the goons and Stapleton following behind. Stapleton was calling out to him. "You might as well give up, Mr. Webb. You're in a sealed box, in total darkness. You're only going to hurt yourself." Which, Spider thought as he pelted along, gasping for breath now, his lungs starting to burn, was rich coming from him. Once they caught Spider, they'd likely kill him. So he ran on, his arms pumping, doing his best to keep his legs going, trying to keep to a straight line, reasoning that it was the quickest path to the edge of the room.

And still he couldn't find the wall. *This is getting ridiculous,* he thought, getting seriously short of breath now, wheezing, slowing down, getting a stitch in his side that hurt like mad. He did remember the time he was told that Dickhead had really great ships, millions of them, which of course was preposterous, but now Spider was starting to believe it. Previously he'd figured this Display Room was not much bigger than a large master bedroom in a house back in his own time. Instead, this place was enormous, bigger than a bloody gymnasium; it must be the size of an arena. He was slowing, just about out of breath, thinking he was one dead Spider. Thinking, they couldn't be far behind. He wished the Room was set for a bright summer's day, the way it had been last time, with thousands of triffid-like sunflowers looming everywhere. They'd be great to hide amongst.

He was thinking, knowing he was done for, of Molly, bloody Molly. *What the hell was he going to do about her?* He thought, too, of Iris, who had disappeared. *Where was she?* He realized, stopping now, leaning over, hands on his knees, gasping, that finding Iris was important, that he was more concerned about Iris than about Molly. Whatever the hell Molly was doing, it was likely her own choice. But Iris? He was responsible for her. He had to find her. He wanted to find her; he missed her, he realized. He missed her something fierce, and that gave him pause, too, the depth of his desire to get back with Iris. Behind him, not far away, he heard Stapleton and the goons coming, making no effort to sneak or conceal their movements, so he took off again, running badly, hurting, hurting all over, his chest burning, his head aching, his heart protesting. This whole plan was not going so well, and wasn't that just typical of the day he was having? Everything gone wrong. Bloody everything, and nothing sorted out. He swore to himself. Still, he thought, getting desperate now, staring ahead of him, straining to find the wall, maybe he'd find the Time Machine around here somewhere. Maybe it had crashed, and Iris might be stuck, trapped under the wreckage. Maybe, in fact—

Spider went full-tilt straight into an invisible wall. "Shit!" he cried out, hearing and feeling his nose crunch and break. Then, even as that was happening, the rest of his body hit and crumpled and he fell against the wall, sinking to his knees. "Oh fucking bloody shit!" The pain in his nose was blinding, dazzling, in the dark, so intense and bright it was as if he could see by its light. He put his hands over his face, aware of blood emerging through his nostrils, and he slumped there, back to the wall, winded, wheezing, breathing through his mouth, shaking, still feeling all that adrenaline fizzing in his blood, trying to burn off. He tried not to make too much noise as he sat there, in gigantic pain like nothing else he'd ever known, like a religious experience of acute, sticky misery.

Spider struggled back to his feet, fell back, and he tried again, his whole head now throbbing with pain, his vision spinning, but he tried to look around. Where were those bastards? He was sure they were just behind him. Meanwhile, where was he? It looked like he was still in the middle of the field. Far as he could tell, it went on forever. So what had he run into? He reached out, and yes, there it was, solidity. It felt warm. It must be a display surface illusion of some kind, because he could feel, now he took a moment, despite his heaving breath, his racing heart, under his trembling hands a surface studded with hexagonal patterns that he guessed were some kind of emitters. *Fine, who cares?* he thought to himself, and set out again, trying to run, as best he could, this time keeping his right hand against the wall, searching for some kind of exit. Behind him, he heard Stapleton and his goons. They were close now; he could hear them breathing hard. He was glad they didn't have dogs. That at least was lucky. He kept going, found a corner, and kept going, following the new surface, churning along, his face on fire, his mouth all dried out from the mouth-breathing, his teeth starting to ache now—

The wall gave way. He tumbled in a tangle into the recessed exit, landing hard on his left shoulder — felt something in the joint go *thunk* — then the side of his swollen face hit a wall or the floor, and it was like a fireworks of pain going off in his head, glittering bursts of agony, and he lay here, howling with surprise and dismay, and he tried, despite everything, to get back to his feet. The ground under him was solid, a real floor, but when he put some weight on his shoulder it, too, sent up a particularly spectacular blast of pain, and he gasped, but struggled up anyway, knowing he was in real trouble, but his feet slipped, and he toppled once more, hitting his nose.

Then, the smell of breath and sweat. Stapleton and the goons had arrived. "Mr. Webb," Stapleton said, pausing for breath. "How lovely to see you again." The voice came out from the dark. Then a boot collided with the side of Spider's head, a study in the physics of momentum, but not for Spider. He was out cold, lost to darkness.

CHAPTER 19

And, *boom*, back in the Time Machine, at the controls, in a lot of pain. Iris was sitting up on the control panel. Oh, God, his head. Hard to focus on anything. Coughing hard; taste of blood. Very little light. The pain. It was everywhere. Last thing he remembered … curled up on the floor? A moment of sickening pain-beyond-pain. And they'd arrived somewhere. The air smelled different. He could taste things, in the air, but his nose — God, everything hurt. Mostly what he could smell was blood, but that was just him, he realized only after a long, puzzling moment. The room spun. The air tasted metallic. Oily. Iris was getting down off the Machine. "Is this it?" she said. "Doesn't look very futuristic." Then she turned, saw Spider, who was starting to subside back into the dark. "Oh, God! Spider, oh my God…" He became aware, as from far away, that Iris was trying to get him out of the Time Machine, without hurting him, which was impossible. She was talking to him, reassuring him, telling him to take it easy, it was going to be fine, just hang on a bit and she'd get him out of the damned thing, and there you go, good you can stand on your own, although — oh, whoa! Okay, maybe not on your own. She helped him to the floor. You've probably got a concussion. When did this happen? Did you see what happened? God, Spider. The floor was hard and cold. He could see fuzzy red lights. Everything hurt. My God, what happened to you? You look like, God, you've just been smashed to bits here. Jesus Christ, Spider. What you need is an ambulance, and I'm pretty sure they don't have those here. Look, maybe we can get you back to our own time, do you think? No, probably not a good idea to move you again, not in this state. Okay, think, Street. Think. Let's see. Patient is breathing. Good. Very good. Blood loss not serious, not hemorrhaging. Good. Spider, you still with me? He murmured something. It was dark, and cold. He was shivering, and shivering hurt. Machinery, all kinds of wicked machinery up there, tucked away, in the ceiling, he could see it, kind of. One of his ears was a howl of piercing agony, and he wondered if he'd lost an eardrum, maybe. He wanted to hold his hand over his ear, but moving his arm … oh, God, no, that wasn't going to happen. He could hardly move that arm at all.

He was dizzy. He was barely awake. His head, the whole upper part of his body, hurt so much it felt normal, like it had always felt this way. When he went to speak, what came out sounded pathetic and stupid, and he was self-conscious, and resolved to speak no more. It embarrassed him to be like this in front of Iris. He tried to look around, but could only make out dim red lights, darkness, cables draping down out of the dark ceiling, a sense of huge, restless machines over his head. He let his head settle back against the floor. "Are you cold? Do you feel cold? Spider? Can you hear me?"

Nodding, he managed to open his mouth enough to say, "Fine. Fanks."

"What happened to you? You were fine, just a minute ago, back home, you were just fine, I saw you, you were fine!"

He shrugged as expressively as he could without killing himself with fresh waves of nausea-inducing pain.

Iris crouched there next to him. He'd never seen this side of her. She looked upset at what had happened to him. She looked, and this was a little bit frightening, even: she looked lost, confused. Working through checklists in her mind, asking him first-aid questions, testing what he could see and what he couldn't, checking his hearing, did he know who she was — of course he knew who she was! Did he know they had been in a time machine? All these questions. She examined the rest of his body, looking for signs of injury. From her examination, and the way he flinched and gasped when she touched various parts of his body, it became clear that Spider had been given a sound thrashing. Oh yeah, that's right. He remembered running in a field. Still, he was awake, more or less, fading in and out, and he could see, a little, though his eyes were mostly squeezed shut from swelling. In his mouth he could feel loose teeth, and teeth fragments. When he tried spitting them out, it only made everything hurt worse, so he considered swallowing them, revolting as the idea seemed. The best news from Iris's examination was that he could still feel his fingers and toes. His back was greatly abused, but still working. He would, in time, get over all of this.

"Help me, Spider. Promise me..." Dickhead had told him. "Avenge me," he'd said. It was funny, thinking about it, in the way that things can be bitterly funny when there's bugger-all you can do about them, when you're helpless before limitless power, when it's either laugh or cry and cut your wrists. He remembered Dickhead, how something had happened to his neck, that there had been a whooshing-swooping sound, like a skipping rope moving at full speed, followed by Dickhead's whole head, huge like Uluru, sliding sideways, not like Uluru at all. And Dickhead still aware, reaching out to Spider to tell him, to remind him, of his responsibility to "Kill John Stapleton". *Fuck, Dickhead! How the hell do you expect me to kill anybody like this?* Spider thought. *A newborn baby would have a better shot at the bastard!*

Then, two things happened, neither of them good:

The first was that the room abruptly lit up with spinning red lights, klaxons blared ocean-liner-loud — so loud he felt the fragments of his teeth vibrating in his mouth — followed by Iris staring up, wide-eyed, as the machinery in the ceiling unfolded out of the darkness — robot arms with laser-guided power tools and grabbers — and set about dismantling the Time Machine.

Iris screamed, "No! No you fucking don't! That's our way home! You — stop that!" She had her side-arm out, aimed into the guts of the darkness, held in both shaking hands. She fired once, then twice. The gun's retort rang and rang in the confined space of the room. Spider's bad ear felt like someone had driven a knife into it; the other merely felt abused. And he smelt burnt propellant. Iris frantically tried pulling the robotic arms away from the Time Machine, but was gently pushed back. A recorded voice asked her, politely, in English, to stand well back, behind the black and yellow striped line, for her own safety.

She came to Spider, knelt next to him, in tears. "I couldn't. I tried, but—" She wiped at her eyes with the heel of her hand, delicate, careful.

Spider reached out, took her free hand. It was cold. She was shaking. He squeezed, which was about all he could do. Iris did not pull away.

The second bad thing was this: some unknown time later, long after the ceiling-machines had folded back up into the seething mechanical darkness overhead, taking the parts of the Time Machine with them, a door opened, revealing John Stapleton. Iris said, "Who the hell are you?" and Spider, still fading in and out, losing all track of time, managed a brief glimpse, and recognized him. Spider tensed up, and felt unwanted adrenaline blast through his abused body, making his heart go nuts as he lay there. He tried to tell Iris who the guy was, but he couldn't speak properly, and it came out all wrong, and hurt. Stapleton looked different, Spider noticed. This time he was a tall strapping fellow, looking a far cry from the hunted, refugee figure he'd met in that virtual Calgary diner, and even a long way from the leather-clad crime lord figure he'd met in Dickhead's Display Room. This version of Stapleton was clearly older, and not in a good way, more worn, bone-tired, and was dressed in a white jumpsuit which appeared to be glowing in the low light. This, whenever this was, was clearly years and years later after Spider had last seen the murdering bastard. And, thinking that, Spider wondered if this version of Stapleton still had that invisible wire device that he had used to slice off Dickhead's enormous head.

Iris had her side-arm out and up and directed at Stapleton before Spider could so much as blink. "Stop right there," Iris said, starting to get up. She positioned herself between Stapleton and Spider.

Stapleton stopped, looked momentarily embarrassed and said, "Oh, I'm sorry," and put up his hands. "I just wanted to say hi to our newest arrivals. We've been waiting for a long time. Especially for you, Spider Webb. *The* Spider Webb. Wow!" John Stapleton seemed to relish the significance of Spider's name. "I never realized, that the first time we met, who you were, and, truly, I'm sorry about that. It was a misunderstanding. We got caught up in what we were trying to do, and it's a damn shame you got hurt like that. I'm really sorry. And of course, for you, it's like it just happened, yes? Yeah, thought so. As I say, please accept my apologies. We have a sickbay. Really, there's no time to lose. Things are getting a bit tight."

"Just who the fuck are you, again?" Iris said, still aiming the gun at Stapleton.

Stapleton looked surprised that she didn't recognize him. "Spider didn't tell you? Ah, well, I'm John Stapleton. Hi." He smiled, all charm, hands still more or less up, as he approached her. "You're Inspector Iris Street, of the Western Australian Police Service, right? I've never been to Australia, I hear it's really a lot like Canada..."

"Just stop right there." Iris said. "What happened to our time machine? Give it back, and we'll be on our way, out of your hair. No problems. No questions. Okay?"

Stapleton took another step forward as he spoke, doing his best to sound friendly, even a bit folksy. "Well, that's a bit of a problem. We need the parts. All the other time travelers who've come here, they've had to give up their machines, too. Every bit helps, you know?"

"Oh no, we're not staying. Spider needs urgent medical attention."

"Yes, and he'll get it, once you put down the gun."

Spider managed to rasp out, "*He* attacked … *me.*"

Stapleton said, "What was that?"

Iris was looking at Stapleton and at Spider, back and forth. To Spider, she said, "He did this? How could he possibly have done this? You've been with me the whole time."

"It … wath him. Thome goonth. They…"

Iris turned back to Stapleton. "Is that true? You did this to him?"

Spider was starting to drift away. His eyes felt heavy. His back hurt. He wanted to go to sleep. But somewhere in the back of his mind he knew that sleeping when concussed was not a good idea, but he wasn't sure he was concussed, not really, and in any case, he was terribly tired. He could hear Iris and Stapleton still going at it. Iris sounding more and more alarmed, but trying to hide it. Spider could hear it in her voice, and he was sure Stapleton could, too. He tried to tell Iris what had happened, but realized, after a bit, that he dreamed that part, that he had actually been asleep, so he tried to snap back awake, to shake himself out of it. Then, darkness, and torn dream fragments, and a gunshot. And he was awake. "You stupid bitch!" That was Stapleton, shouting. Iris yelling, "I told you to stay where you were and explain yourself."

Stapleton: "You fucking shot me!"

Iris: "You'll live."

Stapleton: "Jesus! You shot me!"

Spider, his good ear still ringing, and his bad ear screaming, tried to contort himself, to see what had happened. He could smell the propellant from Iris' gun. She really had shot the bastard! *Good for her!* he thought. *Plug him for me, too, would you?*

Iris: "Keep your hands where I can see them. Yes, that's it. Now. Some straight answers."

Stapleton: "I'm bleeding out here."

Iris: "Is there someone I could call for you?"

Spider thought she sounded hesitant there, nervous. The situation going out of control. He imagined Iris cursing herself for shooting the guy. Stapleton said something Spider didn't catch. For what seemed only a moment Spider blacked out again, during which he experienced a sensation of movement, of being swept along. There was a voice muttering something about "BP". He thought he heard Iris say "Hang in there, Spider. Just hang in a little longer. Come on, mate. Make us an effort". He also, and he was sure he was dreaming at this point, the sort of dream where you know perfectly well you're in a dream, and you can sit back, inside the dream, and watch the craziness unfurl around you, he thought he heard Iris tell him, "Come on, Spider. I love you, okay? You got me to say it. I swore I would never say it. But, God, come on, mate. Come back to me. It's been over a week now. I love you, I love you, I love you!" Yes, that was some strange dream he was having. Iris, he knew, would never say something as sentimental as "I love you". She wasn't that kind of woman. Even when they had their brief affair, those words had never entered into it. He had almost said it once, he remembered, in the so-called "throes of passion", but held back, because he knew it would only piss her off, and he didn't want that. At the time, though, he'd believed it, and felt it. Molly had been "difficult", stuck on a commission project that wasn't going anywhere, and the block was making her crazy. Even when he was home, she was almost always off in her studio, swearing, throwing things round, swearing some more. It was hard. She'd go to bed early, sleep badly, toss and turn, get up in the wee hours to go and throw stuff around some more, swearing something awful, always in clear, ringing tones that only emphasized the foulness.

So, yes, Iris telling him she loved him. Clearly a dream. But she'd said something else, hadn't she? Just then. What was that she'd said? He tried, from inside the dream, to rewind and listen again, and yes, there it was. She'd said, "…it's been weeks now." *Weeks*? What? Only a moment ago he'd been lying on the floor and the Time Machine had been taken apart, and Iris shot bloody Stapleton — yay, Iris! — and now it's weeks later? That didn't make a speck of sense. She must be mistaken. Then again, it was a dream. Of course, when you're in a dream, everything makes perfect sense. Yes, of course you'd be bobbing for apples with the British Prime Minister; doesn't everybody? Only when you wake up and you think about it, and you realize, and you go, "What the hell?"

In any case, Spider thought it might be wise to try and wake up now. He was in control of this whole thing, so getting his body to wake up should be easy. Here we go, on the count of three, one, two, three, and wake!

Nothing. Nothing at all. He had a faint sense of Iris sitting there with him, talking to him, reading to him, telling him things about her life here in Colditz. Something about working on repairing a crashed timeship. She knew nothing much about chronotechnology, just what she needed to know in order to do her job in the Time Crime Unit back home, but she could work out plans of action, delegate jobs, prioritize manpower, work out schedules and timetables, and she was a whiz with project management. She told him one day that John Stapleton "wasn't such a bad old stick once you got to know him a bit." And it was "such a shame about his wife". Which, when Spider heard it, he hardly took any notice. Spider at that point was a long way from anywhere, arguing with Dickhead about some damn thing, and he heard Iris as if from a great, echoing distance. Even so, he put Dickhead on hold, and paid closer attention. Iris was talking about John Stapleton, who wasn't such a bad old stick … Iris? At that point Spider began to think about things. He'd been wandering around in the wilderness of his unconsciousness for quite some time, it seemed to him. Dickhead aside, it was lonely, and strange. And now Iris was getting cozy with Stapleton? All at once he felt himself banging on the underside of an ice floe, struggling to breathe, trying to get someone out in the world to see him, struggling to get out of his own useless head.

And so it went. Iris came to see him every chance she had. She talked about the ship repairs. It seemed the ship's massive time engines might well be stuffed; something about trying to restart the magnetic containment for the singularities. The prospect of getting the whole ship running again, leaping about in time, was receding. Repair efforts were shifting to the construction of, maybe, a reusable lifeboat sort of thing. He heard Iris tell him one day, "We could really use your help here, Spider. Everyone's pretty much had it. John's got us working round the clock, and if that's not bad enough, there's that Vore thing you told me about. I don't exactly know what he's doing to it, but you can feel it howling when you sleep. We hardly ever see John these days. He's always doing something with the trap controls, God knows. Are you getting it, locked away in there?" He was right there, pounding against the ice; the ice seemed so thin. It was as if he could see the room; his eyes must be a bit open. Now that he concentrated, he could see dim light, shapes, then something that must be Iris' face. It was hard to tell, but it looked like her hair was longer. In any case, it looked as though there was a lot more of it than there had been. That shocked him, seeing that, no matter how imperfectly. How long had he been here, under the ice, in this place? Surely his body must be healed by now? He could not tell, and he certainly had no motor control as far as he could determine. Iris was talking to him again, very close to his face, right by his ear. "Spider, come on. We're dying out here. Power's going. The winter is closing in. We can only use five percent of the ship, it's too expensive to heat. We really need you. God, I need you, Spider. God, listen to me, how pathetic am I, going on like that. Me, a fully-grown police inspector, 'needing' a man — I'm a bloody disgrace to the sisterhood, but I can't fight how I feel, can I? It's hard out here. John's crew, the ones who worked you over, are working us hard, double-shifts every day, trying to restore power, restore the time engines, life support. When you look out the windows, it's — what's the word for something between beautiful and terrifying? It's like that. I run the project schedule, and I can tell you, we're way behind. Estimated time to a complete energy failure versus estimated time to system resuscitation? Not looking good for us. Did I mention the food's shit, literally, recycled. It's lovely, thinking about that every time you eat or drink your rations. I know we have recycled water back home, but this stuff has a texture even you wouldn't like. Water really ought not to have texture. Grittiness. Things that get stuck in your teeth. The other time machine geeks— which reminds me, I've met the kids, the children you were looking for? Vijay and Phoebe? They're nineteen years old now. Looks like they're planning some kind of family, 'once they're back home,' of course. You'll have to imagine me doing the air-quotes there. They're nice. I don't understand a word they say. Advanced time theory. Oh joy of joys. Beyond my poor addled brain, that's for sure..."

He wasn't sure what else Iris said. He was off dreaming again, no longer trying to punch through the thin ice that separated him from the outside world, lost down in the dark deeps, somehow able to breathe underwater. He heard a voice calling to him, from further down. He figured out how to dive, the pressure of the cold dark pushing against his ears, and he could easily make out the seaweed-draped figure of a naked woman with no eyes, hair swirling and tangled around her head. As he maneuvered closer, he saw it was Molly, snared in sea-wrack and long strands of kelp, her skin, even in this darkness, seemed to glow, but not in a good way. He tried to pull back from her, but she managed to snag his foot in seaweed, and pull him closer.

"Al, you're here. Thank God. You have to help me." It sounded like Molly. It had Molly's voice. Though, as he drew near, he could see her mouth wasn't moving; the voice he heard was in his head, with him. He tried and tried to get away, but she kept pulling at him. Now he could see her eye-sockets, like small fleshy mouths, themselves (he imagined, in the dark) lined with sharp teeth.

"I'll help you, but you have to let me—"

"Come closer, Al. I need you to do a little job for me. Can you do that for me, Al?" She had hold of his head now, and they were face to face, down in the deep. He shivered and shook. With growing amazement, he realized she was going to kiss him. And the horrible thing was, he liked the idea, and he wanted to kiss her, too. There was no way this was Molly, his Molly, but, maybe, in his mind, it was close enough. He'd always wanted Molly, even during the worst times, but now, yes, even like this, he still wanted her. They kissed, embraced, bound together with long cold strands of kelp. She told him, inside his mind, that he had to get Stapleton to stop torturing the Vore. She and the Vore had become an item. "The Vore is howling in pain. Can't you hear it? It's screaming across the universe. And there are other Vores coming to help it. They'll be here soon, and they will liberate it, and destroy everything around it. They'll destroy me, Al, because now I'm part of it. It's up to you. You have to stop Stapleton. You have to get him to release us, no matter what it takes. I'm counting on you." She reached down with one of her weed-draped hands to touch him, to take hold of him—

Spider snapped awake, blinded by the room's light, silently screaming, his mouth dry, voice hoarse; throat burning. He tried to get up, but was weak, almost helpless, covered in stick-on sensor pads. He tried to move, and fell off the bed, and tumbled onto the cold steel floor, still feeling Molly's tendrils wrapped around and around him, binding the two of them together in the cold abyssal darkness at the floor of his conscious mind.

CHAPTER 20

Spider managed to get up, climbing the structure of the bed. It was hard, and he was weak, but much of the pain he remembered was gone. At last, he got back onto the bed, exhausted, breathing hard, clutching at his chest. Remembering Molly. "The Vores are coming," she had said. "Bloody Hell."

Looking around, he took in the salient details of his "room". He and the bed were in what looked like a utility storage room. There was room for the bed, a chair, and not much else. The door was open. He could hear noises from beyond, and saw people rushing about, all of them in shapeless blue overalls, all of them thin, even emaciated, carrying things, pushing trolleys. There was a constant industrial din in the background, and there was a voice talking over some kind of public address system, but softly. It took him a moment to recognize that it was Stapleton's voice, but he couldn't quite make out what the guy was saying, only that he was saying it a lot. Spider, who realized he was hungry, his stomach growling and dyspeptic, tried calling out to the passersby. "Hey, I'm awake! I'm up! I need a little help. Hello?" This got him nowhere. His voice was weak. Swearing, he slid off the bed, taking his time, doing his best to hang on for support. His legs almost went out from under him, and he gasped, trembling, standing there, clutching at the bed frame. The bed, he noticed, had been cobbled together from stray bits of steel. The whole thing could have collapsed out from under him at any moment.

Disconnecting himself from the monitor leads, Spider shuffled out the door into a long, drafty corridor, and propped himself against a wall, breathing hard, sweating. Someone came up to him, a nurse. "Mr. Webb! I was just coming to—"

"I appear to be up," Spider gasped, and felt exhausted. His knees shook.

The nurse helped him back to his bed, checked him out, examined his eyes, waved fingers about, asked how he was feeling, if he knew who he was, and if he knew where he was. "Yeah." He stared at her, annoyed. "This is 'Colditz', isn't it?"

The nurse winced at the name. "That's what the geeks call it, yes," she said.

"Look, I need to see my ex-wife, Molly Webb. She's here, right?"

This appeared to surprise the nurse. "She *is* here. She arrived with everyone else."

This interested him, despite the state he was in. "Let me guess. She was none too pleased."

The nurse allowed herself a small smile. "She said she thought she was going to the Louvre. Something about an exhibit?"

"Right. Good. Can you please tell her I'd like to see her."

"Okay. Um. Will do. Is there *anyone else* you'd like to see?" The nurse leaned on the "anyone else", as if trying to give Spider a hint.

Spider still remembered his dream, could still taste Molly's mouth. *The Vores are coming.* "Well, yeah, now you mention it. I need a word with John Stapleton. Got a bit of unfinished business I need to discuss with him, you know, if he's free."

"You want to speak to John Stapleton?"

"Yeah. He's an old pal."

"*The* John Stapleton."

Spider was baffled. "The Canadian physicist bloke. Big fella. Tall. Got a stupid little beard thing. Last I heard he was your Big Cheese around here. That's him on the PA all the time, isn't it?"

"He's busy with the Guest, Mr. Webb, but I will pass a message up through channels. He has been inquiring after you, while you—"

"How long was I out?"

"Thirty-four days."

Thirty-four days? He looked down at himself. Other than understandable weakness from being bedridden, he seemed okay, if a bit thin.

"Yes."

"But I'd been beaten to a pulp."

The nurse did her best to provide a smile. "There was nothing serious."

Spider flexed his fingers and toes, touched parts of his head and his teeth. "Nothing serious?" He was sure he remembered John Stapleton's goons tracking him down, and kicking him senseless. That was right, wasn't it? He didn't dream that, did he? He remembered being in the Time Machine, with Iris up on the "handlebars" just in front of the status lights on the control panel, and he remembered pushing the lever forward to start the Machine off on its leap into the future, but after that, things got a little murky. Something about Dickhead, and vengeance. Such a strange word, that, "vengeance". Like something people did in old movies. And there was Stapleton himself, and... He struggled to recall anything. Something about running through a field, in the dark? Spider shook his head, as if that would clear out some cobwebs. While he couldn't, at least right now, remember any clear details about this so-called beating that he mentioned to the nurse, something about it sounded right. And he had been out of it for, what, more than a month? Or at least that's what she was telling him. For a moment he did stop and look around, taking in the cramped surroundings, that droning voice in the background he could not quite hear clearly, the cold-ness, the smell of something not quite right, something stale in the air.

The nurse brought him a steel bowl full of a dreadful cereal-based gruel, body-heat-warm, and a steel cup half full of room-temperature water. The cereal glop had a mouth-feel something like melted ice-cream, but there was a hint of some 'texture', he thought, a grittiness, a sensation he associated with broken dental fillings in his mouth, and he remembered Iris talking to him, while he was out, telling him about this stuff. Putting the thing together with the memory helped make it real, and helped make those memories of Iris telling him stuff real, as well. He began to feel more "here", wherever here was. He hadn't been dreaming; he'd been awake, just not fully conscious. He could remember a fair amount of what Iris told him. They were on a crashed timeship. Engines stuffed. Winter closing in. Only five percent of the ship in use. Right. Everybody buggered from working round the clock. Yes, he thought, looking around. That made sense. He looked at the food, and the water, nodding to himself. And the water! He tried some, hoping to get that grit out of his mouth, but it had a smell to it that reminded him of the urinals in his old primary school boys' toilets. Not that it smelled like urine, or even stale urine, but there was something in the water's smell that caused his mind to leap to this image. He imagined the nurse telling him he'd get used to it.

Then, a knocking at his open door.

"Iris!" he said, delighted to see her, and waved her in.

They swapped greetings, tried with great embarrassing awkwardness and elbows to hug — neither Spider nor Iris had ever been huggers, much — and Iris finally settled for kissing Spider on his grizzled cheek, close to his mouth. Astonished, his cheek burning, he looked up at her, and saw Iris blushing, then looking away for a moment, hands over her face, swearing under her breath. After an awkward moment, Iris got him to shift over in his narrow bed, and she hopped up and perched on the side of it. She sat there, smiling at him, smiling like sunrise, and he felt a great warmth filling his heart that he had not felt in... He could not remember when he last felt like that. His cheek tingled. He smiled back at her, unable to help himself. It was lovely to see Iris, even if she looked terrible: lean, hungry, dark rings under her tired eyes.

"So how are they treating you?" she said to cover the moment of embarrassment.

"Good. No worries. Of course, I've been out cold most of the time, so I have no idea, really—"

She turned back to him, looked at him, and her stoic mask dropped away. She said, "God I'm glad to see you awake."

"Um, it's great to see you, too," he said, even though he kept thinking about how it felt kissing the Molly-thing.

"I thought you were gonna die on me," she said.

"I wasn't going to die, Iris."

"You were gone so long. The ship's medic, Jameson, he was telling me not to get my hopes up. He said if you were going to come out of it, you would have after just a few days. The longer it went, the less likely..." She stopped, and discreetly dabbed at her eyes with the heel of her hand.

"I was right here the whole time."

"Yes, but you—"

"I remember you talking to me," he said, by way of changing an awkward subject. It was upsetting seeing Iris like this, so not in control and not brimming with her usual brisk and daunting confidence. That in itself told him everything he needed to know about the sheer grinding awfulness of the situation here in Colditz. It scared him, but he wasn't about to let on to Iris that he felt that way.

"You remember that?"

"Sure, at least some of it."

"Really?"

"Yeah. You talked about the ship, and John, things being shit, all kinds of stuff. I thought I was dreaming."

"Silly Spider!"

"I remember looking forward to your visits."

"Oh, God," she said, hands over her face again. "You remember everything I said to you?"

"I don't know. There was a lot of stuff, and I was fading in and out, you know…" He was lying. Spider remembered Iris telling him she loved him. He remembered her pleading with him to come back to her. And, looking at her, he wished he had been here for her.

"I'm sure you hallucinated a lot of it," she said. "I wasn't here all that much. I've been busy."

"Oh, I know. Of course. Lots to do."

"That's right," Iris said, nodding, as if she couldn't run far enough from those moments of weakness when she confessed things she wanted kept hidden.

"I understand, Iris," he said, intending multiple meanings.

She allowed him a small smile, as if accepting his gracious exit. "No worries."

There was one small problem: just as he remembered Iris' visits, he also remembered Molly, or at least the Molly-thing, down in the deepest ocean trenches of his mind, calling to him, enfolding him against her cold body, telling him about the Vore, that it was in pain, and its buddies were coming to "liberate" it. "Iris," he said, feeling awkward, knowing this would not go over well.

"Spider," she said, looking glad for a change of topic.

"I gather Molly's here. Yes?"

"Molly? Your Molly?" She looked confused for a moment. "Yes, of course. She's been asleep almost since she got here, more or less like you. Can't get her out of bed, won't do a bloody thing to help out. Just lies there, talking in her sleep. A pain in the arse."

"She turned up with all the other time travelers?"

"It was a side-effect of the system John and his people used to capture the Vore's worldline. Future-bound time travelers, anywhere on Earth, departing between the two threshold dates, and who happened to be between, wait a minute; let me get this right..." She thought a moment. "Yeah. Between point-of-origin and destination, while the thing was running, all their world-lines intersected here, so all kinds of folks, but mostly hotrod geeks, they all turned up, all at once, along with the Guest. You'd be surprised how many time travelers got caught. Anyway, the Guest was shunted into its 'quarters', and everybody else, well, we all did our best to fit in. John's crew, the few who were left, did what they could to make us comfortable. Wasn't easy, what with the lack of power, resources, the endless freezing hell outside, the food situation inside — and of course, you two snoozing away, needing constant care."

Spider felt mortified, thinking about it, but put that aside. "Okay, about Molly. I need to see her."

Iris did not look pleased, but put her best professional face on. "You can see her, sure, but, you know, she's—"

"Asleep? I know. Thing is, she spoke to me, while I was out."

"She did? How the hell did she do that?"

"That's what I need to find out. I need to find out if she was just dreaming, in which case what she said is just dream-bullshit, or whether she was telling me something that needs addressing."

"What'd she tell you?"

"She told me the Vores are coming."

"Oh. Shit," Iris said.

"So, can you, um...?"

Iris rounded up a makeshift wheelchair that had been built in case either Molly or Spider couldn't walk properly once they woke up. Spider thought he didn't need it, that he could get around just fine, but in practice he was able only to walk about four steps, and then had to stop and get his breath back, preferably while sitting. He put up with the wheelchair.

As Iris propelled him along through cramped, low corridors, often so narrow that only one person could pass at a time, and frequently so cold that he was grateful she had brought a blanket from his bed.

Iris said, "Did she give you any kind of timeline for their arrival? Like a time and a date? Some sign we might look for?"

"No, nothing. That's what I need to find out."

"How bad could it be?"

"Bad."

"Great. Fucking great. Like we haven't got enough to worry about."

When they reached Molly's room, Iris wheeled him up to her bed, and asked if he wanted some time alone, to talk to her, but she left before he could answer — for a long moment he found he could not speak: just seeing Molly unconscious, lying, tense, under enormous pressure, in bed, hardly breathing, so shrunken, her whole face screwed up hard, as if to keep out something horrible, or as if she were in terrifying pain... It was harder to see her this way than he'd expected. He could not look away. Iris, waiting for him outside, was forgotten. Molly lay there, in the grip of something dreadful, from which she could not escape. Spider stared and stared at his sort-of ex-wife. He remembered how he had once, a long time ago, found her at the End of Time on Dickhead's flagship, pale and apparently frozen and dead like all the others, and how that had felt, the wrenching guilt, the wanting for things to have been different, for Molly to have been left out of the whole thing. And she had forgotten it all, once she came back to him. Dickhead, somehow, had fixed things with his magical timeline manipulations. All Molly had been left with was that terrible arthritis, and frustrating dreams of pain and anger that, awake, she could never articulate, and tried instead to express it in her work, all these wretched partial creatures, bent over, shivering with agony. Spider hated seeing them, knowing what Molly did not, knowing what really had happened to her. And now here he was again, a vile circle complete. Molly before him, close enough to touch, cold, her mind filling with the Vore's presence, like a monstrous file downloading from a remote server, all checksums complete. What would happen when the Vore was finished? Spider wondered, looking at her, wishing he could take it for her. He already had experience with things getting injected into his head. He could take it. It would be okay. But Molly? This was not her battle. She did not deserve whatever it was that was happening to her, deep within the vault of her own lonely mind. Spider sat there, shaking his head, trying to keep from weeping, and not having much luck. Wiping his eyes on his arm, he maneuvered his chair over closer so he could reach out to her, and touch her face — and she flinched. "Oh, shit," he said, startled, and pulled back, eyes wide, staring. "Sorry, Moll," he said. The last thing she needed was for him to be adding to whatever was going on in there. So he sat there, and wondered when he'd last touched her face, but couldn't remember. All he could remember was Molly yelling at him, telling him he was useless, but still wanting him to mow her backyard, or paint her fence, or, good grief, look after her sick goldfish while she went to New York. And hadn't that worked out well? "Geez, Moll," he said, hardly able to speak. "What have you done now?" He remembered hearing from Stéphane Grey about Molly's adventure in New York, and her meeting with, he assumed, a future version of herself, luring her into the wild beyond. Why would Molly have gone along with that? Molly's idea of using time travel was to make sure she had set the timers on her lawn reticulation; she wasn't inclined to go off on grand adventures. She had too much work to get through, grants to apply for, meetings with potential clients to go to. That nurse had mentioned to him that Molly had said she thought she was blipping off to a visit to the Louvre, and instead wound up here.

Then, Molly was speaking to him. "Al," she said, her voice coming from far away. She rotated her head, opened her eyes, and looked at him, only this was the Deep Sea Molly, the Molly-thing from his dreams, the one with the gouged-out eye-sockets, like hungry mouths, shadowed and cold, staring at him. "You're running out of time. It's almost finished moving into my mind. Not long now. If you're going to help me, if you're going to get off your comfortable arse for once, you have to do it now. Do you understand me? Can you hear me? Al?"

Electrified, shaking, cold all the way through, Spider sat there, unable to move, staring and staring into those gaping, bottomless sockets. "Moll, I-I'm here. I heard, but I don't—"

Then, a new voice, male, booming, right behind him. "Hey, Spider! There you are!"

Spider jumped, yelling, clutching his chest, almost falling out of the wheelchair. Turning, he saw John Stapleton, in those same white overalls, picture of a man who'd lost his way, just barely this side of nuts — Spider had seen that look before, and not just on Dickhead. Spider remembered attending the scenes of domestic disputes, back in his days as a copper, turning up, and finding strung-out housemates, wasted on meth, or psychotic from too much dope, with kitchen knives, holding his or her other housemates at bay, screaming abuse at them, telling them to keep back, or else, you understand, or else! People who'd been awake, for days or weeks, well past their own mental use-by date. Stapleton looked like that, but he was trying, hard as he could, to conceal it, even from himself. He remembered Iris saying something, while he'd been out of it, that Stapleton had been spending all his time with "the Guest", trying to commune with it, to coax

out that Final Bloody Secret of the Cosmos, tuning the confinement field of the trap to hurt the Vore, to make it talk. Iris had
told him nobody saw Stapleton much. Day-to-day operations in
the timeship were left to his few remaining followers, who in
turn bossed about the surviving time machine geeks and the
others who'd been swept up along with the Guest.

"John," Spider said, once he'd put together his shattered
composure once more. "Good to see you again. See you've recov-
ered from that gunshot." Spider did not trust Stapleton. In his
mind he saw, by starlight, Dickhead's head starting to slide away
from his blood-spurting neck, and noted the look of fevered
hatred on Stapleton's face as he did it, as he saw the results of
it, watching the blood; watching the head. He remembered
Stapleton taking the head before it fell to the ground, and holding it up, intending to show it off like a hunting trophy, like
something he'd won after a long battle. "See the mighty hunter,
triumphant at last!" Except the head vanished, after a final, discreet wink at Spider, leaving Spider with the command to "kill
Stapleton".

Stapleton flexed the leg that Iris shot, and Spider could see it
wasn't quite right. "Yeah, good as new. Nothing to worry about.
Bit of a graze. Iris and me, we're buds now, no problem. The
whole thing was a misunderstanding. I should've realized at the
time."

"Oh, good," Spider said, "I'm so glad you guys are buds now."

Stapleton confected a smile. "Yeah. So, you're back in the land
of the living yourself at long last. That's great! I hear the tech
guys could use your expertise," he said, pronouncing "expertise"
with a hard "s" sound, rather than the more familiar "z" sound
Spider would have used.

"I'm no engineer, you realize. I just—"

"Of course, obviously."

"There's a limit to what I can do. Domestic time machines?
Yeah, no worries. The time engines on a ship like this? I dunno."

"Yeah. I know. It's okay. We have help files."

For a crazy bastard with messianic dreams of acquiring the
most sought-after nugget of information in the universe, no
matter what it took to get it, Stapleton seemed surprisingly laid-
back about it. He was putting up a great front. The man went
on. "I've scheduled a tech briefing for you later this evening. Just
to go over the current situation, where we're at, things we've
tried; options we're still looking at. Get you up to speed fast as
possible."

"Oh, good," Spider said, thrilled at the prospect and thinking if it involved PowerPoint slides, he might just shoot himself.

Meanwhile, Spider noticed that while Stapleton was standing there, towering over him in his white jumpsuit, he was watching Molly, as if waiting for something to happen, and worried about what it might be. It occurred to him that maybe Stapleton knew what was going on between her and the Vore. But if he knew what was happening, why hadn't he stopped it? More to the point, how had some earlier self of his failed to warn him it would happen? Surely... Spider lost track of his thinking when he saw Molly. Her face was as it had been before, scrunched up, as if with great pain and internal torment, as if fighting something, and losing the battle. God, Molly, he thought. Then he had a closer look. Her eyes looked, for all that her face was all screwed up, like there were *normal* eyes staring out from under normal eyelids. There was no sign of the Molly-thing that had spoken to him, that had warned him *"You have to stop John tormenting the Vore."* The Vores were coming to the rescue and to lay waste to everything they found in their way. Things that ate space and time, that ate the stuff of the universe itself. It occurred to him that he had never found out just what kind of creatures or things these Vores actually were. Were they monsters? Were they insanely intelligent aliens, plotting the destruction of the universe, or what?

"Mind if I ask you something, John?" he said, as if unconcerned about anything at all — just a guy shooting the breeze.

"Sure, anything," Stapleton said. His eyes looking like broken glass.

"Why the hell is Molly even here? What's with that?"

Stapleton looked, for a fractional moment, like he was going to snap, and show something of his true face, but he pulled back. "Damned if I know, to tell you the God's honest truth. I think she was doing a time-jump and got caught in the worldline driftnet—"

"This Guest everyone keeps mentioning..."

"Yes?"

"It's a Vore, right?"

Stapleton appeared surprised at Spider's information. He thought a moment. "You know about the Vores? Who—"

"Dickhead. Dickhead McMahon? My former employer and personal nightmare? Big head, cheap suits, obsession with keypoint indicators and the end of the universe itself. He told me all about 'em. Angelly thingies out to burn down the universe, because God wanted to start over, get it right this time."

"Ah, I see. You believe him?"

"About what? Vores as such, or the whole angel thing?"

"The angel thing."

"Fuck, no," Spider said, and managed a convincing skeptical laugh. That crazy Dickhead and his wacky ideas!

Stapleton managed a laugh, too, though it looked like it hurt him. He was lost in his own brittle thoughts for a long, cold moment, and Spider remembered him killing the bastard. "Good old Dickhead, eh? He and I met—"

"I know how you met. Calgary bar. Hockey night in Canada on the telly."

Stapleton went pale. "Oh, right. Yeah. You said that, that night, on *Destiny*."

"Yeah. The night you murdered Dickhead. The night you did your fucking best to kill me, too."

"Hey, now wait just a minute there, Spider. I apologized for that. That was a misunderstanding. That—"

Spider nearly laughed. "A misunderstanding? You and your mates nearly kicked me to death!"

"It was a bad time for all of us—"

"I know! I was bloody well there. Twice! I saw the bodies, the ship's crew, all dead and frozen. I had to dig my wife, yes, *her*, right there, her, Molly Webb, I had to dig her out of a pile of frozen corpses. You know what that's like, John? Can you imagine what that might be like, sorting through corpses?"

"Spider, I'm really sorry, I am, it's just—"

"Yeah. You're really sorry. Me, too, mate. Me, too. Oh, and here's a memo: that D6 of yours? You filled up my head with all this nano-shit, just so you and I could have that little chat in the diner, aw, poor old Canadian me, misunderstood Dickhead victim, poor, poor me, waaah! Sometime, when you can manage it, I'd love it if you could get someone to remove that shit from my head, thanks."

"Spider, we will absolutely see to that, no problem. Just as soon—"

"Mate, don't give me 'soon', okay? I have it on good authority that your time is up. You're finished. You know that Vore you've got on ice downstairs in the basement? The one you've been torturing all these years? Yeah, its mates are coming. They're coming here as we speak. Express delivery. And they're gonna burn all of this, and all of us, down to the ground."

At this, Stapleton stared down at Spider, and by the look on his face, Spider figured the guy had just concluded that Spider clearly needed his medication, because he was nuts. Stapleton said, "Oh, I see."

"You don't believe me?"

"Sure I believe you, Spider. Sure I do. Why wouldn't I?"

Spider hated being patronized, but he could see the guy's point. Where was Spider getting this information? On what evidence did he base this outrageous claim? The Vores are coming! Oooooh, scary! Yes, it sounded crazy. And the fact that Spider had been told this by Molly, who right this minute was away with the fairies, and had been for a long time, did not exactly bolster the credibility of his case. Spider was, he knew, one of those old guys who stands near traffic lights with big placards proclaiming "The End is Nigh'" and "Repent Now, Sinners". And until such time as the Vore cavalry arrived, Spider was screwed. He'd blown it. Looking up at Stapleton, he saw that his captor now looked very much like a man who'd won something. He stood taller, looked confident. He looked like someone ready to go about his business, leaving Spider to it.

"Well, if that's everything, Spider, I do have a busted time-ship to fix."

Spider considered his position. The fight had gone out of him. He was exhausted, and sagged in the wheelchair. "You mentioned a tech briefing later tonight?"

"Yeah. That's right. Just a brief overview."

Nodding, Spider said, "Okay. I'll be there."

"Unless the Vores come and kill us all, of course," Stapleton said, and laughed, shaking his head, amused. He turned to leave.

That, Spider thought, was uncalled-for. The bastard had won the day, left his opponent on the field of battle, lame and bleeding. There was no need to get in one last stab for good measure. Watching Stapleton leaving the room, still giggling a little, Spider called after him, "You've been interrogating that Guest of yours for ages, haven't you?"

Stapleton paused in the doorway, turned halfway, glanced back at Spider. "Eight years, give or take."

"And so far, bugger all, right?"

"It's taken longer than I thought it would to establish the right level of tuning for the containment fields, but I'm—"

"Eight years. Eight long years. Eight years of sitting down there, working the controls, trying this, trying that, trying every damn thing you can think of, burning up God only knows how much power that you might otherwise have used to get your ship going again, or maybe just provide your crew with decent living conditions, something better than food that tastes like liquid shit and water that smells like urinal cakes—"

"You going somewhere with this, Spider, or can we just take it as read that you're a bit cranky today?"

"What makes you think that Vore thing is even conscious, in any way? Huh? How do you know it's got language? Sure it might know the elusive Final Secret Blah Blah, but could it tell you even if it wanted to? How do you know it's not basically just some kind of dumb animal, or maybe even some kind of bug, or an insect, like maybe a tick? When Dickhead first told me about the Vores, they kinda sounded like ticks, I thought, stuck in the skin of the universe. How do you know there's anything in there at all? How do you know there even is a Final Secret? Suppose it's just some shit Dickhead dreamed up—"

"There *is* a Final Secret, Spider," Stapleton said, again patronizing him, giving him that tone in his voice, that I-know-best vibe that Spider hated more than just about anything.

"There is? You sure?"

"Yes, I'm sure."

"How sure?"

"I spent eight years on this. I know it's there. I just haven't—"

"Haven't found quite the right way to inflict pain and suffering on this creature you've got downstairs?"

"I have to tell you, Spider, as a man of science, I do resent this assertion of yours that I'm torturing it."

"Oooh, man of science!"

"I'm not a torturer."

"No, 'course not. Silly me."

"That's right."

"So what is it you've been doing down there all this time, until the wee hours, every day, causing the thing to scream and howl in everyone's sleep?"

"I'm just attempting to find a mutual communications modality—"

"Ooooh, modality!"

"Stop that now."

"Stop what?"

"Stop mocking me."

"What else should I do?"

"You could be damned grateful I saved your useless life, grateful that I allocated valuable and scarce resources to healing you — and for caring for your useless wife, someone who has absolutely no value to our community here, who is worthless…" Stapleton was watching Spider as he was saying this, watching the way the blood drained from Spider's face, the way his hands gripped the arms of his chair white-knuckle tight, the way he stared back at Stapleton, fire in his eyes. "Yes, Spider? Something you want to say before I head off to go about my business keeping your ass alive?"

"Yes, actually. Thanks, by the way, for fixing me up after trying to kill me. Much appreciated. Jolly decent," he said, but before Stapleton could speak, Spider continued. "About my ex-wife here. Molly. Her name is Molly. She's an artist. Back home, that is. A sculptor. She's pretty good. And yes, not much of a contributor to your little project here, that would be true. Even if she wasn't asleep, and about that more in a minute, there wouldn't be much she could do for you, except maybe make coffee with a certain passive-aggressive manner. That's not the point, though. The point is Molly has no business being here. She's here by mistake, John. She's here because she met a future version of herself who lured her into making a jump in time, and in doing so she got scooped up in your little cross-time driftnet."

"I know you've got a point in there somewhere," Stapleton said.

"The point is this: you want me to work for you, you treat her with respect. She's not a parasite soaking up your terribly precious resources. She's my wife, still, technically, and you talk to me about her the way you just talked about her, I'll punch your fucking lights out." Spider was out of his wheelchair. He was taking cautious, crazy steps towards Stapleton. His legs felt like they would collapse out from under him at any moment, and the adrenaline was surging through him, and he could feel his booming heart in his ears. He was right on the red-line of what he could possibly do, taking a giant risk.

Stapleton looked at Spider dismissively. He snorted, and began to turn away again. Spider said, "Awfully sorry to hear about your wife, by the way."

That got the man's attention. His head snapped back towards Spider. "I beg your pardon?"

"You said you lost her."

"I said what?"

"Yeah, it was back when you were telling me how you and your ragtag group of conscientious objectors to Dickhead's mass-murder campaign — sorry, the 'ascendancy program'

— up and fled, rather than carry out Dickhead's orders. You told me how you guys ran off from the End of Time, hurtling into the past, and Dickhead's minions, the loyalists, gave chase. Sounded terribly exciting. Except for losing Ellen, of course. That had to really suck."

Hearing that last bit, Stapleton went pale, stricken, showing a glimpse of his true, fried, self. The interior Stapleton who was hanging on by his bitten-back fingernails, who was obsessed with the damned Vore in the basement, with the promise of the power he could access if only he had that Final Secret of the Cosmos. Spider saw all this flicker over the guy's face, and it wasn't pretty. And that whole chatty, friendly mask was starting to crumble. "*I* told *you* about Ellen?" His contempt for Spider could not have been plainer.

"Yeah, you told me all about it at the diner. Real shame." Spider shook his head, all sympathetic. Spider could smell Stapleton now, the pain and the desperation, the longing, the cracking eggshell of his mind.

"It was… It was an accident," Stapleton said, shaken to his marrow, withdrawing into himself.

"You think Ellen would want to see you torturing the Vore, John?"

"I'M NOT A TORTURER," he said.

"I don't see why not," Spider said, smooth and calm. "You're already a murderer. The way you killed Dickhead. That was something. You remember that night on Dickhead's ship?"

"He wanted us to kill everyone."

"You said Dickhead told you it had to look, how'd you put it, 'inviting'."

The man stood there, clutching at his head, eyes squeezed closed, rocking a little, Spider noticed. "He had to make way," Stapleton said.

"Yeah, 'cause you figured there was no need to wait for the end of the universe to get your special magical treat from the Vores when you could just go and bag one right now and torture it into telling you everything, eh?"

"I — That's not how it was!"

"You know, Dickhead's head wound up in my fridge, at work? Did you know that, John?"

"No, I, er, you, oh God," he said, struggling for composure now, and beginning to lose the fight.

"Dickhead was a right bastard, a tyrant, a bad husband, and a pain in the arse in every way, but he'd never harm a helpless creature. Unless of course he drove over it in his Hummer, but generally, no. He told me stories about rescuing spiders from his shower cubicle. Funny bloke."

"He was a monster. He had to go!"

"But you could just have waited with him, up there at the End of Time in your mountain fastness, all you Zeropoint people. The Final Secret was coming. You just had to wait. Why couldn't you do that?"

"He — I..."

"I reckon," Spider said, "deep in your black heart, you know, you've figured out already, that there is no Final Secret, haven't you?"

"What the hell are you—"

"You know. You're a man of science. You believe in evidence and reason and all that Enlightenment stuff. You must have concluded, by now, after years and years, that that Secret thing is bullshit. There's nothing there. It was just Dickhead's stupid wet dream all along — only you've come all this way, with all these people, and you've lost so many of them, and now you know it's all for sweet bugger all, and you can't face the reality of it, so you carry on, killing that creature, punishing it. That's what you're doing now, isn't it? You're just punishing it. Making it suffer, for no good reason at all."

"There is a Final Secret!"

"But what if it's just bullshit? God, you're a mess. You're coming apart at the seams, and for what? Come on, mate. Give it up. Let the thing go. It's had enough. Nothing deserves that kind of pain and wretchedness. What do you reckon?"

"*There is a Final Secret.* Dickhead would never have lied to me about that."

"Prove it."

"I don't have to prove it to you," Stapleton said, clawing back a tattered remnant of his former cocky manner and trying to make it cover his true face. "I believe Dickhead because I have heard them, too."

This surprised Spider, and he hesitated a moment. "Oh, what?"

"I've heard them singing to me, late at night, singing in my mind."

"Bull*shit*!"

"I am their Chosen Vessel!"

"No. You're a torturer and a murderer!"

"I AM CHOSEN!"

"Oh, fuck off, you are not." It was Spider's turn to laugh.

Stapleton clobbered Spider in the face, once, twice, and again. Spider fell back, bloody, hit the back of his head on the wheelchair, banged heavily against the frame of Molly's bed, and collapsed to the floor, the pain barely registering, consciousness collapsing in on itself, huddling, curling up inside his damaged brain. The pain, and there would be plenty of that, was still on the way. Right now, he lay there in a stunned numbness, a tingling raw, wet, blood-in-the-eyes confusion, curled up, struggling to get back up, but his hand slipped, and he fell again, hard. Stapleton, meanwhile, loomed over him like a sinister building, and pulled something from his pocket — Spider heard a familiar whipping, whooshing sound, it reminded him of … something, oh God, what did it remind him of? Fading in and out. Fragments of waking detail and action. Disconnected awareness. Bits of a dream. Eyes stinging with blood. The far-off sound of Iris yelling something.

Stapleton roared, flung himself at her, huge, his arm sweeping down, and there was that swooping sound. Iris screamed, "That's my fucking arm!" Spider saw a great spray of blood. Then Stapleton was coming for Spider. "You want evidence. I'll show you evidence," the man said, from far away, his voice almost lost in the roar of pain and confusion that was Spider's mind. Stapleton added, spit flying as he spoke, "I. Am. Chosen, damn you."

Spider, his mouth full of blood and pain, said, "Bull. Shit."

The bed frame moved above him. The blankets folded back. Two legs appeared next to him, legs he recognized through the bloody mist. "Molly…?" It was Molly. She was getting up. Spider saw her feet on the blood-slick floor, saw the freckles on her pale skin, the tiny tattoo depicting a winged death-head skull, on her ankle. He remembered what the Molly-thing had told him. Time was short. Soon the download would be complete. The Vore would merge with Molly, and now it looked like it had at long last arrived.

Spider, struggling to stay conscious, heard someone scream. He thought it might be Stapleton. "No, no, no fucking way. No fucking way!" Spider watched those freckled feet advance towards the shadows. He saw Stapleton slip in a smear of blood, and fall. But Stapleton managed to back away, still saying, "No, no, this is not happening. This is not happening." He made it to his feet, looking shit-scared, and glanced at Spider. "What have you done to your wife, man?"

The creature which had been Spider's sort-of ex-wife paused as Stapleton bolted off, screaming instructions, and for a cold moment it looked down at Spider. This was the eye-less face he had seen before. There was no sign of the Molly he knew. She was gone. Whatever drove her body now was vast and ancient; it had time. The Mollyvore's cold, stone-hard hand reached down, touched Spider's face, gently. A faint, passing hint of a smile flickered across its face, and Spider realized, in a sudden moment, an oasis of clarity, that Molly was indeed still in there. She was fine. She would be okay. He should not worry about her. He said, "Okay," and the Mollyvore, shedding the flimsy surgical gown of the helpless patient, left the room, blood on its feet, looking to Spider like the Greek goddess of cold and furious vengeance, trailing ruin.

As darkness settled over him like a blanket, Spider heard, in the distance, thunderous explosions, screams, running. "Ah, Molly," he murmured, with a weak smile.

CHAPTER 21

Cottesloe Beach, Perth, dawn. It was chilly. Towering Norfolk pine trees stood around in a park up on a bluff. Down on the beach, before the morning sun arrived, even as the usual gang of crazy dawn swimmers went about their painful business, a wedding was taking place. The groom, nervous, happy, clad in a tux one size too small, kept fiddling with the too-tight neck of his shirt; the bride, luminous, in a sheath of antique white lace, her hair hanging loose and free around her pale shoulders, was annoyed at the groom, and trying to pay attention to the celebrant before them. Arrayed around the bridal party, a rowdy crowd of well-wishers, muttering about the early hour, wondering if five in the morning was too early to get pissed.

Far up on the bluff, among the pine trees and the black cockatoos feasting on cones, was a park bench affording an unmatched view of the beach, the rocky groyne, the pavilion, and the old pylon out in the water. On the bench sat two people: one, a middle-aged man, weary, beaten-down, dressed in old grey overalls and well-worn Doc Marten boots, touching his face with great care, as if worried about broken bones; the other, a woman of great, venerable age, with no eyes, white hair hanging loose around her shoulders, blowing in the gentle breeze, wearing cargo pants and a black turtleneck sweater, focused on the wedding party down on the sand, far below.

"You're fine, Al," the old woman said. "This isn't strictly speaking real, kind of."

This confused him. "It's not? So, what? I'm dreaming?"

"No, you're here, inside a memory. Your unconscious body is at Colditz."

"Oh, good. I was worried," he said, deadpanning. He watched the proceedings down on the beach. "You looked gorgeous."

"I wished you'd stop fidgeting with your bloody collar."

"The bow tie was too tight. I couldn't breathe."

"The most important day of your life, and you didn't plan ahead and maybe, just maybe, get your neck measured?"

She was right. He should have had a proper fitting before buying the damned thing.

"All you had to do was stand there and look good in the suit and say, 'I do'. That's it." She shook her head, watching.

"We got through it, didn't we?"

The Molly part of the Mollyvore was in charge here, in his memory. She looked at him. It was the damnedest sensation. It was exactly as if she still had eyes. Those dark and empty sockets somehow bored right into him. There were no secrets, and could be none. She saw everything, now that the troublesome eyes were gone. He shuffled a little on the bench, uncomfortable, knowing that only a moment ago he had been left for dead in a pool of his own blood on the floor of a crashed timeship in the Year Eight Million. He realized this, all of this, this scene around them, was an illusion, which the Mollyvore had laid on for his benefit, to remind him of something, and by way of it saying goodbye. He knew that in what passed for a real world, his ex-wife had turned into an avenging demon of some kind, and that she had gone forth to kill John Stapleton, and who knew what else. Maybe the entire ship was gone by now, taking Spider, and the children Mr. Patel had sent him to find, and everybody else, with it. Maybe this was the afterlife. The Mollyvore had not said, and this was, he knew, its meeting. It was weird to see his and Molly's earlier selves, down there on the beach, two crazy kids totally unaware of the observers here, up among the pine trees. They were foolish young people who should never have married, but had been full of hope and something resembling happiness, a shade of happiness, at any rate. Spider's police career had taken off and Molly's artistic endeavors were starting to gain recognition. She had been hailed in various industry magazines as "a talent to watch", "a star in the making". Great things lay before them both.

"I've decided to forgive you," the Molly part of the Mollyvore said, her voice mild, as if she were commenting on the cool weather.

This got Spider's attention. Guiltily, he looked at her. "Um, what?" he said in that tone you use when you know you're in trouble, but you're trying to "act natural", thus demonstrating that you are indeed far from "natural". He heard that tone in his voice, and cursed himself.

"When I was in New York, my future-self showed me what you did at The End of Time, and it all came back to me."

Something heavy and cold settled deep in Spider's guts. She knew. Crap. "Oh?" he said, still playing all innocent, but starting to bead up with cold, cold sweat.

"It's all right. I said, I forgive you." Mollyvore touched his arm; her hand was like ice.

"You forgive me?" It was hard to speak; his mouth had gone dry.

"But you should have told me. That was wrong. That was nineteen kinds of wrong. I was — God, I can't begin to tell you how angry I was — even though it explained so much, it was kind of liberating in its way. It made sense. I even, sort of, understood why you did it. Even so, if you'd been in New York with me, at the time, I probably would've killed you stone dead. I would've grabbed someone's gun and shot you, full magazine, right in the guts, where it would hurt, where you'd take a long, horrible time to die — and I'd have gone on from there, seeing what else I could do to you."

"But, you forgive me," Spider said, suspecting he might be running out of time, and that the Molly part of the Mollyvore might soon be gone forever.

"I need to know one thing," he said, trying to understand his new unreality. "Why did you go with your future-self, knowing what had happened to you in your subjective past?"

"Vanity, I guess. Future-me told past-me that in fifty years I would be making a big splash in France, and that there was an exhibition of my work at the Louvre. How could I not go?" A faint hint of a smile flickered over her ancient face.

"And so you were caught in Stapleton's driftnet."

"Yes, and that's when the captured Vore decided to become a part of me. It was my destiny."

"You had to be because you already had been," Spider said, thinking about circularity, cause and effect, and hating the whole miserable thing.

"Time's funny that way," she said.

"Okay," Spider said, fully aware of who, and what, he was sitting next to. He understood in that instant why the Mollyvore had chased John Stapleton back through time to the park in Midland, why it had to kill him, and how Stapleton must have used the "escape" time machine the prisoners built to clear Colditz security, and the Time Voyager software in his head to blip back, hoping to elicit Spider's help in dealing with Molly. Stapleton must have hoped that he, Spider, could in some way reach the Molly part of the Mollyvore. Hell, maybe Stapleton even expected him to kill Molly, and keep her from going to New York and meeting Future Molly. It made sense. And he hated that it made sense. Like everything in the world of bloody time travel, it was circular; with fanciful baroque curliques and ornate twists and turns in the time-space continuum — but which always ended with Stapleton being torn to snack-sized bloody chunks in Midland.

The only puzzling detail in the whole thing was this: Stapleton was, as far as he could tell, still alive. He thought long and hard about what the Mollyvore had told him so far, and the way she had said it, still with that cool, calm voice. She had had a very long time to think about the matter. "Why?" he said, at last. "Why forgive me, when you could kill me with a glance?"

"Nothing I can or could do to you would be as bad as what you've been doing to yourself, knowing what you did and why you did it. You betrayed me, your wife — not once, with that stupid affair with what's-her-face — but twice. Even though we were separated at the time, I was your wife. We had vows. Promises. I treated you like shit, and you liked it. That was the deal. And then you pulled that number on me. Do you know how long Dickhead had me hanging there at the End of Time? Hanging by my wrists, bent up behind my back. Only a centimeter or two off the ground, so close, agonisingly close. You remember that, Al?" She stood up and demonstrated, gasping at the pain as she showed him, again, what had been done to her. "I was hanging there like that for hours. All to get you to cooperate with Dickhead's monstrous schemes. Which you did!" She was disgusted. "How weak is that!"

"I'm so sorry," he said, hardly able to speak, remembering only too well.

"It's all right. I said I forgive you. And I do. Completely. Must have been hard living with that."

He nodded, sniffling, and hating himself.

"It was," he said, hardly able to speak. He wiped at his eyes.

"Yes, and now I remember, too," she said.

"I'm—"

"Yes, I know. It's all right." She reached over, and touched his knee. He flinched, as if he'd been shot.

"How can you be..." he struggled to say, "...so reasonable?"

"Al, I saw what you did, and I understood. You were in an impossible situation."

"That's not the bloody point," he said.

"Bloody Dickhead, what an arsehole!" Molly said, deadpan.

Shocked, he laughed out loud. Molly laughed with him, and touched him again.

"His poor wife," he said.

"You should talk to her."

Nodding, he said he would.

"I'm sorry I was so awful to you," Molly said. "At the time, I justified it to myself. You were boring. You were soooooo boring."

"Um," he said, in the awful position of hearing said aloud things he had always suspected she thought, but had never dared ask about.

Molly went on. "I wanted someone, I don't know, a bit dashing, exciting somehow. Someone who'd sweep me off my feet, but instead it was just you, plodding old Al, always on tap to paint the laundry or fix the fence. You were always so available. It was easy to mistreat you. It was like you were queuing up for it."

"Pardon me for being dull," he said.

"It's okay. It was a long time ago." The way she said it, as if you'd have to be a fool to still be all upset about such ancient business. Spider nonetheless felt like just such a fool. Too available? Too ready? Queuing up for it? Guilty as charged, he thought.

Molly was staring out beyond the breakers. The wedding party down on the beach, ceremony concluded, was moving on. The bride and groom, trying to keep control of their hair in the gathering wind, were posing for wedding photos. Spider remembered those photos. He hadn't looked at them in years.

There was something he didn't understand. "You and the Vore. You..." he started to say, then trailed off, thinking about it. "Is it possible," he began, thinking hard, "that you could find yourself in such extreme pain, such a marginal state of mind, that you could disassociate, that you could leave your body, that you could..."

"It was something like that. Me and the Vore. Our eyes met across a crowded space-time. We were both disassociated, no

longer tied to our own space and time; atemporal, drifting outside the flood of the universe. The past and the future were all
mixed up and confused. And we bonded for a brief time, then
went our different ways. Later, when I turned up on Stapleton's
ship, it found me again. It was just this side of madness, barely
hanging on. And we helped each other again."

"You let it into your mind."

"Say what you like about me, Al, but I will not stand by while
a helpless creature suffers."

He thought about Mr. Popeye, how she, as part of the
Mollyvore, had spared the little guy. Trashed the house, but the
fish was perfectly fine, a mild case of fin rot aside. "That's how
I knew it was you," he said, and when Molly seemed confused,
he explained about Mr. Popeye. "When we examined the house.
You spared the fish. Only you would do that."

Molly smiled. It seemed to glow with the sunrise. He stared
and stared, then looked away, sad, knowing this was the end.
This was the last time he would see her. She had not said as
much, and he had not asked, but there was a sense of melancholy about it, about her choice of this moment to revisit. The
strange thing, he thought, was that he felt all right about it. If this
was the end, he could accept that. He was ready to move on, just
as Molly had already done. It was startling, to understand that
about himself. It made him look at Molly differently. She was
someone he'd never really known, let alone understood.

They sat in silence a while, listening to the wind in the trees.
Spider thought and thought, turning everything over like com-
post in his head. A few things stuck out.

"So what the hell are they, anyway? The Vores."

"Living, conscious singularities."

"Shit," Spider said.

"Incapable of anything like language."

"And this Final Secret of the Cosmos? Is there one?"

"Dunno. It never came up."

"Dickhead said they were burning down the universe, that
they were Angels, you see, making way for God to create the
universe again, bigger, better, with more of everything He liked.
Is that true? Do you know?"

"Beats me," she said, smiling, watching the waves, not a care
in this world nor any other.

Spider nodded

"Right. So what about, er...?"

She indicated vaguely at her face. "The eyes? My peepers?"

"Yeah."

"Gave 'em up when I took on the Vore."

"Did it hurt?"

"It was quick."

They sat in silence a while longer. Spider listened to the early morning wind in the trees, the calls of the cockatoos, the occasional thump as a falling pinecone hit the roof of a parked car. This was nice, he thought. Peaceful. It was the most substantial conversation he'd had with Molly in, well, he couldn't say how long. Possibly ever. Certainly the first time he'd spoken with her when everything she said to him didn't come with that subtext of bitter disappointment. Without that constant scowl, and even without the eyes, she was beautiful. He was going to miss her.

"Will I ever see you again?"

"You want to see me again? Really?" She appeared surprised.

"Just wondering."

Down on the beach, the shadows cut deeper and darker. The sun in the east was above the horizon; someone's flowers were tumbling across the sand, driven by wind, towards the lapping water.

"In the course of your long, surprisingly long life, Al, you will see me three more times."

He had to sit and process that; there was a lot to unpack. "I live a long time?"

"Crazy long time, yeah."

"I didn't know." He wasn't sure whether to thank her for telling him, or not. "Three more times, eh?"

"Give or take. Depends."

This was maddening, but he didn't want to blow it. Breathe, Spider. Long life. Three more meetings. "Okay," he said at last.

"Good."

"What about your art?" He imagined her moving stars around, building nebulae and molding liquid dark matter in her weird, post-mortal hands.

"I gave it up."

"Gave it up? How could you give it up?" He was shaken at the news. Molly no longer an artist? He didn't know artists could even do that; he thought it was a lifetime thing, like a sentence.

She said, without a care, "I had to make room in my mind for the Vore. It wasn't a hard choice."

"Shit," he said, amazed, and strangely disappointed. "Is that why you…" he started to say, thinking about Molly's destroyed sculptures at her house.

"They were rubbish," she said. "Derivative. Lame. I saw, at last, my gaping lack of talent. It was kind of a relief to get rid of them."

Spider was astonished. "You miss it?"

"Nope. Too busy."

"Are you, I don't know, are you happy?"

"Define happy, Al."

He couldn't. "Three more times, eh?"

"No, I'm not telling you when. I don't do appointments."

"Right." He watched the beautiful bride running, barefoot, into the water to go wading after her lost flowers; he could hear her swearing, those ringing tones carrying all the way up to the pine trees. His earlier-self stood there at the edge of the water, shouting after her to leave the bloody flowers, she was ruining her dress, and she was shouting back at him that it was hers to bloody well ruin. Spider remembered it well.

When he looked back at the Mollyvore, it was gone. He blinked, his eyes closing for a fraction of a moment, and when he opened them again, he was back in the wreck of the ship, cold and weak, shivering, in a lot of pain, and he could smell blood and burning. It was dark. He was lying on some kind of cot on the floor somewhere. When he touched his face, he discovered his injuries were not as bad as he'd expected. There was a hot tingling feeling in his cheeks, and he realized there were constructor agents at work, rebuilding everything.

"Hello?" he called out. There was a lot of noise, and the burning smell was bad. There was a fire nearby. So much smoke in the air he found himself coughing as he tried to call out. And it was cold, inexpressibly cold, so cold his hands and feet felt numb. Hull-breach, he thought, and struggled to his feet, thinking that if the hull was compromised and the seals on the doors weren't completely air-tight, things might be a bit urgent. He got to his feet, hit his head on an overhead pipe he never saw, and swore. It was nothing serious. Someone had covered him with a blanket, so he grabbed it and wrapped it around himself. "Hello? Hey! I'm up! Hello? Anyone?"

Then, a moving point of light, some distance away, lighting up a nearby passage. Someone was coming. Someone tall. The light approached. "Mr. Webb? I thought I heard you. You're back with us again?"

Spider didn't recognize the male voice. "Yeah, sorry, um. Yeah, I'm fine, I think. Someone gave me something for my—"

"Yeah," the voice said, the light coming close. Spider, squinting, saw it was a very tall young man, rugged up with blankets, gloves, wearing a sort-of hat. "I'm Vijay Patel? I think you knew my dad? Iris told me—"

"You've seen Iris?" he said, seizing on the news. "Is she okay?" He remembered something bad had happened to her, that Stapleton had done something to her.

"Iris, yeah, she's fine. No worries, Mr. Webb. She's looking after Phoebe for me while I'm checking on things."

Spider nearly lost it, hearing that Iris was all right. For a long moment he couldn't speak, he was so overcome with happiness. "Thank God, that's great. Thank God, oh that's so good to hear. Um, can you take me to her? Is that…?"

"Of course. That's where I'm going. I was just making the half-hourly round to check everything, and to stop in and see if you were awake yet. Keeps me busy, off the streets," he said, and laughed a bit.

Spider liked him. "You got me this blanket, and the…" He gestured around his face, referring to the constructor-bots. "Bit of a medic, are you?"

"Something like that, Mr. Webb. Can you move under your own steam, or do I need to get help?"

"I think I'll be okay."

"Okay. Good. We'd better get moving."

"Call me Spider," he said, and stuck out his hand, and they shook, very quickly.

They set off. Vijay told him that Iris would be very pleased to hear that he was awake at last. "She's been talking about you non-stop this whole time," he said, and Spider caught, in the flickering light, the hint of a smile on Vijay's face.

Embarrassed, Spider seized on something he remembered Iris telling him, that Vijay and this Phoebe were a bit of an item, having grown close after many years stuck here in Colditz. "How is Phoebe?"

"Iris is taking good care of her, given the limited first-aid facilities, sir. Phoebe was caught in an explosion. It was during your wife's rampage through the ship. She pretty much totaled it. Before, we had a bit of a chance of getting her going again, to some degree, but once Mrs. Webb was finished, before she left, well it's a miracle anybody was left alive, to tell the truth." He was leading Spider through access ways, maintenance hatches, and areas where they had to crouch to an uncomfortable degree, and go single-file. Everywhere they went, hardware and machinery blocked the easy ways through, and some doors were sealed shut. Vijay knew his way around the maze, he was full of confidence, and chatted away at Spider as easily as if he'd known him all his life.

Apparently Spider had been out for four days. Iris had dragged him, one-handed, from Molly's room to safety, even as the Mollyvore set about her campaign of destruction. Vijay remarked that the Mollyvore actually turned away from one strike, once it saw that Spider and Iris were in the way. The thought of his Molly, as part of the Mollyvore, destroying every-thing in its path, everything that smacked of a connection to its former confinement and torture, gave him the horrors — none-theless it had turned away from an attack that would have hurt him. Just like Mr. Popeye, he remembered again.

Vijay tried to fill Spider in on what had happened during those four days after the Mollyvore had vanished. Section by section the ship fell apart. Vijay, Phoebe, Iris and Spider had been cut off from the area Stapleton and his crew had been work-ing in. "They probably didn't survive," he said. There had been hull-breaches and large sections of the vessel had been rendered inaccessible. When Spider asked why he'd been kept so far from where Vijay, Iris and Phoebe were based, Vijay told him there simply wasn't room. They had to find the best possible place, the safest possible place, for him. Iris had been very insistent on that point, he said. When she wasn't looking after Phoebe, when the girl was asleep, Iris spent a lot of her time watching over Spider. "Apparently," Vijay said, "you talk in your sleep. Iris thought you were either talking to or about Molly."

Spider felt mortified, thinking of Iris hearing such things, and doubtless not understanding the context.

Vijay was working his way through engineering, almost as far aft on the ship as one could get. Spider realized they were a long way from the singularity containment section, which was one of the first things the Mollyvore had destroyed: the ship's time engines ran on power extracted from the gravity waves emitted by two small artificial singularities orbiting one another. Once containment failed, the two singularities, each of infinite density and zero dimension, had dropped out of the ship and started orbiting the Earth's core, devouring everything they encountered. Vijay estimated that they had no more than a month before the twin singularities consumed the planet's core, which would lead to the breakup of the whole world.

"Well, crap," Spider said, helpless before such unthinkable power.

"Indeed, yes," Vijay said. They moved on. "You know," said Spider, "Your dad sent me here to find you, and Phoebe. To bring you back home."

Vijay abruptly stopped and turned to faced Spider. "*Dad* sent you?"

"I told him I couldn't promise anything—"

"Dad sent you?"

"Yes, I just—"

"Sorry, it's — you're sure he didn't send you to get *Kali* back?"

Spider remembered Patel telling him that *Kali* was more important than his own son. It seemed the son was only too aware of where he fit in the scheme of things. "Yes, he sent me to get you."

"Really?"

"Vijay, I'm freezing my bits off here. Can we talk as we go, please? And yes, really."

"Sorry, yes of course. Sorry, Mr. Webb. It's just..." Vijay led Spider out of an access port in the side of the duct and indicated they had to climb a nearby ladder that led up into the freezing darkness. "It's just hard to believe my dad, of all people—"

"Giving a shit about you?"

Vijay pointed his light at him. "Yes, sir, exactly."

"Dads can be full of surprises," Spider said, trying to wrap the blanket around his hands to keep them from the freezing rungs of the ladder.

"It's not much farther," Vjay said, with renewed confidence.

CHAPTER 22

Iris, who had heard them coming, was pleased to see Vijay back safe and sound, but when she saw Spider, she just stood there, staring at him, not saying a word, and not needing to. He had just noticed that most of her left forearm was missing, and that the stump was tightly bandaged, when Iris was in his arms, warm but shaking, and they embraced, and Iris surprised him by kissing him, properly, full-on, and at first he simply stood there, more astonished than he could have said, but gradually, as he felt himself warming to the idea, began to join in. At length, Iris pulled away, her eyes huge, shining, a knowing look on her face. Spider went to say something about her arm, but she stopped him, put her remaining hand softly against his mouth, and looked away for a moment. He understood, sort of, too many emotions swirling through him. He said, feeling his whole body waking up as if from an eternity of cold slumber, "Good to see you, too, Iris," and, though he intended it as a wry comment, something to lighten the mood, he immediately felt like he'd just said the stupidest thing a man could possibly say to a woman, and at the worst possible time. Not sure what to do with his hands and arms, and seeing that Iris might be feeling a little the same way, attempted a hug — and felt her ribs, which chilled him afresh. "Iris…" he said, intending to say something fine and winning and hopeful, but she again placed her hand over his mouth, and held him close, sharing her warmth with him.

Vijay was tending to the sleeping form of Phoebe, a flimsy young woman whose head was covered in bandages. She lay there, her mouth open, hardly breathing. Iris told Spider she'd been that way since the explosion at the singularity containment facility. Phoebe, in the long years she'd been here in Colditz with Vijay, had become a reasonably competent technician, someone who, with the backing of a proper university, could have been an engineer. Spider felt the impulse to apologize to her, for his ex-wife, and saw that he would have to get past that sort of thinking.

Now Iris and Vijay were talking, discussing the state of things. Spider didn't understand or follow a lot of it, but he could tell that things were as bad as bad could be. Iris asked Spider, "How tired are you?" and at first he misunderstood the point of her question, and thought she was talking about something entirely else, and felt not at all sure how to respond, considering, but then he woke up to himself, and realized this was all-business Iris. This was Inspector Street, taking charge of the situation. He said he was okay, at least for now, and asked why.

She and Vijay exchanged a few words, and Vijay said, "I want to show you our lifeboat. You feel up to having a look at it?"

"You have a lifeboat?"

"It's what's left of an emergency escape vehicle we've been trying to build. Stripped down to the chassis. Just enough power to get the four of us home. Iris was very insistent that we were not leaving without you."

Spider looked over at Iris and Phoebe. Iris had not been expecting him to look her way, and he saw her with her guard down, sitting there on a box by the weak electric light next to Phoebe's blanket-strewn cot, clutching the stump of her right arm. It was healing, but Spider could see, in that rare moment, that Iris was in terrible pain, holding it with her remaining hand, biting her lip, stricken, her face drawn. Then she glanced up, saw Spider looking at her, and blushed, scowled at him, and sat up straighter. She yelled at him, "Don't just bloody well stand there like an idiot. Go and help Vijay! Christ!"

He went, but felt awful for Iris, even as he knew she would not, not ever, not under any circumstances, want anything even smelling of his pity or concern. She would be resolute and strong and carry on like the Black Knight in that Monty Python film, losing his limbs one by one, and fighting on, blood spraying everywhere, insisting the missing limbs were mere "flesh wounds". That was Iris, no question. She would be fine. Spider got on with it.

Vijay led Spider on another trek through the nooks and crannies of the engineering department, taking great, even pedantic, care to explain to Spider the full nature of every possible hazard. It was still shockingly cold, the air thin, and there was that smell of burning electronics in the thinning air. *That can't be good*, Spider thought. At length, they arrived outside at a lab to which Vijay had a key. Inside — and Spider recognized the smell of a time machine workshop immediately — Vijay showed him the lifeboat.

It was all Spider could do not to laugh.

"Took me ages to find the parts," Vijay said, walking around it, switching on a couple of lights.

"I can imagine," Spider said, nodding.

Vijay had, apparently, set out to rebuild *Kali*. This turned out not to be possible. That fabulous hotrod time machine had been stripped down to component screws and washers, and all of the custom spintronics, the chromed translation engine cluster, the heat dissipation vanes, and recycled in various ways in the course of trying to rebuild the timeship's mighty engines. And, once used, it was not always easy for one skinny nineteen-year-old guy to scrounge them back. So he'd "liberated" whatever he could find from the parts of every time machine that had been brought here while the driftnet had been running. The result, Spider thought, was a machine sculpture the old Molly might once have found fascinating. Spider could see parts of *Kali*, but he could also see some of the more elegant parts of the Wellsian Time Machine he and Iris had used to get here. There was the big spinny dish, now mounted horizontally. And there was an enormous scanning/translation engine connected by thick insulated hoses to a power-source the size of a small car. It was, he thought, the ugliest, most grotesque monster of a machine he had ever seen. The contrast between the brute functionality of some parts and the studied elegance of others, and the electric blue, lightning-bolt styling of still others was stunning. Spider walked around and around the machine, marveling. From what Vijay told him when he asked pointed questions about system integration and the memory-depth of the scanning engines, about the specific curve and limits of the Fenniak Transform, and the sheer computational grunt of the translation engines, this shambolic contraption should be able to take the four of them on a single, mind-hurting leap across the vast airless gulf separating their current time to any point, any time, any place eight million plus years ago.

This contraption was their ride out of here. All he had to do was get it running. The wreck of the timeship around them wasn't going to stay even as relatively intact as it was for much longer. And the singularities now swirling around the core of the planet were only going to get bigger and hungrier.

Spider said, at last, "What have you figured out, so far?"

"Power supply works. Green lights on the board."

"Good. How much power?"

Vijay told him, and Spider did some calculations in his head, based on passenger load, the computational requirements of storing the vector-state data for each particle in the human body, in the machine itself; then there was the energy-cost of translating — editing — that data to reflect the destination's time-coordinates. By the time he finished his sums, Spider whistled, or tried to whistle. His mouth was not quite fixed yet, and he made an embarrassing tooting noise. "How are the data processing connections?"

Vijay told him, and in fact told him about every key system and subsystem. The kid knew his time machines. His old man would be proud. And, listening to Vijay, Spider found himself running out of objections for why the beast should not fly. Vijay said he had a full board of green lights, all systems operational, everything working the way it should — but still it would not go. It was, Vijay suggested, as if the beast was maybe a little afraid.

Spider climbed into the unlikely structure, asking Vjay if he'd tried x, if he'd tried y. Spider tested individual components, checking voltages and current, and basic connections, plugs and ports, making sure nothing was loose or had come undone. It always paid to check the basic stuff, Spider had learned, because sometimes a job that had been baffling you for days turned out to be a loose lead deep inside the translation engine. And on this Frankenstein's monster, where few of the parts were meant to go together, it was worth checking.

That sorted, Spider moved on to more systems-level issues. Number one: software. Had Vijay managed to scrounge up or hack viable drivers for these components. Careful inspection, and beady-eyed questioning of Vijay revealed that he had performed wonders. "I've been writing custom drivers since I was five," Vijay boasted at one point, and Spider shook his head and wagged a finger.

"That kind of thing, young man," he said, trying to keep his face straight, "could lead to a life of criminal time machine hackery." Vijay grinned, but said nothing.

Finally Spider said there was nothing left to do but pull the entire scanning engine, and examine it piece by piece. It was possible that the machine was failing to start the scan cycle for the good reason that the scanning process was out of phase with the translation engine. Though how that could be, when the status lights on the control panel all showed green, Spider did not know.

Pulling the scanning engine took time. It was laborious, tedious work, compounded by occasional tremors shuddering up from the growing singularities below. When Vijay went on his routine patrols to check air-tight door seals, he found one had been bent out of alignment during the quakes, and fixing it became a matter of higher priority than the time machine. The repair took two days.

At night, while Spider slept, he pulled the time machine apart and, like a Chinese Puzzle Box, put it back together again. Over and over and over, dreaming he would find the fault.

The cold was brutal, and felt personal, mean, like the universe outside was pressing in, hammering at them all the time, trying to find its way through the fragile, broken hull of the timeship.

Back at the lab, Spider opened up the status board. Holding a weak light between his teeth, he examined the connections feeding the indicator lights, and found a loose solder. "You bastard!" he muttered, now holding the light close to the circuit grid so he could see the fault as clearly as possible. "You bloody bastard!" The circuit grid was receiving signals from the out-of-sync scanning engine, but the defective solder was allowing a false-positive signal through when it should have indicated a red light.

The re-soldering took longer than it should have done, Spider's hands were so clumsy and hopeless, dropping tools and having to go fossicking about in the works of the beast to find them. In the end, though, he completed the job. His multi-tool showed that circuit now worked properly and the light showed red. At least the panel was now working.

During the next four days, as Spider and Vijay struggled around the clock to figure out how to get the lifeboat going, there were two major earthquakes, including one which threatened to cut off Iris and Phoebe. It took another day and a half of hard, difficult work to make sure the access between the two sites was safe, and to ensure that there had been no further ruptures to the fragile hull of the timeship. "We have to shift everything into the lab," Spider said, horrified at the idea of being cut off from the others. That evening they moved everything, including Phoebe on her cot, through the labyrinth and into the lab.

The lab was much colder than their closet. "I don't know if I can take much more of this, Spider," Iris told him, and he noticed her mouth was turning blue. The shakes now were constant for all of them, no matter what they did, how much they "rugged up", and they were aching and dizzy from hunger. Phoebe's condition was marginal at best; the girl was barely breathing, her pulse was thready, and Iris thought the girl had a mild fever. "Soon," Spider told Iris. "We'll get it soon. Hang in there."

CHAPTER 23

The next day they heard the machines outside, on the time-ship's shattered external hull.

"What the f-fuck is that?" Iris said, more from deathly weariness than anything. They were used to the hulk's constant groans and creaks, but these new sounds were different: they were purposeful.

"Are those footsteps?" Vijay said, staring up into the dark of the high ceiling. Far above, faintly, yes, the sound of something with what sounded like heavy boots clomping about on the outside.

Then, amid the shuddering and clanking as some sort of unthinkable hardware engaged with the hull, the unmistakable screaming howl of industrial power-tools, carving through wreckage, off in the distance, echoing through the remaining air-spaces and connecting linkages of the ship. "Shipbreakers," Spider said.

"What?" Iris said.

Vijay, though, understood only too well. "Salvage guys. They're cutting up the ship, stripping it for whatever they can sell. Must be pretty desperate if they're interested in this old heap."

"They sound close," Iris said, staring upward, listening, even as the ground trembled and rumbled beneath them.

Spider thought so, too. "They probably don't know we're here."

Vijay, who'd been lying underneath the lifeboat time machine, inspecting joints and connections, rolled out. "We need to—"

Iris needed no further encouragement. She got up, demanded the biggest, heaviest damned tool Spider had — the best he could do was a spanner half a meter long — and Iris got to work with her good arm, pounding the spanner against the wall, screaming, shouting, *"We're here! Hey! We're here!"* The noise was spectacular, and the impacts were taking their toll on the wall. When she paused after a few minutes, there was no change in the sounds of outside activity, so she went at it again, in bursts of two to three minutes, until she had to sit down, a long while later, sweating, breathing hard, her breath steaming before her. "Oh, look, my sweat's starting to freeze," she said, horrified and amazed. Her efforts appeared to make no difference. The shipbreakers kept at it, the power-tools coming closer. Spider was shocked at the speed of it. The way things were going, the shipbreakers would reach this part of the timeship's engineering section in a couple of days, long before the singularities finished their hungry work.

Iris kept at the hammering, as much as she could. Spider and Vijay worked on the lifeboat around the clock. Phoebe's condition deteriorated. Iris told Vijay, "I think she's now actually comatose. I'm so sorry."

"Yeah, but she could wake up, right? People wake from comas all the time."

"I'm no doctor, okay? But I know a bit about this stuff; there are key signs to look for. In my opinion, she's hardly there at all. I don't know…"

"But we're so close, Iris!"

"I don't know if she could survive a time-jump, is my point, Vijay."

Vijay was staring at the dimly-lit alcove where Phoebe lay, with her blue lips and hands marbled blue and white, no steam visible from either mouth or nose. She lay too still for words. "But it's just teleportation. It's nothing. There's no health impact, there've been studies. My dad—"

"Let Spider carry on. I'll hand him tools. You sit with Phoebe."

Spider called out, "Talk to her. She can probably hear you."

Iris shot him a look, and he shrugged, and got back to work.

The next day, Spider was back working on the control panel. He had a very pretty row of green lights. He'd checked everything, at least three times. Despite Vijay's concerns, he had managed to disassemble and test the vast majority of the

lifeboat's systems. There was, as far as Spider could tell, nothing wrong with the machine. It ought to work. The shipbreakers
were almost upon them. The noises of their grinding and banging and dragging grew louder, closer. It sounded like a lot of
machines were out there, and a lot of people, all working hard,
no doubt hurrying to cut up the timeship and grab the valuable
bits before the planet became too unstable. And all the while, as
they worked and listened to those sounds, sometimes stopping
what they were doing and just looking up at the ceiling as if they
could see through the layers of internal infrastructure between
them in this lab and the workers climbing around outside on the
hull, there was that one profound terror: at any moment a team
of those guys out there were just as likely to bring their gear to
bear on the hull directly above this lab. How quickly would the
stuffy air in here disappear? How quickly would unconsciousness hit? Would they freeze before they asphyxiated?

There was nothing wrong with the bloody lifeboat. It ought
to work, so why wasn't it? Spider had tried everything, gone
over every possibility. In a moment of desperation, he muttered,
"Open the bloody pod bay doors, Hal!" It was only too tempting
to grab Iris's spanner and smash this useless piece of shit to bits
for all the good it was doing them.

Vijay said, "What?"

Spider never heard him. As soon as he'd said it, he felt something in his head wake up, just the way he remembered from his
old police days, when he'd have a keen moment of insight about
a difficult case. "Open the pod bay doors, Hal," he said again,
and then supplied Hal's response, *"I'm sorry, Dave, I can't do that."*

"Spider?" This from Iris, who flashed a worried look at Vijay.

Spider had not had any sleep in at least three days. He'd barely
eaten, was trying to ignore signs of frostbite in his toes, and was
running on adrenaline, so maybe, who knows, maybe that had
done something interesting in his head, connected stray ideas
together, things he'd heard a long time ago, back when he was
at TAFE learning about time machine theory, about weird but
incredibly rare anomalies. He climbed down and stood in front
of the lifeboat, even as the shipbreakers stomped and clomped
and worked and cut the wreck of the timeship out from under
them, even as the growing singularities shook and trembled and
threatened to swallow up the very ground on which the wreck
of the timeship was perched. Spider stood there, staring at the
lifeboat. "Open the pod bay doors, Hal," he said, and he cracked
a smile.

Vijay came up to him. "Um, Spider, sir? You're—"

Spider turned to Vijay. "It's Schwartzmann's Ghost!"

Vijay was baffled. "Ghost, sir?"

"Yes, Schwartzmann's Ghost. Also known as Schwartzmann's Complete Fucking Pain in the Arse."

"I'm, um—"

Spider saw that Vjay wasn't getting it, and further that Iris was looking at him funny, as if worried that he'd lost it. He said, trying to explain, "No, look. Not any kind of actual, you know, ghost-ghost, like a spook, a haunt, nothing like that."

Vijay clearly didn't like the look on Spider's face. "O-kay…"

"Trust me, and I might just get you home to see your dad before he goes to prison. Look, it's like this. This time machine is the most absurd, convoluted, mess of a time machine ever built, but it should work, and it's a brilliant tribute to your good self, Vijay. You're a genius. But the thing is, in the course of building this fabulous beast, the scanning and translation engines have developed an emergent behavior. You follow me? It's *as if* the thing's haunted. Not by an actual ghost, no. It's a metaphor. It's *like* there's someone in there, holding the machine back, refusing to cooperate. You get me?"

"You're saying the lifeboat can fly, but it just … *doesn't want to*?"

"That's right. Well, no, it's *as if* it's become self-aware, and that metaphorical self just doesn't want to. Do you see?"

"So why not just give us a red light for the scanning system? Why all the bullshit?"

"Because it's cussed. Because it's just one of those things about time machines, particularly a home-made one like this, bolted together from cannibalized bits of other time machines. There's all kinds of machine history in the thing, all kinds of machine memory. It's a strange and spooky thing, machine memory."

"Uh-huh…"

"We have to lobotomize it."

"What?"

"Cut out part of the memory. Essentially, remove the Ghost in the machine."

Iris came over. "What the hell are you saying, Spider?"

"I know it's weird. It's rare, it's weird."

Vjay said, "Who the hell is this Schwartzmann guy?"

"Time travel theorist from the old days. When the Email-From-the-Future turned up with the instructions on building Time Machine 1.0, this guy Dr. Robert T. Schwartzmann, PhD, led the skeptics who insisted the whole thing was an elaborate hoax. He maintained you couldn't build a working time machine based on the theory provided. There was no closed timelike curve; no rotating Gödelian universe; no Wigner's whatsit — none of that crazy shit. The prospect that you could change the past he particularly hated, what with the whole Timeline Preservation Conjecture, and all of that. 'Causality must be preserved!'" For this quote Spider affected a comedy voice, then went on, trying to explain. "Schwartzmann and his mates just didn't like it — and they were wrong. The man's been a laughingstock ever since, and he continues to insist time travel is just an illusion, that it's all in our heads, and one day we'll wake up and—"

Heavy footsteps, directly overhead.

"Oh, shit," Vijay said, looking at the ceiling. As they stood there, shivering, staring up into the darkness, they heard industrial machinery clunking into place.

"Vijay," Spider said, getting to grips with the situation. "Listen to me. It's like this. We have to make more than one trip. We can't all go at once."

"But—"

"Listen. If we pull half the memory to 'kill' the Ghost, there won't be enough translation capacity for all four of us. You and Phoebe, you go first, okay? Then, when you get to safety, send the machine back to us, and I'll send Iris through, and then I'll follow."

"What." This from Iris, now in his face, so furious she was whispering.

"It's how it has to—"

"I'm not going without you!" It was remarkable, Spider thought, how Iris could get so much furious determination into such a quiet utterance.

"I'll be coming right behind you, it'll only be a few seconds, tops, and I'll be there, okay? It's just I don't want to take the chance the machine chokes on the idea of sending us together."

"You're sending them together!"

Spider was glad it was dark. He figured Iris's gaze at this point would turn him to stone.

"They're relatively small and skinny and all undernourished. Look at Vijay, he's skin and bone! Now look at me. Even with all this, this…" He gestured around impatiently at the greater environment. "Even with all this, I'm still a big-boned lad, and I can't take the chance that the machine refuses to take us both."

"You can't make that choice on my behalf—"

"For God's sake, Iris, someone has to be in charge. Listen, listen — can you hear them out there? They're coming. They're going to open up this whole section at any time. We have to do this now!"

Vijay, not needing to be told twice, picked up Phoebe and struggled to bring her to the lifeboat. Iris said she'd come this far, and now she wanted Spider and herself to work together. "Don't you want that, too?"

Spider knew exactly what she was asking him, and it terrified him almost as much as the prospect of imminent frozen death. He did his typical thing, and temporized, and made a show of pulling half the scanning memory out of the translation engine.

Vijay entered the destination date on the control panel. Green lights lit up the panel and the whole unit came alive. Spider gave him a thumbs-up. Vijay saluted him, and hit the go button. The lifeboat howled, glowing, started to look oddly blurred—

And before Spider could say anything, they were gone, as if they had never been there at all. By now, even as Spider stared at the empty space, they would be home, powering down, the machine ticking. Come *on*, Vijay. Send her back!

The machines above were cutting into the hull overhead.

"We are not done with this, Spider. You listening to me?"

"Yes, I'm listening to you. But I can't take the chance of us going together. It's too—"

The expression on Iris's face shifted, and she looked at Spider differently. "It's too what, exactly?" she said.

"It's too risky, is what exactly. All right? It's—"

"Too risky?"

"That's right. I can't—"

"Can't what?"

He stared at her, listening to the machines overhead, and still waiting for the lifeboat's return. This was not the time for a discussion like this, he was thinking. "Iris, we can talk about this later, once we're home safe and sound."

"No, no, no, you don't."

"Where's the bloody lifeboat, Vijay? Come on, kid. Send it back!"

"We're going together," Iris said, with forbidding certainty.

"No. Just no."

"No? That's it? Just no?"

"I just said goodbye to Molly, okay?"

"Fucking Molly again!"

"No, it's not that. It's… God, Molly's gone. She's out of my life. But now I—"

Mildly mollified, Iris said, "Yes?"

He knew what she wanted him to say. He wasn't stupid. He knew exactly the thing she was trying to get him to say, but as much as he wanted to, in the present circumstances, he couldn't. "I just can't take the chance, Iris. You're too pre—"

"Who the hell says you even get a say?" Iris was saying before she heard what he'd just said, at which point she stopped, glared at him. "I'm too what?"

With no warning, no hint of its return, the lifeboat was back, as if it had never gone, filling up the lab with its home-made bulk — except for one little detail. Acrid electrical-fire smoke was pouring out of the lifeboat's translation engine bay.

"Oh, no, no you bloody don't…" Spider said, climbing up on the lifeboat to inspect the situation, but it was indeed as bad as it looked. The lifeboat was dead. He glanced back at Iris. She didn't have to ask. Taped to the control panel was a photo, showing Vijay, Phoebe (awake, smiling, in a hospital bed, lit by sunshine), Vijay's dad, Mr. Patel — and an old man, scowling, sitting next to the bed, who Spider guessed was Phoebe's father.

"There's a photo," Spider said, coughing, woozy from all the smoke.

Iris came over; she'd been trying not to cry. "They made it?"

"Looks that way," he said carefully climbing down from the burning machine, "Fried the unit doing it, but yeah." He felt crushed, and huddled with Iris in the corner, staring at it.

The cutting was coming close now; it sounded like they were through the infrastructure, and had started to work on the ceiling above. The whine and scream of the cutting machines was harrowing. Iris stared at Spider, the fumes from the lifeboat filling the lab. Spider held a blanket over his nose, staring at the machine, knowing it was dead, and knowing they, too, were finished. Iris held him. "You gave it your best shot," she said.

"Go back to hammering on the walls."

"You think there's a point?"

"There's always a bloody point!" he said, shouting but not meaning to. He was just feeling so frustrated, so useless. To come this close and then fail at the last moment — it was a hard thing to bear. He was boiling with bitterness.

Iris continued to hold him, and he held her. She said, "You did good."

"I got us fucking killed!"

"We're not dead yet," she said, in the most reasonable tone in the world, even as the first shower of sparks rained down from the ceiling.

By the flickering light of the cutting torch and that fall of sparks, Spider stared at Iris. "I'm sorry," he said to her. It was killing him that he couldn't save her.

"Shh, no need for that," she said, and touched his lips with her finger.

Spider saw sparks reflected in her eyes. "It'll be quick." He wondered what it would feel like, the remaining air in the room, and all this filthy smoke, rushing up through that hole and out.

The cutting torch worked its way around to where it started, and a roughly circular piece of ceiling crashed and clanged against the burning time machine and hit the floor. The smoky air in the room did not immediately leave. Spider felt his guts in knots; he was shaking with anger and sadness. Any minute now... Such an odd feeling, facing one's imminent death.

"Hello? Hey! Hello?" This was Iris, letting Spider go for a moment, and going to see if she could see anything up there, through the hole. "Spider, have a look at this!" Bright light shone down into the lab through the smoke, lighting up Iris's face. Seeing her like that, Spider's heart filled with warmth and happiness, in crazy defiance of the circumstances, or perhaps because of them. He went to join her, wondering what she could see up there. Iris was yelling, "We need some help down here! Oi! Hello!"

Under the broken and stripped hull of the timeship, the ground shifted, and sent Spider and Iris sprawling in the darkness. The remains of the ship tipped to one side, creaking and shaking, its torn spaceframe twisting, buckling. Spider got back to his feet and helped Iris, called up into the light, "Hey, if you guys up there can hear us? We'd like some help." Distantly, he could hear something like an alarm klaxon, and thought he might be able to hear voices shouting to one another.

A ladder appeared out of the light, and dropped to the floor of the lab; its legs hit the floor with a resounding thunk.

"Is that for us or for them?" Spider said.

Iris took his hand again. "Maybe they're waiting for us."

"Not exactly welcoming, are they?"

Iris was coughing, her eyes watering. "Come on, I can't take much more of this."

"It's almost certainly trouble," Spider said, even as he felt the floor beneath his feet trembling again.

The ladder, from what Spider could see, appeared to be made from aluminum. The rungs were spaced apart in such a way that it looked entirely suitable for human-shaped users. Either they're human, too, or they've got a special kit for dealing with different types of aliens, Spider thought, and then paused a moment, his mind boggling that he could think such a preposterous, crazy thought in this context without his brain exploding. *This ladder,* he thought, *would not look out of place in Dad's shed.* In fact, now he took a close look, it might have come from Bunnings. And that, once the thought appeared in his head, gave him far more pause than any development so far. He'd been working on the assumption that the shipbreakers were, if not aliens, then some kind of way-far-future humans, or post-humans. But what if they were just regular guys? What kind of sense did that make?

A voice out of the smoky light above. "Did I hear someone calling for some help down there?" A male voice, far off.

"You speak English?" Iris called up into the opening.

Something moved to block the light from above, and soon a figure in a dark outfit started climbing down the ladder, coughing as he descended through the smoke. Spider rushed to help, coughing himself, and Iris rallied round, too, helping the new arrival down the ladder. Between the smoke from the burning time machine and the light streaming in, it was hard to see who or what was coming down the ladder, except it was obviously human, and wore a dark suit. For a brief, crazy, even desperate moment Spider found himself wishing it was Soldier Spider, his far-future all-action alter-ego. Except, of course, Soldier Spider was dead at the End of Time, a long way from here.

It was not Soldier Spider, as Spider soon learned. Even as he saw the man's ample backside in those trousers, Spider knew who it was, and all the rage, the bitterness, and black furious anger filled him afresh, as if it had never gone away, and far from helping the man safely traverse the ladder, Spider reached up and grabbed the back of his ill-fitting suit jacket, and yanked him down, so that he fell from the ladder to the floor, where he landed with a terrible thud, complaining and shouting. *"You!"* Spider said, hardly able to speak. *"You!"* He was pointing and coughing now. Iris shouted at him, but he was hardly even aware of her.

Dickhead McMahon lay there on the floor, trying to get his breath, rubbing his elbow, staring up at Spider and Iris. He smiled that enormous smile that was bigger than his very considerable head. Iris helped him to his feet, and maneuvered him clear of

Spider. Once upright, his suit adjusted and his hair tidied back into place, Dickhead thanked Iris, winked at her, and turned to face them both. "Spider! It's been so long!" he said, arms out as if for a hug.

Spider kept his distance, shaking and not only from the cold, breathing through his blanket. "I saw you murdered. John Stapleton, he killed you, he took your head off, you … you time-traveled your head into the break room fridge at the shop. You, you were *dead*, Dickhead!" It beggared belief. It was impossible. Or so he thought. Until he stopped, watching the bastard, the way he seemed quite unperturbed on hearing this news. This was not the garish future Dickhead from The End of Time. This Dickhead appeared younger, energetic, and perhaps still idealistic. "Ah, right, yes. Stapleton. Hmm. I've been getting some worrying notes about him from my future self. Man seems like trouble, has done from the beginning, I should have seen it myself, I'm normally much better with people than this, you know, aren't I good with people, Spider? I was right about you, after all." He stopped a moment, thinking. "Stapleton, you say? Took my head off? Bloody hell, that's not kosher, is it? Why not a simple knife in the guts like a decent person? What kind of murderer takes a man's head off? That's, my God, I swear to you, Spider, that's not on. I hope you've dealt with him."

Spider glanced at Iris. "He's been taken care of, yeah."

"Good, very good. Still, thanks for the tip. He's just up there, you know, in the ship, waiting for me, taking care of things while I'm down here sorting you two out. Bloody Stapleton, eh? Those Canadians, you can't trust 'em, can you? You mark my words, Spider, they're bloody trouble." Dickhead popped his watchtop and jotted some quick notes. "Stapleton. Must kill. Right, yes, okay!" He furled the watchtop and looked back at Spider and Iris. "You two look like you're about ready for a rescue, I must say. We've been patrolling the timeline, looking for scrap to help with the effort. There's a war on , you know, and all that, and we're always short of vital gear. Metals, paper, components."

"Dickhead, for God's sake, I think my eyes are starting to freeze," Spider said, hardly able to speak. He was looking at Iris, who could barely stand, and knew she desperately wanted to go up there, where it was warm, where there was food, and shelter, but she would not go without him. He'd tried to explain to her about Dickhead, and he thought she understood. But this situation, he knew, was different. It was not like they could refuse whatever the hell Dickhead was going to want in return for this rescue. He had them in a spot, and Spider hated that, hated having to depend on Dickhead's kindness — again.

Meanwhile, Dickhead had noticed Iris's state, and was chumming up to her. "Hello, my dear, I'm assuming you're the illustrious Inspector Iris Street of the Western Australian Police Service? Yes? Yes, I thought so. Lovely to meet you, heard lots about you, all good of course," he said, chuckling, doing his best to appear "charming". "I'm Dickhead McMahon, please just call me Dickhead, everyone does," he said, and managed a laugh despite the choking smoke. He held out a hand for Iris to shake, but she declined the offer, looking to Spider like she might keel over at any moment. Why couldn't the bastard see how serious this was? Dickhead went on, as if this was a chance meeting on a sunny day, perhaps in a lovely park. "Well, this is a pretty pickle we've got ourselves in, isn't it, Spider? And here I am to bail you out once more. Getting to be a bit of a habit."

Spider managed to clear the screaming burning noise in his head long enough to say, in a somewhat coherent state, "What do you want?"

"What do I want? I want you, my good man! Like I've always wanted. I want you, at my side, my Numero Uno, my second-banana, my right-hand man, right where you belong, I've always thought so, haven't I, Spider?"

"So it seems," Spider said, thinking about the ascendancy event Dickhead would host in years to come, and how it was important to make mass-murder look "appealing", because otherwise nobody would want to participate. That was the role Dickhead had in mind for him, the role currently held by Stapleton, the guy Dickhead went to when Spider wouldn't cooperate.

This made Spider think. If he went along with Dickhead on this, went up the ladder — Stapleton would presumably find himself kicked out of an airlock, and thus would never stage a mutiny in the future, never set about to capture the Vore, never travel back to Spider's own time. Hmm, he thought. Perhaps we're at one of those nodal points in time where a change of events is actually possible.

Seen in this light, Spider thought, he was just about *obliged* to go with Dickhead. Except, what would happen to Past-Molly? Would she still become Future Molly? Did some events truly want to happen, or did it just work out that way sometimes through the sheer inertia of cause and effect? He imagined a great bristling sheaf of possible timelines spraying out from this point, all of them different, except for one grim detail: they likely all led somewhere Spider did not want to go.

Dickhead was talking again, this time to Iris. "...Very slow to make a decision is our Spider, have you noticed, Inspector? Always off in a world of his own, full of plots and schemes and conspiracies and nonsense. Well, the time to put aside childish things is past. It's time to take on adult responsibilities, I'm sure you'll agree. Ah, Spider. Yes, it certainly is warm and cozy up there. Why don't you come up and let me show you around? You'll be so much more comfortable than, well, here. The singularities are eating the planet's core, Spider. Our studies show this whole continent will buckle and fail within days, so you really don't want to stay here do you? I'm all about the future, Spider, and you can be a part of it, and of course your good self, too, Inspector. I'm sure I can find a challenging position for someone of your esteemed talents in the Zeropoint hierarchy, you mark my words!"

"Not ... interested," Spider said, before he even knew he was going to say it. He knew it was crazy. He knew staying here was suicidal. But maybe suicide was the correct choice here. The thought of Dickhead's epic corruption leaching into him, no matter what steps he might take to fight it off, to watch for it, to try to work within Dickhead's mad system, it made him ill.

"Spider," Iris said, touching his shoulder.

Spider shook her off and shot her a look of darkest anger. "No. Just no," he said, starting to huddle down towards the ground, where the air was still somewhat clear, even if so cold he could feel his lungs burning in pain with every breath.

Spider knew attacking Dickhead was pointless. The man was a whack-a-mole game gone mad. Every time you kill him, he pops up again, and again, each time more terrifying than the last. Spider could hardly breathe. "No, not again. Not. Again. I won't."

"Spider, come on now. Let's not do this. Come on."

"No," Spider said, glaring at Iris, daring her to look upon Dickhead sympathetically. Iris, standing there, wrapped in her blankets, implored Spider with her eyes. And that did it, in the end. Against all his better judgment, indeed, against all his bitterly won experience of Dickhead, the mass-murderer, the cult leader, the madman, the cracked genius, Spider looked at Iris, who was barely hanging on, and hanging on just for him. He knew it, understood it, and felt ashamed of himself. There was more at stake here than his own precious conscience. He met Iris's gaze, struggled to his feet, and managed to produce, for Iris, a small smile, perhaps the hardest thing he'd ever done. He said, looking at her, but talking to Dickhead, "Excuse my poor manners. My old mum would be appalled."

Dickhead winked at Iris, put on a smile that seemed to swallow the whole room, and swept Spider into a tight, suffocating bear-hug. Spider didn't care. Dickhead was warm. That warmth felt good, and he hated himself for finding something about Dickhead that he liked. Spider said, "Let's talk, eh?" and knew, right there, that he was doomed.

Dickhead beamed at him, and at Iris. He said, "Step right this way, people." He helped Iris and Spider negotiate the ladder, an ordeal for them both with their near-frozen hands and feet.

As he followed Spider up the ladder, Dickhead called up to him, "Oh, and by the way, Spider, I've got this little job for you, thought you might be able to help me out."

Spider hesitated, still on the ladder, climbing towards the warm light, bright without being dazzling or harsh. He was leaving behind all hope of ever returning to his own timeline. It was a turning point for him, the end of one life, and perhaps the start of another, whether he liked it or not. Everything he'd ever loved or cared about was gone. No, wait, he thought, and looked up, and there was Iris above him, hanging on to the ladder with her stump so she could reach her hand down to help him up. She was smiling down at him, aglow in the light, despite the pain. "Come on, Spider, you can do it." He felt warm at last in the light of her smile.

Not everything he loved was gone. He managed a smile back at her, and kept climbing, one rung at a time.

It was hard, but wasn't everything in this life? Dickhead, he knew, was right behind him. "A little job, you say?" Spider said, forcing himself to keep his voice light, telling himself he was doing this for Iris. "What sort of little job?"

Our titles are available at major book stores
and local independent resellers who support
Science Fiction and Fantasy readers like you.

EDGE Science Fiction
and Fantasy Publishing

www.edgewebsite.com

Our titles are available at major book stores and local independent resellers who support Science Fiction and Fantasy readers like you.

Alphanauts by J. Brian Clarke (tp) - ISBN: 978-1-894063-14-2
Apparition Trail, The by Lisa Smedman (tp) - ISBN: 978-1-894063-22-7
As Fate Decrees by Denysé Bridger (tp) - ISBN: 978-1-894063-41-8
Avim's Oath (Part Six of the Okal Rel Saga) by Lynda Williams (tp)
    - ISBN: 978-1-894063-35-7

Black Chalice, The by Marie Jakober (hb) - ISBN: 978-1-894063-00-7
Blue Apes by Phyllis Gotlieb (pb) - ISBN: 978-1-895836-13-4
Blue Apes by Phyllis Gotlieb (hb) - ISBN: 978-1-895836-14-1

Captives by Barbara Galler-Smith and Josh Langston (tp)
    - ISBN: 978-1-894063-53-1
Children of Atwar, The by Heather Spears (pb) - ISBN: 978-0-88878-335-6
Chilling Tales: Evil Did I Dwell; Lewd I Did Live edited by Michael Kelly (tp)
    - ISBN: 978-1-894063-52-4
Cinco de Mayo by Michael J. Martineck (pb) - ISBN: 978-1-894063-39-5
Cinkarion - The Heart of Fire (Part Two of The Chronicles of the Karionin)
    by J. A. Cullum - (tp) - ISBN: 978-1-894063-21-0
Circle Tide by Rebecca K. Rowe (tp) - ISBN: 978-1-894063-59-3
Clan of the Dung-Sniffers by Lee Danielle Hubbard (tp) - ISBN: 978-1-894063-05-0
Claus Effect, The by David Nickle & Karl Schroeder (pb) - ISBN: 978-1-895836-34-9
Claus Effect, The by David Nickle & Karl Schroeder (hb) - ISBN: 978-1-895836-35-6
Courtesan Prince, The (Part One of the Okal Rel Saga) by Lynda Williams (tp)
    - ISBN: 978-1-894063-28-9

Danse Macabre: Close Encounters With the Reaper edited by Nancy Kilpatrick (tp)
    - ISBN: 978-1-894063-96-8
Dark Earth Dreams by Candas Dorsey & Roger Deegan (comes with a CD)
    - ISBN: 978-1-895836-05-9
Darkness of the God (Children of the Panther Part Two)
    by Amber Hayward (tp) - ISBN: 978-1-894063-44-9
Demon Left Behind, The by Marie Jakober (tp) - ISBN: 978-1-894063-49-4
Distant Signals by Andrew Weiner (tp) - ISBN: 978-0-88878-284-7
Dreams of an Unseen Planet by Teresa Plowright (tp) - ISBN: 978-0-88878-282-3
Dreams of the Sea (Part 1 of Tyranaël) by Élisabeth Vonarburg (tp)
    - ISBN: 978-1-895836-96-7
Dreams of the Sea (Part 1 of Tyranaël) by Élisabeth Vonarburg (hb)
    - ISBN: 978-1-895836-98-1
Druids by Barbara Galler-Smith and Josh Langston (tp)
    - ISBN: 978-1-894063-29-6

Eclipse by K. A. Bedford (tp) - ISBN: 978-1-894063-30-2
Even The Stones by Marie Jakober (tp) - ISBN: 978-1-894063-18-0
Evolve: Vampire Stories of the New Undead edited by Nancy Kilpatrick (tp)
    - ISBN: 978-1-894063-33-3
Evolve Two: Vampire Stories of the Future Undead edited by Nancy Kilpatrick (tp)
    - ISBN: 978-1-894063-62-3

Far Arena (Part Five of the Okal Rel Saga) by Lynda Williams (tp)
- ISBN: 978-1-894063-45-6
Fires of the Kindred by Robin Skelton (tp) - ISBN: 978-0-88878-271-7
Forbidden Cargo by Rebecca Rowe (tp) - ISBN: 978-1-894063-16-6

Game of Perfection, A (Part 2 of Tyranaël) by Élisabeth Vonarburg (tp)
- ISBN: 978-1-894063-32-6
Gaslight Arcanum: Uncanny Tales of Sherlock Holmes
   edited by Jeff Campbell & Charles Prepolec (pb)
   - ISBN: 978-1-8964063-60-9
Gaslight Grimoire: Fantastic Tales of Sherlock Holmes
   edited by Jeff Campbell & Charles Prepolec (pb)
   - ISBN: 978-1-8964063-17-3
Gaslight Grotesque: Nightmare Tales of Sherlock Holmes
   edited by Jeff Campbell & Charles Prepolec (pb)
   - ISBN: 978-1-8964063-31-9
Gathering Storm (Part Eight of the Okal Rel Saga) by Lynda Williams (tp)
- ISBN: 978-1-77053-020-1
Green Music by Ursula Pflug (tp) - ISBN: 978-1-895836-75-2
Green Music by Ursula Pflug (hb) - ISBN: 978-1-895836-77-6

Healer, The (Children of the Panther Part One) by Amber Hayward (tp)
- ISBN: 978-1-895836-89-9
Healer, The (Children of the Panther Part One) by Amber Hayward (hb)
- ISBN: 978-1-895836-91-2
Healer's Sword (Part Seven of the Okal Rel Saga) by Lynda Williams (tp)
- ISBN: 978-1-894063-51-7

Hell Can Wait by Theodore Judson (tp) - ISBN: 978-1-978-1-894063-23-4
Hounds of Ash and other tales of Fool Wolf, The by Greg Keyes (pb)
- ISBN: 978-1-894063-09-8
Hydrogen Steel by K. A. Bedford (tp) - ISBN: 978-1-894063-20-3

i-ROBOT Poetry by Jason Christie (tp) - ISBN: 978-1-894063-24-1
Immortal Quest by Alexandra MacKenzie (pb) - ISBN: 978-1-894063-46-3

Jackal Bird by Michael Barley (pb) - ISBN: 978-1-895836-07-3
Jackal Bird by Michael Barley (hb) - ISBN: 978-1-895836-11-0
JEMMA7729 by Phoebe Wray (tp) - ISBN: 978-1-894063-40-1

Keaen by Till Noever (tp) - ISBN: 978-1-894063-08-1
Keeper's Child by Leslie Davis (tp) - ISBN: 978-1-894063-01-2

Land/Space edited by Candas Jane Dorsey and Judy McCrosky (tp)
- ISBN: 978-1-895836-90-5
Land/Space edited by Candas Jane Dorsey and Judy McCrosky (hb)
- ISBN: 978-1-895836-92-9
Lyskarion: The Song of the Wind (Part One of The Chronicles of the Karionin)
   by J.A. Cullum (tp) - ISBN: 978-1-894063-02-9

Machine Sex and other stories by Candas Jane Dorsey (tp)
- ISBN: 978-0-88878-278-6
Maërlande Chronicles, The by Élisabeth Vonarburg (pb)
- ISBN: 978-0-88878-294-6

Moonfall by Heather Spears (pb) - ISBN: 978-0-88878-306-6

Of Wind and Sand by Sylvie Bérard (translated by Sheryl Curtis) (tp)
  - ISBN: 978-1-894063-19-7
On Spec: The First Five Years edited by On Spec (pb)
  - ISBN: 978-1-895836-08-0
On Spec: The First Five Years edited by On Spec (hb)
  - ISBN: 978-1-895836-12-7
Orbital Burn by K. A. Bedford (tp) - ISBN: 978-1-894063-10-4
Orbital Burn by K. A. Bedford (hb) - ISBN: 978-1-894063-12-8

Pallahaxi Tide by Michael Coney (pb) - ISBN: 978-0-88878-293-9
Passion Play by Sean Stewart (pb) - ISBN: 978-0-88878-314-1
Petrified World (Determine Your Destiny #1) by Piotr Brynczka (pb)
  - ISBN: 978-1-894063-11-1
Plague Saint by Rita Donovan, The (tp) - ISBN: 978-1-895836-28-8
Plague Saint by Rita Donovan, The (hb) - ISBN: 978-1-895836-29-5
Paradox Resolution by K. A. Bedford (tp) - ISBN:978-1-894063-88-3
Pock's World by Dave Duncan (tp) - ISBN: 978-1-894063-47-0
Pretenders (Part Three of the Okal Rel Saga) by Lynda Williams (tp)
  - ISBN: 978-1-894063-13-5

Reluctant Voyagers by Élisabeth Vonarburg (pb) - ISBN: 978-1-895836-09-7
Reluctant Voyagers by Élisabeth Vonarburg (hb) - ISBN: 978-1-895836-15-8
Resisting Adonis by Timothy J. Anderson (tp) - ISBN: 978-1-895836-84-4
Resisting Adonis by Timothy J. Anderson (hb) - ISBN: 978-1-895836-83-7
Rigor Amortis edited by Jaym Gates and Erika Holt (tp)
  - ISBN: 978-1-894063-63-0
Righteous Anger (Part Two of the Okal Rel Saga) by Lynda Williams (tp)
  - ISBN: 897-1-894063-38-8

Silent City, The by Élisabeth Vonarburg (tp) - ISBN: 978-1-894063-07-4
Slow Engines of Time, The by Élisabeth Vonarburg (tp)
  - ISBN: 978-1-895836-30-1
Slow Engines of Time, The by Élisabeth Vonarburg (hb)
  - ISBN: 978-1-895836-31-8
Stealing Magic by Tanya Huff (tp) - ISBN: 978-1-894063-34-0
Stolen Children (Children of the Panther Part Three)
  by Amber Hayward (tp) - ISBN: 978-1-894063-66-1
Strange Attractors by Tom Henighan (pb) - ISBN: 978-0-88878-312-7

Taming, The by Heather Spears (pb) - ISBN: 978-1-895836-23-3
Taming, The by Heather Spears (hb) - ISBN: 978-1-895836-24-0
Technicolor Ultra Mall by Ryan Oakley (tp) - ISBN: 978-1-894063-54-8
Ten Monkeys, Ten Minutes by Peter Watts (tp) - ISBN: 978-1-895836-74-5
Ten Monkeys, Ten Minutes by Peter Watts (hb) - ISBN: 978-1-895836-76-9
Tesseracts 1 edited by Judith Merril (pb) - ISBN: 978-0-88878-279-3
Tesseracts 2 edited by Phyllis Gotlieb & Douglas Barbour (pb)
  - ISBN: 978-0-88878-270-0
Tesseracts 3 edited by Candas Jane Dorsey & Gerry Truscott (pb)
  - ISBN: 978-0-88878-290-8
Tesseracts 4 edited by Lorna Toolis & Michael Skeet (pb)
  - ISBN: 978-0-88878-322-6
Tesseracts 5 edited by Robert Runté & Yves Maynard (pb)
  - ISBN: 978-1-895836-25-7

Tesseracts 5 edited by Robert Runté & Yves Maynard (hb)
- ISBN: 978-1-895836-26-4
Tesseracts 6 edited by Robert J. Sawyer & Carolyn Clink (pb)
- ISBN: 978-1-895836-32-5
Tesseracts 6 edited by Robert J. Sawyer & Carolyn Clink (hb)
- ISBN: 978-1-895836-33-2
Tesseracts 7 edited by Paula Johanson & Jean-Louis Trudel (tp)
- ISBN: 978-1-895836-58-5
Tesseracts 7 edited by Paula Johanson & Jean-Louis Trudel (hb)
- ISBN: 978-1-895836-59-2
Tesseracts 8 edited by John Clute & Candas Jane Dorsey (tp)
- ISBN: 978-1-895836-61-5
Tesseracts 8 edited by John Clute & Candas Jane Dorsey (hb)
- ISBN: 978-1-895836-62-2
Tesseracts Nine edited by Nalo Hopkinson and Geoff Ryman (tp)
- ISBN: 978-1-894063-26-5
Tesseracts Ten: A Celebration of New Canadian Specuative Fiction
edited by Robert Charles Wilson and Edo van Belkom (tp)
- ISBN: 978-1-894063-36-4
Tesseracts Eleven: Amazing Canadian Speulative Fiction
edited by Cory Doctorow and Holly Phillips (tp)
- ISBN: 978-1-894063-03-6
Tesseracts Twelve: New Novellas of Canadian Fantastic Fiction
edited by Claude Lalumière (tp)
- ISBN: 978-1-894063-15-9
Tesseracts Thirteen: Chilling Tales from the Great White North
edited by Nancy Kilpatrick and David Morrell (tp)
- ISBN: 978-1-894063-25-8
Tesseracts 14: Strange Canadian Stories
edited by John Robert Colombo and Brett Alexander Savory (tp)
- ISBN: 978-1-894063-37-1
Tesseracts Fifteen: A Case of Quite Curious Tales
edited by Julie Czerneda and Susan MacGregor (tp)
- ISBN: 978-1-894063-58-6
Tesseracts Sixteen: Parnassus Unbound edited by Mark Leslie (tp)
- ISBN: 978-1-894063-92-0
Tesseracts Q edited by Élisabeth Vonarburg and Jane Brierley (pb)
- ISBN: 978-1-895836-21-9
Tesseracts Q edited by Élisabeth Vonarburg and Jane Brierley (hb)
- ISBN: 978-1-895836-22-6
Those Who Fight Monsters: Tales of Occult Detectives
edited by Justin Gustainis (pb) - ISBN: 978-1-894063-48-7
Throne Price by Lynda Williams and Alison Sinclair (tp)
- ISBN: 978-1-894063-06-7
Time Machines Repaired Whie-U-Wait by K. A. Bedford (tp)
- ISBN: 978-1-894063-42-5

Vampyric Variations by Nancy Kilpatrick (tp)- ISBN: 978-1-894063-94-4

Wildcatter by Dave Duncan (tp) - ISBN: 978-1-894063-90-6